MAGGIE

To Beth,

Enjoy!

Diane

D. L. Rogers

Maggie

Diane L. Rogers – Author
June 2012 Release
All Rights Reserved;

THE WHITE OAKS SERIES: by D.L. Rogers

Tomorrow's Promise: Survival on the Plains – Book 1 in the original trilogy, released 2008
Brothers by Blood – Book 2 in the original trilogy, released 2008
Ghost Dancers – Book 3 in the original trilogy, released 2007
Caleb – Book 4 in the continuation of the series, released 2010
Amy – Book 5 in the continuation of the series, released 2011
Maggie – Book 6 in the continuation of the series, released 2012
Beginnings: Into the Unknown – Book 7 (and prequel) in the continuation of the series, released 2013

Other Books by D.L. Rogers

Elizabeth's War: Missouri 1863 – Released 2014
The Journey – Released 2009
Echoes in the Dark – Released 2009

Cover design by Glen Dixon

DLRogersBooks
www.dlrogersbooks.com

Dedication

To my Dad, for his encouragement, pride, and being one of my biggest supporters. Thanks, Dad, I love you.

"Social science affirms that a woman's place in society marks the level of civilization."

-Elizabeth Cady Stanton

"Resolved, that the women of this nation in 1876, have greater cause for discontent, rebellion and revolution than the men of 1776."

-Susan B. Anthony

Riding in a Stage

Creeping through the valley, crawling o'er the hill,
Splashing through the branches, rumbling o'er the mill;
Putting nervous gentlemen in a towering rage,
What is so provoking as riding in a stage?

Spinsters fair and forth, maids in youthful charms,
Suddenly are cast into their neighbors' arms;
Children shoot like squirrels darting through a cage,
Isn't it delightful, riding in a stage?

Feet are interlacing, heads severely bumped,
Friend and foe together get their noses thumped;
Dresses act as carpets-listen to the sage;
"Life is but a journey taken in a stage."

-From: *Six Horses* by Captain William Banning
& George Hugh Banning, 1928.

PART I

BOSTON

Chapter One
1879

Maggie raised her hands to protect her face from the barrage of flying fruit heading straight for her. Jerking left to keep from being hit, she wrenched her back when a rotten tomato sailed past and splattered against the wall in a drippy glob of flesh, seeds and juice. Ignoring the pain racing up her spine, Maggie straightened and glared down at the crowd. Heart pounding, waiting for the next assault, she jerked right as an egg flew by to explode in a yellow and white oozing mass beside the tomato. Dodging left then right to avoid more airborne fruit, Maggie Douglas, born of a well-respected ranching family whose spread was located northwest of Kansas City, Missouri, tried to remember *why* she was standing alone in front of this hostile audience being pummeled with rotten fruit and insults. *Was it because she believed so strongly in women's rights that she was willing to risk life and limb to help gain the freedom to vote, as black men who were slaves little more than ten years ago now voted? Or was she running away from an overbearing father and brothers? Or from George, the man who, by his own misfortune, had fallen in love with her?*

She lunged forward and landed on her belly as a moldy melon whizzed overhead to join the collection of fruits and vegetables decorating the wall and floor behind her. Maggie pushed to her knees, stood up, brushed off her drab dress and glowered at those laughing in front of her. In her glaring silence, she dared them to continue. *She would not be easily driven away. She had something to say and she was going to say it, whether they liked it or not!*

Maggie took a deep breath, pushed a stray lock of her raven hair off her heart-shaped face, squared her slender shoulders and stood her ground. Deep blue eyes gazed out from yet another little stage in another unremarkable town whose name she couldn't even remember—one of many she'd visited in the last year after hearing Lucy Stone speak when Maggie first arrived in Boston from Kansas City. Miss Stone's impassioned speech had caused a surge of responsibility to run through Maggie. It was time for her to *do* something about the ideals she'd been

spouting at her father and brothers for years about her rights—
about the rights of *all* women. After spewing those beliefs for so
long, it was time to make her stand. Trained by Miss Stone,
Maggie traveled from one small town to another, trying to
educate its inhabitants about what women's rights offered for
both sexes, and getting nowhere fast, it seemed. On rare
occasions she left town with a feeling of accomplishment,
hoping she'd sparked a fire in some young woman to go out and
spread the word; but most of the time, she left wondering what
she was doing and why—as she did tonight. The novelty of her
quest had worn off with its reality.

She continued to stare down at the crowd, daring them to
continue the assault on her person. Tonight had begun the way
most of her previous speaking engagements did. First came the
cat calls when she walked on stage; then the whoops and hollers
and fist waving when she tried to speak. Then the dirty names
and assaults upon her character from the men assembled. It
progressed, as usual, to the barrage of rotten fruit and vegetables
hurled at the stage. The twenty or so women in the audience, a
mixture of all shapes, sizes and ages, looked angry and horrified
at the same time. They were in a hard place, and Maggie knew it,
but by God *it was time to be heard*! If they *ever* wanted more
than to suckle babies, do laundry and take care of their children,
homes and men for the rest of their lives, they *had* to make a
stand—and now was as good a time as any! If they ever wanted
land, a home, or a business to call their own, they had to start
someplace, and here was that place.

Maggie Douglas was fighting for *them*. Fighting for a
woman's right to take possession of her own home if her
husband died because, right now, women *had* no rights to that
home. Neither could she take possession of a piece of land
deeded to her if her husband died on their way to claim it.
Women were non-entities, faceless and kept by men to wash and
clean and take care of their homes and babies. A black *man*
could now vote, yet a *woman*, of any race, could not! Maggie
was fighting to pull them from their lives of toil, drudgery and
subservience. She was fighting for *those women* as much as for
herself!

The ladies who'd invited her to speak had run from the stage as soon as the fruits and vegetables started to fly, but Maggie stood fast. She'd seen more than one dress ruined by worse harassment than this. She'd seen more than her share of rotten fruit and vegetables; had been on the receiving end of too many rotten eggs to count and even had manure hurled at her! She'd stood then and intended to do no less now.

A tomato hit her in the chest while she mused over her situation. The men in the crowd roared with laughter and the women cowered. She knew her face was as red as the stain spreading across the front of her dress, but she refused to back down. She ducked when another object sailed toward her head, bringing more guffaws and shouts from the crowd. Women tugged at their husband's arms, trying to make them stop or pull them out of the hall, but they only jerked away, laughing harder.

"Why don't you run like those spinster gals who asked you here, Miss Douglas? They haven't got husbands so they figure to make our wives as miserable as they are," a tall, thin man in the middle of the hall yelled.

"Go back where you belong," shouted a rotund man in the first row.

"We don't want you here!" a man waving his fist cried.

The crowd howled.

Maggie noticed a young woman trying to stand, but her husband kept shoving her back onto the seat, his face red, his nose flaring as he shouted at his cowering wife. Maggie could only imagine the threats he laid upon her.

"Why don't you pull up them skirts, Miss Douglas, and show us some ankle on your way out the door?" another man yelled, followed by more whooping and laughter.

Maggie took a deep breath, dodged another projectile and another before she came to attention. "I will not leave this place!" she shouted in a deep voice that resonated throughout the hall. "I was invited by the ladies of this town to speak on an issue which has bearing on you all and I intend to have my say. You may either listen…" she looked around the hall at the men standing poised and ready to throw their next item, "or leave!"

There was a unified gasp. Eyes bulged with disbelief that she had the audacity to stand so boldly in front of these men in *their* town and shout orders. Maggie prayed her bold show would cow some of the lesser-spoken men, and give strength to some of the women who stood beside their husbands, backs straight and their eyes riveted on her.

"Do you men feel better now? Do you feel stronger and more superior because you've thrown a few rotten tomatoes—and even hit me with one?" She brushed at her soiled dress. "Because if this is what makes you feel superior to a woman...?" She let the words hang.

Grumbling, the men began to sit down, the wide-eyed women sliding down beside them. When all was quiet, their attention turned back to the stage.

"Thank you." Maggie's eyes searched the crowd and fell upon the three women standing at the back of the room who had invited her there. "Come now. Please return to the stage with me." One by one the ladies returned and stood on either side of her, hands clasped together.

"Ladies and gentlemen, we stand before you, a united front," they raised their linked hands high for all to see, "wishing for one thing and one thing only. To be recognized. To be taken seriously. Many women are uneducated and misinformed, but certainly they're not stupid. They are uneducated because they're not allowed to *be* educated and misinformed because no one informs them. We are wives, mothers, and sisters who want our voices heard. Who want to stand with our men to vote and..."

"Women are too stupid to vote!" a man shouted from the back row. "My wife is only good for two things—taking care of me and mine and, well, you all know what else." Laughter erupted throughout the hall and Maggie's chest tightened, but she would not be thwarted.

Maggie waited until the hall quieted once again. "And have you even tried to speak with your wife about what goes on in your town or country?"

"Why should I? She's just a woman; the only thing she needs to worry about is me and mine. Nothing should concern her except that." There was general agreement amongst the men in the hall, while the women openly seethed from what Maggie could see.

"That's all your wives are good for?" she asked.

"Damn right!" someone else yelled.

"Not good for anything else," shouted another.

It didn't take long for the squabbling to begin between husband and wife instead of being focused on Maggie. Many a woman turned her back on her husband with arms akmibo and toes tapping, and Maggie heard more than one threat from a wife to withhold her "wifely" duties if her husband didn't start to take her seriously. While waiting for the hall to quiet again, Maggie found herself thrown back to the day she'd made her decision to leave her home, the Lazy D Ranch outside Kansas City, on the quest that had brought her to this place.

"Damn it, George, why won't you listen to reason?" Maggie stared at a determined George. She'd been mucking stalls for what seemed like hours, hoping to figure things out in her head and decide on a plan, before he'd tracked her down and confronted her. Maggie had things to do and George wasn't part of those plans, but he just wouldn't listen. She knew George cared about her, maybe even loved her, but she didn't love him back. She couldn't, at least not now.

Softening her tone, *hoping* to make it easier for him to understand, Maggie continued, "Sure, my father and brothers *like* you, but they wouldn't want you for a son-in-law. They've made it painfully clear they won't settle for someone like—you."

"What the hell do you mean someone *like me*?" Anger swept across George's usually calm, handsome face.

Maggie sighed when the memory of George's appearance at her family's ranch popped into her head. Her brother, James, had hauled George home from Fort Leavenworth after saving him from a pounding by angry soldiers. Having refused to follow an order given by his commanding officer to kill a Lakota woman and her child during a raid on their village, as well as not carrying out General George Crook's overall order to "destroy the village, everyone and everything in it," George had been forced to resign his commission as a cavalry lieutenant to avoid a general court martial for disobeying orders and conduct unbecoming. Relating the story behind his resignation had made Maggie's stomach turn, and she'd felt an immediate kinship with the shy, sandy haired, principled man. He'd come to the Lazy D and worked for her father as a ranch hand and, in his shy, boyish way, had wooed Maggie until she, literally, threw herself at him. To her great disdain he rebuffed her—twice—before she was forced to let him to court her the "old-fashioned way." During that courtship, Maggie grew quite fond of George and respected him greatly for his stand on the Indians, but not enough to give up her plans.

Maggie stared into George's confused and angry face. She didn't want to hurt him, but there was no other way. She straightened her back to gather the courage it would take to do just that. It was the only way she could to do the things she had to do, without his interference.

"What do you have to offer me, George Hawkins?" A home? A future? Security?" she drawled, her voice thick with sarcasm.

"We can get those together, Maggs." He'd used her childhood nickname, the only person allowed to do so without getting a tongue-lashing to remind them she was no longer a little girl.

"I've saved a little money," he continued.

She wanted to cry at the look of hope on George's face, but she could not, would not, spend the rest of her life known only as Stuart Douglas' daughter or the little sister of Edward and James Douglas or, worse yet, as the wife of a ranch hand with "a little money."

She closed her eyes and took a deep breath for patience. "'A little money' isn't what my father has in mind for my future." No, he intended for his only daughter to marry someone who could give her the kind of life she'd been raised with. Of course he wanted her to marry, have children and care for her husband and children, as all women were intended, but he wanted her to marry within her own station. But Maggie was meant to be more than just a wife and mother regardless of who she married, be he cowboy or rich man. She'd told her father and brothers that many times, but they wouldn't listen. She was a woman who wanted, needed, a life of her own; one helping other women, as well as herself, to obtain a voice in this emerging country.

She looked back at George's hopeful face and snapped, "I've told you time and again, we can't tell my family."

"Well I'm damn tired of sneaking around, stealing kisses, afraid of getting caught and having my head blown off by someone in your family. I still think you're exaggerating." George's chin raised a notch, silently questioning whether she was telling him the whole truth about her father and brothers.

Her chin lifted in response. "Exaggerating, am I? Let me tell you what happened to the last man I introduced them to. He was a gentleman from St. Louis in Kansas City on business. He was refined, well-dressed and, seemingly, everything my family wanted in someone for me to marry. He came from a well-known family, but he didn't have property. He was only beginning to establish himself. But it wasn't good enough. They grilled him like a common criminal about his life, his family and his ambitions until the man finally tucked tail and ran like a rabbit." She threw her hands up. "And he was someone I thought they'd find acceptable!" She was losing patience. *Why couldn't he understand?*

George took a deep breath. "Then why are they always harping on you about finding a husband?"

"Oh they want me married off, sure enough. They just want to be sure it's a man *they* approve of. Since the episode I just told you about, I've never again brought anyone home to meet my family. Never. I think they realize what they did by chasing away my last suitor, which is why they constantly remind me I need to find someone." She looked deep into George's eyes. "That's why we can't tell them."

George stared at her a few moments before he stepped into the stall, reached over and took her hand. "Maggs..."

"What?" She snapped again. "I know that tone, George." *She couldn't let him take her in his arms and kiss her thoughts away. She couldn't!*

"I want you to marry me."

"Haven't you heard a word I've said?" She stabbed the pitchfork into a pile of soiled hay, snatched her other hand away from him and stomped out of the stall. Her heart was pounding when she whirled back to face him and said through gritted teeth, "My father and brothers will *not* approve of our relationship, nor will they accept it. What do I have to do to make you understand that?"

"Ask them."

She closed her eyes and shook her head in disbelief. "Ask them? Ask them?" She ran her fingers through her hair and spun around on her heel. "Ask them?"

"Yes. It's as simple as that."

"Simple as that," she parroted. She couldn't believe he thought it could be that simple.

"Maggs," George tried to interrupt.

Maggie ignored him and continued her tirade.

"Maggs!" he shouted, jerking her to a halt. She stood staring, uncertain what more she could do or say to make him understand. Her family simply would not accept George Hawkins, dishonorably discharged, former U.S. Cavalry lieutenant and now an employee on *their* ranch, as the husband of their precious daughter and sister!

"What are you so scared of?" he finally asked. "Of what they might say? Or of me?"

She stood stock still. Her eyes bore into him. One hand eased to her hip while the other slipped to her forehead and pushed a lock of hair back. Her right toe kicked at the hay in front of her. She looked away, unable to give him the answer he wanted.

George stepped in front of her and grabbed her shoulders. "Which is it, Maggs? I thought you loved me. Have you just been playing with me all this time? Like all the others?"

"No," she managed, her throat tight, her heart breaking. He *wasn't* like the others whom she *had* toyed with for one reason and one reason only—to make her father and brothers crazy and teach them a lesson for butting into her life. George *was* different. If she allowed him to change her mind about leaving, she might very well wind up loving him and spending her life with this simple cowhand in defiance of her father and brothers—and missing out on all she wanted for herself. She had things to do and she intended to do them, whether George, her father or her brothers approved or not. "No, George. I care about you a great deal." *But I can't love you; I won't love you.*

His eyes went wide. "You *care* about me. A great deal!" he shouted.

"But I don't love you." *There, she'd said it out loud. That should be enough to make him understand.* Intent on ending this conversation she added, "At least not enough for marriage, whether they approved or not."

"Well, thank you for telling me," George ground out, his nose flaring his teeth gnashing.

"Please understand, George. I have things to do." She tried one last time. She meant to strike out and help with the women's movement. It was time men realized women had a mind—and a voice.

"Oh, yes, I remember," he drawled. "You have to follow your precious Miss Elizabeth Stanton and Miss Susan Anthony. You have to run around the country shouting about your rights."

Her concern about hurting his feelings dissolved like a spoonful of sugar in a hot cup of coffee. She drew up her back and stepped directly in front of him, her nose only inches from his.

"You're damn right, George. And, as a matter of fact, I was about to tell you I'm leaving on the next train to do just that." She hadn't made up her mind until that moment and was as surprised as George at her revelation.

"What?" George shouted. "Next train where?"

"There's a rally scheduled in Boston and I intend to be there to lend my support." Her heart was pounding, but she would not back down. She'd made a decision and intended to stand by it.

"Boston! Are you crazy? That's hundreds of miles away."

"I know where it is, George. Remember me? This is Maggie Douglas, not some dull-witted female who doesn't know the geography of our country. And no, I'm not crazy. It's time I make a real stand for what I believe in. I'm going, and not you nor my brothers or my father will stop me."

She spun on her heel and started out of the barn, needing to get away before she changed her mind, or before George changed it for her. Before she could get far enough away George grabbed her by the arm and turned her back to face him.

"And what about us? Is what we've got so easy to forget?"

Her heart was breaking as she looked into his pleading face and remembered all the secret times they'd shared at the pond behind the bunkhouse and other secret places around the ranch. Snuggling in the cold at the pond she'd learned how George was with Custer at the Little Bighorn. There, she'd confided in him all she'd suffered with her mother's death and how an old Indian chief had befriended her and whose young granddaughter perished because he couldn't get the medicine needed to help her. Sadness overwhelmed her, but she refused to give in. It was her time and she intended to take this chance. It might be her *only* chance.

"No, George Hawkins, it's not easy to forget. But this is something I must do. Just like you had to do what you did at the Little Bighorn to save your friend Blue and later defying Colonel MacKenzie's order in that Cheyenne village. You have ideals. Well I do, too, and it's about time I put my time and effort where my mouth has been. I've been shouting my beliefs and now it's time to do something about it. I have to, George. Allow me this and who knows what'll happen when I return. Perhaps we can rekindle what we have then, but not now."

Maggie gently removed her arm from his grip and left him standing there gaping, all hope drained from his face. She turned and strode from the barn, fearful of all she would leave behind, anxious and hopeful for what lay ahead.

Laughter and insults jerked Maggie back to the present. Everyone was on their feet. The men shuffled from the room, the women leading the way with their backs turned against their men, arms crossed over their chests and the threat to withhold their duties on their lips. Many an angry man waved his fist at Maggie to let her know how much trouble she'd caused with his now departing wife. She wanted to raise her hands high and shout at them like an impassioned preacher that *someday there would be a reckoning and women would emerge to take control of their own lives*! Instead she shouted, "Please! If you would just listen to what I have to say!"

The snickers and insults continued as the hall emptied. A few of the women threw Maggie apologetic glances as they passed, until she and her three companions were the only ones left in the quiet, empty room.

Chapter Two

Maggie had followed Miss Susan B. Anthony's teachings from the time she realized she was not like her brothers. After her mother's death when Maggie was thirteen, she was treated differently, and she didn't like it. She could rope and ride just as well, if not better, than either of her older brothers and most of the hands on the ranch by the time she was sixteen. She thought fast on her feet and handled any situation that came along as well or better than anyone; but when it came to political thinking, her opinion didn't matter in the Douglas household. She was a girl, and girls 'didn't need to worry about such things' she was told over and over by her father and siblings.

Curled up on the bed in her tiny room following tonight's disastrous meeting, Maggie surveyed her surroundings. Not much bigger than her closet at the Lazy D, her eyes settled on what was left of the barely palatable food on the little table beside her. This is what had become her usual, every day meal instead of thick cuts of beef from cattle raised on her family's ranch. Tasteless fare instead of plump chicken legs fried to a crispy, golden brown or juicy ham slices swimming in thick gravy. A knot formed in her stomach and she suppressed a sigh. *Was it worth it? Would she ever see any success from tromping around the country, shouting her beliefs about women's rights? Or would she spend the rest of that life in little rooms eating horrible food, alone?*

Thinking about the meals she was missing at the Lazy D caused another memory to form and, although she tried to push it away, Maggie couldn't help but smile. She would never forget the first night George came to the Lazy D. On a tirade about the Indians and women's rights, Maggie and her father and brothers were shouting at each other across the dinner table. Exasperated with the whole conversation and hoping for some support from George, Maggie pointed her fork at her brother James and said, "Ask Mr. Hawkins what he thinks."

"Call me George, please," their guest said uneasily.

Maggie cocked her head to take a better look at the man sitting across from her. He was handsome, in an odd way, with his unruly, sandy colored hair and despite the glasses that sat awkwardly on his nose. *Perhaps she would make him her next conquest and watch her father and brothers go crazy,* she'd mused. *Yes, that was it.* "Very well," Maggie conceded with a condescending sigh. "George. Now please, answer my question."

"Which was?"

Maggie sighed again. *He had the attention span of a gnat!* "As to whether or not you feel women should be given the right to vote."

"Oh, that question." Color crept into his face as Maggie and her family awaited his response.

"Well, Maggie, that's something I haven't given much thought," he finally answered.

"Do you think women are unintelligent?" She was warming up now.

"Of course not. But to be honest," he cleared his throat, "I haven't had much experience around women. I've spent most of my life around men, in the cavalry. It was only my pa and me growing up, and the only women I'm familiar with are my adoptive mother, Sarah, and my best friend's wife, Amy."

"And what would they say on the subject?" She leaned her elbow on the table, drawing a harsh look from her father. She waited until it seemed he'd fallen asleep or forgotten the question all together before Maggie prodded, "George?".

He sighed again. "I just don't know, Maggie. I haven't thought much on it."

"Do you know a black man can vote, but a white woman can't?" The thought still irritated her a great deal.

"Of course I do, Maggie. That's part of why we fought the war."

George's answer annoyed her even more and she rolled her eyes, pursed her lips and drew a heavy breath for strength. "I won't debate *that* issue with you right now, George, but why should a black man vote, and not me? Am I less able to decide the direction of this country than him, someone who was a slave only little more than ten years ago?" She couldn't keep the sarcasm from her voice.

"Well, no," George sputtered.

"Then why don't I? I'll tell you why. Because men forbid it! Do you know Miss Susan B. Anthony has been fighting for women's right to vote since *before* the war? Do you know she tried to vote back in '72 and was arrested? But she refused to pay the fine and they let her go. What do you think of that?" She knew her cheeks were aflame as she waited for his response.

"Well, I'd heard something about it, but paid it little mind."

He was almost squirming now. Maggie leaned in and stared directly at him. "Because it doesn't concern you. Just like all men." She threw her fork onto her plate, sat back and crossed her arms over her chest. "But it does, Mr. Hawkins, concern me." Her heart was pounding. She was getting into dangerous territory and knew her father and brothers would jump in any time. But it wouldn't be to her defense—oh no. It would be in the defense of *men* and not her rights to anything, except to have children and take care of a husband and family.

George took a deep breath. "Maggie. I believe if a woman is well-informed, she should have the same right a man does to choose who runs this country."

Maggie sat bolt upright she was so surprised at his response. But so, too, were the others at the table.

"What?" father and sons shouted in unison.

George shook his head and Maggie *almost* felt sorry for him.

"To a degree, I do," he added in a rush.

"To a degree?" Maggie drew the words out slowly, her eyes large.

"Now wait just a darn minute everyone. I haven't given this subject any thought prior to today and you're all expecting me to be an authority."

Maggie only wanted to know how he really felt. "Not an authority, George. Just honest," she said, disappointment heavy in her voice.

"Stay here awhile, George, and you'll be an authority before you know it." The laughter in her father's eyes told Maggie how he really felt.

Maggie watched her brothers and father exchange glances before all three laughed out loud. It was all she could do to keep from lashing out, but kept her tongue for the sake of not ruining the rest of the meal and looking like a shrew in front of their guest.

It was her father who leaned forward and said, "You don't see *Godey's Lady's Book* publishing articles about the good of the women's suffrage movement, Maggie."

Maggie took another deep breath for strength as her father continued.

"On the contrary, I believe Mrs. Hale, its founder and a proponent on all kinds of other women's issues, has made it clear she feels crusaders for women's suffrage to be nothing more than ill-bred, unladylike hooligans."

Maggie's back went up. "Like me? Besides, how would you know, Pa?" Maggie spread her hands on the table and her eyes sparkled with mischief. "Do you read *Godey's* when no one's looking?"

Her father's cheeks flared red. "Of course not! I heard it from the widow McCaffery," he explained.

James and Edward snickered, but hid their smiles behind their hands as Maggie continued.

"The widow you've been sparking the last three months?" she shot back, knowing her father thought their relationship a secret. "And why were you speaking on such a subject to her anyway?" Maggie asked, curious.

"It so happens I was asking her opinion following one of our rather lengthy discussions about *you* and your foolish ideas. She agrees that the women's right to vote is utter nonsense. She believes women shouldn't be filling their heads with political ideas. They should be at home taking care of their family."

That was it! She couldn't listen to any more. Maggie jumped to her feet, almost toppling her chair, and slammed her fist down on the table. "There it is again. That notion that all women should be home making babies and taking care of their men! What rubbish. God gave me brains the same way he gave them to all four of you. And I can use them as well as any man. I ride better than any hand on this ranch. I can shoot and mend a fence as well as any man here. But I don't have a brain big enough to figure out who should run this country because I can't understand the political nature of it?" she shouted in disbelief, her heart racing.

"Now, Maggie, honey. We didn't say that," her father tried to placate her.

"Don't you 'honey' me!" she raged, shaking her fist. "Someday we women will rise up and you'll understand the real meaning of fear. You mark my words." One by one, she stared down each man at the table before she stalked out of the dining room and stomped up the stairs, slamming the bedroom door behind her.

Maggie giggled with the memory. She raised her head and looked around the darkness in the room that stretched from corner to corner, save the light from one small gas light on the wall beside the bed. "Not even enough light to read," she chided aloud before thinking with a snort, "even if I had something *to* read." The only thing she had with her was a much-read copy of Miss Lucy Stone's *Woman's Journal*, one she'd read so many times she could almost quote every line of every article. Almost.

George's face haunted her. *How much had she given up to defy her father and brothers so she could voice her ideals on women's rights? Where was he? Had he forgotten her? Would she ever see him again?* She curled into a ball and before she could stop them, tears flowed. *Had she traded George's love for barely edible food, tiny cold rooms with too soft beds to sleep alone in every night, with vegetables and insults thrown at her on a regular basis?*

She was absorbed in a raging bout of self-pity when a knock at the door startled her. It was late; it had to be close to midnight and she wondered why someone would be at her door now? Wary, she wiped the tears from her face, stood up and pulled the belt on her tattered robe tight around her waist and went to the door.

"Yes?"

"Miss Douglas, it's Jasper Warren. I was at your talk tonight. I'm sorry for the lateness, but I wanted to apologize for the men being so mean to you. If you have a minute I'd like to talk to you."

Maggie was uncertain. "It's late Mr. Warren. You should be home with your wife."

"She threw me out. Told me to find someplace else to sleep until I could talk with her about her rights. She's a strong-willed woman, Miss Douglas." There was a pause before he added, "I was hoping you might help me out. That you might tell me what it is you're trying to do so I can go home and talk to my wife about it better."

Maggie felt pricks of warning run up and down her spine. *What respectable man would be at her door at this time of night? Then again, this could be a start for the rest of the men in town,* she thought with hope. *If she could sway just one man who might sway another man...*

"Just a moment." She slid the bolt and opened the door enough to peek through.

That was all he needed. The door burst open, hit her in the shoulder and hurled her backwards onto the bed.

"What are you doing?" Maggie screamed through her panic, scrambling upright. She pointed at the door. "Get out of here this instant!"

A big, burly man with a thick beard and dirty brown hair shot with gray stood in the doorway. "I've got other ideas, Miss Douglas," he hissed. "You want to shout about your rights to vote and do everything a man does. You want to shout about being equal to a man; well I'm gonna to show you how un-equal you are!"

He took two steps to the bed, grabbed her arm and jerked her to her feet. He reeked of alcohol and real panic set in. Maggie'd dealt with drunks before and there was no reasoning with them.

"Let go of me!" she shouted at the top of her lungs, hoping someone would hear. "Someone help me!"

The room was so small the man took one step backward and slammed the door shut with his booted foot. "No need to bother anybody else. This is between us."

He pulled her to his chest and wrapped his arms around her, but she managed to keep her right arm from being caught in his embrace. He licked her cheek then smothered her in a slobbery kiss that made her gag. She thought she'd lose the tasteless dinner she'd tried to eat earlier, but managed to keep the gorge down, although thinking it would serve him right if she did throw it all up in his face.

She shoved against his chest. "Let—me—go!" she cried, but it was like pushing against the side of a mountain. Her mind was rolling like a building thunderstorm when she opened her hand and slapped his ear as hard as she could. He stopped kissing her, shook his head, but held on tight. Boxing his ear had *not* had the desired effect she wanted, she almost whimpered out loud.

"Ah, a fighter. I like a fighter," he drawled with a new gleam in his eyes. "But I'm bigger'n you and this is one fight you won't win, lady."

The light in his eyes frightened her as much as anything she'd ever experienced before. She struggled and tried to push him away, but he was built like a small bull with as much strength. "Let me go!" she screamed again before he claimed her lips in another rough kiss.

The door burst open again and in a heartbeat two men were dragging Maggie's assailant off her.

She stood rooted to the floor, gasping, trying to understand what had just happened. The big man fought against the other two, but his drunkenness was beginning to undermine his determination and they were able to subdue him.

"Come on, Jasper, you're drunk and need to leave this lady alone," one of the men said.

"She ain't no lady!" Jasper shouted, jerking against their hold on him. "She's the one that started this. Filling my wife's head with all kinds of foolish ideas about not having to cook and clean or take care of me." He stopped struggling and looked Maggie square in the eyes. "She even told me she won't service me any more until we come to an 'understanding' about this," he almost whined in his muddled state.

"That's between you and Rosie, Jasper," Maggie's rescuer said. She noticed how well-dressed and well-groomed he was in a black suit with polished black boots, a white shirt and a black string tie. He spoke well and, in her instant assessment she thought him very handsome. "Just go on home, Jasper," he continued. "Tell your wife you're sorry and that you understand now, but you need to get some sleep before you two can talk about it in the morning."

"It's all her fault," Jasper whined like a little boy, held up between the two men. "Coming here, filling the womenfolk with foolish ideas…" The big man heaved a heavy sigh, turned to Maggie—and spat at her.

Maggie didn't even have time to react. His spittle barely missed her, landing on the bare, planked floor in front of her, just beyond where her toes peeked out from the robe.

The big man threw his head back and guffawed before he was jerked backwards. "You had it coming, standing up on that stage, spouting all your lies. Women were put on this earth to serve men!"

Maggie snapped. She stepped up and slapped him square in the face.

His look of surprise was almost humorous, but once past the shock of her striking him, he started to struggle again. "If you were a man I'd kill you for that!" he shouted.

Her heart beating a wild race, her knees feeling like they'd buckle right under her, Maggie stood firm. "If I were a man, you wouldn't get the chance, because you'd already be dead. Don't think just because I'm a woman I won't kill you if you *ever* accost me again. I'm a crack shot and not afraid to use a gun." That said she pulled a five shot, .31 caliber, Colt Pocket Model pistol from the pocket of her robe. "You don't know how lucky you are these men came in here and rescued *you* from *me*! Otherwise, your wife might be in black tomorrow morning."

Jasper tried to break free again and Maggie took a step backward, hoping the other two men could contain him so she wouldn't be forced to use the pistol leveled at Jasper's chest. "Get him out of here please," she said, weary.

"Come on, Jasper, be a good boy and let's get you home," the handsome man said.

The big man continued to struggle as he was dragged out of Maggie's room. "It's all her fault, I tell you. If she hadn't come to town…" was the last thing Maggie heard before she slammed the door shut and slid the bolt home.

Maggie slept little that night, reliving Jasper's visit over and over. It wasn't the first time she'd been accosted by a drunken husband intent on 'teaching her a lesson' for interfering in his and his wife's life. After a similar incident a few months ago she'd bought the Colt, she affectionately called Wally, and kept it hidden in her reticule all day then transferred to her robe as soon as she got to her room each night. She was never without it and practiced whenever she could to keep up her skills.

The sun was peeking through the flimsy curtain covering the thick-paned window of her room when another knock sounded at the door. Maggie sat bolt upright, her body tingling with warning.

"Miss Douglas?"

Maggie shook her head to clear it of last night's events. "Who is it?"

"It's Paul Thornton, Miss Douglas. I was one of the men who helped you with Jasper last night. I've come to check on you and make sure you're all right."

Maggie swallowed with relief then remembered how Jasper had insinuated himself into her room on the premise of only wanting to talk.

"How do I know you've only come to check on me?" she shot back, her heart thudding again, her fingers wrapped around Wally's handle in the pocket of the robe she'd slept in.

"You don't have to open the door, Miss Douglas. I just wanted to make sure you were all right." There was a pause before he added, "I'd like to make up for Jasper's rude behavior. He doesn't represent the thoughts of *all* the men in town. Perhaps I could buy you breakfast? There is a nice restaurant downstairs. If you'd be willing to meet me there in, say, an hour, I'd be happy to purchase breakfast for you, as a way to apologize for last night's meeting and Jasper's despicable behavior."

His language alone gave Maggie pause. He sounded polished, polite and educated. Her curiosity piqued, she got up and stepped toward the door. "How do I know you're not trying to bull your way in here like Jasper did?"

"You don't, that's why I've suggested we meet downstairs. I remember you, so you don't have to try and find me. I'll see you when you come down. One hour?"

Maggie sighed. She glanced at the table where her half-eaten dinner still sat. She hadn't had a good meal in—how long? She couldn't remember and her stomach chose that moment to growl as if to remind her. "Very well, I'll meet you in the restaurant in one hour."

"Excellent. I shall see you then."

"Thank you, Mr. Thornton." She leaned her ear against the door and listened to his footsteps go down the stairs. She sighed and lay back down on the lumpy mattress with a smile on her face. If nothing else, she'd get a good meal out of this inhospitable, dung heap of a town.

Maggie had on her best day dress, which wasn't very good these days. It had grown thin and almost raggedy in her travels, but the plain green muslin was the best she had. She hefted the weight of her reticule and felt better knowing Wally was close at hand.

Standing at the door to the bustling restaurant she reassured herself there were too many people in plain view for her to be taken advantage of and relaxed. Scanning the crowd, she pictured her handsome, well-dressed rescuer and hoped he was the one who had extended the invitation. She counted eight tables in the room, each with one to four patrons. Several business-looking types talked in close proximity, making deals, she presumed, while other cowboy types were wolfing down what was probably their first good meal in weeks. Then there was him. Their eyes met and he jumped up and hurried to greet her.

"Miss Douglas, I'm so glad you decided to come down. Please." With a light touch on her elbow he guided her toward his table. "Join me."

Maggie's heart was pounding again. She'd grown up around opulence and wealth, knew how to comport herself around such, but this man oozed money, arrogance and charm. She had to be careful. She wasn't some green calf who'd never been outside the paddock before, but it had been a long time since someone had shown her kindness, and she couldn't let it cloud her judgment.

"Please." His arm flowed across his chest toward a chair at the table he'd just vacated. "I'm so glad you decided to join me, Miss Douglas. I was rather distressed to find you in such a difficult situation last night. Jasper can be, well, he can be impetuous for a man of his age. And, of course, drink doesn't help." His eyes sparkled, but Maggie didn't know whether it was because he was telling the truth or weaving a lie.

"It was very fortunate you and your friend showed up, Mr. Thornton. If you hadn't, I don't want to think about what might have happened." She paused and her eyes hardened when she added, "To Jasper, of course, as I was completely prepared for the worst." She patted her bag to let him know the Colt was within reach.

Thornton chuckled and leaned back in his chair, assessing her. "You are a woman, Miss Douglas, I would not want to cross."

"No, Mr. Thornton, you would not."

He leaned forward again. "Well, since that is not my intention, perhaps we may start again." He offered his hand. "Miss Douglas, I am Paul Thornton. I was born and raised in the middle of Boston and I am currently the sole owner of the White Stag, a gentlemen's establishment across the street. I'm afraid Jasper spent a good part of last evening after your meeting at my place drinking. He was rather loud in his intentions so one of my employees and I followed him when he left. I feel somewhat responsible for what happened, since he did, in fact, become quite inebriated at my place of business."

Maggie listened intently as the soft-spoken gentleman went on to tell her how Jasper had railed against Maggie's speech, what little she'd been able to give, and how it had enflamed his wife to throw him out until her rights were discussed. She watched his mouth, the thin upper lip covered by a thick, black moustache, as he enunciated each and every word. His dark eyes were expressive, and dangerous, she decided. Light black hair was clipped evenly at the nape of his neck. High cheekbones accentuated his handsome face and pulled all his features together in a nice package. Maggie almost sighed. It had been a long time since a man had paid her any attention—polite attention—who didn't want to teach her a lesson for what she was attempting to do for their wives.

"And what about you?" he asked, drawing her from her perusal of his face and enjoyment of his obvious charm.

Maggie lifted her chin a notch and sucked in a breath. "I've come to fight for the God-given rights of women to think and learn and vote, just like a man." She paused and waited for his reaction against what she'd just said, like every other man—even George—with scorn. He only smiled and nodded.

"Go on," he prompted, taking her by surprise.

"Well…Women are just as smart as men, only they're not given the chance to prove it because from a tender age we're taught our only worth is to marry and take care of our children and some man." She felt her face color, knowing she was including Mr. Thornton in her description of *all* men.

He waved his hand. "Please, do go on," he said with a smile.

Maggie almost shook her head and shouted at his refreshing attitude at allowing her to speak her mind and not be looked down upon because of her ideas. She smiled and nodded. "It will be a difficult battle that must be won if women are ever to be allowed to think on their own or allowed the vote." She paused again, wondering exactly how much she should tell him about herself. She decided to trust him and continued. "I grew up on a ranch with two older brothers and learned early on that, although I could do everything they could, I was treated differently because I was a girl."

"Is that so?" Thornton leaned closer as though to absorb every word she said.

Maggie was warmed up now and began her usual tirade. "Just because I'm a woman shouldn't mean I can't vote, drink, smoke or even curse if I want to."

Thornton guffawed and Maggie's face went hard.

"My dear, Miss Douglas, I'm not laughing because of your ideas, I'm laughing because I enjoy hearing you say them out loud! I employ many women who feel the same way you do, but, unfortunately, because of their profession, they are not taken seriously."

"And what is it they do, Mr. Thornton?" Maggie was certain she already knew the answer, but she wanted to hear him say it, that, in essence, they earned their living doing sexual favors for men for payment. "Are you comparing me to a harlot?"

Thornton cleared his throat. "Not at all, not at all. I…"

Maggie took pity on him and laid her hand over his, noting its smoothness and warmth. "It's all right, Mr. Thornton. I've been compared to as much or worse many times because of what *I* do."

He closed his eyes and nodded understanding. "I must agree with you, Miss Douglas, that from all I've seen over the years, women are not weak, by any means. However, ours is a society run by men and it will take time for them to absorb new ideas before embracing them, especially when it means relinquishing some of their power and control. Hopefully, as the years pass, you, as well as my—employees—will be taken seriously and reap some of the benefits."

Maggie watched the play of his face and couldn't help but grin. "I hope you're right, Mr. Thornton; that all it will take is time and perseverance to have our voices heard." She hoped so for herself and every other woman out there trying to get their message across and hoped it happened before she was too old to enjoy it.

Maggie and Paul ordered and ate their meals while easily conversing on their similar views of how badly the Indians had been treated, her right to smoke, drink and curse if she wanted to and, of course, her right to vote.

Before she knew it, it was heading toward noon and the lunch crowd began to arrive. Paul stood. "Unfortunately, I must end this most enjoyable conversation. Alas, I must return to my establishment and prepare for the day. Would it be too forward of me to ask you to join me tomorrow morning for breakfast and a carriage ride? I find you stimulating and very much enjoy your company, Miss Douglas."

Maggie knew she was blushing—and Maggie *never* blushed! This handsome man completely unnerved her. She was only in town two more days and then it would be time to move on and start all over again. She sighed and disappeared into Paul Thornton's eyes, imagining them together, losing herself in the pretty picture of another wonderful breakfast and a morning carriage ride, the sun high above them, birds singing in the trees and a slight breeze before he touched her hand and brought her back to reality.

"Miss Douglas?"

There was a rakish grin on his face, as though this wasn't the first time a woman had lost herself in his eyes. She waved her hand and tried to clear her head. "I'm so sorry, Mr. Thornton…"

"Paul, please."

"Very well, Paul. I must apologize. I was imagining a lovely ride in the country with a handsome man at my side. It's been a very long time since I've enjoyed a ride of any kind, other than on a loud, dusty train, or the companionship of someone who understands my ideas and agrees with me."

Paul bowed. "I'm happy to accommodate you. Shall we meet at eight so as not to be rushed before I must return to the White Stag?"

Maggie felt things she'd almost forgotten, hope and excitement, but most of all respect for this man. He was educated and agreed with what she believed in. Her body sang with anticipation. For the first time in a very long time, tomorrow seemed a long way away.

Chapter Three

After a restless night, morning broke bright and warm and Maggie's former depression dissipated with the darkness. She dressed with a smile, anxious for the day. Looking forward to her outing more than she had anything in months, she stopped her preparations to think about where she was and what the day might bring. *Paul Thornton is a handsome, polished man and the owner of a successful establishment—an establishment that uses women, sex and liquor to make money,* she reminded herself. *Was he the kind of man she wanted to become further acquainted with? He was the kind of man who used women instead of promoted them. Was he the kind of man she might fall in love with?* Her head snapped up. *Fall in love! Where had* that *come from? She couldn't fall in love with anyone. Or could she? Had she given enough of herself to walk away from all this?* She looked around the dismal, unwelcome room. *Fall in love?* she snorted. *And what about George? Was she willing to forget George for another man? Hadn't she told George they had a chance* after *she finished what she had to do?* Guilt rose in her belly. She hadn't even given George a chance to tell her he'd wait or even support her in her decision. Instead, she'd hurried away without looking back.

She shook her head. *She didn't want to think about any of it. She just wanted to go for a carriage ride, spend a nice, quiet day with a handsome man then move on to the next town to do what she did—which was? Educate? Help other women by planting the seeds of knowledge in them so they would explore the possibilities on their own? Or cause dissention between husbands and wives, as Jasper had so astutely made her aware? Falling in love wasn't part of the bargain for what she had to do.* Sucking in a deep breath, she ran her hands over her body, wondering what it would feel like to have Paul Thornton's hands there. Or George's....

"Stop!" she shouted out loud. "No more. I'm going to spend a nice, quiet day with a handsome man and that's all," she muttered aloud. "And nobody, not even me, is going to talk me out of it!" Maggie checked her hair and face in a small, cracked, oval mirror hanging on the wall next to the pitcher and bowl she'd used earlier to wash. Satisfied she'd done all she could for her appearance, she grabbed her bag, stepped into the hallway and closed the door behind her.

Walking down the stairs Maggie's heart pounded with anticipation. She wasn't going to let anything ruin today. They would start with a nice breakfast and stimulating conversation, followed by a carriage ride into the country and more conversation. *An innocent day that would do what? Remind her of everything she gave up when she left the Lazy D, including George, security, and decent food and clothing, or a day to discuss her views and beliefs with someone of a similar mind? A day to dream about her future or remember her past?*

There was no more time to dwell on it. Paul was coming her way, hand extended, a huge smile on his face.

"Good morning, Miss Douglas. I'm so glad you could join me. Shall we?" He guided her to a corner table, helped her get seated then sat down across from her.

"Thank you for inviting me, Mr. Thornton," Maggie said, suddenly nervous. *Why in this world was she nervous? She traveled the country speaking in front of hostile crowds getting pummeled with bad words and rotten food, why was it this handsome man made her insides feel like quivering jelly?*

"I thought we agreed you'd call me Paul." His disarming smile calmed Maggie's nerves.

"Yes, we did. And if I'm going to call you Paul, please, call me Maggie."

He tilted his head, closed his eyes and nodded. "Very well, Maggie." He studied her a moment then asked, "Are you hungry? I woke up starving this morning," he said, an odd smile on his lips.

Maggie studied his face and wondered if there was a double meaning in his statement. *Could he be alluding to a hunger for her?* She mentally shook herself. No one had wanted her that way for a long time. Thinking about it caused George to pop into her head and she forced him out before she gave Paul a blinding smile. "I'm very hungry, Paul," she managed. "I don't generally eat well when I'm traveling. Not enough funds from my sponsors." The moment it was said she wished she hadn't. *She made it sound like she was starving!*

"Well, we're going to take care of that, Miss—Maggie," he corrected. "Order whatever you like. I enjoy a woman with an appetite."

He let the words hang and again Maggie wondered at his meaning. *Was he baiting her? Letting her know he desired her, or was he just being honest about what he liked in a woman?* It'd been so long since Maggie had enjoyed a man's company, she was afraid she could no longer distinguish the difference.

"Shall we?" Their breakfast was brought a few minutes later and little was spoken during the meal. As good as the food tasted, Maggie forced herself not to wolf it down, but quickly polished off several eggs, a slice of ham, fried potatoes and two pieces of toasted bread slathered with peach jelly before she sat back, a cup of coffee in hand.

"So, tell me about yourself, Maggie." Paul slid back in his seat.

"There's not much to tell."

"I don't believe that. A beautiful woman without a story?"

She was blushing again and she knew it. *What was he doing to her?* She could stare down an angry crowd without flinching, but given a few compliments by this handsome man, she turned into a big pile of mush. Drawing a deep breath to control her racing heart and, hopefully, regain the correct color in her face, she said, "I grew up outside Kansas City where my family owns a ranch."

"And your family? Do they approve of your roaming the country, doing what you're doing?" he asked, mischief in his tone.

Maggie laughed out loud. "Certainly not! They're part of why I'm here, doing what I do."

Paul crossed his arms over his chest. "I'm listening."

Was this man really interested in her and her story, or was he setting her up for something else? He was disarming with his charm and good looks. She had to be careful. She was a smart woman who would not be taken in by a handsome face. "My father and two brothers," she began, drawing a sigh of understanding from Paul before she continued, "don't believe in the women's movement."

"I can imagine. Growing up with three men and only your mother as a buffer…"

Maggie shook her head. "She died when I was thirteen. It nearly destroyed us, but we survived. After her death I was treated differently by my father and brothers, like I was fragile, which I certainly was not." Memories of her childhood flooded her mind, the pain of her mother's death, the good times, the hard times, and her father and brothers, which brought a pang of loneliness to her heart.

Paul leaned forward again, propping his elbows on the recently cleared table. "It sounds to me like there was a bit of rivalry there. Men, regardless their age, do not like to be upstaged by a girl." He smiled rakishly.

Maggie couldn't help but grin. He was charming and her heart skipped a beat every time he gave her that confident smile. "I admit there was a rivalry. I've always been as good or better at whatever my brothers did, even when we were little. Whether it was shooting, riding, fencing or other chores around the ranch, I was always able to keep up, and I think they resented that— especially after my mother died. Then all of a sudden I was a *girl*, too delicate to do those kinds of things anymore, which I continued to do whether they liked it or not," she added, her voice rising in pitch. "I suddenly couldn't think on my own or have ideas about being equal to my brothers. Even my father began grooming me to get married, have babies and take care of my family. But I was restless. I've always been restless, even before my mother died. I wanted more. I was as smart as any man. I'd proven that time and again and wouldn't let them dictate what I could and couldn't do. It made me to work harder to be better than all of them, Father included."

"I'm sure that ruffled a few feathers." There was a sparkle in Paul's eyes.

"It certainly did!" Maggie laughed. "We quarreled all the time over my strange ideas and I left many a dinner table stomping up the stairs to my room, slamming the door behind me." George's first dinner snapped into her head again and she sighed, realizing she missed George as much, or more, than her family. Again, thoughts of where he was and what he was doing assailed her.

"So what finally caused you to do what you do?" Thornton asked, pulling her back from her musing.

"Well, there was this man."

"Ah, the mysterious man. Did he love you? Did you love him? Did he understand your drive to do what you're doing and support you, or disagree like your family?"

His insight made Maggie uncomfortable. She swallowed and took a deep breath. "He and I believed in many of the same things, such as how badly the Indians are treated, but when it came to my rights as a woman, he just didn't understand how important it was to me. He tried," she defended, "but when I made my decision to come east, he, well, he no longer understood."

"Because he was threatened with the possibility of losing you." Paul laid his larger hand over Maggie's and squeezed. His eyes bore into hers. "When a man is threatened with losing something he wants, nothing makes sense to him and he'll do whatever he can to keep it."

Was he speaking in double entendres or was it just her imagination? Maggie withdrew her hand and leaned back, suddenly uncomfortable and anxious to be away from the table and end this discussion. She pulled a battered watch from her bag. "Look at the time. Shouldn't we be going so you don't have to rush to get back?" Her heart was racing again and she was uncertain why. *Was she anxious to spend the rest of the morning with this dashing man, albeit a possibly dangerous man, or did she want to run from him—like she had from George?* She told herself fear would not dictate her life so she quickly added, "I'm looking forward to that carriage ride. Where are we going?" she asked, hoping she wasn't being too forward.

Thornton crooked his head, his eyes sparkling again. "I love a woman who speaks her mind. I'm very much looking forward to our ride, Maggie. Shall we?" He stood and offered his elbow.

A carriage with two matched bays waited for them at the livery a few blocks away. Paul paid the livery man then helped Maggie onto the seat. His touch was light and Maggie told herself his innuendos at the restaurant must have been in her imagination. He was a perfect gentleman. It had been so long since a man paid her any attention, she just didn't know how to perceive his words, she told herself.

"Comfortable?" he asked, settling beside her.

"Very." Maggie raised her face to the sun. It was a warm, sunny day, the temperature nearly perfect.

"Shall we, then?" Paul clucked the horses out of the livery lot and onto the main street.

"Where are we going?" Maggie ventured to ask again, not having received an answer at the restaurant. She didn't really care where they went, as long as it was away from town, away from people, and away from the memories of George suddenly jumping into her head, making her feel as though she were betraying him. She shoved thoughts of George from her mind. *George was no longer part of her life. She was a big girl and needed no one's approval to go for a carriage ride with a handsome man!*

"I thought we'd go that way." He pointed toward a grove of trees about a half mile from town. "Toward the river."

Maggie nodded, closed her eyes and turned her face into the sun again.

"Aren't you afraid your skin will darken?" Paul asked. "Aren't women supposed to avoid the sun and keep their skin milky white?"

Maggie huffed. "Most women prefer to stay out of the sun, but I *like* my skin tanned from working outside and..." she sucked in a breath, realizing she was talking like she was back on the ranch, working side-by-side with the ranch hands, riding her favorite mare, Beulah, or out-shooting her brothers in a test of skills.

Paul threw his head back and laughed loudly. "My, you are a puzzle Miss Douglas! So how well *can* you shoot?" His eyebrow lifted curiously.

"Better than you, I'd bet."

He laughed again. "Well, when we get where we're going, we may have to test your boast."

Maggie nodded. "I'd like that. It's been a while since I've had the chance to practice. It's not always easy to do so in some of these small towns." She paused. "But it's important I keep up my skills. Never know when I might need to use them."

"One must be prepared for anything," he said with a gleam in his eyes.

Maggie suddenly felt uncertain. He agreed too easily with everything she said. Again she wondered at his motives for being so kind to her. She had to be on her guard. A handsome man would not take advantage of her—unless she wanted him to. Patting her bag with Wally concealed inside she relaxed and enjoyed the movement of the carriage.

The buggy rolled out of town, into the woods, and clattered onto a canopy-lined road so thick with trees they blocked out most of the sun. It was cool on the shaded road and Maggie pulled her wrap around her shoulders. "So, Paul, you know all about me. What about you?" she asked, wanting to keep him talking, afraid of where her mind might go if she wasn't engaged in conversation—straight to George.

Paul held the reins lightly and the horses forged ahead without prompting. He turned and offered another blinding smile. She marveled at the whiteness of his straight teeth, at the perfection of his face, the chiseled cut of his cheeks and jaw, the dark, mysterious eyes, the strong forehead and his well-groomed hair and moustache. Without a doubt, he had to be the most handsome, perfect-looking man she'd ever seen. She was watching his lips, not hearing a word he said, when George popped into her head again. She frowned and groaned. "Not again," she whispered under her breath.

"I beg your pardon?" Paul asked.

"I'm sorry, Paul. I was distracted. Please continue."

"As I was saying…" Maggie caught the annoyance in his voice. *Apparently he doesn't like repeating himself,"* Maggie thought as he continued on a sigh. "I was born in Boston as I said last evening. I left when my parents died and was on my own when I was barely twenty years old. I left with a small inheritance. Why I landed here, I have no idea. It was just the first place I came to that I didn't get up the next morning and move on. I got a job working at the White Stag as a bartender." He stopped to acknowledge Maggie's look of surprise. "Yes, I tended bar. It's how I knew there was trouble with the previous owner and how I wound up owning it."

"And how did that happen?"

Thornton cleared his throat. "I used some of my inheritance to buy part of the Stag. The owner had deep gambling debts, so he accepted my offer without much thought. I paid off his debts and came in as an equal partner."

"But you're the sole owner now, is that correct?"

Paul nodded.

"And how did you manage that?"

"He couldn't control his gambling and fell back into debt as soon as I'd bailed him out. He thought he'd win back the money to buy everything back, but it didn't work that way. It didn't take long before he owed a lot of people a lot of money and the only way out was to sell more of the Stag—to me. He had nowhere else to go, so I bought him out and the rest is history. In ten years I've made the White Stag the successful establishment it is today."

"Selling alcohol to irate husbands and sex to men willing to pay for it." Maggie could have bitten her tongue for spouting off, but it was said and there was nothing she could do but wait for his response.

"You have a very sharp tongue, Maggie. The White Stag is a respectable business. Yes, I sell spirits, but I don't control who purchases them. I rent rooms upstairs to ladies who, well, enjoy the company of men. I don't know if they sell their favors or not, they are merely my tenants."

"Oh please, Paul. Yesterday you as much as admitted they sell sexual favors. I'm a big girl, I can handle the truth."

A strange light flickered across his eyes before he smiled brightly. "No fooling you, Maggie. Of course the girls are paid for their favors. It's part of the establishment's," he sighed, "nature."

"And what do you get out of it? A percentage? Do they live there for free and give you favors in return?" Maggie snapped her mouth shut. *What is* wrong *with you?* she almost shouted out loud, but groaned instead. "I am so sorry, Paul. I have no right."

Paul turned a frosty smile her way. "No apologies are necessary. You're a smart girl, Maggie and, apparently, you're quite aware of what goes on in the White Stag."

Maggie nodded. "Obviously, I don't know what goes on first-hand, but I have seen enough establishments like the Stag in my travels to have a good idea."

Thornton chuckled. "It's a business, just like running a dress shop or a bakery. I have stock I need to keep and orders to fill."

"Except those orders are for girls and time, am I correct?"

Paul shifted in his seat. He turned his head to the left then right, making his neck snap. "I take care of my girls. I protect them. They feel safe at the White Stag."

Maggie wanted to slap herself for opening her big mouth—again. *Why oh why did she always have to ruin everything by saying whatever came into her mind without thinking!* "Paul, again, I apologize. It's none of my business what you or your girls do. I feel very strongly about this because, as you know, it's part of what I speak about in my travels. Women having a choice, being able to take care of themselves, without having a husband and, well, without having to sell themselves." *How had this conversation turned so badly? The tension between them was as thick as the jelly she'd smeared on her toasted bread earlier. She decided right there she was going to let Paul do all the talking from now on. She was merely along for the ride.*

Paul surprised Maggie by throwing back his head and laughing again. "I have never, ever, met a woman like you Maggie. You're beautiful, courageous and smarter than I'd give credit to most men. You say what you think, sometimes *without* thinking, but you're as honest a woman as I've ever seen."

Maggie stared, and possibly for the first time in her life, she was speechless.

Chapter Four

The carriage rolled through the trees, but following Maggie's outspoken observances conversation lagged. She wasn't sorry, though. She was who she was and any man interested in her for any reason had to know that and accept it. Maggie sighed and lifted her face to take in the intermittent rays forcing their way through the canopy of trees. It was a day made in Heaven as far as she was concerned and she was thankful to be enjoying it in such a way, as opposed to sitting alone in her lonely room or wandering around town with nothing to do but window shop and think about the things she no longer had.

"We'll be to the river soon," Paul said.

Maggie smiled and nodded, unwilling to relinquish the hold the sun had on her or open her mouth and put her foot in it again. She was warm, content, and at peace with herself and the world.

Paul chuckled beside her. "I see you truly are a woman of the outdoors, Maggie. It is a glorious day and I'm happy to be sharing it with you."

She took a deep breath and lowered her head. "Thank you, Paul. It's been wonderful so far."

"As will the rest of the day. Look." He pointed. Perhaps a quarter mile away the trees disappeared and Maggie could see the river. Birds soared high above on invisible streams of air darting up then down again on a different stream. Ships sailed the far channel and the trees and bushes lining the shore stood out in a deep, shimmering green against the rippling river. Maggie sucked in a breath of the fresh air and smiled, *this was a day she would remember for a long time.*

"The shore is nice and sandy. You'll be able to take off your shoes and stick your toes in the sand."

"Umm." It had been a long time she'd felt so carefree. At the ranch there were always chores to be done, some thing or some one to occupy her. In her travels there was always anxiety about her next speech and the next town; but today—today she was going to enjoy lazily and leisurely and without a care.

Paul nodded and flicked the reins over the horses' rumps to pick up speed. When they reached the river Maggie jumped from the carriage before it stopped. Paul tied off the team and followed her to the edge where the sand was warm and soft.

"Oh it's glorious!" Maggie twirled in a circle, arms extended, face toward the sky, enjoying every ray the sun offered before plopping down in the sand. Sucking in a deep breath of the clean, river air, she unlaced her boot, pulled off her sock and drove her toes into the soft, white sand.

"Did you doubt me?" Paul asked, stepping beside her, feigning injury.

"Of course I didn't doubt you, but this is even better than my imaginary carriage ride," Maggie trilled, unlacing her other boot.

"Here, here, there's no need to sit in the sand. I've brought a blanket and some cheese and bread and wine to snack on before we head back."

Maggie groaned. "I couldn't eat another thing. I rather stuffed myself at breakfast, in case you hadn't noticed." *He must have noticed. Although she'd done it slower than yesterday, she'd eaten like she was starved!*

Paul eyed her, an unusual sparkle in his eyes. *Had she seen what she thought she saw?* Maggie wondered, momentarily unnerved. She'd seen it before in many a cowboy's eyes. But at the Lazy D she was in control and no one dared accost her, lest they deal with her father and brothers. It was lust she'd seen and reminded herself to be careful. She was not about to fall prey to a handsome face and charming ways.

"You couldn't have asked for a better day if you'd ordered it," Paul quipped, that blinding smile on his face again, all traces of the mysterious sparkle gone.

Maggie cocked her head, wondering if it had even been there. Chiding herself once more she swore to have a wonderful day—a day she would remember for a long time.

The masculine smell of Paul's cologne distracted Maggie enough that her shot flew untouched into the river.

"Is that it? I can beat that easily," Paul challenged over her shoulder.

"You're not playing fair. I was distracted," Maggie pouted, unused to being beaten.

"Who said shooting is fair?" Paul chucked her chin. "You must be able to hit your target, regardless of what's happening around you, Maggie. Care to try again?" He stepped back five feet and bowed at the waist.

"Humph. I'll show you." She raised her arm, looked to make sure he was still at a distance, took a breath and fired, the shot shattering the top branch of a budding tree at the river's edge. "There! I told you I hit what I aim for."

Paul smiled and bowed again. "I never doubted that, Maggie. I never doubted." He strolled back beside her and laid his hand on the small of her back, causing a ripple of excitement to run up her spine. *Was it from fear, or did she* want *him to touch her*?

She stepped aside. "Your turn. Beat that."

"Alas, I have no weapon."

Maggie handed him Wally. "Use mine. It sights a little high, but other than that, it fires true."

Paul hefted the short barreled gun, tossed it between his hands then spun it back and forth and around on his right forefinger. Before Maggie took a breath, he'd fired the last three shots, taking out the last of the already shattered branch and two branches below. He spun the gun around and around before he wrapped it in his hand and held it out to Maggie. "Does that qualify?"

Maggie gaped in stunned silence. *He shot better than anyone she'd ever seen, and certainly better than her!* She blinked. "I must say, it does. I had no idea."

"Nor do many people, Maggie, so let this be our little secret." He tapped the end of her nose. "I needed to know how to protect myself when I left Boston, so I bought an old Colt, very similar to this one in fact, and practiced every day on my travels. Soon, I had it mastered. I play the fopish dandy to avoid unwanted confrontations at the Stag; but forced to protect myself, I can do so easily."

"Apparently so," Maggie said on a sigh, unnerved by his skill and realizing he'd spent the last of her ammunition. First thing she would do when she got back to town was purchase more.

"I hope I haven't upset you." That charming smile was back on his lips.

"Not at all. I'm just not used to losing."

"Nor am I." He sidled up beside her and ran his hand up and down her arm. "May we dispense with the coltish innocence now? You're surprisingly beautiful, Maggie. Not at all what I expected of a woman spouting suffragist drivel. I've admired you since you walked on stage the other night. You're educated and strong-willed…"

Maggie stepped away. "Stop right there." The hairs on her neck pricked with warning. *What the hell was he alluding to?* "What are you doing and what do you want from me, Paul?"

"The same things you want. Good food, a safe place to live, lots of money, love."

She put up her hand, palm out. "Whoa. I know where you're going with this, but I'm not here looking for love. I did my job and I'm leaving soon. Romance doesn't play any part in my life." *If it did, I certainly wouldn't be here*, she berated herself, memories of George assailing her, piercing her with guilt and remorse.

Thornton slid toward her and grabbed her around the waist. "You have no time for love?" he drawled, that strange gleam back in his eyes. "You and the ladies you associate with run around the country spouting about 'free love,' yet *you* don't practice it?" He snorted. "You entice a man then spurn him? Do I look like a man to be spurned by a woman, Maggie?" His once handsome face was hard, his jaw flexing in controlled anger.

She jerked away and drew her worthless gun, realizing everything he'd done had been a ruse to use up her ammo. She nodded in acknowledgement. "So that's why my shooting skills intrigued you so much. It didn't matter whether I could shoot the eye out of a squirrel at 300 paces. All you wanted was to make my gun worthless."

Thornton bowed and before she could blink, grabbed Wally and tossed it aside. "Guilty, as charged. Again, let's dispense with the innocence, Maggie. You're a woman, I'm a man. We're all alone out here with no one to disturb us."

Maggie stumbled back several paces. "That's *not* why I came out here," she said, her voice an octave higher than normal.

"Why *did* you come out here, Miss Douglas? To convert me to your cause or use me to sway the other men in town to your beliefs that a woman is equal to a man? Hah! The only thing a woman is good for is lying on her back and pleasuring a man."

Maggie felt like she'd been gut-punched and she had to draw a deep breath to keep from doubling over. "I want to go back now," she said through gritted teeth. She needed to keep a cool head if she was going to leave here the same way she came.

Thornton laughed, quietly at first before he threw his head back and howled. "You would like to go back, would you? Well, that's not what I have in mind." He strolled toward her and Maggie almost tripped backing away from him. "I have many other things in mind for the rest of our morning, which," he looked at his pocket watch, "is slipping away."

"Let it slip. It's time to go back." Maggie ran for the blanket where he'd tossed Wally, but Paul grabbed her by the arm, stopping her in mid-stride, whirling her around to face him.

"There's plenty of time yet, Miss Douglas."

The use of her formal name sent shivers of warning up and down her spine. "I beg to differ," she said, her throat tight. "I just remembered an appointment with one of the ladies who asked me to speak," she lied. "If I don't show up, she's liable to send someone looking for me. The livery man will tell him which way we went."

"Tsk, tsk, tsk, Miss Douglas. You're a terrible liar."

"It's true. I must leave now." Her heart was thundering and she was breathing like she'd just tried to out run a team of horses.

He jerked her into his chest, his face only inches from hers. Looking into the depth of his smoldering eyes she wondered how she could have thought him handsome. Right now she'd more easily compare him to an evil demon than the man she'd arrived with.

"We're not going anywhere, Miss Douglas. You dare to lead a man on and when it's time to follow through you deny him?"

"I did no such thing. I haven't led you on. You asked me to breakfast and then for a carriage ride. All I wanted was a carriage ride!"

"Are you so naïve to believe an unsupervised carriage ride was all I had in mind?" he asked, his eyes gleaming. "You know who I am, the kind of business I run, the kind of women I employ." He snorted. "I thought you a woman of the world, Maggie. I'm *highly* disappointed."

Angrier now than afraid, she garnered all her strength and shoved him away. "I never believed you intended anything more than a simple breakfast and a quiet carriage ride, *Mr.* Thornton! Now take me back. If you don't I'll…"

"You'll what?" He tilted his head and sighed. "Scream?" His arms encompassed the empty, open country around them. "Tell everyone I brought you out here, alone, to do what? If you were a proper lady, you wouldn't have accepted an offer to come out here without a chaperone." He paused then drawled, "You want this as much as I do, Maggie. I've seen it in your eyes."

"I didn't come out here with any intentions other than those I've already told you!" she shouted, unable to believe his accusations. "And you haven't seen a damn thing in *my* eyes!" Her mind was spinning. She couldn't believe she'd been so stupid! "I did not come to this town to start trouble, either. Women have rights, and one of those rights is saying *no* to men like you who think all you need to do is buy a meal, snap your fingers and we should be ready and willing to fall into your beds."

"It's always worked before." He cocked his head, as though unable to comprehend why his charming ways weren't working on Maggie. *Or had they? She'd fallen into his trap and she was helpless at the moment to get out—but she* would *get out.* She scanned the area for something to help in her escape, noting how far away the carriage stood and where Wally glistened in the sunlight only a few feet from where she stood. *She had to get to it.*

"What do you intend, Miss Douglas? Will you reach your gun before I do?" Thornton was chuckling now, which made her angrier. "And what good is it if you *do* reach it?" he snickered.

"Stop this right now, before something happens we both regret."

"The only thing that's going to happen, Miss Douglas, is I'm going to teach you the difference between a man and a woman. I'm going to show you the rights I have as a man, and how few rights you have as a woman. I'm going to show you what little worth you really have."

He lunged, wrapped her in his arms and slobbered kisses up and down her face, nothing like the kisses Maggie had imagined. He was rough and hurtful. She struggled wildly as he trailed wet kisses over her cheeks to her ears then down her neck. He was not to be denied. She'd thought herself a woman of the world, but had proven herself nothing more than a mere babe left in the care of a wolf.

"I'll show you how unequal to a man you are, Miss Douglas," Thornton growled before claiming her lips in another bruising kiss.

She tore her mouth away and spat in his face. He shoved her backward and she stumbled, but managed not to fall.

"You arrogant son-of-a-bitch!" She'd had enough of this ill treatment by this pompous bastard. She feinted left, the same way she'd out-smarted her brothers many times, as though to run for the road. He shifted to stop her, but she pivoted right and ran for Wally. *It may not have bullets, but it will leave a hell of a gash when I slam it against his thick skull!* her mind screamed, running for the only weapon she could see around her.

Almost there he tackled her from behind. She landed on her belly, the gun just out of reach. Digging her fingers into the soft sand she scrambled toward it, but the sand only gave way and she slid backward when he jerked her legs. She rolled onto her back, kicking and thrashing. Her skirt slid up, exposing her legs, and Thornton's eyes gleamed in anticipation. She kicked harder with her bare feet, but he only grunted and yanked her closer.

"This—will—not—happen!" She stopped struggling, waited long enough to feel him relax a little, jerked her right foot free and planted it square in his groin. Thornton doubled over, screaming in pain.

"You bitch! You rotten bitch!" he groaned, dropping to his knees and curling up in a ball.

Maggie jumped up, grabbed Wally and the rest of her belongings, ran to the horses and untied them. She stopped, her foot on the step-up of the carriage and turned to the writhing man. "You'll find all your things at the livery." She turned her back, tossed Wally and her shoes on the seat, and climbed up. Before she sat down her arm was yanked back in a painful grip.

He jerked her off the carriage and threw her to the ground. She hit hard, but had been thrown off too many horses and knew how to land. Going limp the moment she realized she was going to hit the ground she rolled and sprang back to her feet.

"I'm not done with you, Miss Douglas. Not by a far measure."

"You're as done as you're going to get, Paul. If you don't stop this right now, I'll ruin you in town."

He threw his head back and laughed, a sound that resonated evil instead of mirth. "And if you run back to town crying about what I did or tried to do to you, whose story do you think they'll believe? I'm a respected member of their community who brings in a lot of revenue. They'll believe me, not some hussy who came to town spouting about women's rights and stirring up trouble."

"Some respected member of town. You run a brothel! You exploit women for money!"

Thornton charged. Before he could wrap his arms around her shoulders she slammed Wally into the side of his head. With barely a whimper Thornton slid to the ground.

Maggie wasted no time. She jumped into the carriage, turned the team around and raced back to town, thankful her naïvete was the only thing she'd lost today.

Chapter Five

The surprise in the livery man's eyes when Maggie returned the carriage told her he'd seen Paul Thornton return more than once with a disheveled young woman in the seat, but this was the first time he'd seen his carriage come back without *him*. She gathered her things and jumped down, a spring in her knees when she landed. "Tell Mr. Thornton I've returned his carriage and belongings safely." There was a smile on her lips.

The plump, white-haired man snorted and nodded. A wide grin spread across his face, a grin he didn't try to hide. "Yes, Ma'am!" He led the horses into the barn, his laughter echoing through the rafters behind him.

Maggie hurried toward the hotel, thinking it prudent she catch the evening train to her next destiny of Taunton. After she finished her business there, she was engaged to speak in the surrounding towns of Norton, Mansfield, and Easton in the days following. Although her departure would be a day early, she hoped to leave Mr. Paul Thornton and any revenge he may wish to seek on her behind. She'd wire her benefactors of her change of plans as soon as she arrived and hope there was a room available when she got there. Otherwise, it was going to be a long wait until her reservation opened. Although low on funds, she had to escape before Thornton made it back to town, bringing his anger and possibly that of every other man in town down on her.

In her flight from the river, she gauged the distance to be five or six miles, but could easily be mistaken by the quick pace she'd set. She hoped five or six miles afoot was far enough to allow her the time she needed to catch the seven o'clock train and be gone before Thornton made it back.

Inside her hotel room she shoved what little she had into her two satchels, paid the surprised clerk for her early departure, and went directly to the train depot to wait. She sat in a corner trying to be as inconspicuous as possible. When her stomach growled about six o'clock, she told it to be quiet. When her bottom went numb from the hard seat, she ignored it, as she did the hard stares of the men and women who passed her, apparently remembering who she was.

Anxious to be gone, she checked her watch often, praying her time wasn't running out. At 7:05 there came the labored chug, chug, chug of the train as it slowed coming up the tracks. Maggie closed her eyes and said a prayer of thanks that she'd surely be gone before being confronted by an angry Paul Thornton.

Her prayer was premature. Thornton stepped out in front of her when she stood up and started toward the train. "Going somewhere, Miss Douglas?" His controlled anger was obvious below the surface of his calm smile. His once handsome face was hard and an angry blue and black bruise ran from above his jaw to the top of his cheek on the left side of his face and around his eye. Maggie's heart nearly popped out of her chest. Deciding her only defense was to show no fear she took a deep breath and drew up her back. "I'm leaving. I'm due in Taunton in a few days and decided today was just as good a time to leave as any." *She about bit her tongue off yet again, realizing she'd told him exactly where she was going. Nothing she could do for it now.* She stepped forward.

He stepped closer and stopped only inches in front of her. "But *our* business isn't finished, Miss Douglas." His voice was cool and deep.

"I told you earlier, Mis-ter Thornton, we have no business."

"You're wrong." He grabbed her elbow in a painful grip and dragged her aside. "We have lots of business to conclude."

She jerked her arm away. "Mr. Thornton, I don't understand why you insist on continuing this charade. People are staring." She looked around the platform. People hurried toward the train, but curious eyes watched them.

"You said out by the river you aren't used to being beaten, well neither am I."

Maggie stepped to the side, angling toward the train, but he moved with her. "This isn't a game, Mr. Thornton; however, it *is* getting tedious. I have a train to catch." She stepped toward the platform again.

He stepped with her. "There's another one tomorrow."

"I'm leaving now—thanks to you." She stared him down, unwilling to give in. If there was one thing Maggie knew, it was how to be stubborn. There were people all over the platform now so he was in no position to try and force himself on her like he had earlier.

His nostrils flared, his eyes widened and his lips worked, but it took a moment before he swallowed, bowed and said, "Miss Douglas, I do apologize for my actions today. Please, let me make it up to you."

She laughed in his face. "No thank you. Your apology doesn't change anything. I'm still getting on that train. If you'll excuse me?" She tried to push by him, but he stepped in her path again.

"No."

Maggie felt a rush of uncertainty, but mostly she was angry. *Who the hell did he think he was?*

"Listen, Paul, our morning didn't turn out quite the way either of us intended. Let's just leave it at that. No one knows what happened out there—unless you tell them. This train is leaving and I'm going to be on it, whether you like it or not."

He grabbed her arm so hard she knew there'd be marks later. "You're not going anywhere. I'm not through with you yet."

She glared down to where he was crushing her arm between his curled fingers. *She'd had enough of this.* "I'll scream," she threatened, her voice rising with each word. "People are staring. Let me go!" She jerked free again.

He scanned the platform, only then seeming to realize they weren't alone and that people were stopping to stare, some even stepping forward as though to offer aid. His calm demeanor slipped and he backed away. "You think you're pretty smart, don't you?" he said through gritted teeth. "Well, you're not as smart as you think. I won't forget you, Maggie Douglas, don't you forget *that*."

He turned and stalked away, his back stiff his stride long. Maggie watched him go in stunned silence. Chills ran up and down her spine until the loudspeaker blared a second time the train was in its final boarding. Hurrying aboard, she placed her things on the seat beside her, sat down and forced herself to breathe normally. Laying her head back against the rough seat she closed her eyes and prayed Taunton would be better. *It couldn't be worse.*

Taunton was only about 30 miles away and seemed to be a town of some distinction. Leaving the train station, Maggie headed toward the center of town where a sign told of Taunton's history, one established by members of the original Plymouth Colony back in 1637. Called Cohannet by the Indians before the arrival of Europeans, it was now referred to as *Silver City* for its vast silver industry. Signs hung along the main street with names like Reed & Barton, F.B. Rogers, and Pool Silver.

This must be a forward-thinking town, Maggie thought hopefully, scanning Main Street and its bustling businesses. Down the road was the town hall where she would speak in two days. Forward-thinking meant she might actually be heard. Hope rose in her chest. *Perhaps this town would be different.*

She couldn't have been more wrong.

The lights were high and bright, nearly blinding Maggie from where she sat at the back of the stage. Well-dressed men and women, most likely leaders of the community, sat at the front of the hall, while the rear was filled with what appeared to be the "every day" people; those who worked hard for what little they got and didn't get it off the backs of others. Everyone was reserved and respectful and Maggie prayed they would remain so, at least long enough to hear what she had to say. She was growing weary of the constant drudgery of moving from town to town, speaking and not being heard, and being used for target practice by angry men. *Perhaps tonight will be different,* she hoped again, looking out into the sea of faces.

Eustice Wilson, the reed-thin, hawk-nosed, unattractive woman who had invited Maggie to speak, stepped to the front of the stage and raised her hands for silence. The room quieted within moments. "Thank you for coming this evening ladies and gentlemen. We have a very distinguished guest with us to speak about an issue important to everyone here. The rights of women—our women, any woman."

Maggie searched the room that held about thirty people and waited for the usual cat calls and insults toward Miss Wilson and herself, but everyone remained calm.

"Miss Maggie Douglas, a young woman tutored by Massachusetts' own Lucy Stone, is here with us to tell us more about this great movement. A movement that cannot be stopped—only understood."

The men in the room squirmed. The women raised their chins and smiled.

Without further ado, I introduce to you Miss Maggie Douglas."

Maggie stepped up to the edge of the stage and looked out into the hall. A group of six or eight young women of all shapes and sizes stood at the back of the room, wide smiles on their faces, clapping excitedly. The rest of those gathered clapped politely, but remained seated, their faces expectant.

She cleared her throat. "I'd like to thank Miss Wilson for inviting me to speak, and I'd like to thank everyone that came tonight to listen." She stopped and waited for the first insult that always came after her opening remark, but the room remained silent. "I speak to you about a very important issue, that of the rights of women, the right to vote, to have a voice and to be heard." Still there was silence and with that silent encouragement, Maggie launched into her speech.

"It began long before the Civil War," she explained, telling the audience how Miss Lucy Stone, Miss Elizabeth Cady Stanton, Miss Susan B. Anthony and many others formed the Woman's National Loyal League of 1863 and had been instrumental in getting the Thirteenth Amendment passed in 1864 abolishing slavery. "Following the war, your very own Miss Stone helped form the American Equal Rights Association, whose main goal was to achieve equal voting rights for *all* people of *any* race." She paused to let what she's said sink in. "Yes, ladies and gentlemen, *all* people and *all* races. And they succeeded—to a point. Men who were slaves now have the right to vote, but a woman does not. Whether a Negro woman or a white woman, we are the same, all are disallowed the right to vote."

"Women aren't educated to vote, Miss Douglas. They're born and bred to bear children and take care of their families. Why should they be allowed to vote when they don't understand politics?" a well-dressed man asked politely from the second row of the audience. The men beside and around him nodded agreement, while the women nearby pursed their lips in anger.

Maggie took a deep breath to keep from screaming in frustration. He sounded like he was discussing the breeding of prized livestock rather than the rights of women and his words brought back memories of too many heated discussions around the dinner table at the Lazy D. Although the man was well-dressed and well-mannered, he was as ignorant as any of the hundreds of other men she'd spoken to in the past.

"Sir, you have hit on a very delicate subject for me. Part of the reason I'm here is because my father and brothers told me from a young age that birthing babies and taking care of a husband and family was all I was good for. However!" she shouted, raising her arm, and pointing her finger in the air for dramatic effect that jerked many a wandering eye back to the stage. "I am much more than a baby maker. I have a brain, gentlemen, that is as whip smart as anyone here that can think and decide the politics for my town or country as well as any of you!"

The men squirmed in earnest now, but Maggie didn't give them time to rebut before she shouted, "An education, gentleman, an education is the key! An education is all it takes for a woman to understand the politics necessary to vote."

A middle-aged man stood up at the center of the hall and doffed his slightly tattered hat. He, too, was well-groomed, but his suit was worn at the elbows and around the collar and pockets. He was not under-weight and neither was he fat, but his eyes had a tired, used up look. "It is more promising and productive for me to spend what meager funds I have to educate my son and not my daughter," he began, twirling his hat between his fingers. "I'm not a wealthy man, Miss Douglas, not all of us are. I must be selective with how my children are educated and how I spend my hard-earned funds. My daughter will always have the option of marrying and thus being taken care of by her husband. My son will not. He must know how to take care of himself *and* his family."

Maggie thought a moment before responding. "Sir, I agree your son must be educated; however, not all women want to be married, have children and raise a family, at least not until later in their lives. In the interim, will your daughter live with you until that decision is made or will she take a job, find a home of her own and support herself until she does marry? In my travels, I must take care of myself. I must be educated to do so, and in that education I must know about my surroundings, about my town and my government."

The room grew silent and for the first time Maggie thought someone might actually be listening. She continued with more history, telling the crowd how Susan B. Anthony had tried to vote in 1872, but was arrested, instead. "After a change of venue she was brought to trial where the judge instructed the jury *to find her guilty with no discussion!*" Maggie shouted, letting the words hang before continuing a few moments later. "She was fined $100, which she refused to pay, and was eventually released. That gentlemen, is how our system of government treats a woman who wants a voice in the running of her country!"

Grumbling erupted throughout the room and Maggie waited for the explosion of insults. Her head cocked in surprise when none came. Drawing in a fresh breath, she continued. "It is time for women to be recognized and to give them a voice in what matters to all of us. Our families are important, yes, but our communities and what happens in our country should concern us, as well. Our time of drudgery is behind us and it's time we speak out and make ourselves heard!"

The door to the rear of the hall burst open with a resounding crash. Eight or ten raggedly dressed men poured in across the back of the room. Maggie's jaw dropped when the last man stepped inside. Her skin bubbled and rolled with fear as Paul Thornton followed a few steps behind the others along the left-side of the room toward the stage. All conversation halted as the men sauntered toward the front, their eyes gleaming with mischief—save one. Thornton only had eyes for Maggie, glaring at her with open hatred. His eyes pierced her like a spear as he ambled forward, a wide smile on his face, as though he had not a care in the world.

He stopped five feet from the stage, grabbed the lapels of his finely cut suit coat and turned only half way toward the audience. "Ladies and gentlemen of Taunton, I am Paul

Thornton. I am a successful business owner who has dealt with this woman before." He raised his hand to where Maggie stood on the stage. "I give you warning! Do not be taken in by her. *This* is what happens when you are deceived by her words!" There was a unified gasp when he turned so all could see his grossly black eye and the purplish, blue streak that covered the whole left side of his face.

"That's not true!" Maggie screamed from the stage. "He attacked me," she defended. "I only protected myself!"

Thornton laughed that deep, low chuckle that made Maggie's skin crawl. He swept his arm across his chest with a flourish and shouted, "A quiet carriage ride, everyone, was all I expected, but before I knew it I had a gun slammed against my skull and my possessions stolen!"

"That's not true! He attacked me I tell you and I did *not* steal his belongings!"

Thornton snickered. "So she says. I took, what I thought was a finely bred lady, to breakfast and then for a quiet carriage ride. The next thing I knew, I was out cold, my money *and* my carriage were gone, and she was on the next train out of town!" he shouted for extra show.

The audience grumbled and Maggie knew she had to stop this now or she was in serious trouble. "Please! That's not how it happened. We went to breakfast and for a carriage ride, but I did *not* attack him. It was the other way around! And I certainly did *not* take his money or his possessions. I returned his carriage and belongings when I got back to town!"

"So you say, Miss Douglas," Thornton drawled. "I woke up to find everything gone and had to walk the six miles to town dazed with my head splitting. Here is the evidence of what happened!" He pointed to his face with flourish.

"It's not true! You attacked me. You tricked me into using all the ammunition in my gun so I couldn't protect myself when you attacked me!" She watched the eyes of the audience turn hard and realized the moment she mentioned having her own gun, she'd lost them. They were beginning to believe Thornton's story. "He's lying. I went for a simple carriage ride and once we stopped he attacked me!"

"I'm sure you did nothing to lead him on, did you, Miss Douglas?" shouted one of the rabble who had arrived with Thornton.

"Of course I didn't. I only wanted to enjoy a quiet ride before I departed the next day to come here."

"You went alone, with no escort?" another of the men asked, a snide smirk on his lips, adding fuel to an already growing fire.

"I'm not a child. I don't need an escort. What's wrong with you people? Can't you see he's lying? Why would he have brought all these other men with him if not to stir up trouble?" Maggie pointed out.

"We've only come to make sure you don't stir up trouble for the fine people of this town." Thornton waved at the men accompanying him.

"Seems to us, Miss Douglas, you're the one stirring up trouble," was shouted from the audience.

"I'm telling you, it's not true! He attacked me. I merely defended myself."

"Is this what women like you preach?" a well-dressed man in the front row shouted, shaking his fist. "What were you hoping for when you took this man's offer of a carriage ride, alone?" The man stood up. "I'll not have my wife listen to this kind of talk. Come Ruth, we're leaving." He roughly grabbed his wife's arm and led her out, followed by others.

Maggie shook her head. "That's not what I wanted. I merely agreed to a meal and a carriage ride. I'm a grown woman who does *not* need an escort!"

"Apparently you do, Miss Douglas!" someone shouted from the crowd.

"We don't want you here!"

"Get out of our town. We don't want to hear anything you have to say!"

"Get her boys!"

Maggie knew she was in serious trouble. She ran toward the stairs at the back of the stage, but one of Thornton's men blocked her way. She whirled and ran in the other direction, but Thornton was already on the stage.

"Paul, don't do this. You know the truth. You know I didn't do what you say I did."

His eyes gleamed with malice. "I only know what you didn't do, Maggie. Now it's time to pay the debt you owe me—one way or another. Just say the word and I'll make this stop."

"I will not!" She ran toward him and shoved him aside, but another ruffian was right behind him. She slammed into the man and he locked his arms around her like the thick branches of a tree. "Let go of me! You have no right," she screamed, trying to break free.

"Last train outta town leaves in a thirty minutes," someone shouted from the audience.

"How about she's on it?" Thornton asked, standing beside her and the man holding her.

Those remaining in the audience erupted with cheers of agreement. "Get her out of here!"

"We don't want her in our town."

"Run her out on a rail…"

"How can you? You know what happened? This is wrong," Maggie shouted at Thornton, staring into his disfigured face, disbelieving he was the same handsome man she'd imagined a quiet, carriage ride with only days ago.

"What I know is that I don't like to lose."

Maggie had never known real fear until that moment. She was hoisted up by several of Thornton's men and carried to the middle of Main Street kicking and thrashing. "I didn't do what he says. I took his carriage back with everything accountable *after* he attacked me. I didn't do what he says. You must believe me!"

Maggie was set on her feet in the street. Thornton sidled up beside her and whispered. "I told you you'd pay, Maggie. It's a shame you doubted me."

Maggie spit in his face. He raised his arm to strike. "Do it! Show these people who you *really* are."

Thornton pulled out his kerchief and wiped his face instead. "I have no intention of striking you, Miss Douglas. We have something else in mind for you."

Coming from an alley between two buildings Maggie spotted two men carrying what looked like the top rail of a fencepost. She caught her breath. *They were going to ride her on a rail!* She'd heard about it, even heard some of the other suffragist women speak their fears of that very thing happening in their travels, but Maggie never dreamed...

Thornton laughed beside her. "We won't be *too* hard on you, Miss Douglas. You haven't murdered anyone, but we are going to remind you of what you are and that is *not* a man. Charlie!" Thornton bellowed. A squat, balding man ran up to him with a bucket brimming with what looked like syrup.

Maggie squirmed against the men holding her, but she was powerless to break free. The crowd was growing and the people's faces appeared hard and angry, not ashamed or guilty. The insults on her person were being flung like the rotten fruit she'd borne so often, and she knew this was one time she wasn't going to talk her way out of trouble. In light of that realization, she drew up to her full height, took a deep breath and shouted, "I see your intent and I will bear it with strength and dignity, but know this, you are punishing the wrong person!" Maggie squared her chin and shoulders and stared out over the crowd, looking everyone in the eye.

"Let her have it boys." Thornton's voice was the last thing she heard before the bucket of cold maple syrup was dumped over her head and the contents of a feather pillow emptied next. There was syrup and white chicken feathers from her head to her waist, the feathers stark against her black hair and the dark syrup, but she stood stoic, bearing their torment with dignity. *She would* not *allow them to humiliate her for something she did not do*!

Maggie felt like she was being torn in half when she was hoisted none too gently onto the fence rail. There were feathers in her mouth and eyes. She spat and coughed and kept her eyes closed tight to bear the humiliation. *Feeling* it was almost more than she could take.

"Get out of our town, *Miss* Douglas. We don't want you here."

"Go corrupt some other town!" faceless voices taunted.

The post was hoisted into the air. Maggie wrapped her arms around it and held on tight to keep from rolling upside down. Her heart was thundering, her body was shaking, and she couldn't keep the tears from streaming out of her eyes. Her father's face jumped into her mind and the shame he would have felt if he saw her now nearly made her throw up, but the vengeance he would reap made her smile. Although they differed in views, he and her brothers would never tolerate such actions against their daughter and sister and would have quickly straightened out this crowd. With her eyes closed, hugging the post to keep from sliding under it, she was paraded up and down what she presumed was Main Street, bearing her shame in silence. She would *not* allow them to see any guilt, for she had none, nor would she beg forgiveness or admit to something for which she was innocent. Taunted up and down the street to admit her guilt, Maggie remained silent. Her teeth clattered from the rough handling of the rail, her womanly parts hurt more than she imagined a woman experienced in childbirth, her inner thighs screamed in agony, and her spirit nearly broke. But she refused to give in. *She was innocent and before she left this place they would know it!*

It seemed like hours, although she knew it had been only minutes, before the bone-wracking torture stopped and she was jerked down. She managed to stand straight and proud before opening her eyes for the first time since her "punishment" began. Standing tall she shouted, "I am innocent and when you realize the kind of man my accuser is, you will know every one of you is as guilty as he for having done this shameful deed."

Thornton, standing across from her, clapped. Some of the ruffians who had arrived with him clapped, too, but Maggie realized the rest of the crowd was already gone. The only ones remaining were the men who had arrived with Thornton—*paid thugs.*

His smile turned malicious. He stepped forward and dropped her two satchels at her feet. "Here are your things. The train leaves in ten minutes. Your ticket has been paid for, be on it."

Maggie grabbed her bags and hurried to the depot, yanking off as many feathers as she could on the way. By the time she arrived, she'd managed to pull most of the feathers off her chest and arms, but her hair was a syrupy mess and feathers stuck out in every direction. She cared not and ignored the stares of those she met. The only thing she wanted was to be as far away from here as fast as she could. She had no idea where the train was going, but wherever it stopped she'd bathe and wash Paul Thornton and Taunton out of her life forever.

Chapter Six

On her knees, Maggie grabbed the side of the round metal tub, closed her eyes, took a deep breath, and plunged her head into the already dirty water. She shook her head back and forth then scrubbed her scalp one last time to be sure she'd gotten rid of the last vestiges of her humiliating experience. Her lungs ready to explode, she slung her head back, the sopping mass of wet hair slapping her body like a whip. Gasping, gripping the side again, she let the water sluice down her face and over her neck and shoulders. She wanted only to be rid of any remnants of Paul Thornton and Taunton, both physically and mentally.

She didn't know the name of the town she'd landed in and didn't care. Getting off at the first stop, she'd hurried to the only hotel in the tiny, dusty town, gotten a room amidst amused stares, and used almost the last of her cash to have a bath brought to her room. All she wanted was to be clean again, to crawl into bed and—do what? Her eyes popped open and she squeezed the tub tighter. *Yes, do what? Forget Taunton happened?* She knew it was easier to hope for than do. *Should she track down Miss Stone and ask her for help? Should she pretend it hadn't happened and go on to the next town and possibly get ridden out on a rail again?* Maggie sighed and pushed to her feet, her knees popping. Staring down at the swirling, murky water, she wished for a new bath, but knew she'd been lucky to get what she had. There was no choice but to use the already dirty water. She scooped out as many feathers as she could then closed her eyes and tried to imagine she was in one of the clear creeks at the Lazy D and stepped in. She sat down and pulled her knees tight in the murky, cooling tub. Ensconced in the brown liquid, she let her head rest against the rim and allowed the water to soothe her aching muscles and wounded pride. *I can continue on this course—or I can do something else. But what? I can go home. But I'd have to go with my tail tucked between my legs, never to speak of what happened to my family and,* her heart suddenly leapt at the thought, *I can find George and beg his forgiveness for how badly I treated him!* The realization of how much she missed him hit her like a blow. Tears streamed down her face and sobs wracked her chest. *What a fool you've been! You gave up George's love to be spat upon, insulted, used for target practice and, finally, run out-of-town on a rail! For what? To* educate *strangers about women's rights! To* educate *people who don't* want *to learn about such things!*

Her tears continued until her eyes were so puffy she could barely see. She finished her bath, pulled herself out of the cold water and wrapped the shabby towel around her. Not even remembering how, she dried off and crawled into the mushy bed in nothing but the sheets and slept without moving until the sun warmed her face the next morning.

After days on more than one dirty, hot train, and using the last of her money to pay a livery to drive her to the ranch from the depot in Kansas City, Maggie was home. Standing on the front porch of the Lazy D, she looked around the only home she'd ever known. Things appeared the same—yet they were different. The corral where she'd worked many a horse and baited George on more than one occasion, stood empty. The bunkhouse was deserted, but it was the middle of the day she reminded herself, so the hands would be working elsewhere. The barn door was closed, the yard quieter than she remembered it should be even in the middle of the day. *Where were the men working the yearlings or breaking the two-year-olds?* she wondered. Dropping her bags, she took a calming breath and knocked. The door was flung open and there stood Judith, the plump, gray-haired housekeeper who had been at the Lazy D for over twenty-five years. In a heartbeat Maggie was enveloped in Judith's arms, the woman's hands smoothing the hair that only a few days before had been filled with maple syrup and feathers.

"Bless the Heavens, child. You've come home," Judith cooed in her ear.

Maggie pulled away, tears sliding down her cheeks. She couldn't speak, only managed to nod before Judith pulled her into another embrace. It took several minutes before Maggie was able to step back and ask, "Where's Pa and the boys?"

"They're checking fence in the north pasture."

"Why are *they* riding fence? Where are all the hands?" Maggie asked, the curious feeling about the desolation of the ranch striking her as odd.

"We're running slim these days, Maggie." The housekeeper poked Maggie in the side. "We could sure use your help. The new hands just don't measure up these days, according to your Pa and brothers. Half don't know how to fix a fence and the other half don't know how to brand or rope. And the other half don't know their asses from…" She raised her chin and blushed. "Things just aren't the same since you left, Maggie girl. Your Pa and brothers went half-crazy with worry when you when you lit out of here."

Maggie sighed. The last thing she wanted was to discuss her family's feelings about her hasty departure, although once they returned, she'd have no choice. She made a decision and she'd stuck by it. What she wanted to know now, was about George.

"What about George?" she asked her heart beating faster.

"George? George who?"

Not a good sign. Maggie steeled herself. If Judith didn't know who George was, there was a good chance he wasn't here anymore and that she was too late. "George Hawkins, the man I brought home from the fort who'd had a tussle with some of the soldiers there. He was a guest for a few days then went to work for us." Maggie waited, her heart still pounding.

"Oh, him." She grimaced before she said, "Your Pa and the boys were pretty mad at him after you left. They were sure he knew where you went or knew you were leaving and didn't tell them."

"But he didn't know. He had no idea, about anything. Even I didn't know I was leaving until that very day."

"Well, they were pretty mad at him."

"Did they fire him?"

Judith shook her head. "He stayed on a little while then left on his own, but your Pa didn't fire him."

"Where did he go?" Maggie asked, knowing it was already too late.

Judith frowned and shook her head again. "I don't know, child. He was just a hired man. I don't keep track of the cowboys. They come and go so quick through here, I'm lucky to know their names when they're here!" She wrapped her arm around Maggie's shoulders and led her toward the stairway. "Come on now, enough talk about missing cowboys. Let's get you settled so you can surprise your Pa and brothers when they come in."

Maggie had no choice. Her hopes of finding George were gone. She had no money of her own, her dreams of being a motivating force in the women's movement were over—and she'd lost George. She forced a smile and let Judith lead her up the stairs to her old room, the woman chattering like a magpie the whole way.

Maggie stepped inside the bedroom behind the housekeeper who continued to ramble about how Mr. Douglas had not allowed her to straighten or move a thing.

It was as though Maggie had stepped back in time and she'd been there only this morning. Clothes she'd discarded in her rush to pack for her ill-fated journey were strewn across the beige canopied bed, her only concession to being a girl. The fancy French armoire that had once been her mother's stood open, her riding clothes hanging haphazardly from their wooden hangers, her boots lined up in a neat row on the floor below and two cowboy hats on the shelf above. Her dressing table stood empty; everything there she'd taken with her, the chair crooked, the mirror dusty. The left curtain over the bed hung limp while the right was drawn up. A waterless pitcher and bowl sat in front of the window to the left, a towel draped over the top, right where she'd left it. Nothing had been moved or disturbed. The only thing that had changed was her.

Judith left to start dinner and Maggie re-hung scattered clothes, folded others and put them in the dresser before she unpacked what few belongings she'd come home with. The room in order again, she laid down on her belly on the bed, cradling her head in the soft pillow, a luxury she hadn't felt in a long time. Surrounded by feelings of warmth and belonging, although defeat nipped close at her heels, she quickly fell asleep.

"Get up, Maggs! Let me look at you!" Stuart Douglas's voice thundered through the haze of sleep.

Maggie jerked up, rolled onto her back and sat up, her head spinning. "Pa," she croaked, rubbing her eyes, her mouth tasting like an army had tramped through it.

"Get up girl and let me see you."

Maggie struggled to her feet, not wanting to leave the comfort she'd found in her bed.

"You look like you been rode hard, girl. Seems your new life doesn't quite agree with you."

Maggie bit down on a sharp reply. "Nice to see you, too, Pa. You don't look so great yourself." She poked his stomach and brushed her hand across his still-thick hair. "Got a bit of a paunch there, eh? And there's an awful lot of gray in that black mane you're so proud of."

He grinned. "Nothing gets past you, does it Maggs?"

Maggie frowned at his use of the nickname she thought she'd long ago broken her family from using, but she let it pass. It was her homecoming and she didn't want to spoil it.

"Where are James and Edward?" Now that she was home, Maggie was anxious to see her entire family—at least until they started badgering her about getting married and raising babies again.

"They're right behind me." The words were no sooner out of his mouth than Maggie heard them clattering up the stairs.

"Maggie!" James, taller and stockier than Maggie remembered, his hair as black as hers and in need of a haircut, charged into the room, swept her off her feet and twirled around in a circle. "You're home! Why didn't you let us know you were coming?"

Maggie chuckled and hugged her brother. "Thought I'd surprise you," she lied. She kissed his cheek and hugged him again before pushing at his chest. "Let me go so I can say hello to Edward."

James put her on her feet. She turned and gave her oldest brother a warm hug and kiss, eying him closely. He was the tallest of the three men and fair. Where Stuart, Maggie and James were dark-haired with deep blue eyes, Edward's hair was barely brown, with eyes as green as sprouting pasture grass in the spring, like their mother's had been. She'd heard them called "smiling eyes" and Maggie agreed; when Edward smiled his entire face lit up, including his eyes.

"Don't forget your Pa." Stuart opened his arms and Maggie stepped into them, easily accepting the warmth he offered. She laid her head on his chest, taking in the smell of sweat and leather, dust and hay, smells Maggie had forgotten she loved. Her eyes still closed, she realized just how many things on the ranch she'd missed. Regardless her brothers and father drove her insane with their constant badgering, she was glad to be home and looking forward to getting back to some kind of routine, until she decided where she wanted to go with her life.

She lifted her head and sighed. "I must admit, it's good to be home."

"We're glad you're back. I probably shouldn't ask, but are you home for good?" Stuart ventured.

Maggie pursed her lips and shook her head. "I honestly don't know, Pa. I hadn't thought past getting here. Let's see how things go." Knowing she was too late to catch George sent a twinge of regret through her. *What would she do now? Stay and pretend she never experienced everything she had in her travels? Or should she relent and just do what her father and brothers wanted? Find a man, get married and have those babies they wanted her to have? It wasn't that she didn't want children; it was just that she didn't want them* now. And with another twinge of regret, she realized that if she did have children, she wanted them to be George's.

James poked her, pulling her back from her regrets and what ifs.

"Judith's got a huge welcome home meal ready, Sis. Your favorite; fried chicken, green beans cooked in bacon grease and fried taters." James's eyes glittered and he smacked his lips.

Maggie's stomach growled, reminding her she hadn't had a good meal since the breakfast she'd shared with Thornton days ago.

"Sounds like you're in need of a good meal," Edward teased, poking her in the belly.

She knew her face had to be aflame. "I didn't realize just how hungry until right now. The thought of Judith's fried chicken is making my mouth water and my stomach growl." She turned her back on her family.

"Race you!" she called over her shoulder, already out the door.

Judith's fried chicken tasted better than Maggie remembered and she ate until she thought she'd pop. Her father and brothers watched her covertly throughout the meal, saying little, allowing her to enjoy every bite. She was just finishing when her father finally spoke.

"It's good to have you home, Maggie, but we're curious about what brought you back."

Maggie thought she'd choke on the last piece of meat in her mouth. Forcing herself to stay calm, she said, "I just got tired of hot trains, tiny rooms, and lousy food." She waved her fork across the empty plate. "It's been way too long since I've had a meal to rival one of Judith's."

"That's it?" James asked, seemingly disappointed. "You were never insulted in your travels or had rotten food thrown at you like I've read about in more than one accounting of those suffragist rallies back east?"

Maggie finished chewing. "I won't say there weren't insults or rotten food thrown; but you know me, when I put my mind to something nothing is going to stop me until I'm ready."

"You must have worn more of that food than you ate, Sis," Edward said. "You're thin as a rail."

Edward's innocent reference to a rail made Maggie flush. She knew her cheeks had to be red because she felt the heat racing up her neck.

"Like I said, the food left little to compare with Judith's cooking, and living in hotel rooms not much bigger than my closet didn't offer much in the way of comfort. When I wasn't speaking boredom was the order of the day. Most of the towns were so small there was little more to do than speak and wait for the train to wherever I was going next. There was more boredom than excitement to complain about."

Anxious to change the subject before too many questions came up that Maggie didn't want to answer, she turned to her father. "The ranch seemed awfully deserted when I got in this afternoon. Where are all the hands, Pa?"

Stuart frowned and the brothers snorted. "Gold fever Maggie girl. They come through here, work long enough to make the fare to catch a train west to find their fortunes in gold, and they're gone."

"Are they heading for the Black Hills? George told me all about the gold Custer found there before the Little Bighorn in '76." Her heart jumped at the mere mention of George and she realized this was the perfect opportunity to ask about him. "Speaking of George, is he still around?" she asked, knowing full well he was already gone.

James shook his head. "He left out not long after you did, Sis. I think he was pining for you," James said with a grin.

"Why would you say something like that, James?"

"Because it's true," Edward said before James could answer. "Come on, Maggie, you may not *think* we knew, but we were all aware you and George were, well...."

"What?" Maggie felt like her heart had dropped to her feet.

"We all saw it the first night George got here. There was electricity between the two of you nobody could miss," Stuart said, trying to suppress a grin and failing.

Maggie sighed. Her shoulders drooped and she shook her head in disbelief. "I can't believe this. We sneaked around trying to hide because I was sure you would disapprove of him. What about that night you confronted me? You asked me right out if we were sneaking around. Of course I lied, and I could tell you didn't believe me, but you certainly didn't *sound* like you approved if we *were* involved!"

"We figured if you *thought* we disapproved, you'd run even faster toward him—the way you did everything else. From the time you were little, Maggie, the more we told you no, the more you wanted something. Hell, that's how you became so good at everything. Whenever we told you you couldn't do something, you went out and practiced until you were better than anybody else." Stuart frowned again. "Initially we wanted someone from our own station, but after all, you weren't a young girl anymore. Twenty years old is no spring chicken, girl, and we wanted better for you. We had to hope for someone that would at least love you and we all decided we might as well root for George. We liked him well enough and figured the rest would follow since you two did seem to like each other." Her father raised his shoulders. "He didn't have money, and we knew it, but we figured we'd pushed too hard in that direction already, so we decided to go for love. I was going to give you two a stake and figured the rest would take care of itself." He sighed. "And then you left."

Maggie couldn't believe what she was hearing. *They were talking like she'd been a prized mare and they'd been hunting for the perfect stud. And when they couldn't get the specifications they wanted, they decided George would do because he cared about her. They'd actually known their secret and kept quiet about it. Had she thrown everything she might have had with George away chasing dreams of making a difference in the women's movement because she believed they wouldn't approve of him for a husband? Had she been a fool for throwing everything away to pursue her dreams or had she done what she had to do because of who she was? What did she have to show, other than bruised pride, for traipsing around the country for two years being disrespected and abused?*

She swallowed and looked at her family. "Where is George now?" She felt deceived and that she'd left for no reason. *But was that wholly true? Wouldn't she have gone anyway? She'd had things to do and had been willing to give up George to do them. She even used his love as an excuse to go.* Everything was suddenly all mixed up!

James shook his head. "We don't know where George is, Sis. He moped around here for weeks after you left."

"We were pretty rough on him," Edward cut in. "Even though he told us you'd gone to Boston, we thought he'd known beforehand you were leaving and hadn't told us. We were angry with him, but we were angrier with ourselves for not letting you know we were happy you and George were getting together and we took it out on him. Because we'd kept quiet—you were gone."

"George had no idea I was leaving," Maggie defended for the second time today. "*I* didn't even know I was going until he and I fought that day about our being together. He wanted me to tell you about us and I told him he was crazy. He even asked me to marry him!" Their faces registered shock at how much their interference had cost before she added, "I told him *no* because you all wouldn't approve! I even told him about your running Albert off to make him understand how much you wouldn't approve. I never dreamed you were rooting for us, otherwise, I *might* have stayed." Maggie had never felt so betrayed. And by her own family!

Her brothers and father grew uncomfortable. *Good. Let them squirm. They deserve it for interfering in my life, yet again!*

"You have no idea where he went?" Maggie ventured, hoping to get some scrap of information.

Stuart shook his head. "He never told us. Just said good-bye and headed west."

West, Maggie thought. *That's a lot of territory, but at least it's a direction. She would stay here until she was ready then head west. Maybe someday she'd find him. Now all she had to do was figure out how to get there, how to find him, and what to do in between.*

Chapter Seven

Maggie let Beulah have her head and the two raced hell-for-leather across the flat, open pasture. The light palomino mare had been rank at first from lack of riding, but after a few minutes of lunging in circles around the corral and lots of loving, the horse relented. She'd let her master know how much she'd missed her and the two now rode like they'd covered the terrain yesterday. The mare stretched out, nostrils flaring, feet pounding and Maggie flattened herself against the horse's neck. The wind whipped through Maggie's unbound hair and the sun was hot on her back and shoulders. She felt free racing against the wind, feeling as though Beulah's legs were hers, and she wondered how she could have gone so long without realizing how much she loved and missed the ranch.

She slowed Beulah to a lope and then a jogging trot. Maggie grimaced at the discomfort it caused in her still-tender thighs and buttocks before she finally brought the horse to a walk to cool her down. Maggie stroked the animal's neck. "I've missed you, Beulah girl." The horse threw her head up and down as though in agreement.

Maggie'd been home for two weeks. After her father and brothers' confessions at dinner the first night, they hadn't spoken again about George or her travels, which suited Maggie just fine. She had no intention of letting her family know that being run-out-of-town on a rail had really prompted her return. It was bad enough they knew she'd been insulted and used as a target on a regular basis, but her pride couldn't handle letting them know how badly she'd been mistreated—and knowing she'd get more than one "I told you so" in response.

She'd spent the last two weeks rediscovering the ranch, what needed to be done and what she could do to help. The lack of hands was obvious. She jumped in and did her share to help as soon as she could. She pulled fence with her brothers, culled out acorn calves to be fed extra grain and molasses-covered ground-up corn to fatten them up. She'd even roped strays that had gotten through the fence before they'd been able to fix it. She loved being on Beulah's back, doing what was needed around the ranch and appreciated coming in at night smelly and sweaty just like her brothers and father after a hard day's work and sitting down to one of Judith's well-prepared and well-deserved meals.

Maggie was taking some time for herself on this beautiful Sunday afternoon, trying to decide what to do with her life. *Could she stay at the Lazy D, doing what she loved, yet knowing there was so much more out there to be learned and experienced? And what about her need to find George? Was there even a chance?*

Turning Beulah around and giving the horse her head again, it took them only an hour to get back to the ranch. At the barn Maggie removed the horse's tack and hung it in its proper places. She pumped two buckets of water and poured them over Beulah's back to cool her down then grabbed a brush. With long, deliberate strokes, Maggie smoothed Beulah's sleek coat and in the time it took to finish, she made a decision. She was going to find George and it was time to tell her father and brothers. They'd grumble and argue and try to talk her out of it, but her mind was made up.

Maggie gathered her family in the front room after dinner that night to tell them her plans.

"What's the big secret, Sis?" James plopped down on the brown and black, cloth-covered settee nearest the front door.

Edward sat down in one of the black overstuffed, leather chairs beside the floor-to-ceiling gray rock fireplace, Stuart in the matching chair on the other side of the hearth. The elder Douglas sighed and picked at his nails with a small knife. "We're all here, Maggie. What's so all-fired important?"

Annoyed with her family's lack of attention, Maggie took a deep breath and plunged in. "I've come to a decision about what I want to do with my life."

All three men's heads popped up, their eyes riveted on Maggie.

"Here we go again," James mumbled.

"Let her talk," Edward chastised.

Maggie ignored James and smiled at Edward. "I'm leaving."

All three men jerked forward in their seats. "And going where?" Anger was heavy in Stuart's question. "We're short-handed. You're needed here. You just got back and you're going to abandon us again already?" Her father paused then added harshly, "Do you at least plan to give us the courtesy of a good-bye this time?"

Maggie ground her teeth together and almost backed down. Instead, she straightened her shoulders and raised her chin. "I'm going to find George."

The floor reverberated with the thud of feet hitting it when they all three men jumped up at the same time. "You're what?" they shouted in unison.

"I'm going to find George." She enunciated each word for clarity.

"You will not! You're home and you're going to stay. We need you here."

Maggie looked away from the anger in her father's eyes. "Pa, I'm sorry it's been hard to find good hands to run the ranch. As much as I love the D and would like to stay, I have things I still want to do, need to do, away from here."

"Like running around the country spouting off about women's rights?" James chided.

Maggie felt her face flush and anger boiled in her belly. Her eyes pinched and she pointed at her brother. "Yes, that's right. I'm not a little girl anymore in case any of you have noticed! It's my choice what I want to do with my life and no one else's. I'm sure as soon as this crazy gold rush is over you'll have more than enough hands to run the ranch, but right now, I have to go."

"To find George." Stuart ground out.

"Yes." She glared at her family. "And, I'd like to point out that you're all partially responsible for my having to go. If you'd minded your own damn business and left George and I alone, maybe something more would have happened between us. Maybe!" she shouted, stopping a retort from James. "But I still had things I wanted to do and probably would have left anyway, so I won't put *all* the blame on your shoulders, but you all played a big part so don't try to deny it." One by one she stared her family back into their seats.

They stewed a few moments before Stuart said, "We may have liked George and hoped you might eventually marry him, Maggie, but it was never intended for you to chase him across the country to do it!" Stuart crossed his arms over his chest to show his authority like he used to do when she was a little girl.

Maggie's back stiffened as both her brothers crossed their arms and nodded like their father. "I'm going Pa and you can't stop me. You can't tell me what to do anymore."

"The hell I can't! You have a stake in this ranch after I'm dead. If you leave I'll…"

"You'll what?" she asked, unable to believe he would actually threaten to disinherit her.

Her father growled deep in his throat and threw his hands in the air. "Damn it Maggie, I'm not going to do a damned thing and you know it. We can handle running this ranch. Hell, your brothers and I have been doing it since you left the first time without a word."

Maggie grimaced at the well-aimed jibe.

"We're just concerned for your safety." Stuart sighed, shook his head and ran his fingers through his still-thick hair.

Maggie went to her father and dropped to her knee beside his chair. "I know, Pa, and I love you all for it. But I have to do this; just like I had to go on my adventure to Boston. It made me stronger. Everything I learned in the time I was gone made me stronger."

"Stronger?" Her father's head jerked up, his eyes wide. "Girl, you're stronger than most men I know. You get any stronger and nobody'll realize you're a woman!" he growled, but with a slight grin.

"They'll know, especially George when I find him, *if* I find him. He'll know." She pursed her lips. "I treated him badly, Pa. I used you and James and Edward as an excuse to run away because I did care so much about him. Maybe I even loved him, but I had things I wanted to do, and if I hadn't done them and became his wife, I would have resented him for it. Can you understand that?" She took his hand and kissed it. "I love you all, but I have to expand myself beyond this ranch. I just have to. I don't know why. I love it here and I love you all, but there's something more for me out there."

Her father smiled weakly and kissed her cheek. "I understand, Maggie." A heavy breath soughed from his chest.

"I'll do whatever I can to help you. So tell us what it is you have in mind."

"I want to go to Cheyenne. The west isn't as wild as it used to be and that's where…"

"The hell it isn't!" Stuart was shouting again. "Cheyenne may be a new hub of the west, but there are still wild Indians around those parts. The Black Hills aren't that far from there, Maggie, only 300 miles, and there are still plenty of Indians there. And it's not just the Indians," he added. "Cheyenne is full of gamblers and ladies-of-the-line plying their trade. And since it's become the capital of Wyoming Territory and the Union Pacific goes through it now, it's a jumping off point for hundreds of men making their way to the Hills to find their fortunes in gold. Rough men, Maggie, very rough men."

"Pa, part of what I've been shouting about for years is the way the Indians are treated. Maybe I can make the public more aware of what's happening to them in the Black Hills."

"You mean when they're not murdering prospectors?" Edward said for the first time during the heated conversation. "Maggie, they find prospectors murdered every day by savages between Cheyenne and Deadwood."

"Well I don't intend to be one of them. I'm not planning to go racing into the Hills, Edward. I intend to go to Cheyenne, gather information and, hopefully, find George from a safe distance." She stepped to her brother and laid her hand on his shoulder. "I promise. You won't read about my hair being lifted in the Black Hills." Edward's face scrunched in a scowl as he eyed his sister.

Maggie turned back to her father. "And Pa, there may be rough men in Cheyenne, but do you think I haven't handled rough, angry men in the past couple years? I'm not afraid of any man." A twinge of self-doubt raced up her spine when she spoke the words, remembering Thornton and his gang of ruffians. She'd survived his torment, but barely.

"That's part of what *I'm* afraid of," Stuart admitted. "Maggie, you're tougher than any woman I have ever known, but you're still *not a man*. In a one-on-one confrontation with a man—you'll lose, just by sheer strength.

Maggie wanted to disagree, but knew he was right. Thornton had proven that. But she wouldn't be swayed, her mind was made up. She was going to find George and, like him, she hoped to make a difference in the doing.

"And how do you plan to get to Cheyenne and survive while you're there?" Stuart asked.

"I was hoping for a little help in that endeavor."

"You're actually asking me for help?" Stuart muttered, shaking his head, running his fingers through his hair again.

Maggie nodded. "Yes, I need your help to find George *and* make a difference while I'm doing it."

"What do you want Pa to do?" Edward asked.

"Like I said, I want to start my search in Cheyenne. I found Mr. Robert Strahorn's pamphlet, *The Hand-Book of Wyoming,* and read everything I could about it. The city has come a long way since becoming the capital of Wyoming Territory. I'm hoping since George wanted to help the Indians he decided to start where there was the most trouble for them, and that would be the Black Hills and the Dakota Territory. I would probably have a better chance of finding him if I went to Deadwood or Custer City, but I know those towns are still too rough, even for me, so I figure Cheyenne is as good a place to start as any."

"How do you plan to live?" Stuart asked. He cleared his throat and added sternly, "I won't send you out with a satchel full of money. I won't help you that way. You keep reminding us you're a grown woman so if you think…"

Maggie shook her head and raised her hand. "Of course not, Pa, but I do want to know if you have contact with any of the newspaper men in Cheyenne. My thought is if one of them would take me on as a reporter I could work for the newspaper and look for George at the same time."

No one said a word. Afraid her father was going to flat out deny his help, Maggie plunged forward. "Wyoming Territory is very forward-thinking, Pa. Mr. Strahorn says so in his pamphlet. Did you know that Wyoming Territory was first to give every woman that lived there who was twenty-one years or older the right to vote back in '69?"

The three men glanced at each other and sighed. They'd butted heads too many times on this subject and she was happy to let them know she planned to go to a territory where the folks took women seriously!

"I plan to place advertisements in newspapers all over the territory to find George," she began.

Stuart raised his hand for silence and Maggie snapped her mouth shut with a frown. "You're not going to help me are you? Well then, I'll figure it out on my own." She turned to leave the room but was stopped cold by her father's bellow.

"Stop right there, Maggie Douglas!"

Slowly she turned around. "I have a number of connections in Cheyenne," Stuart began, on his feet again. "A few of them have relocated from Denver and report that Cheyenne is actually becoming quite civilized, although it still has its rough element. They tell me it may even someday overtake Denver in sophistication. So, whether I want to admit it or not, you've chosen well. And," Stuart stopped.

"Yes Pa?" Maggie's heart was racing. She could scarcely believe her father might help her on this journey to find George.

"I know the owners of both the *Cheyenne Daily Leader* and the *Cheyenne Sun*. I'll send a telegram to see if either would be willing to give you a position—considering Wyoming is so forward-thinking towards women and all." There was a sarcastic gleam in his eyes.

Maggie stepped forward to give him a hug, but he raised his hands again. "Wait, there's more. I may also contact Jay Gould, who runs the Union Pacific, to arrange comfortable passage for your trip out there. And," he added quickly, keeping Maggie from running to him. "Barney Ford, another acquaintance, owns the Inter-Ocean Hotel that's not far from the UP depot. I'll set you up there for one week. That's how long you'll have to learn the lay of the land and find a place to live. Know this Maggie, I will not do any of this if you don't have a means to support yourself *before* you go," he said.

He pursed his lips and swallowed hard. Maggie knew he was having trouble speaking so she stood where she was.

"As much as it pains me to see you go—again," he said, "I know you'll never be happy unless you find your own way. You're a stubborn girl—woman," he corrected quickly, "and I'll do whatever I can to make sure you're safe, but you'll have to earn your way just like any man."

Maggie smiled, squealed like a little girl and threw herself into her father's arms. "Thank you, thank you, thank you, Pa!" she cried over and over, placing kisses on his cheeks and face. "You won't regret it."

Stuart groaned and pulled her into a crushing embrace. "I already do," he said on a cracking sigh.

PART II

CHEYENNE

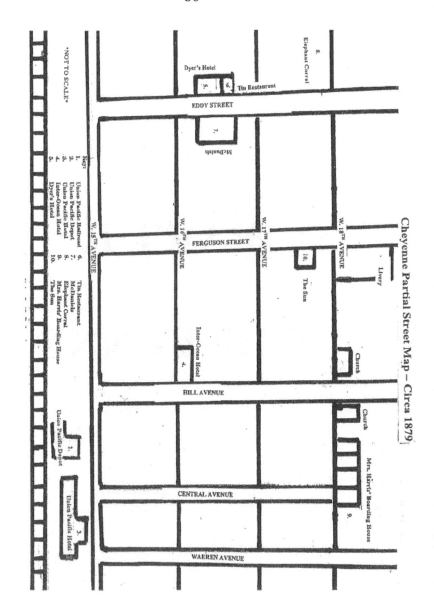

Cheyenne Partial Street Map – Circa 1879

Chapter Eight

A new wardrobe of the latest fashions replaced the simple, ragged one Maggie had worn during her suffragist days. A shopping spree to Kansas City funded by her father gave Maggie the confidence she needed to make this new journey and the encouragement her life would finally fall into place. She hoped so, jerking the skirt of her full dress that had caught on the stairs of the train behind her. *Who thought up these silly fashions?* she wondered. *It* had *to be men who didn't have to* wear *these ridiculous contraptions!* She tried to breathe, but felt like she was being suffocated by the tight, hip length corset. *At least it's not bustled,* she mused, that style having passed earlier this year.

However, having read so much about Cheyenne as a new up-and-coming city of the plains, Maggie was looking forward to becoming part of its society, which called for a new wardrobe, regardless how silly and restrictive it seemed.

Her chest tight with anticipation, she stepped down from the Pullman car onto the platform and scanned her surroundings. The long, two-storied, white-washed Union Pacific Hotel was to her right, with rows of sparkling windows on each floor and hacks full of people coming and going out front. Spread out behind the Union Pacific Hotel was Cheyenne. Several taller buildings were visible in the distance, one of which was the Inter-Ocean Hotel where she would spend a week while looking for permanent residence.

"May I take your bags, ma'am?" a black, crisply uniformed porter asked.

"Of course, thank you." She handed him a penny. "The rest are still in the car, seat number three." She pointed inside. "Might you also arrange for a hack to take me and my things to the Inter-Ocean?"

The porter nodded and bowed. "Yes, ma'am. I kin do that." He disappeared inside the car to retrieve the rest of her bags.

Maggie sighed. How different this adventure, as she'd come to think of it, would be than when she ran off to Boston with her wild ideas of becoming a force in the women's movement. Following her shopping trip to Kansas City, her father had surprised her by announcing he would give her a generous stake to get started in Cheyenne. It would be more than enough for a roof over her head while looking for a place to live and awaiting her first pay voucher as a new reporter for the *Cheyenne Sun*. Her father had come through in more ways than she dreamed he could—or would. Through a mutual friend, he'd contacted Mr. Jay Gould of the Union Pacific Railroad and arranged passage on one of the luxurious Pullman Palace Sleeping Cars for the trip from Kansas City to Cheyenne. Maggie had never seen such opulence on wheels and enjoyed all the amenities offered in the rolling car she shared with few other travelers. Separated from the regular passengers, her car boasted over-stuffed, bright red upholstered seats that folded out into a bed for sleeping with long curtains that went from ceiling to floor allowing privacy to each traveler. Walnut paneling rose from floor to roof, thick carpeting padded the floor and silk drapes covered the windows. An abundance of kerosene lamps afforded plenty of light, and friendly porters walked the aisles, making sure the needs of every passenger were met. She ate exquisitely prepared food in a newly designed dining car and was treated like nobility. Comfort during Maggie's trip from Kansas City to Cheyenne had *not* been difficult.

She was to meet Mr. A.E. Slack, the owner of the *Sun*, first thing Monday morning and, therefore, had two full days to explore her new surroundings, it being Friday night. Maggie smiled and sat down on a bench on the train station platform, her bags beside her, to await the porter with word of a hack.

The porter returned a few minutes later and took her and her bags to the carriage he'd hired to take her to the Inter-Ocean.

"Thank you again for your help." Maggie handed the porter another penny.

"Glad I was to be of service, ma'am." He nodded and smiled. "You has a nice day, ma'am."

Maggie was helped into the back seat of the carriage by an old, bent-over driver with a long beard and a plug of chew inside his cheek. Assured it was a short distance to the Inter-Ocean, the hack turned right out of the depot behind the Union Pacific Hotel, went a short distance then turned left onto Central Avenue. Waiting at the first intersection, several wagons rumbled past, overflowing with men and every implement imaginable for finding gold. Dust billowed out from the wheels, leaving a cloud of dust heading right toward Maggie's carriage.

Maggie covered her nose and mouth and coughed as the cloud surrounded the hack. "Where are they going in such a rush?" she managed between coughs.

"They're headed for the Hills, ma'am." The driver said on a cough of his own before he spat a black stream of tobacco juice to his left. "The Deadwood Stage depot is right across from the Inter-Ocean." He pointed left up the street. "It goes from here to Deadwood six days a week. You'll be a seein' plenty of wagons and stages comin' and goin' if your room is on the 16th Street side of the hotel, ma'am. Them prospectors come ever' day by the hunnerds by rail and wagon." He fell silent a moment, coughed like his insides were coming up, then spit again over the side before continuing. "And hunnerds more leave ever' day. Some take the stage to the Hills to find their fortune. Others go in wagons filled to the brim, like them that just passed. A few find what they're a lookin' fer, but most find only Injuns and their own demise."

Before she could ask any more questions, the conveyance jerked forward and the driver turned left down 16th Street. He pulled to a stop in front of the Inter-Ocean Hotel, the tallest building on the right-hand corner of the block at 16th and Hill, directly across from the Deadwood Stage depot just as the driver had said. Although quiet now, Maggie imagined it would be lively enough in the morning when it loaded for its next trip toward Deadwood and she intended to be up and about to see it.

The Inter-Ocean appeared to be a respectable establishment. Windows glistened in the sun from each of its three stories. A wooden roof in the middle of the building between the first and second floors covered the entrance where people hurried inside and out, and a pinnacle with a thin spire rose from the middle of the roof at the center of the building like a church spire. Hitching rails lined the Hill Street sidewalk where horses awaited the return of owners who might be taking their evening meal at the hotel's restaurant or trying their luck in the Inter-Ocean gaming room, Maggie surmised.

"We're here, ma'am." The driver locked the brake, stepped down and offered his hand to assist Maggie from the buggy. She waited on the planked sidewalk in front of the hotel as he pulled her bags down and set them beside her. "I'll let 'em know you're here, ma'am." The driver hurried off as fast as his crooked legs and crooked back allowed. A few minutes later a porter dressed in a fancy uniform arrived with a cart to take her bags. She paid and tipped the driver and followed her bags inside. Indeed this was the beginning of a new adventure, she thought, stepping into the fancy hotel.

The focal-point of the large lobby was the glass chandelier hanging in the middle of the high ceiling. The papered walls were lined with thick, multi-colored chairs and sofas. An impeccably-dressed man stood behind a long desk at the far end of the room, smiling widely, waiting for her to reach him. She followed a dark brown carpet runner, laid over the lighter brown carpet, to the desk.

"Good afternoon, ma'am, and welcome to the Inter-Ocean." The man continued to smile, his white, straight teeth prominent. "Your name please?"

"I'm Maggie Douglas."

He checked his records. "Yes, Miss Douglas, we have your room all ready." He turned, grabbed a key from those lining the wall behind him and handed it to her. "You're in room 206, Miss Douglas. Please sign here." He turned a big book toward her.

"Thank you." She took the offered pen and signed her name on the huge register filled with flowery signatures of those who, she supposed, were wealthy visitors to Cheyenne.

"If you're in need of anything, Miss Douglas, you be sure and let us know. Will you be dining in the restaurant this evening?" He waved his hand to encompass the dining room to her right. "Or if you prefer, you may have your meal brought to your room."

She pondered his question then decided what she really wanted was a bath first then a meal and then a bed. Although she'd traveled in luxury, she was bone-tired and wanted nothing more than to settle in and get a good night's sleep before starting tomorrow's exploration of Cheyenne. She had two whole days to discover her new home and she intended to use every minute doing just that. "If you don't mind, may I have a bath brought to my room and a meal?"

"Certainly, Miss Douglas, I shall take care of everything. And what would you like for supper? We have an excellent steak available."

"Steak would be fine, thank you." She wondered absently if the steak might be beef from the Lazy D, knowing her father had worked many deals for the sale of Lazy D beef in this hotel.

He nodded, snapped his fingers and the porter stepped forward. "Take Miss Douglas's bags to room 206." He turned back to Maggie. "Enjoy your stay, Miss Douglas."

"Thank you, I will. Oh, before I retire, can you tell me where the telegraph office is located?"

The man gave her directions. "Please have my bags taken to my room. I need to send a telegram before I go up."

"Please, Miss Douglas, I can handle that for you. Just give me the message and I'll be happy to send it for you."

"Thank you." She scribbled out a short message to her father letting him know she'd arrived safely, handed it to the man then followed the porter up a wide, carpet-covered staircase to a room on the second floor. It was elegant with a double-sized bed with an ivory-colored canopy and long, sheer drapes tied back on each side. The bed was positioned in the center of the wall between two tall windows and matching ivory curtains fell from ceiling to floor over the windows on either side. Walking to the window on the right, Maggie pulled back one of the curtains and looked out over 16th Street and the empty stage depot, imagining the excitement there would be tomorrow morning when the stage loaded for Deadwood.

She hooked the curtain on a nail at the side of the sill then raised the window to allow in the breeze. Turning back into the room, she continued her perusal of what would be her home for the next week or so. A four-drawer dresser stood against the wall on the right at the foot of the bed and a tall armoire stood against the opposite wall on her left. Carpet covered the floor between the door and bed and the armoire and dresser.

The porter placed her bags by the armoire. She gave him another penny and closed the door behind him. Leaning against it, she looked around and whispered, "Thanks, Pa."

She put her clothes away and just as she finished, there was a knock on the door and her bath was delivered by two burley men. They set the round tub in the middle of the room, returning three times with hot water to fill it before she was left alone. She threw her restrictive traveling clothes on the bed, happy to be free of them, and slid down into the hot water. Allowing the bath to swallow every part of her she could fit into the small tub, she reveled in the luxuriousness of her surroundings. Comparing where she was now to what she'd lived in for so long in her travels, she realized how much she'd given up to traipse around the country trying to convince everyone women deserved the right to vote and do whatever a man had the right to do.

Finishing her bath, dinner arrived. "Please leave it outside the door," she called, not dressed yet. "Also, please inform the desk the tub and water may be removed tomorrow after I've left for the day." She wanted to eat and have a good night's sleep before she took on the city at first light. She scooted another penny under the door for the waiter, put on her night gown and robe then ate her dinner in silence, her mind going in circles as to where she wanted to go and what she wanted to see when she headed out in the morning.

Although exhausted from her long trip, sleep eluded her. Having read Cheyenne might soon pass Denver as the *Queen City of the Plains and Mountains* with its growing new sophistication, Maggie wondered if the city was truly beyond its *Hell-on-Wheels* days with its rough and wild ways. It had been the capitol of Wyoming Territory for three years now, *had it grown respectable in those three years*? Her mind tumbled with unanswerable questions. *How long would she stay? Would she be here long enough to witness such momentous changes in this blossoming city? Would she be successful in finding George? Had she done the right thing in leaving the Lazy D and her responsibilities there?* Tossing and turning, it took several hours before she fell into a fitful sleep full of raucous cowboys, wild Indians, rumbling stages, and lost love.

Maggie stepped out of the Inter-Ocean onto the 16th Street sidewalk into the already warm sunlight. It was going to be a hot one and she was happy she'd made the extravagant purchase of a parasol during her shopping spree in Kansas City. She might very well need it in the coming days. Her brothers and father had laughed themselves to tears when it fell out of the bag she'd tried to hide it in, but she'd ignored them. If she was going to *be* a lady in this emerging territory, she had to *act* like a lady—and ladies wore fashionable dresses and carried parasols. *Her days of roping and riding like a man were behind her. She was a woman and it was time to act like one!*

Activity across the street drew Maggie's attention to where a tall red stagecoach bearing the words *Stage Line to Deadwood City,* was loading in front of the depot. A dozen or more passengers, mostly rough-looking men, were climbing on along with a few hard-looking women. Every man had a pistol strapped to his hip or carried a rifle, but the passenger that stood out most was a woman dressed in buckskins with a six-shooter on each hip and a Winchester rifle in her hands. The woman's dark, coppery-colored hair was cut short or tucked tight under a dirty, small-brimmed hat. She was cursing a blue streak and Maggie grinned, remembering a tirade of her own at Fort Leavenworth shortly before she'd met George when a storekeeper tried to short her weight of flour by putting rocks in her sacks. She'd exposed his fraud then cursed till her jaw hurt, loud enough for everyone nearby to hear. She grinned at the memory, imagining she must have seemed as unfeminine and crude as this woman did today.

The woman's fringed buckskin jacket and pants had seen better days and she slurred her words like she was on a two-day drunk or just coming off one. Her oval face was hard, her dark eyes pinched and her prominent nose and cheeks flamed red.

"Damn it, Bill, get this over-sized heap o' horse-shit rollin'!" she yelled at the driver, shoving her way through the crowd. "Git the hell out o' my damn way you bunch o' yeller-bellied, churn-twisters! I got to git to Deadwood, damn it!" She pulled herself onto the side of the stage, climbed over the driver and plopped down beside him, the rifle cradled in the crook of her elbow, taking the position Maggie had learned in her studies was "shotgun."

There were almost as many riders on top of the coach, squatting on boxes, sacks and all manner of belongings strapped to the top and rear, as there were inside. A team of six blacks stood with heads bobbing and snorting, ears pricked and hooves pawing, waiting for the signal to go.

Maggie watched the last of the passengers settle as best they could on the over-burdened stage and, amidst the jingling of the horses' traces, the whip cracking, and shouts from the obnoxious woman riding shotgun, the animals surged forward. The stage lurched behind it and rolled away in a flurry of churning dust, the sun reflecting off the guard's rifle as it disappeared down the street.

Still watching the stage, deciding which direction to take in her exploration, Maggie felt a presence near her. She turned to a man dressed in a pearl gray suit with a matching derby standing beside her, his head cocked, watching the stage, as she was.

"It's quite a sight, isn't it?" the stranger asked without taking his eyes from the departing stage.

"Yes, it is, especially some of the odd-looking people on it."

"You mean the hayseeds, punkin' rollers and cowboys looking to find their fortune in the Black Hills?"

Maggie nodded, understanding his references to farmers and cowboys, but most curious about the woman guard. "What about the woman riding shotgun?

"Ah, you're referring to Calamity. She often makes the run to Deadwood riding shotgun."

"*That* was Calamity Jane? I've heard about her." Maggie turned to the man still looking down the street. "Is she as notorious as they say?" she asked in her curiosity.

The man chuckled and turned to Maggie. If she'd been walking she would have stumbled. He looked eerily like a younger Paul Thornton with his dark hair and dark eyes and her hackles went up.

"She's quite the character," the man said. "She's been known to out drink, out shoot and out curse any man, even Bill Hickock, rest his soul, before his demise."

Maggie felt something akin to shock rip up her spine. Recalling Calamity Jane's demeanor, dress and language, she wondered if people saw her, during her fight for women's rights, the way Maggie just saw Calamity Jane, as an oddity, doing exactly what Maggie had fought to allow women to do for so long.

"Are you all right, ma'am?" the gentleman asked. "You look like you just stepped in front of a herd of buffalo."

Maggie shook her head and smiled. "I'm fine. Miss Calamity just—reminded me of something."

"Or someone?" he asked, a sparkle in his eyes.

He was too smooth, and even though he *wasn't* Paul Thornton, he reminded her all too much of the man she wanted only to forget. "Thank you for your explanations, sir, but I must be going now." She just wanted to be left alone.

She turned to walk away, but he hurried around in front of her and stopped, forcing her to stop, too.

"Forgive me. I only want to make your acquaintance." He bowed low. "I'm Luke Short, presently of this fine city, although I've called many places home in my quest to find my fortune."

Maggie rolled her eyes. There it was. He was another user intent on making his fortune, probably off others, just like Thornton. *He didn't* look *like any of the prospectors she'd already seen coming and going through the city, though. Did he have some special plan to strike it rich in the Black Hills? Was he waiting for a rich relative to die to inherit his or her money? Why was he so cocksure he was close to finding his fortune when so many never did? Again, Thornton's face flashed before her and Maggie's body sang with warning.*

"Doing what, may I ask, Mr. Th…Short?" she corrected. "Have you already struck gold in the Hills or are you waiting for a silent partner to inform you he's hit the vein that will make you both rich?" The sarcasm in her voice shocked even her, but she couldn't help it, he reminded her too much of Thornton.

Short cocked his head and raised his chin a notch. "I'm a gambler, ma'am."

Gamblers were regarded highly out west. Why even in Kansas City and Dodge City, Maggie knew gamblers still made a living dealing cards out of the Marble Hall or the Long Branch Saloon. Perhaps this Luke Short had visions of becoming the next Bat Masterson or Wyatt Earp, which was the *last* kind of man Maggie wanted to further acquaint herself with.

"So, Mr. Short, where have you called home?" Maggie asked, curious now.

"Well, I was born in Arkansas, but moved to Texas when I was very young. It was in Abilene, Kansas, at the tender age of sixteen that I got my first taste of cards. From there I wound up in Kansas City…"

"Kansas City?" she interrupted, intrigued. "You lived in Kansas City?" This was just *too* strange a coincidence.

"I wasn't there for long. I was on the Kansas side where my brother got me a job dealing at the Marble Hall. Perhaps you've heard of it? Or him?"

"I've heard of it. And who is your brother?" she asked, more curious now that she knew he'd lived not far from the Lazy D.

"Charlie Bassett."

"Charlie Bassett the famous lawman? *He's* your brother?"

"Yes, ma'am. Guess he figured if I was going to make my livelihood as a gambler, I might as well be good at it, so he set me up at the Marble Hall to learn the trade. Wound up in Nebraska for a little while and now I'm here."

Suddenly uncomfortable, like Fate was somehow guiding him, Maggie turned the conversation. "And where do you currently ply your trade, Mr. Short?" She couldn't stop the sarcasm again when she added, "Shingle & Locke's or McDaniel's perhaps?" If he was on his way to becoming some famous gambler, he must work at one of the bigger, more well-known drinking and gambling establishments she'd read about. Maggie was more curious than ever now, yet leery of the smooth-talking gentleman.

"I deal Faro for Mr. Ed Chase—at the Inter-Ocean Hotel."

"The Inter-Ocean?" Again, if she'd been walking she would have stumbled.

"I confess. I was outside the hotel before my shift last evening when I saw you arrive and decided I wanted to meet you."

"Did you now?"

"I stand guilty, Miss Douglas."

"You know my name?" Warning shot through her. He was all too smooth and reminded her entirely too much of Thornton.

He grinned. His long, bushy mustache curled around his lips, his dark eyes softened and his rounded cheeks reddened slightly. "I looked at the register after you checked in, Miss Douglas."

"Well, you seem to be quite an industrious fellow."

"This industrious fellow would like to accompany you on your discovery of Cheyenne."

"And how do you know I don't have an appointment?"

Short pursed his lips. "I'm a personal friend of Mr. Slack who owns the *Sun*. He frequents my table often and we—talk. Although Cheyenne has grown considerably, she's still small enough that her inhabitants know what's going on in their city. You're arrival has been awaited by many."

Maggie took a sharp breath. "And do they look forward to my arrival with anticipation or dread?" She knew Wyoming accepted women more readily than most territories or even states back east, *but would they accept a woman reporter nosing around in their business?*

"That remains to be seen, Miss Douglas. The ladies of our fair city are most anxious for your arrival. However, the men are, well, more reluctant and wait to judge you upon your abilities. However, once they've met you in person...."

"Meaning?"

"You're most charming, Miss Douglas. And, if I may be so bold, not at all what I expected. Mr. Slack told me about your suffragist connections and I didn't expect someone quite so lovely."

Maggie flushed and she knew it. Warning crept up her spine. She was many things, but charming and lovely were neither of them. Loud, rash, adventurous, sarcastic, obnoxious, and a woman who spoke her mind was more like it—but charming and lovely? She remembered all too well Thornton's easy ways and wouldn't allow another man to sweet-talk her so easily.

However, she *did* need to find her way around Cheyenne. *What better way to do so than with someone who knew it well? They would always be in plain view and not alone in a carriage out in the country.*

"Miss Douglas?" Short prodded.

"Very well, Mr. Short."

"Luke, please."

"Very well, Luke. However, I must warn you my *only* intention is to learn my way around Cheyenne and nothing else." She wanted him to know right off she had no romantic inclinations whatsoever. Besides, she had more reasons for being in Cheyenne than just working for the *Sun* and she intended to follow through. First thing Monday, before her meeting with Mr. Slack, she planned to put an ad in every newspaper she could find in her efforts to locate George.

"Well then, I'm your man and I promise to be nothing but proper."

Maggie pursed her lips. "Very well, Mr. Short, show me Cheyenne." She placed her arm around his proffered elbow and they headed west down 16th Street where saloons, stores selling books, toys and clothing lined the block. Crossing Ferguson Street there was a shoemaker, a barber shop and more saloons, all of whose owners Short could name.

Reaching the next crossroad, Maggie was guided to the right. "Eddy Street houses several of Cheyenne's more well-known establishments," Short said.

"Such as?"

"Dyer's is one of Cheyenne's most elegant hotels."

"My father's spoken of Dyer's. He's stayed there on previous trips here."

Short cocked his head. "Well, it's my good fortune he put you in the Inter-Ocean when you arrived and not at Dyer's, otherwise, I may not be enjoying your company."

Maggie smiled, reminding herself to beware. A handsome, smiling face had betrayed her too recently and she wasn't about to allow it to happen again. "Preordained, perhaps?"

"Perhaps." They continued up Eddy Street until Short stopped and waved his hand toward the left side of the street. "I give you Dyer's Hotel." They stood across from a wide, two-story, brick building with a large DYER'S HOTEL sign displayed prominently under the ledge of the roof, just above the second level. The main entrance was covered by a small, railed balcony that jutted out from the second floor and braced by two round columns at the road. Well-dressed patrons stood on the sidewalk or loaded into fine carriages out front.

Short pointed at a slightly taller building to the right of Dyer's. There were three long, thin windows on the second floor and two large, wide windows on either side of the door at street level. "That's the 'Tin Restaurant,'" he instructed, "named such because of the tin dinnerware they used when it first opened. Many a cowboy has been pressed into service there as a bullwhacker after losing all his money at McDaniel's."

He certainly knows this town, Maggie thought as Short whirled and, with a flourish pointed to the building directly behind them. "And this, Miss Douglas, is the McDaniel's of which I speak."

Maggie turned to the building that took up a good portion of the block. It was quiet outside because of the early hour, but Maggie easily imagined many a cowboy losing a month's pay inside. Although early, a number of men lounged outside and along the street.

Starting up the sidewalk again, the front door to McDaniel's opened and out stepped a portly, well-dressed man just ahead of them. He smiled widely when he spotted Luke. "Luke Short!" He hurried over and pumped Luke's hand. "Good to see you man. You're out and about early this morning." He grinned, eyeing Maggie.

"Morning, Mr. McDaniel." Short turned to Maggie. "May I present Maggie Douglas, the new reporter for the *Sun* Mr. Slack is expecting."

"Yes, yes, I recall. Welcome, welcome, Miss Douglas." He doffed the black bowler hat that matched his well-tailored suit to expose his balding head when he bowed. The man seemed to Maggie more like a small town preacher trying to fire up his congregation than a man who ran an establishment of gambling, drinking, and uncertain moral behavior.

"Mr. McDaniel." Maggie forced a smile and offered her hand. McDaniel took it and held it overlong, making her more uncomfortable.

"I look forward to reading your work, Miss Douglas. Perhaps you might do a piece on my establishment?" He waved his free hand at the marquee above their heads with *McDaniel's Theatre* painted on it. "With the proper escort, of course," he glanced at Luke, "a personal tour of my theater would be appropriate, perhaps?" He waved toward the door he had just exited.

Maggie felt like she was being undressed right there. She saw a familiar light in his eyes she didn't ever want to see again, especially from him. Lust sparkled there and she wanted to guide him right away from her. "Thank you for your offer, Mr. McDaniel, perhaps sometime in the future once I'm settled in. Right now I'm just trying to find my way around, but later I may visit."

"Glad to hear it." He leaned forward conspiratorially, "You know, I run a proper establishment and I want everyone to know that. Unfortunately some unsavory characters have been known to frequent my place, but I do try to keep it respectable."

Maggie withdrew her hand, took a step back and forced another smile. "I'll remember that, Mr. McDaniel. Thank you again for your offer."

Luke must have seen Maggie's distress. "We must be going now, Mr. McDaniel. We've enjoyed speaking with you. Have a nice day." He tipped his hat and started forward, not allowing McDaniel the chance to waylay them further.

Maggie followed quickly, happy to be away from the uncomfortable man.

"Thank you."

"Don't mention it. He can be a bit off-putting."

"To say the least." Maggie continued up the sidewalk beside Luke Short, wondering if there was anyone in Cheyenne that *didn't* know she was coming.

Chapter Nine

Maggie and Luke strolled up Eddy Street, Short pointing out this business and that until they stood across from a holding area where horses, mules and even a few oxen, milled inside numerous corrals and pens.

"That's the Elephant Corral over there." Luke pointed to his left at the big corner lot where the animals were held then pointed out the structure beside it. "See that building? A hotel and saloon used to stand there, but a fire wiped them out a few years ago and the owners replaced it with that new brick building. They have dances and public gatherings upstairs. Perhaps you'll consider attending one of the dances sometime as my guest?"

Maggie didn't like where he was going. She smiled slightly and nodded almost imperceptibly then turned the conversation back to the corral itself. "I thought the Elephant Corral was in Denver. I've heard my father describe the one there many times."

"There is one in Denver, but there's one in Council Bluffs, Nebraska too. I've heard they named the one in Denver from the one in Council Bluffs, but then I've heard it was named such from an old gold rush term, too. I guess they just called this one the same thing because it's big. Used to be they bought, sold, traded, and shipped all kinds of stock right from here, but now that the railroad has come they take the animals to the depot, load them on freight cars and ship them from there."

A couple of dust-covered cowboys with long, leather chaps and wide-brimmed Stetsons were climbing into one of the corrals where four horses ran back and forth to avoid the encroaching men and the rope halters they had in their hands. Four other cowboys, inside another larger pen were, themselves, cursing and wrestling eight or ten wild-eyed animals also unwilling to be haltered. Maggie decided the horses had to be young and green, just brought in off the range, or both, to be acting so wild. They wouldn't stand still long enough to allow a rope to be put over their heads and as soon as one moved, the rest moved too, kicking up dust and bellowing. They were giving the cowboys fits as they tried to get the snorting, frightened animals roped.

"There's a funny story that goes with this Corral if you're interested." Short said with a sparkle of mischief in his eyes, drawing her attention away from the Corral.

"Of course. I love stories."

"It happened about the time I arrived here in '76, just before the Union Pacific came when they still used freight wagons to haul the stock from the Corral. It happened that one of our local freighters found out some of the hotels in Deadwood were infested with rodents, making business for their, ah, tenants difficult."

Maggie raised an eyebrow, presuming those tenants were most likely Soiled Doves and their clients.

"The freighter, Phatty Thompson was his name, figured out a way to help and paid a bunch of boys here in Cheyenne twenty-five cents each to gather up every stray cat they could find. He loaded up a freight wagon and off he went with all those cats. On the trip to Deadwood the wagon overturned somehow and the cats escaped."

"So are these cats and their descendants still running wild between here and Deadwood, attacking miners on their way to find their fortune?" Maggie asked with a giggle, enjoying the story, and Luke's company, more than she wanted to admit.

"Actually, he managed to get them back into the freight wagon and all the way to Deadwood."

"How did he manage that?"

"When you're scared and hungry, food is a tremendous enticement. Luring the cats with food he got them back into the wagon and all the way to Deadwood where he sold them for ten dollars each. The story goes on that he even had a fancy Maltese in the bunch that he sold for twenty-five dollars, much to the dismay of a woman here in Cheyenne who's Maltese cat had mysteriously disappeared just before Thompson's trip to Deadwood!" Luke grinned and snorted.

"What a fun story. Do you have more?" Maggie was enjoying hearing about Cheyenne's history, albeit humorous.

"Well…" Short put his hand on his chin and looked skyward. "Have you heard the one about Colorado Charley's famous—or infamous, depending on how you look at it—wagon train from Denver to Deadwood?"

Maggie shook her head. "No, but I hope you're going to tell me." She was warming up to Mr. Luke Short and reminded herself to be cautious.

"In June of '76, Charley Utter, otherwise known as Colorado Charley, had a wagon train that went from Denver to Deadwood. On this particular run, he carried an interesting group of passengers."

"Yes?" Maggie asked, wondering if they could they have been more colorful than those she'd seen leaving on this morning's stage.

"Although their destination was Deadwood, several of the passengers—and their girls—decided to stop in Cheyenne when the train held over for the night."

"And?"

"They stayed for good."

Maggie cocked her head and grinned. "More Soiled Doves?"

Short grinned back and nodded. "It was then Cheyenne became the new home to some of Denver's most noted, er, ladies, including Madam Mustache and Dirty Emma. So when you go looking for a place to live, have a care who owns the 'boarding house' where you make inquiries, Miss Douglas." Short winked and Maggie couldn't help but chuckle in response.

"Cheyenne gained another well-known person from Charley's wagon train, too."

"And who was that?" Maggie was thoroughly enjoying Luke's history lesson.

"Wild Bill Hickock came to our fair city on Charley's train. He wore out his welcome pretty quick, though, after he beat up the Boulder Saloon's owner because he was losing at cards and the owner wouldn't raise the house limit so he could win it back. After holding off the bouncers with his revolver, Bill scooped a handful of cash out of the money drawer on his way out and headed to Deadwood—and we know what happened there."

"He was killed by Jack McCall." Maggie wanted Mr. Short to know she'd done her homework and had some knowledge of the territory's history. "Is it true about Wild Bill and Calamity?"

Maggie asked, even more curious after seeing the famous Calamity Jane earlier.

Short clucked his tongue. "I don't think Bill had quite the same affection for Calamity she held towards him. Those who knew him said he always swore they were just friends, but nobody knew for sure. Who's to know a man's heart?" he asked with a gleam in his eyes.

Maggie's mind was spinning with the colorful stories when Luke started across the street and she hurried to keep up. In her rush the bottom of her dress snagged on something in the road.

"My dress is caught," she said to Luke, a few steps ahead of her. Grabbing her skirt, she bent over and tried to unhook the material without tearing it. At the Corral the swearing and yelling had intensified, but Maggie ignored it, intent on freeing her dress—until the high-pitched squeals of horses and splintering of wood drew her full attention. She stood up and, in the few seconds she'd been trying to free her dress, the frightened horses had crashed through the corral gates and were racing right toward her! Standing in the middle of the road, all she saw were flared noses, wild eyes and churning hooves heading right at her from inside a swirling cloud of dust.

"Get out of here!" Luke ran back, grabbed her arm and pulled her toward the sidewalk, but she jerked to a halt when her dress wouldn't tear away from whatever held it.

Maggie well-knew what one crazed horse could do with its hooves and she surely didn't want to find out what this many could do! "My dress is still stuck! I can't break free!" She dropped her parasol and she and Luke tugged and pulled on the skirt until it tore free. Maggie gathered as much of the material as she could in her arms, inappropriately showing her ankles and calves, and ran!

"Come on!" Luke yelled from the sidewalk, reaching for her.

Maggie was only a few feet from safety when her heel caught, she lost her footing and dropped the bottom of her dress. She'd chided countless other females for stumbling and falling at the most inopportune times and now she was doing the same thing! Cursing her luck, she teetered back and forth, trying to keep her balance, but the bulk of the confounded dress worked like an anchor to drag her down. She fell on her hip and rolled, the skirt wrapping around her ankles like an old-fashioned bundling bag.

"Damn, damn, damn!" she shouted in a panic. *She was in serious trouble!* She sat up and tore at the dress, trying to disentangle her legs, but it seemed the more she pulled, the tighter it got. Someone was screaming and she realized it was her. Certain her time had come she closed her eyes, but strong arms gathered her up and hauled to the sidewalk only seconds before the horses tore by in a rush of dust and slicing hooves. A half dozen cowboys on saddled horses raced behind them, shouting and cussing, trying to get a rope on one or two of the lead horses to slow them down. All the way up the street people scrambled to safety on both sides of the road as more horses broke free from hitching posts or bucked off hapless riders to join the crazed herd racing down Eddy Street.

Down the sidewalk in front of Dyer's, the four horses pulling an elegant, open black carriage Maggie and Luke had passed only a few minutes before were rearing and pulling at their traces then suddenly took off down the road with the rest of the herd when the reins broke loose when the brake snapped. Above the din of the racing herd, Maggie heard the panicked screams of the woman caught inside the out-of-control carriage. One of the cowboys chasing the runaway horses rode his mount onto the sidewalk, screaming for people to get out of the way, and around the thundering herd until he caught up with the team. Standing up in his stirrups he leaned left and flung himself onto the back of the lead horse on the right, grabbed the bridle, and forced it onto 16th Street. The woman's screams faded as the carriage disappeared up the street and out of sight, while the terrified herd continued down Eddy Street with more cowboys joining in the pursuit, whooping and hollering after their prey.

When the cloud finally cleared Maggie was sitting in the middle of the sidewalk, her hair askew, covered from head to toe with dust, and the bottom of her new dress shredded. She felt like she *had* been run over by those horses. Everything ached. With shaking hands and coughing up dust, she pushed her disheveled hair off her face and tried hard not to cry. *She'd been around horses all her life, but she'd never faced down something like this!*

Luke was standing over her, a frightened look on his face. "Miss Douglas, are you all right?"

The dust in her mouth kept her from answering right away. She cleared her throat and almost spat before she said, "Thanks to you, Luke, I'm fine. If you hadn't dragged me to the sidewalk, I would have been, well...." She glared down at the dress still wrapped around her ankles, snorted and waved at the offending material. "Would you mind helping me out of this mess?"

It took a few minutes to untangle the material and when she raised her hand for Luke to help her stand, she did so on shaky knees. Her left ankle was tender and the hip she'd landed on throbbed. *She could well imagine the bruise that would be there tomorrow morning!* Other than that, she'd come through the ordeal with little more than a ruined dress, badly bruised pride, and a smashed parasol that was sticking up from the middle of the street like skeletal fingers pleading for help.

Luke smiled and her heart melted against him. He'd saved her life at peril to himself and she was grateful. From now on she would judge Luke Short on who he was and not who he reminded her of. He'd risked his life to save hers—she could do no less than give him a chance.

"Are you sure you're all right?"

Wetting her dry lips and shoving pins back into her hair, she nodded. "Truly, Luke, I'm fine, thanks to you."

"You're more than welcome, Miss Douglas. I shudder to think what might have happened if,"

"But it didn't," Maggie cut him off, unwilling to think about what could have happened.

Luke cocked his head and smiled devilishly. "I'm sure this is not the greeting you hoped for on your arrival." He waved his arm at the retreating horses. "Welcome to Cheyenne, Miss Douglas."

Regardless her heart was still pounding and she could have been killed Maggie smiled—her grin as shaky and lopsided as her hair and clothes.

"Let's get you to the doc so he can check you out." Luke grabbed Maggie around the waist and draped her arm over his shoulder to help her down the street. A few minutes later she was sitting on the doctor's examining table being assessed for possible injuries other than her throbbing hip, twisted ankle and battered pride.

The white-haired, elderly man shook his finger at Maggie. "Young lady, you were very lucky today. You could have been seriously hurt, or worse," he added as though telling her something she didn't know!

Maggie coughed to cover her disdain. He was treating her like some fragile female! "Doc, I was raised with horses and know all about what they can do to a body. I've come off the backside of one more times than I can remember." She slapped at the dirty, ruined dress. "It was this rig that caused my near death and you can bet it won't happen again. As soon as you get me fixed up, I'll be heading straight for the closest dress shop to get a pair of sensible boots to replace these things they call shoes and some comfortable, well-fitting clothes." She slapped at her heeled shoes and dress, causing plumes of dust to float into the air. "Fashion be damned," she snarled, watching the doctor draw back in shock at her harsh language. "I intend to buy skirts I can move in and comfortable blouses to go with them and intend to shove my fashionable, albeit worthless dresses into a trunk until such time as I *may* have need of them!" She grabbed the bottom of her dress and tore at it until the whole underside popped off.

"Aren't you being a little hasty, Miss Douglas?" Luke asked.

"No, I'm not," Maggie snapped. "I could have been killed today because of a stupid dress! If nothing else it reminded me you have to be ready for anything and, if or when something like this *ever* happens again, you can bet I'll be able to get the hell out of the way of whatever is coming! Shoot, I might even jump onto the back of one of those horses and ride *with* those cowboys to stop the runaways the next time! Long trains, corsets and parasols are for fancy ladies and I am *not* one of them—never will and don't want to be. I'm a rancher's daughter and damned proud of everything I can do, which doesn't include worrying about the latest fashions. I want sensibility and comfort—and I intend to get them."

The doctor's face was red with embarrassment and Luke was looking at Maggie askance, too. "Have I shocked you, Luke? In reality I'm more like the unladylike woman you *expected* to arrive in town, maybe even more like Calamity, than the 'lady' you met earlier, but this is who I really am, like it or not, and I intend to get myself clothed properly before the day is done."

Luke shook his head and chuckled. "Miss Douglas, you haven't shocked me." He hesitated. "Well, maybe a little. Truth is I like you just fine. Whether you wear fancy dresses, sensible boots or speak your mind, I like you just fine."

Maggie sighed. That damn sparkle was back in his eyes.

Maggie studied Luke from across the table where they were waiting to order dinner in the Inter-Ocean restaurant. She'd only seen such patience before in one other man—George. He'd been as patient as the day was long in his courtship of Maggie. She'd thrown herself at him, challenged him, even insulted him and he'd always remained true to his ideals. He was a gentleman and treated Maggie no less than a lady, no matter how much he'd wanted her or she'd offered herself to him.

"Maggie?" Maggie jerked back to the present with the touch of Luke's hand, remembering it was his patience that had sent her mind toward memories of George. Luke had followed her from one dress shop to another after they left the doctor's office until she found everything she needed. She had new boots, new skirts and new blouses. It took three different shops to satisfy what she wanted before they returned to the Inter-Ocean hauling almost a dozen bags of new purchases.

"I've only ever seen one other man with such patience, Luke."

Luke smiled, one that was quickly disarming Maggie of her fears. "If you recall my profession, patience is something a gambler must have. Without patience I wouldn't be successful. It's an important tool in reading other players' 'tells.' You know, when they chew on their lip if they have a winning hand or curl their mustache when they don't. Without the patience to discover that, I'd be a loser instead of a winner." He paused before adding, "Besides, I feel somewhat responsible for what happened this morning and want to lend as much assistance as I can."

"Don't be silly, you had nothing to do with what happened. It was an accident and we just happened to be at the wrong place when it did. You saved my life, Luke."

Short actually blushed and Maggie felt her insides melting.

"I guess I did, but if we hadn't been there…"

"If *we* hadn't been there together, I might have been there alone, as I had intended when I left the hotel this morning. If you hadn't been with me, I might very easily have been killed. No more talk about it. What happened was no one's fault, certainly not yours, and I'm safe thanks to you."

He gave a quick nod. "As you wish, Miss Douglas."

Maggie sighed. "Please, call me Maggie."

Luke's eyes brightened and she surveyed his face. He looked to be about the same age as she, but Maggie couldn't be sure because of his self-assurance and the way he comported himself. Most men in their early twenties were still awkward, trying to figure out who they were and what they wanted to do with their lives. It seemed Luke Short already knew who he was and was about doing it.

Two well-dressed men strolled past their table.

"Did you hear what happened this morning?" one man with a long, drooping mustache asked the other.

"Heard a bunch of horses broke out of the Corral and headed hell-bent-for-leather straight down Eddy Street. Must have been a sight."

"Was anyone hurt?" the first man asked.

"Heard no one was badly hurt, but I *did* hear that new woman reporter took a tumble and got her ankle twisted getting out of the way." The men chuckled.

"Do tell. Maybe it's a sign she shouldn't be here. All a nosy woman reporter is going to do is stir up trouble."

The two men passed and selected a table in the corner where they sat down and continued their conversation in private.

Maggie groaned. "It seems most everyone in town knows I'm coming or have arrived, and not everyone is looking forward to it." She shook her head. "How can one woman be such a threat?" she asked no one in bewilderment.

"Don't judge all the folks here in Cheyenne by those two. There are plenty of folks who will accept that you're an intelligent woman who, it seems, can do just about anything she sets her mind to. Maybe even better than most, be they man *or* woman," Luke finished with a grin and that already familiar sparkle in his eyes.

"I don't want to brag, but I am better than most anybody at whatever I try. The way I was raised, I suppose."

Luke reached out, like he was going to touch her hand again, but pulled it back. "Tell me about it," he whispered.

Maggie spent the next hour, between mouthfuls, telling Luke about her childhood growing up with two brothers and an overbearing father, trying to prove she wasn't a helpless little girl that had made her tough instead. She told him how she'd taken off to Boston, been insulted and assaulted and some of the people she'd met, but skipped the part about being run out-of-town from sheer embarrassment.

"So why our fair city?" he asked.

"I guess it was time for a new adventure, so here I am," she said, not being totally honest.

"Is there someone special in your life?" Luke asked with reluctance when the conversation lagged.

Maggie pursed her lips, unsure how much to tell him, but decided the truth was best. "There is someone." Luke tried to hide his disappointment, but failed, so she added quickly, "But I don't know where he is, which is part of why I'm here."

He cocked his head. "Sounds mysterious."

"Not really. He worked for my Pa at the Lazy D. George was a soldier, caught up in the war with the Sioux. He was at the Little Bighorn and with Crook on his Horsemeat March afterward chasing the Sioux. But," she paused and Luke waited patiently for her to continue. "He didn't feel the same way about the Indians most soldiers did. As a kid his best friend was a half-breed named Blue and they were inseparable. At the Little Bighorn Blue saved George's life when Blue found him hiding in a cave." Maggie felt that now familiar pang of regret she got when she thought of or talked about George.

That regret must have shown on her face because Luke touched her hand. "Go on."

"When they were following the Sioux after the Little Bighorn George disobeyed a direct order to kill everyone in a village his cavalry unit had attacked — everyone — including a mother and her child. He wound up being forced to resign his commission to keep from being dishonorably discharged for 'dereliction of duty' and 'conduct unbecoming an officer.' My brother, James, found him at Fort Leavenworth about to get pounded by the men in his company, some of whom had rather enjoyed following the order to kill everyone in that village." Maggie looked away, knowing her face showed the loss she felt at having thrown George away.

"Hey," Luke turned her face back to his. "Where is George now?"

Maggie sniffed and swiped at an errant tear. "Gone. He asked me to marry him, but I sent him away because I had things to do. I told him my family would never accept him." She snorted. "The joke of it is that my family was secretly rooting for him!" She lapsed into silence, remembering the first time she left the Lazy D and left George behind.

"Don't stop now," Luke prodded. "Tell me the rest."

"Before he met me he had things he wanted to do, too, just like I did. Once I left for Boston I guess he decided it was time for him to figure out what to do and how."

"And what was that?"

"Help the Indians."

"Help the Indians! After fighting them at the Little Bighorn?" Short asked, incredulous.

Maggie nodded. "Especially after the Little Bighorn and riding with Colonel Mackenzie afterwards. Knowing what he knew about the Lakota from Blue, he never fought with the same passion the other soldiers did. He became a soldier because it was his father's dream from the time George was a little boy and *not* because he wanted to kill Indians."

"Go on," Luke said when Maggie lapsed into silence again.

"Once I left for Boston I never looked back. I didn't try to reach him at the Lazy D, didn't even contact my family." She looked up. "Rather selfish, don't you think?" she said then quickly added, "I've grown up since then."

"I'm sure you had your reasons for not contacting anyone. Go on."

"When I decided I was done running around the country trying to convert men to a way of thinking that may take decades, I realized I wanted George. So I went back to the ranch to tell him so but by the time I got there, he was gone. Of course, it had been two years and I was arrogant enough to think he'd still be waiting for me." Her thoughts drifted off.

"Where did he go?" pulled her back to the present. She frowned and shrugged her shoulders. "I don't know. I'm hoping he set out to help the Indians like he originally planned. Since there are still Sioux in the Black Hills, I'm hoping he might be out there somewhere." She waved her hand toward Deadwood and the Black Hills. "And since Cheyenne has a stage that takes people there every day, where better to start?"

"Sounds like a good place to begin. How do you intend to find him? There's a lot of territory out there."

"I'm going to put personal ads in every newspaper I can find between here and Deadwood and hope he sees one. I'll use my position at the newspaper and keep my ear to the ground about anything or anyone that might know something about him."

"Sounds like you've got it all figured out."

"It's going to be difficult, especially if George doesn't *want* to be found. He may have forgotten all about me and moved on with his life." Maggie sighed heavily. "What a fool I was."

"Not from how I see it, Maggie. If you hadn't done the things you needed to, you would never have been happy or settled—with George or any man. You'd have been restless, wondering what you missed and you'd have been right. Look at everything you've learned and experienced—good or bad. If you hadn't done what you did and settled for marriage instead, you might very well have driven him away." He pursed his lips. "You and I are alike in that respect, Maggie. If I don't stretch myself to find out what I can really do, I'll wither away. We're the kind of people who always need to reach for something more."

Maggie smiled. "Thank you, Luke." She touched his hand and, although he said he understood about Maggie's feelings for George, she saw hope flicker in his eyes for something more than she could offer. At least not now.

Chapter Ten

Maggie and Luke stood on the porch at the front door of the boarding house. After making inquiries during her shopping trip on Saturday, Maggie was referred to the place by a well-dressed lady in one of the shops where she'd made several of her clothing purchases.

"It looks respectable," Maggie said to Luke, who was helping her get around on her sore hip and ankle. She eyed the exterior of the clean, whitewashed, two-storied, clapboard building. White linen drapes flapped inside the two open front windows on either side of the green front door.

"Looks can be deceiving," Luke reminded her with a grin. "But, if I were a betting man," he drawled with a devilish smile, "I'd bet the woman in the shop yesterday wouldn't have sent you to one of the," Luke cleared his throat and chuckled, "*questionable* boarding houses we talked about yesterday."

Maggie grinned. "I believe you're right. Shall we?" Maggie knocked and a heavy-set woman with graying hair and plump pink cheeks opened the door.

"Yes, may I help you?"

Maggie stepped forward. "Mrs. Harris? My name is Maggie Douglas. I've just arrived in town and I'm looking for a room to rent. I was referred by Mrs. Donnelly who thought you might have one available."

"I do, indeed." The woman locked her arms under her massive chest and glared at Luke.

"May I see the room?" Maggie asked, drawing the woman's harsh perusal from Luke.

"Follow me." She waved a hand, turned and started up the stairs in the middle of the foyer. Before she made three stairs she whirled around and Maggie almost ran right into the big woman. "He waits in there." She pointed at Luke then toward the parlor to Maggie's right.

Luke's neck drew up like a surprised crane. Eyes wide he backed down the stairs and pointed to the room. "I'll just wait in there."

The woman turned around with self-importance and headed back up the stairs, Maggie two stairs behind her. She opened the door to a freshly painted yellow room with a single bed in the left-hand corner and covered by a yellow and white quilt. A short, four-drawer dresser with a yellow runner on top sat opposite the bed, a cream-colored pitcher and bowl on top of it. An armoire stood in the corner against the wall and yellow and white curtains matching the quilt flapped in the single, open window beside the armoire.

"This is my yellow room," the woman said. "Each room is a different color." She smiled, but Maggie saw sadness flicker in her eyes before she could mask it.

"Why colors?"

The woman's lips quivered causing her second chin to jiggle. "Just that a way is all." She paused and took a few moments before she said, "Fact is, the colors remind me of my dear departed boy and husband. Lost 'em both in the War." She sniffed. "My boy, Roscoe, loved blue and red from the time he was a small child, and green and yellow were my husband, Arnold's, favorites. Got four rooms to rent—one red, one blue, one yellow and one green." She sniffed again. "Have a hard time goin' into that blue room, though. Hate that color since the war. Reminds me of those blue bellies that killed by husband and my boy."

"I'm so sorry."

It must have been the opening Mrs. Harris wanted, for the woman launched into a tirade against the Yankees and how they killed her son and husband at the Battle of Shiloh. "My boy was only sixteen. He followed his pa into battle and got 'em both killed." She sniffed and dried her eyes with her apron. "I moved in with my sister and her husband outside of Atlanta, who had somehow managed to survive the war so far. They didn't have much to spare *before* Sherman went through, but after..." She sniffed and dabbed at her eyes again. "We struggled for so long just to put food on the table and keep a roof over our heads that when her husband got the gold fever a few years back and decided to come west, I went with them." She sighed heavily. "O' course, he didn't find any gold. All he found was a bullet in his back six months later from some claim-jumpin' coward who wanted his stake. His worthless stake," she added with a wistful shake of the head. "My sister and I struggled for two years, found this house and rented out rooms to keep from going to the poor house. Then my sister took sick and passed on not a year ago and left me with this place. I had a roof over my head and a business to run. Wasn't anywhere else to go back east, no family left, so I stayed." She lapsed into silence and her eyes filled with tears that eventually slid down her plump cheeks.

Maggie stepped inside the room to allow Mrs. Harris a few moments alone. A few minutes later the woman stepped in behind her.

"I'll take it, if you'll have me," Maggie said.

Mrs. Harris wiped the last of the tears from her face, took a deep breath and was back to business. "You seem like a proper young woman, Miss Douglas, but I've got rules in my house, hard rules for some, so hear me out before you decide you want to stay."

Maggie nodded. "Yes, ma'am."

"I run a no-nonsense place, Miss Douglas, for proper ladies. There's no drinkin', no cussin', no smokin', and most especially no men. If a man visits, he is welcome only in the parlor and must vacate by nine o'clock." She raised her chin as though waiting for an argument. When Maggie remained silent, Mrs. Harris continued. "If a man is discovered anywhere in this house other than the parlor—or *in* my parlor after nine o'clock—he will see the barrel of my Winchester pointed at his gut and you will be evicted. Do I make myself clear?"

"Yes, Ma'am."

"Do you still want this room?" she asked, her eyes drifting downstairs to where Luke waited.

Maggie looked around. It was a quiet room, in a quiet part of town according to Luke and Mrs. Donnelly, who had referred her. She didn't intend to spend a lot of time here. Her intent was to spend time becoming a good reporter for the *Cheyenne Sun*, make a name for herself, and find George in the interim—and she certainly had no intention of starting a romantic relationship, although she was sure Luke would be more than happy to oblige.

"Yes, I'd still like the room. Is there anything you want to know about me?" Maggie asked.

Mrs. Harris shook her head and clasped her hands in front of her. "No Miss Douglas. I know who you are. You're that new reporter gal."

Maggie was surprised then wondered why. Again it seemed most everyone in town knew she was coming. "And that doesn't concern you?" Maggie asked.

"Why should it concern me, Miss Douglas? I applaud you for takin' on what has always been a man's realm. I just hope you do a good job and show them women are not empty-headed and can do a job as well as they can, some perhaps better. I'm honored you chose my house to become your home." Mrs. Harris smiled widely, and Maggie suddenly found her endearing, reminding her of Judith, the cook and housekeeper at the Lazy D.

"Welcome to Cheyenne, Miss Douglas. I wish you great success while you're here." Mrs. Harris turned and headed back toward the stairs. "Shall we retrieve your friend and tell him the good news?"

Maggie followed the older woman, not so sure Luke would agree her living in such a strict establishment was good news.

With Luke's assistance and a temporary pass from Mrs. Harris allowing him into her room, Maggie was settled in by Sunday afternoon. She had little to move from the Inter-Ocean and, although sorry to leave the hotel behind so quickly, she was happy to save the money she would have otherwise had to use for the fancy room. She paid Mrs. Harris two month's rent and still had enough to hold her until she got her first pay voucher from the *Sun*.

"May I buy you dinner, Maggie?" Luke asked when she was all settled.

"Dinner would be nice. I've worked up quite an appetite."

Luke offered his arm and Maggie hobbled to him. He helped her down the stairs where they were met by Mrs. Harris.

"Remember the rules, Miss Douglas. Mr. Short was allowed to help you move in, but from now on, he's welcome only in the parlor and must depart by nine sharp."

"I remember, Mrs. Harris. I'll be back in a few hours— alone."

Mrs. Harris snapped her head up then down in approval. "Very well. Y'all have a nice evenin'." She turned and started away, but stopped. "Miss Douglas. I do want to bring the house's schedule to your attention before you leave. Breakfast is served promptly at seven. It's generally eggs, sourdough bread, coffee and bacon. If you don't come down, you don't eat. Lunch is at noon, although I imagine you'll be at the *Sun* at that time of day, and dinner is at six. Again, if you miss it, you are on your own. I don't put plates aside or keep them warmin' if you're not here." She eyed Maggie then added, "We'll get some meat on those bones once you've had a few good meals here."

"Yes, ma'am."

"Very well, have a nice dinner. I'll see you tomorrow morning at seven sharp." She turned and stomped out of the foyer, the floor boards creaking with each step.

Maggie and Luke hurried outside before they broke into laughter. "Lunch is at noon," Maggie mimicked.

"And dinner is at six," Luke parroted.

"It sounds to me like Mrs. Harris intends to fatten me up!"

"Well, if my opinion means anything, I think you look just fine, especially now that you're wearing your comfortable boots and sensible clothes." There was a gleam in Luke's eyes. "How's the ankle by the way? Shall I find a hack? There's a livery down the street."

Maggie shook her head. "I'll be fine. It's a little tender after all the moving and going up and down the stairs, but the doc wrapped it pretty tight yesterday. I'll be all right."

"Where shall we eat then?" Luke asked. "The Inter-Ocean's dining hall is nice, but Dyer's is close, too."

"Hmmm, let's try Dyer's, if you don't mind."

"Dyer's it is. Shall we?" Luke offered his elbow and the two slowly headed right on 18th Street. They passed several churches, crossed Ferguson Street and turned left on Eddy, opposite the Elephant Corral.

"I wonder what happened to all the horses that broke loose yesterday," Maggie mused out loud.

"At my table last night someone told me they made it all the way to the train tracks before the cowboys were able to get around them and slow them down. Thankfully no one was hurt, but by the time they were stopped, another dozen horses had broken loose and were running with them, making more than twenty horses racing down Eddy Street!

"If that cowboy hadn't managed to get that team of horses onto the side street, that carriage would have been down at the tracks right along with the rest of them. I shudder to think of that poor woman trapped inside. At least no one was hurt—other than their pride." She tapped her bruised hip and smiled crookedly.

They stopped in front of McDaniel's, the strains of music and laughter coming through the doors and windows. "Even on Sunday?" Maggie asked.

"Every day is a work day at McDaniels."

Luke pointed across the street to Dyer's and the Tin Restaurant beside it. "Shall we?" He stepped off the sidewalk, but Maggie stood frozen. The sound of horses' pounding hooves coming straight for her suddenly reverberated through her mind.

Luke tugged gently on Maggie's arm. "It's all right." Luke pointed up the street toward the quiet Corral. "Most of the animals have been shipped out. There are only a few in holding pens right now."

Maggie sucked in a deep breath to still her racing heart. *She was being silly.* "Of course it's all right. I was just thrown back to yesterday, is all." She stepped gingerly off the sidewalk beside Luke and they crossed the street without event. Following a quiet dinner she was back at the boarding house by seven, alone.

She washed up and crawled into the not-too uncomfortable bed. Thoughts of what the new day would bring rolled around in her head and kept her awake. Tomorrow would be the beginning of a new life. *Would it be a good life? Exciting? Lonely? Would this adventure turn out as badly as the last one or would she become the kind of reporter she dreamed of becoming? And George, would she find him, one man in this vast territory?* was the last question on her mind before sleep finally claimed her.

She was late! She'd slept surprisingly well once she finally fell asleep and right through breakfast. *Not a good beginning with Mrs. Harris,* Maggie thought throwing on one of her newly purchased outfits of a white, long sleeved, high-necked, form-fitting blouse, a plain, dark brown skirt that fell just below her ankles, and low-heeled, knee-high brown boots that seemed to take forever to button up. They were fashionable *and* functional the shop owner promised before Maggie hired the woman to sew four additional outfits in different colors to be completed and paid for after Maggie received her first draft from the *Sun*.

Hurrying down the stairs Maggie thought about apologizing to Mrs. Harris and the other three boarders for her tardiness, but decided she'd be better served to cross that bridge later. Perhaps tonight at dinner she would give her apologizes and meet the others, but right now she had things to get done before she started her new position at the paper.

Maggie went as fast as she could on her still tender ankle, closing the front door quietly behind her when she exited. The *Sun* was a few blocks away, but she had other business to attend to at the telegraph office first.

There was a man at the counter scribbling furiously when she walked in. It took several minutes for him to finish the contents of his telegram before he looked up. "Thank you for your patience." He tilted his head and said, "You're new in town, Miss…"

"Douglas, Maggie Douglas."

He grinned and nodded. "Ah, you're the new reporter for the *Sun*."

"I am."

He looked up at the clock hanging behind the counter. "Shouldn't you be there now?"

Maggie cocked her head and frowned. "No, I should not, not that it's any of your concern. I'm not expected for thirty minutes, minutes that are ticking away as we discuss *my* schedule, which is none of your business," she added in an exasperated tone. She was sending her first telegram in her search to find George to any and all newspapers in the Territory the telegraph operator might direct her to. Why she was there and what she was doing was her business and no one else's—especially some stranger—and she intended to keep it that way.

The man chuckled. "Guess it's true what they say about you."

Her spine raised a notch, along with her eyebrow. "And that is?"

"That you spent some time with the women's movement and you say what you think. I understand you're pretty tough, too. If that's true, you should make a good reporter."

"Well, thank you, Mr...."

"Glafeke." He grinned and added, "The owner of *The Cheyenne Daily Leader*."

Maggie groaned and her back sagged as she realized her error. "Mr. Glafeke, I'm so sorry. I had no idea who you were. I..."

He raised his hand. "No harm done—on either of our parts. I was overcurious about something that is, as you so astutely pointed out, none of my business." He brought his hand down and extended it toward her.

She shook his proffered hand. "It's a pleasure to meet you, sir. Perhaps we'll become better acquainted, and I may redeem myself, in our mutual association with the *Sun*," she said in a rush, trying to fix her blunder.

He smiled and shook her hand. "No redemption is necessary, Miss Douglas and, if it doesn't work out at the *Sun*, you come see me." He nodded, turned, and strolled from the telegraph office, a wide grin on his face.

She stared after him until the telegraph operator cleared his throat and asked what her message would be.

By the time Maggie finished at the telegraph office, she'd sent out personal advertisements to be put into five different newspapers throughout the Territory, which read: "Trying to locate one Mr. George Hawkins, last known to me in Kansas City. Have relocated in Cheyenne and await your response. Maggie."

Her mind was spinning as she took the last block toward her new place of employment. *Had George moved on with his life, so much so that he would ignore her, even if he did see one of the advertisements? Had she hurt him so badly he never wanted to see her again, even if he was alone? Or had he married, perhaps with a child by now?* Her thoughts were still tumbling when she reached the front door of the *Sun*.

She took a deep breath for courage and pushed open the door. A bell tinkled overhead and she stepped inside a large room. Two desks were to her right and the room was divided by a three-foot high wall with a swinging gate just beyond the desks. On the other side of the wall stood a large printing press and a man wearing a white, ink-covered apron stood behind one of several tables littered with boxes, ink pots and paper.

"Miss Douglas, I certainly hope that is you," the man called without looking up. "I'm in need of assistance,"

"Yes, sir, I'm Miss Douglas."

He glanced up at a clock hanging on the wall behind the desks. Maggie wasn't early, but neither was she late.

"Very good, you're right on time, Miss Douglas. An auspicious beginning." He wiped his hands on a cloth and pushed through the gate to meet her. "There is much to be done. Your counter-part," he pointed at the empty desk closest to the short wall where a wooden nameplate said Mr. Burns, "is off chasing a story; therefore, I will look to you for local news and assistance here until he returns."

"Whatever I can do, sir."

"That's the idea. Your father was very persuasive in getting me to take a chance on you, now let's see how you fare. I must tell you, I've been anxious for your arrival."

"As have a lot of folks in town I gather."

He chuckled. "Yes they have. You are treading new waters, Miss Douglas. There are many who want you to succeed, and succeed well, myself included. However, there are those who wish you would fail and do so miserably just to prove a woman cannot do a man's job. You're a sign of progress, Miss Douglas, and many will fight that progress. But Cheyenne isn't the wild and wooly west any longer. She's becoming sophisticated and I intend to help her toward that progress. Welcome, Miss Douglas, I'm Mr. Slack, the owner, but please call me A.E."

"I'm pleased to meet you, A.E." Maggie put out her hand.

A.E. looked at her with surprise before he gave a quick shake to her proffered hand. "Very well, the formalities are over, Miss Douglas. Let's get to work!" He stepped to the desk closest to the front door and pulled out the chair. "This one is yours. You should have everything you need to get started."

Maggie looked around and noticed one of those new-fangled type-writing contraptions she'd read about on Mr. Burns' desk.

She pointed. "Will I have one of those? I haven't been trained on how to use one."

A.E. snorted. "Neither has Mr. Burns and he proves it every time he attempts to use it. He's tried and tried to get the hang of it, but its use eludes him. If you should somehow master it, I'm sure Mr. Burns will be happy to give it to you—if not throw it!" Slack snorted and slapped his leg and Maggie immediately felt comfortable with her new boss.

"Your first assignment, Miss Douglas, after assisting me this morning, will be to report your arrival."

"Sir?"

"Your arrival has been anxiously awaited by many, Miss Douglas. It's not every day a woman takes on a man's role as a newspaper reporter and I intend to capitalize on it. I hope to sell extra newspapers reporting your arrival with information you deem interesting or pertinent to who you are and why you're here. Your history, your intentions, why you decided to become a reporter is what I'm looking for, Miss Douglas. Let's call it a test to determine how well you report and how I will assign you in the future. It may be a difficult assignment—or not. Depending upon how you handle it will decide if you *keep* this job."

Maggie sucked in a breath. *Keep this job! What if she didn't measure up and he decided to let her go? What would she do? Although she'd paid her board in advance, two months wasn't long and she may not be able to find something else right away.* Mr. Glafeke's offer popped into her mind. She raised her chin. "Don't worry, A.E., you won't regret your decision to hire me."

His head snapped up and down. "Good girl. Now let's get to work. I've got a paper to get out."

A.E. showed Maggie how to set and ink the print for the page he was finishing when she walked in and she spent the rest of the morning inking and printing her first newspaper copy. A boy came by just after noon and picked up the bundle to sell them on the corner. After a short break for lunch, she would work on her story, which A.E. expected completed by the end of the day to run in tomorrow's edition.

Having missed breakfast, Maggie was starved, but she had no idea where to go for lunch. Her quandary was eliminated when a smiling Luke stepped into the office.

"Luke! What are you doing here?"

"I was hoping to whisk you away to lunch."

"You have no idea how wonderful that sounds. I'm starving. I don't have much time, though. I have a story due by the end of the day."

"On your first day? What about?"

Maggie grimaced. "Myself," she whispered so A.E. wouldn't hear. "I have to write a story about my arrival."

"Should be easy, right?"

Maggie quirked an eyebrow. "I hope so. My new job depends on it."

"Mr. Short!" A. E. was pushing through the gate, hand extended. "What can we do for you today?"

"I've just come by to see if I may escort Miss Douglas to lunch. I hope you don't mind."

He cocked his head. "I don't mind, but Miss Douglas has a deadline to meet, so I leave it up to her as to whether she accepts or declines your invitation."

Maggie couldn't help but grin. "I've accepted, A.E.; however, I've already informed Mr. Short it must be quick."

"Very well, I'll see you when you return." He turned on his heel and shuffled back to what he'd been doing before Luke came in.

"Looks like we'd better hurry." Luke offered his elbow and rushed Maggie out the door before she could change her mind.

Thirty-five minutes later, following a quick bowl of chicken soup and a hunk of thickly buttered bread at a little restaurant close by, Maggie was back at her desk trying to figure out where to begin. After a dozen starts that wound up as crumpled pages in the trash can, it was four o'clock before she put down her pencil, sat back and read what she'd written:

A NEW ERA IN REPORTING

"Today a new era in reporting begins at the *Cheyenne Sun*. Many in Cheyenne have anxiously, and some not so anxiously, awaited the arrival of the *Sun's* newest reporter, Maggie Douglas.

"Raised on a working cattle ranch northwest of Kansas City, a few years ago Miss Douglas heeded the call to join the Women's Movement and left the security of her home for Boston to follow that call. After two years of traveling the northeast, working with the likes of Miss Susan B. Anthony and Miss Lucy Stone, it was time to return home. Once there she easily fell back into the daily routine of the family ranch, which included riding the range, herding cattle and roping strays, fixing fences and all manner of chores necessary on a working ranch. Although born to ranching and proficient at it, Maggie knew there was more for her to do, so during this time she was also deciding where and what her next adventure would be. After much soul-searching she realized the West beckoned. Believing Cheyenne to be a forward-thinking town that may someday surpass Denver as the *Queen City of the Plains and Mountains* in sophistication and opportunity, as well as the capital of the great Wyoming Territory, Miss Douglas decided there could be no better place for her future to begin than right here.

"Miss Douglas hopes to continue her coverage of women's issues in this woman-friendly territory, but would also like to spread her horizons to include the Indians' struggle for the Black Hills and how that struggle affects miners who leave Cheyenne every day in search of their own futures and fortunes. Retracing the past by learning Cheyenne's history is on the agenda, as well. No story worth telling will be ignored by Miss Douglas."

Maggie dropped the paper on her desk and sighed. *Was it too much? Not enough? Was it what A.E. wanted? Well, she'd never know until she gave it to him.*

She held her breath as her boss read the article. He cocked his head, frowned and nodded as she stood beside him waiting for the verdict. Maggie knew she was extremely lucky to have been given this opportunity. Although she'd never had any formal training in the art of writing, she'd always been able to express herself well, thanks to her mother's early lessons. During Maggie's suffragist days, because of that ability, she'd been called upon many times to write fliers and speeches for herself and others, including Miss Lucy and Miss Susan.

A.E. lifted his head, pursed his lips and turned to Maggie. She couldn't read his face so she sucked in another breath and held it while waiting for him to speak.

"Miss Douglas,"

"Yes, A.E." Her voice was rough and she swallowed to help retain her composure.

"Miss Douglas," he said again. "For a first attempt this will do. With a few changes here and there, it will suffice. However, you realize it sounds as though you sympathize *with* the Indians in this piece?"

"Yes, I realize that, A.E. It's how I feel. The Indians have been treated horribly—run out of lands they lived on for generations, put on reservations and forced to farm and fish instead of hunt like they have their entire lives, and to become dependent upon government annuities. Why? Because the government believes the white man has a 'manifest destiny,' and regardless of the Laramie Treaty of 1868 that gave the Lakota the Black Hills, the government is trying to take them away, steal them if you ask me, because gold has been discovered there. The Hills are no longer worthless like they were thought to be when the government first ceded them to the Indians. So the miners go in to take what they think is rightfully theirs and the Indians try to stop them. It's the same vicious circle that's been going on for years."

"Well, well, well, Miss Douglas, I am impressed. You've certainly done your homework."

Maggie closed her eyes and nodded. "Thank you sir, I have. I hope it'll help make me a better reporter. I want to show both sides, as mentioned in the article. I know a reporter must report the facts and remain unbiased."

He thought a moment. "Well said, Miss Douglas, although that isn't always the way it works out. On too many occasions newspapers state one point-of-view and don't report the facts for both sides. It sounds, however, like you will work toward that end. Your writing style will improve with time, and with a few changes, your piece will run on the front page of tomorrow's paper." He broke into a wide smile. "Welcome to the *Sun*, Miss Douglas."

Chapter Eleven

After Maggie's article ran curiosity seekers came by the *Sun* for the rest of the week, anxious to get a glimpse at the new female reporter. Maggie tried to ignore their gawking through the windows or when they strolled inside with self-importance to shake her hand. She gritted her teeth, smiled and greeted them warmly, knowing she was just a curiosity they wanted to appease. Some eyed her critically, as though she carried some rare disease and would pass it on if they touched her, while others pumped her hand in welcome until she thought her arm would snap.

Several people were milling inside the *Sun* building awaiting their turn to meet Maggie when a short, squat man with bug-eyes and thick glasses pushed his way through the crowd and made his way to the desk beside Maggie's and stopped.

"You, I presume, are the one causing this stir?" Notebooks, papers, and a leather bag landed on the desk with a thud.

"Guilty. Seems a lady newspaper reporter is big news in Cheyenne."

"And Deadwood and Fort Laramie."

Maggie frowned. All she wanted was to settle in and do her job. She wanted to be known for being a responsible reporter, not known just because she was a woman. "And you are?" Maggie offered her hand.

"Harvey Burns, your counterpart."

"Yes, Mr. Burns. I've been waiting for you to get back." She kept her hand out but her gesture was ignored. *Very well, if that's how he wants it!* Maggie fumed at the snub.

"Were you hoping I wouldn't return, Miss Douglas?" His face was hard, his big eyes pinched, when he looked up and started organizing the items he'd thrown on his desk.

"I beg your pardon?"

"I asked," he drawled, as though speaking to a stupid child, "if you were hoping I wouldn't return?"

Maggie drew a huge breath and leaned toward him. Ignoring the people standing around who looked as anxious to hear her answer as Mr. Burns, she asked, "And why would I hope that?"

"How fortuitous it would be for you, Miss Douglas, if I didn't return and you became the sole reporter for the *Sun*." Her name had rolled off his tongue like his mouth was full of molasses.

Maggie straightened to her full height, bringing her head above his. She put her hands on her hips and took a step closer. Burns took one step back.

"*Mr.* Burns," Maggie responded with the same hard tone he'd used, "I have no intention of taking your job, whether you never came back or not. I came here to do my own job."

"And what, exactly, is that, Miss Douglas?"

Maggie heard a unified intake of breath from the others in the room. She felt her hackles go up because the only "assignments" A.E. had given her since her arrival, other than the piece on herself, had been mundane, unimportant stories that only women would have an interest in reading. He had yet to give her a story to cut her teeth on. To get out there and talk to the people of Cheyenne and find out what was happening in their city and the surrounding territory. She hoped those assignments would be forthcoming and reminded herself she had to be patient.

She smiled, hoping to diffuse Mr. Burns' suspicions, and not give their audience something more to gossip about. "I want to report what you report—what any male reporter reports; stories pertinent to the population of Cheyenne. Stories that matter."

An eyebrow raised and a small flicker of respect darted across his eyes. "Well, well, well. You may have the heart of a reporter after all. But that remains to be seen." He smiled showing a mouth full of crooked teeth and Maggie's anger dissipated. "I thought you were going to come into town full of big ideas and nothing but fluff, but you seem to want what any reporter wants, a chance to prove himself, or herself, by writing good stories." He nodded his head and bowed in acquiescence. "Bravo, Miss Douglas, bravo."

He lightly clapped his hands and was joined by the onlookers surrounding them. Maggie felt heat rush up her neck and into her cheeks. The crowd, having seen enough of the show, began to shuffle out of the building until Maggie and Mr. Burns were alone.

"You knew I was coming, right?" Maggie asked, confused he had no idea what she was about.

"Of course."

"And you know my background? How I grew up and what I've been doing over the past few years?"

"I do not and I don't care. You will be judged on your merit as a reporter now—not on past experiences. Many a soldier has been elected to a position of power in the government he should never have held, elected solely because of his past glories in the military."

"Such as?" Maggie asked, wondering what else had provoked his ire.

He sighed. "Such as former president Ulysses S. Grant. A questionable general at best. He may have won the war— eventually—and helped in the South's 'reconstruction,' and I use the term loosely young lady; however, his economic policies were a disaster and his administration was riddled with scandal. He would have done better to have gone into the private sector and made his fortune on his name and prior glories and left running the government to someone who had the experience to rebuild this nation properly!"

"Do I sense southern leanings?" Maggie ventured. She had been very young during the Civil War, but to this day sentiments still ran hot and quick along the Missouri-Kansas border where the Lazy D was located. She'd witnessed it on more than one occasion while in Kansas City when fists had flown over comments about one or another's heritage, or whom someone had fought for in the war.

"You do. You may as well know I was a war correspondent for the Confederate States of America and saw all manner of horror—on both sides. However, the victors write history, so much will be lost in the telling."

"Where are you from, if I may ask?"

"A little town south of Kansas City, *Missoura*," he clarified, "called Dayton."

"Dayton! We're practically neighbors. Dayton's maybe seventy-five, eighty miles south of the Lazy D where I grew up."

"And which side of the Kansas/Missoura line does the Lazy D lie, Miss Douglas?" Burns' eyes were expectant and his head cocked.

"The Kansas side. The ranch is between Fort Leavenworth and Kansas City." She smiled when his face hardened. "Have you heard of it, the Lazy D?" she hurried on to keep down the wall she saw going up.

"Don't recall that I have."

"It's my family's cattle ranch. I was just a child when the war started, so I don't remember anything about it, and my father hasn't spoken much to me about it, but I know he fought."

"For whom did he fight, if *I* may ask?"

Maggie was treading on soft ground. It was apparent Mr. Burns carried heavy southern sentiments, along with scars from what he'd seen and experienced during the war.

"I believe he fought for the Union, sir."

Burns' lips puckered. "I see." His eyes blinked rapidly and color crept up his neck. He took a long breath and snapped his tongue. "Well, the war has been over for fifteen years. What happened then holds no bearing on what is happening now. Perhaps someday we will speak of it, but not today."

"I'd like that."

"Very well, Miss Douglas, someday we'll speak of it, but right now, let's talk to A.E. and get you a story to 'cut your teeth on'." Burns grinned then headed toward A.E., busily working at the press.

"Please, A.E. I can do it, just give me a chance."

A.E. raised an eyebrow. "It's not proper, Maggie. Not even in these modern times."

"I'll ask Luke to escort me. Please, A.E., I can do it." She heard the whine in her voice and didn't like it, but she wanted this assignment. It was her opportunity to do a story that would interest men *and* women. Who better to interview a woman gambler than another woman?"

A.E. sighed.

"It's a valid point, but I still don't like it."

"What's not to like, A.E.? I'll have Luke escort me and everything will be fine. I'll get the story and prove I can do it!"

He sighed heavily and thought a few moments before he finally said, "Very well."

Maggie squealed and hugged him before he could finish his sentence. "You won't be sorry, A.E."

"I'm already sorry, Miss Douglas. Just do a good job," he said, extracting himself from her embrace.

"Truly, you won't be sorry, A.E. I promise. I'll write a good story, a great story, you'll see."

They stared at each other until A.E. leaned toward her and said, "Well, what are you waiting for?" He shooed her out of the office and went back to his press.

She hurried through the gate and stopped at Harvey's desk. Her skirt swirled around her ankles when she stopped, a huge smile on her face, hands clasped together in front of her. "He gave me the assignment. I'm going to get Luke to escort me so I can get the interview!"

Burns clapped his hands and grinned. "Good for you, Miss Douglas, good for you. Now be off. Destiny awaits and I have a deadline of my own to finish." He dismissed her with a wave of his hand and went back to his article and Maggie hurried from the office.

It was almost five o'clock when Maggie reached the Inter-Ocean. "Luke! I have exciting news."

"Maggie, what are you doing here? You shouldn't be here," Luke said under his breath.

"Oh pooh." She looked around the gaming room of the Inter-Ocean where Luke dealt Faro and sat down beside a man with a long gray beard and graying hair that turned to her with his mouth open. "It's just a bunch of tables with men playing cards. Why shouldn't I be here?"

"Because a proper lady doesn't come to a place like this, and especially not alone."

"I'm not alone, you're here! And whoever said I was a proper lady anyway, Luke Short?" Maggie tried to look as innocent as possible.

Luke grinned and shook his head. "You are one of a kind, Miss Maggie Douglas."

"Thank you, Mr. Short. I'll take that as a compliment."

The man beside her got up and left the table with a grunt of disapproval. "I'm sorry, Luke, I didn't mean to drive your customer away."

"He'll be back, or someone else will fill his seat—or not. It's early, although we've heard half our crowd is over at McDaniel's. Why are you here anyway? What are you so excited about?"

"A.E.'s given me a real story to write, Luke. He wants me to interview Poker Alice while she's in town! Have you met her? What does she look like? Do you know where can I find her?"

Luke grinned. "Yes, I know her and I can help you find her, but slow down first."

"I'm sorry, I'm so excited. This is my first chance to do a real story that doesn't have to do with baking, sewing, church or children. It's a story men will want to read, as well as women."

"Well then, let's get started. What was your first question?" Luke had a gleam in his eyes.

"Do you know where I can find her?"

"That's easy. Do you see how empty this place is?"

Maggie looked around. The usually crowded gaming room, even at this early hour, was sparsely filled, at best. "There's hardly anyone here. Where are they?"

"They're where Poker Alice is, at McDaniel's. Just follow the men and you'll find Alice."

"Can you take me there, Luke? Now?"

"Maggie, I'm working."

"Can't you get away for a little while? Just long enough to introduce me?" Maggie put on her most endearing face, hoping to coax Luke into doing as she asked. She was learning how easily she could bend him with the cock of her head or pouting lips.

Luke shook his head and grimaced. "You know you can always get me to do what you want with that look, Maggie Douglas. Let me ask Mr. Chase if he minds my leaving for a while."

"Thank you, Luke. Thank you, thank you, thank you!" Maggie hopped up and down like a little girl, but she didn't care. This interview was important and if Luke could introduce her…

"Don't thank me yet, I don't know if I'll be able to leave or not. And if I can't, I do *not* want you going into McDaniel's alone."

Maggie's back went up. "Since when do you tell me what to do Luke Short?"

"Since time as you even think about going into McDaniel's by yourself, Maggie Douglas. It's a wild place and even more so when Alice is there. Men come from all over just to get a look at her. Promise me if I can't get away, you won't try and go there alone."

"I will not promise, Luke. I *have* to get this interview or A.E. will think I'm not resourceful enough to find a way."

"We'll find a way *if* Mr. Chase doesn't let me leave. Just wait here, I'll be right back." Luke hurried away.

While waiting for Luke's return, Maggie scanned the spacious room. Fancy wall paper covered the eight foot high walls but, where carpeting covered the floors in the lobby, the gaming room floor was planked. The tables were less-than-full, some of the dealers yawning in boredom. A chandelier similar to the one in the lobby hung from the ceiling and over-stuffed leather chairs and sofas lined the perimeter of the room.

Luke returned a few minutes later wearing a huge grin. "You're in luck. Because we're so slow Mr. Chase told me to take the whole night off. So, Miss Douglas, I'm all yours for as long as you want me."

Maggie smiled, took his elbow and leaned into him. "Thank you, Luke. This means a lot to me. It's one thing walking into the Inter-Ocean gaming room alone, but McDaniel's *is* different and I do realize that. I truly appreciate you acting as my escort."

Luke cocked his head. "Trust me, Maggie, the pleasure is all mine." He grinned again and Maggie knew if she allowed it, she could grow very fond of Mr. Luke Short.

Loud music, raised voices, bawdy laughter, smoke and alcohol filled Maggie's senses when she stepped through the door of McDaniel's a short time later with Luke at her side. She quickly scanned the room as the two worked their way deeper inside.

"Hang on tight. I'd hate for you to get lost in this sea of humanity."

Luke patted Maggie's hand and she couldn't help but lay hers over his. "Yes sir, Mr. Short. I'll do exactly as you say. Now, where do we find Miss Poker Alice in this 'sea of humanity' as you call it?"

Maggie couldn't see much of anything but tightly packed bodies. Following close behind Luke, pushing his way through the crowd, they made it to a long bar and Maggie was finally able to see something other than heads and shoulders everywhere. Beautiful paintings of what looked like foreign lands hung on the wall behind the bar. Maggie appreciated the paintings as long as she could before Luke dragged her away into the main parlor of the theater. The room was filled with tables, chairs and lots of men being served by pretty women with big smiles. A heavy black curtain fell over the stage at the rear of the room and statues of variously proportioned women stood at both entrances to the narrow stage. Six boxes for private viewing with wide, open windows jutted out from the wall in front and to the right of the stage and were accessed by a thin set of stairs. Maggie craned her neck to inspect the boxes, wondering how anyone could *see* anything on stage from inside of one—unless they were hanging out the window!

Luke pointed. "The gambling saloon is over there. She's probably there." Seconds later he was dragging her out of the theatre room.

"If the gambling saloon is over there," Maggie asked, "why did you drag me into the theater room?"

"I thought you would want to see everything. Well, this is everything and what better time to see it than when you have me for an escort?"

"I do want to see it all, but at a time when I'm not looking for someone, it's not so crowded, and I *can* see it. Under those circumstances I might be a bit more appreciative of its overall ambiance."

Luke chuckled just as Maggie was shoved again. She stood to her full height, deciding she'd been bumped, shoved and pinched enough and it was time to find Alice in this massive crowd. She squeezed Luke's hand and dragged him forward.

"My turn." She walked straight to a table where four men played cards.

"Excuse me." she said to a gruff-looking man at the table.

"Excuse what, lady?" His voice belied his confusion.

Pointing toward the bar she asked, "If I offered to buy you a drink, would you retrieve it and allow me to borrow your chair for a few minutes?"

His mouth split in a huge grin. "Lady, if you want to buy me a drink for this chair, why, I'll be more'n happy to let ya." He stood up on wobbly legs, doffed his hat and put out his hand. Maggie dug through her bag, put a coin in his hand and off he went toward the bar, the other three men watching him go.

"You want to buy me a drink, too, lady?" one of the others asked then another.

Maggie smiled and shook her head. "No gentlemen, I have need of only one chair—that one." She pointed to the vacated chair.

"What are you about Maggie?" Luke asked.

"I intend to find out exactly where Miss Poker Alice is in this crowded establishment, and without further rattling of my brains." She jerked the chair away from the table and turned to Luke. "Please place this in the middle of the room for me?"

Luke scratched his head, but did as she asked. He pushed his way through the crowd drawing grumbles and insults against his person as the chair bumped against more than one patron before he set it down in the middle of the room.

Maggie put out one hand and grabbed up her skirt with the other. "Some assistance, please?"

Luke took her outstretched hand and she stepped onto the chair, able to see over everyone from her vantage-point.

"That way!" She pointed and hopped down. Before her feet touched ground she was shoved and tumbled right into Luke's arms. Their eyes met and held for several seconds before she pushed away, straightened her skirt and hurried off, Luke scurrying after her, forgetting the abandoned chair.

In the middle of another smoke-filled gaming room, a crowd was gathered around a single table. The bar at the rear was almost empty, except for the barkeep cleaning what looked like an already clean glass. Long tables along the side walls were mostly empty, too. Everyone was gathered around the one table in the center of the room.

"There she is." Luke waved and smiled when he caught up to Maggie.

"Draws a crowd, doesn't she?" Maggie said in awe.

"That she does. Shall we? Hang on." Luke shoved his way through the crowd again until they stood behind Poker Alice, one of six people seated at the round table. The dealer looked up. "Lookin' for a pickup game, Luke? We're full up," he said with a grin.

Luke shook his head. "No, just want to say hello to this lovely lady." He swept his hand over the lady at the table.

Without taking her eyes from her cards, Alice extended her right hand. "Luke Short. I'm a little busy right now, but give me a few minutes. I'll put these boys out of their misery and we'll visit."

Luke kissed her hand and she continued the game without missing a beat.

Maggie watched the petite woman in rapt silence as the other four players laid down their bets. Alice smiled when the bet came to her. "I call and raise fifty."

The game progressed as one by one the others dropped out until Alice and one other player were left. "Mister?"

"Don't rush me, I'm thinking." The man rubbed his chin and studied his cards.

Although she still hadn't seen Alice's face, Maggie knew the woman had control of the game. They waited a few more moments before the man slung his cards down on the table. "Too rich for my blood," he grumbled. "What you got, Alice?"

"You should know better than to ask that question, not even to a woman, and especially not *this* woman," Alice chastised.

"But I want to know if I lost the last of my money on a bluff."

She clucked her tongue, shook her head and smiled like the cat that had eaten the canary. "Sorry, Mister. A lady never tells." The crowd hooted and the dealer slid Alice's cards back into the deck. With a flurry of harrumphs the man vacated his seat, which was immediately filled by another player anxious to play against the famous Poker Alice.

"That's it for now, boys!" Alice called, sliding her winnings into a pile in front of her.

"Aren't you going to give us a chance to win our money back?" one of the men she'd been playing with asked. "It's still early."

"I need to have a conversation with this handsome young man beside me. Y'all be patient, keep my seat warm, and I'll be back shortly." She pointed at the dealer. "Wiley, keep an eye on my winnings."

"Yes, Miss Alice, I will."

There was a unified groan of disappointment when she stood up and pushed away from the table. She turned around and Maggie got her first look at "Poker Alice," amazed at the small woman's presence. Although she was inches shorter than Maggie, Alice's stance and demeanor commanded respect. Maggie studied the slight woman and easily understood why men flocked to her. Her small, shapely frame was adorned in a frilly, fashionable blue dress. Deep blue eyes sparkled with intelligence, and mischief, and long, soft brown curls tumbled over her shoulders and down her back. In a word she was beautiful and a beautiful, successful, woman gambler was to be respected, if not followed and gawked at.

"How the hell are you, Luke?" she shouted over the din, leading the way out of the room.

"I'm well, Alice. And you?" he asked, trying to keep up with the petite woman while dragging Maggie behind him.

When they reached a back room Alice ushered Luke and Maggie in and shut the door. She flopped down in a chair and lit a cigar!

"Maggie Douglas, I give you Alice Ivers. Alice, Maggie Douglas."

Alice gave a quick nod. "Any friend of Luke Short is a friend of mine, Miss Douglas."

"Maggie, please, Miss Alice."

Alice grinned and pulled on the newly lit cigar. She took out the cheroot, eyed it and rolled it between her fingers. "One of the nastier vices I've picked up hanging around places like this. Bless my dear-departed husband's soul he'd roll over in his grave if he saw me smoking one of these things." She popped it back in her mouth, clenched it between her teeth, slapped her leg and hooted. "But let's not get sullen about my poor Frank. What are you doing here, Luke? Last I knew you were out in Kansas."

"I was, dealt at the Marble Hall for a while, but I'm at the Inter-Ocean right now."

"Working for Big Ed Chase?" she said on a chuckle, blowing out a swirl of smoke. Her eyes sparkled and Maggie saw not only her outer beauty, but her inner beauty, as well.

"For now." The room fell silent a moment until Luke said, "Miss Douglas is a newspaper woman."

"Well, bless my soul! Good for you, honey. What can I do for you?"

"I'm hoping for an interview, Miss Alice. It's my first real assignment. Up till now I've only reported female interests. I've written about more church socials, births and marriages than I knew could exist in one town. I'm ready for something men will be interested in reading, as well as women. I want them to read about a classy woman gambler—a beautiful woman gambler, I might add."

"No need to sweeten up the pot, Miss Douglas. The interview is yours. Just tell me when and where and I'm your girl."

Chapter Twelve

LADY GAMBLER TAKES CHEYENNE
POT BY POT

Alice Ivers, otherwise known around the gambling circuit as "Poker Alice," is earning her nickname every day, proving that a pretty face can have the brains and cunning to win at poker and faro. Since arriving in Cheyenne, Alice has been seen from Dyers to McDaniel's to the Inter-Ocean, bringing her winning ways to each establishment, while her wit, charm and petite frame are admired by men and women alike who gather to watch her play.

Born in Devonshire, England, Alice's family moved to Virginia when she was a small babe. In Virginia she attended boarding school until she was teen-aged when the family moved west in search of silver. Landing in Leadmine, Colorado, Alice met her soon-to-be husband, Frank, a mining engineer with a passion for gambling. Unwilling to stay behind when her new husband ventured to the gambling halls of their resident mining towns, Alice stood quiet and stoic behind him, hands on his shoulders, watching and learning everything there was to know about poker and its players.

"I wasn't going to stay home and play the demure little wife while Frank was out having fun playing cards and making money to boot! I was young and smart and wanted to be with my husband, else I wouldn't have gotten married! So off I went with him to the gambling halls where I studied everything I could about the game until I felt confident enough to play with the men," Alice stated during her interview.

An unfortunate accident took Frank's life only a few years into their marriage, leaving Alice to fend for herself. She might have taught school, had there been one in the vicinity and, although well-educated, there were few other options available to a woman alone in a rough mining town. So Alice picked up a deck of cards and took to gambling like spurs to boots. In the years following Frank's death, Alice proved proficient at both poker and faro, showing that a woman with a pretty face can win a freezout and buck the tiger when given the opportunity.

Dealing or playing, Alice quickly gained her moniker of "Poker Alice."

Miss Alice mostly travels the Colorado circuit, but can be seen in towns between Denver and Cheyenne, and may even consider an appearance in Deadwood someday.

So be on the lookout for Miss Alice Ivers, better known as "Poker Alice," at any of the gambling establishments around town. But don't look for her on Sunday, she'll be doing what the Good Book says to do on the Sabbath—resting—and counting her winnings.

A.E. pinched his lips and took a deep breath. Maggie thought she'd bust, waiting for the verdict on whether her piece would run or not. She'd labored for hours to get the right combination of fact and newly emerging legend. She didn't want men to think of the piece as nothing but a bunch of fluff, to disregard it as more women's news, but something they would enjoy and accept as good writing. This was Maggie's chance to prove she should be accepted as a reporter for what she wrote, the same way Alice Ivers was accepted as a gambler for how she played cards.

A.E. cleared his throat and swallowed. "Well, Miss Douglas."

"Yes, A.E.? Will it run?"

He pursed his lips, prolonging her anguish.

"Please, A.E. You're killing me!"

He broke into a smile and his head bobbed up and down. "It'll run." He clucked his tongue. "Yes sir, it'll run."

Maggie squealed and ran toward him, but he threw his arms up as a barricade. "Miss Douglas, you must dispense with hugging me every time I approve of something you've written or give you an assignment you appreciate. In the future, there will be many such assignments and you can't be hugging me every time I give you one. My wife will get suspicious." He winked, turned and strolled through the gate into the back room. "It'll be tomorrow's headline!" he called over his shoulder. "Now take the rest of afternoon off. You've earned it."

The days blended into weeks and Maggie found herself covering happenings at the Elephant Corral to theater shows at

McDaniel's, escorted by Luke, of course. After the story ran on Alice, Maggie's and Mr. Burns' relationship solidified. He accepted her as a good reporter and respected her for a job well done.

The summer heat intensified and, although Luke and Maggie's schedules conflicted and they spent less and less time together, when they did see each other it was clear Luke's feelings for Maggie were heating up as fast as the weather.

"Maggie, why won't you even consider it?" Maggie's legs were curled under her on a multi-colored quilt. Sitting in a clearing inside a copse of trees on the outskirts of town, Maggie and Luke had enjoyed a picnic dinner of fried chicken, sweet potatoes, corn on the cob and apple pie. "I'd give up everything and settle down for you."

Maggie felt a sense of déjà vu. She'd had this conversation before a long time ago with George, and she was sorry how it ended then. *Would she be sorry again? Although she'd heard nothing from George since her arrival, she wasn't ready to give up her search yet.*

"Luke, I've told you again and again, I can't. I'm still looking for George." *But was that her only reason? She was just beginning to get her legs as a reporter. Was she ready to give it up to become someone's wife, even George's if she found him? Was she too restless with too many things to do to become anyone's wife—ever?*

Luke grabbed her shoulders and pulled her toward him. "I've been patient and played the gentleman for months now, Maggie. George is lost in the wind. You've sent ad after ad with no response. You'll never find him. Stop looking. I'm the one who's here." His lips came down on hers in a bruising kiss.

Deep down Maggie knew Luke was right. *There was no guarantee she would ever find George. It'd been months and she still hadn't had any response to her personal advertisements. Would she ever? This was now and Luke was here.* Forcing herself to relax, she melted into his kiss.

Her encouragement was all he needed and he crushed her to him. He kissed her with all the passion he'd held back, his tongue forcing her lips apart so he could invade her mouth. His hand swept behind her head and he wove his fingers into her hair. He trailed wet kisses from her mouth to her ear and down her neck.

Paul Thornton's face exploded into Maggie's mind. It became Paul kissing her, slobbering on her, not Luke. She couldn't breathe and tore herself away, shoving at his chest. "Please, no," she managed on a ragged breath.

He pulled back and although she saw Luke, she also saw what was in his eyes. Lust. The same lust she'd seen in Paul's eyes that horrible day.

"What's wrong, Maggie? I love you. I think I've loved you from the minute I saw you. Let me show you."

His lips crashed down on hers again and she struggled harder. All she felt was what she'd felt the day of Paul's attack. Panic. Fear. There was no love in her right now, just fear. She had to be free of him. "Stop, Paul! Stop!" She slapped at his face and shoved at his chest and shoulders. She was so afraid, she had to get away!

Her head hurt. *Why were her teeth rattling?* He had her by the shoulders, shaking her. There was fear in his eyes. "Maggie, Maggie, I'm so sorry. Please, Maggie, forgive me."

She came to her senses, took a deep breath and sat back. "Luke…"

He swiped beads of sweat off his forehead, took a deep breath and shook his head in confusion. "What the hell just happened? One second you were responding to my kiss and the next you were calling me Paul, slapping at me, trying to get away from me."

"It's a long story, Luke, one I've never shared with anyone."

"I'm so sorry, Maggie. I had no idea. I thought you've been pining over George all this time. But there's something more, isn't there?"

Maggie swallowed and nodded. "Yes."

"Can you tell me about it?"

She bit her lip. "I don't know, but it's part of the reason I'm here."

"I'd like to hear about it—if you can talk about it." He reached for her hand and she let him take it, realizing how foolish she'd been. Luke loved her; he'd just told her so. Even if she didn't love him back she had to believe he wouldn't do anything to hurt her. She had to trust again sometime, *why not now?*

Unable to look Luke in the eyes, she told him what had happened with Paul Thornton. "I never dreamed he would accost me, Luke, never, or I wouldn't have gone with him. I just wanted to be free for one day without worrying about where I was, where I was going or being insulted and pummeled by rotten food. I wanted to be away from town, any town, to smell some fresh air and feel the sun on my face. I guess I missed the ranch more than I realized." She turned and looked into the depth of Luke's caring eyes, all traces of lust gone. "I never considered myself naïve, but Paul Thornton proved otherwise." She sniffed and wiped a tear sliding down her face.

Luke brushed her cheek with the back of his fingers. "I'm so sorry, Maggie. I never would have pushed you if I'd known." He sighed and took her chin in his hand. "I told you the truth, though. I love you Maggie Douglas. I've loved you since the minute I spotted you in front of the Inter-Ocean." He plucked another tear from her face. "I would never knowingly hurt you."

"I know that, Luke. And it's not just Paul and what he did to me, there's George. I gave my heart to him a long time ago then threw him away because I 'had things to do.' I have to find him or at least try until I've exhausted every resource. That's why I'm here in Cheyenne, why I'm doing what I'm doing. I want to know what's going on in and around the Hills, and who's doing it, because that's where George was headed when he left the Lazy D. It's the only way I can find him. It's only been a few months and I'm not ready to give up yet."

Luke turned away, but not before Maggie saw the disappointment and pain in his eyes. "I understand. If it's time you need I'll give it to you, but know this Maggie Douglas, I don't know how long I'm willing to wait. I have things to do, too. He grabbed his hat, stood up and walked away.

The oppressive August heat slid into September. As much as Maggie hated it, she'd taken to wearing a bonnet and using a newly purchased parasol to keep the punishing sun off her head and shoulders when going from place to place. She wore one, thin petticoat under her skirt, rolled her sleeves up as far as they could go, and unbuttoned her collar in the hot office of the *Sun* when no one else was around. Windows were flung open, but unless there was a breeze, the air was stifling and the sweat poured off her forehead and soaked her clothes.

Maggie was at her desk, trying to stay as cool as was humanly possible when a boy ran into the office, handed A.E. a piece of paper, and ran back out. A.E.'s eyes bulged and his lips twitched as he read the paper.

He crunched the paper in his fist. "Burns! Where's Burns?" he cried running through the gate into the front office.

"He's not here, A.E. He's in Denver remember? Can I help you with something?"

A.E. frowned and cursed under his breath. "Only one of the biggest stories in months."

"What story, A.E.?" With Harvey's absence this could be Maggie's chance for the story she'd been waiting for.

He pointed then let his hand fall as if in defeat. "That telegram."

"Yes?"

"There's been a monumental fire in Deadwood. Early reports are that it's wiped out more than half the town."

Maggie's mind started to whirl. *This was her chance.* "Let me go, A.E. I can cover it," she blurted.

His head jerked up with such surprise, Maggie realized the thought of sending her had never even crossed his mind. "Send you? I couldn't send you."

"Why not? Because I'm a woman? I can catch the stage to Deadwood as easily as any man. If you're worried about my safety, the stage will be full of men to protect me—if I needed protecting," she added as an afterthought. "Don't forget, I always have my pistol close at hand." She stepped up to her boss. "A.E., I'm a good reporter. Haven't I proven that I can get a good story?"

"Yes, you have, but this is different. This could be dangerous."

"Please A.E. You took a chance on me with Alice's piece and look how well it turned out. More people read the *Sun* than ever before, because of me. I've written on everything and anything you've given me since then. This is the story I've been waiting for to really prove I can do this—to you, to the town, but most especially to myself. Please, let me have it."

A.E. stared at Maggie, hard. "*If* I let you go, Miss Douglas, *if,*" the word hung a moment before he said again, "*If* I give you this story, getting there is only one of the problems. It's a grueling, six or seven day trip at minimum and there are still wild Indians on the trail. You'll be riding with any number of rough, hard men..."

"The better for my protection," Maggie interrupted.

A.E. frowned. "That's not the only thing I'm concerned about, Miss Douglas. The telegram says half the town has been wiped out. Every room or hotel that wasn't destroyed in the fire will be full. Where will you stay?"

"I've camped out half my life on cattle drives, A.E. Sleeping under the stars is nothing new to me. I'll bring a canvas, bedroll, and extra food. I'll sleep wherever I can. That's the least of my worries. *Please* A.E. Give me this chance, you won't be sorry. I've proven I can get a good story, let me do this one, too."

It was several moments of sputtering and rubbing his chin and face before A.E. popped his cigar back in his mouth, groaned and nodded. "All right, Miss Douglas. You be on the Deadwood stage tomorrow morning. I want facts, but I want the human side, too. I want to know what happened, how they fought it, what's left and how the people are handling it. I want to *see* the fire and its flames in your story. I want to *feel* its intensity, *choke* on the smoke. In essence, talk to the people, find out what happened and put me there, before during and after." He took a deep breath and shook his head. "I'm taking a big chance on you Maggie Douglas. If anything happens to you I'll never forgive myself." He paused, as though reconsidering then said, "I could wire Mr. Burns and send him straight up there."

"Please A.E., don't. I can do it, I promise."

With a sigh and a grimace, he nodded. "Be on that stage in the morning. Now go home, get packed and get some rest. You're going to need it."

Maggie hurried to the Inter-Ocean to find Luke before she did anything else. His shift didn't start for a few hours, but she hoped to find him playing poker or faro.

"Luke!" He laid his cards down when Maggie came up behind him, huffing and puffing. "Luke, I have exciting news!"

"Slow down Maggie. Let me finish this hand and we'll talk in the lobby. Go wait for me there and catch your breath."

"Hurry, Luke, hurry." She rushed to the lobby, her heart pounding with excitement and from her exertion. Most unladylike, she plopped into one of the over-stuffed leather chairs and tapped her toe while waiting for Luke, who arrived a few minutes later.

"What on earth are you so excited about, Maggie?" He sat down in the chair beside her.

"I got it. A.E. gave me my story!"

He leaned over the arm of his chair toward her. "What story?"

"*The* story. The one I've been waiting for."

"And what story is that?"

"There's been a huge fire in Deadwood and I'm going to report it."

"You're going to Deadwood? Alone? Maggie, you can't."

Maggie raised her eyebrows. "What do you mean, I can't? You know better than to tell me that, Luke Short. Why can't I?"

"It's not safe. Deadwood is still a wild town."

"Well, it's not wild anymore. The fire has wiped out half of it and I'm going there to report on it."

"I'll go with you."

"No!" She wasn't sure why she rejected his suggestion so quickly, but this was something she had to do on her own to prove she could do anything a man could under any circumstances—without someone babysitting her. "No," she said again more calmly. "I have to do this alone, Luke, but I appreciate your offer."

He shook his head and gnashed his teeth. "Maggie, you can't go. I won't let you."

"Pardon me?" Maggie's hackles went up. She knew Luke was in love with her, but he had no right.

"I mean, Maggie, please reconsider. It's too dangerous."

"Life is dangerous. I could have been killed that day in the street when those horses got loose or any number of other times between the Lazy D and here. This is the story I've been waiting for, Luke, and I will not let it get away—for any one or any reason. I leave on the morning stage. I hoped you'd be happy for me, but I can see that's not the case." She started to get up, but he stayed her by laying his hand on her arm.

"I'm afraid for you and that takes precedence."

"Well stop being afraid. Be happy. Encourage me, but don't try to stop me."

"I will try to stop you, any way I can. Maggie, it's too dangerous for you to get on that Deadwood stage alone. It's attacked by Indians on a regular basis. People are killed!"

Maggie knew that, but she wouldn't dwell on it. "I have my pistol and there will be plenty of men on the stage with guns who know how to use them."

"Yes, rough men who are not used to sharing the company of a beautiful woman for days in close quarters. Many who might,"

"Might what, Luke?" Maggie interrupted.

"Try to take advantage of you the same way Paul Thornton did, but this time they could easily succeed."

Maggie was not a quitter and she would not back down from this assignment *or* this argument, especially after she'd begged A.E. to let her go. She pursed her lips and took a deep breath. She patted her bag where Wally was hidden. "Luke, I always have my gun with me."

"Like you did with Thornton?" he interrupted.

"I told you what happened that day. He caught me unawares. I was naïve. I won't be naïve again."

"No, you'll be outnumbered and helpless is what you'll be. And in the end, you could be dead! Whether it's at the hands of men who are out-of-control or Indians, dead is dead, Maggie."

For a moment Maggie hesitated, then stood her ground. She was Maggie Douglas and she had things to do, and right now that was to report the fire in Deadwood. She straightened her back. "I will not change my mind, Luke Short, and you won't make me. I'm going to Deadwood on that stage tomorrow morning. I'll arrive safely, get home safely, write a great story, and no one, not even you, is going to stop me."

"I hope you're right, because when it comes to what you might face on that trip to Deadwood you're still very naïve."

Maggie held her temper. Luke loved her and was afraid for her, she reminded herself. "Please Luke, I have to do this. Be happy for me, don't send me away angry."

He sat without saying a word for several moments before he finally nodded. "All right, Maggie. If you have to do this, just come back alive and *be careful*, can you at least do that for me?"

"I will. And you can bet I'm going to come back with the best damn story you'll ever read!" She gave him a quick kiss on the cheek and raced out the door, missing the sadness that washed over his face.

PART III

DEADWOOD

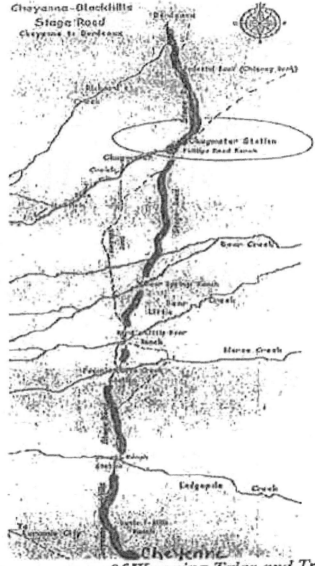

Maps courtesy Of Wyoming Tales and Trails

Cheyenne-Deadwood Stage Map, Bordeaux to Rawhide

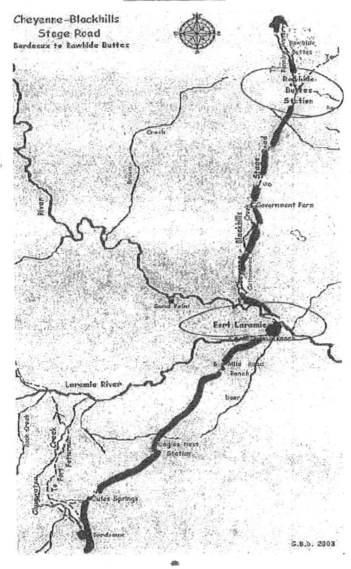

Cheyenne-Blackhills
Stage Road
Bordeaux to Rawhide Buttes

G.B.D. 2003

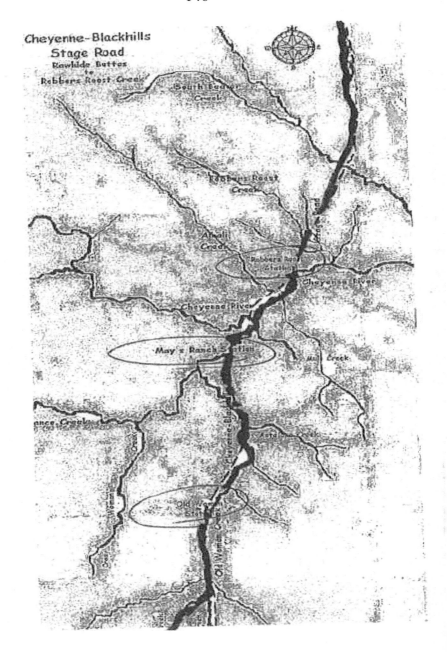

Chapter Thirteen

Not one dress or skirt was going with Maggie to Deadwood. She had on one of six newly-purchased Levi Strauss & Co. denim blue jeans she'd bought the night before at one of the local mercantiles that were selling them to miners like bottles of water in the desert. The other pairs were rolled in a bag along with ten lightweight, short-sleeved shirts, socks and under garments. Sliding on the one pair of riding boots she'd thought to bring with her from the ranch, she felt right at home, her attire bringing more than one stare and stumbled-step when she got out of the hack she'd hired to get her and her gear to the depot. Adjusting her newly purchased cowboy hat, rolling the brim to get it formed the way she liked it, she told herself she was ready for this monumental assignment. She had no idea how long she'd be in Deadwood and hoped she was prepared for any eventuality. Her hand wrapped around the heavy bag holding the oiled canvas she'd also purchased last night for use as a tent or anything else it might be needed for. She'd also bought some canned fruit and two canteens, now filled with water, the straps crisscrossing her chest and slapping her hips with each step. Inside two smaller bags were her writing supplies and her clothes. She planned to stay in Deadwood long enough to see everything she needed to see and talk to as many people as she could to find out exactly what happened and how the community was dealing with it, just like A.E. asked. She would make him proud. He would *not* be sorry he sent her.

Maggie's bags were stowed and she climbed inside the creaking coach, pulled by a team of six black horses. Sandwiched between two smelly men with scraggly gray beards and work-worn, dirty hands, she laid her hat on her lap to keep it from being crushed in the over-full cabin. Three big men crowded the seat opposite and the top of the stage overflowed with men who sat anywhere and held onto anything they could to keep from falling off.

"So, young lady, what're ye doin' headed to Deadwood all alone?" the older man on her left asked. His breath reeked so badly she wanted to pinch her nose.

"I'm a reporter for the *Cheyenne Sun*. I'm going to write an article about the fire."

"Fire? What fire?" the man on her right leaned forward to ask, his breath just as rank as the other.

"There was a big fire in Deadwood yesterday. I'm going to write about it."

"You? A woman?" one of the long-legged men across from her said and everyone in the coach erupted into laughter.

Maggie's eyes pinched and her mouth hardened. She wagged her finger at each and every man inside the coach. "Bet you wouldn't talk like that to Miss Calamity Jane. Well, you shouldn't talk to me that way, either. She's a dead shot and so am I." She patted the small bag where Wally was hidden and lifted her chin. "I can take care of myself just fine, gentlemen."

Her mention of Calamity Jane took some of the starch out of them. "You know Miss Calamity? Can ye shoot like her?" the man on her left asked.

"Can't say as I know her personally, but I hope to meet her someday." She pulled the Colt out of her bag to show them she was serious. "But we do have a lot in common."

"By damn you do, you both wear men's clothes!" one of the men across from her hooted and slapped his leg.

Another of the men added, "Calamity carries a rifle, girl, a *real* gun, and two pistolas to boot. All you got is a puny suicide gun." The coach erupted into laughter again, the men nodding agreement.

Maggie lowered her head, took a breath then raised her chin, a huge grin on her face. "Ah, but gentlemen, I know where to put that bullet into a man to make it count." She slid Wally back into the bag.

The coach went eerily quiet until one of the older men snorted. "Why, Miss, you're jest a funnin' us."

"Am I?" She patted her bag where Wally lay concealed again. Her eyelashes fluttered and she smiled at each of them. She let them think about her statement a few moments before she changed the subject. "And gentlemen, while we're discussing such matters, why shouldn't I wear pants? You all wear them. Why shouldn't I?"

Every man in the stage snorted. "Because you can't ride a horse in a dress," the man across from her stated, as though any dim-wit should know the answer.

"Exactly! I can't ride a horse in a dress, either. Nor can I traipse around a burned out town in a dress. It's just not sensible and I, gentlemen, am a sensible girl." She smiled again and one by one the men nodded their heads and smiled back.

"Ye seem a bright young woman, Miss..."

"Douglas, Maggie Douglas. You remember that when my story is on the front page of the *Cheyenne Sun* once we get back. Maggie Douglas, don't forget it."

"Well, Miss Douglas," the as yet unheard of man across from her said with no trace of a smile on his face. "Let's hope you make it to Deadwood and back with all that pretty black hair of yours still attached to your head—since you can take care of yourself and all."

Her fellow passengers hooted with laughter again, and Maggie wondered for the first time since taking the assignment if she was doing the right thing.

They stopped several times that morning at way-stations along the route to blow the horses. Stuck between the two smelly, jabbering men and dodging the legs of the three silent, insensitive men on the opposite seat, had Maggie on edge. Her legs were so cramped by the time they reached Horse Creek Station for the noon meal, she nearly fell getting out of the stage.

"Come and git it!" The chow bell was ringing when Maggie's boots hit the ground. She grabbed the rail to keep from stumbling, stamped her feet and rubbed her legs trying to keep them from going into a full cramp. Her toes and feet tingled and both of her calves were as tight as a bow string pulled and ready to release. Using the stage for support she limped around the back of it, grumbling. She hobbled to a corral holding the horses that would replace the current team for the afternoon trek and continued complaining until her anger dissipated. It took ten minutes for her toes and legs to stop tingling and her calves relaxed enough to walk without everything cramping.

She was the last one into the depot where everyone was already seated at a long trestle table. A big woman ladled bowls of what looked like chili from a huge pot and loaves of sourdough bread were being passed around and pulled apart as quickly as the men got their hands on them.

"There you are, Miss Douglas!" Sam, Maggie's stage companion to her left, shouted. "Pull up a squat and git ye some grub. What took ye so long?"

"My legs were cramping, so I took a walk." Maggie wanted to talk as little as possible to Sam or Tom, her right-hand stage neighbor. She wanted less to sit near them to eat, afraid she might gag in the effort, but there were no other open spots so she slid in between them.

Sam chuckled, shoved a spoonful of chili into his mouth then tore off a piece of bread with his teeth. "Is a bit cramped inside that stagecoach, ain't it little lady?" he mumbled around his food.

It was all Maggie could do to keep from forgetting about lunch and run back outside. But it was a long trip and she couldn't skip any meals, even if it meant eating them with this raggedy, smelly bunch.

She smiled and took a bowl of chili offered by the hefty woman. "Go on and eat, girl. You're gonna need your strength— 'specially travelin' with the likes of these fellas." The woman slapped a hand grabbing at the plate of bread Maggie was reaching for and smiled, exposing two missing front teeth. "Go on. Grab ye that piece of bread. Helps the chili settle." The woman cackled and walked away.

Maggie took a tentative bite of the chili and, aside from the grease floating on top, was surprised at how good it tasted. Grabbing a chunk of bread out of the basket as it sailed past a second time, she sopped up the grease, tore off the greasy part of the bread, laid it aside, and enjoyed the rest of the meal.

A half hour later they were heading back to the stage. Maggie tapped the driver on the shoulder before he climbed up. "Mr. Lathrop, is there any chance I could ride up top with you and Mr. Noonan?"

"Call me George, Miss Douglas," he said with a grin. "Interior aroma gittin' to ye? It has been known to get a might rank inside."

"Yes, George, and I'm afraid it's going to get worse after our meal." Maggie felt a wave of sadness wash over her just saying the man's name and she wondered absently if she'd ever find *her* George.

The driver grimaced. "Wish I could accommodate ye, but I can't let you up top, miss. Rules is rules. Only my guard is allowed to ride with me, an' John don't like to share his space with nobody."

"What about on top of the stage, is there any room up there?"

He shook his head and snorted. "It's full up. Ain't no more room a-tall." He flung his hand up to encompass the top of the stage where men were already sprawled about, claiming their small patch of stage.

She closed her eyes, sighed and walked back to the coach. Taking a deep breath of the last fresh air she'd have for a while, she pulled herself inside and grabbed her hat off the seat where she'd left it.

"There you are, Missy! Saved yore seat for ye right chere," shouted Maggie's lunch partner.

"Here I am Sam, ready and rarin' to go." She slid down between Sam and Tom.

"Glad to hear it, glad to hear it! We're gonna git to know each other real good afore this trip is over!" Sam snorted, laid his head back and closed his eyes.

Maggie swallowed and tried not to breathe too deep. She closed her eyes, laid her head back and covered her face with her hat. The stage jerked forward. *This is going to be a long trip—a very long trip indeed.*

Chapter Fourteen

Sam helped Maggie from the stage that night when they
stopped at Chugwater Station. Everything was tight again, her
toes trying to curl up inside her boot. She was sure her legs
would cramp this time and she'd drop to the ground like a stone,
writhing in pain.

"Thank you, Sam. I need to walk around." She let go of his
hand and grabbed the rail, praying she *could* walk. Maggie was
anxious to get away from the reeking coach. She'd covered her
nose with her bandana and hidden her face with her hat in an
unsuccessful effort to block out the odors permeating the stage.
Her eyes watered and bile threatened more than once. She didn't
know which was worse, the constant swirling of tobacco smoke,
her companions' body odors, or their seemingly continuous
passing of gas and the guffaws that followed each round.

"It is a might ripe in there, Miss Douglas," Sam said. "Wish
it weren't, but that's jest how it is." He shrugged his shoulders
and rolled his dirty hat in his hands, his face red with
embarrassment, having been a major contributor to Maggie's
discomfort.

Although the old geezer was unkempt and smelled as bad
as a pair of socks worn for a week on a cattle drive in a hundred
degree heat, he was winning Maggie over. His heart was kind. In
their discussions so far she'd found out he was headed to the
Hills in search of gold to send back to his daughter who'd lost
her husband from consumption and was left alone to raise four
children. Tom, the man to her right, she'd learned in the rare
times he'd joined the conversation, had a life of leisure in mind
after finding his fortune. Her other three companions were hard
with no redeeming qualities as far as Maggie could tell. They
spoke little, even to each other, never smiled, kept their arms
crossed over their chests, and took whatever space they wanted,
mostly hers, which was one of the reasons her legs continued to
cramp so much.

"We'll have supper and spend the night here," Sam said,
helping Maggie get her footing.

She scanned the station. A white, two-storied depot with four
columns and a porch offered food and comfort for the night.

Beside the depot was a nicely-kept home, the manager's she presumed, as she walked in circles to get the feeling back in her legs and feet. A short distance from the house was a corral where horses milled.

Anxious about missing any supper, Sam hurried her along as fast as he could, Maggie becoming aware for the first time of his heavy limp. *What had caused it?* she wondered as he helped her along. *Had he fought in the war and been injured or was it just part of his being old?*

Ten minutes later she was sandwiched between Sam and Tom, as was becoming her usual place, at another rough-hewn trestle table. Maggie forced down beans and dry cornbread and washed it down with cool water that must have just come out of a well or pump. Locating the pump after the meal, she filled a bucket and washed up as best she could behind the corral. Feeling somewhat refreshed and a little cleaner from the chilly water, she went back inside where Sam grabbed her as soon as she stepped through the door. She couldn't help but smile at the old man. He'd appointed himself her personal guardian, whether because she reminded him of his daughter or because he was just kind, she didn't know. Whatever the reason he was sweet and, despite the fact he was water-shy, Maggie liked him.

"Hurry up, Miss Douglas. I saved ye a spot over there." He hustled her to a piece of floor across the room where her bedroll was laid out and her bags sat on top saving the spot.

"Thanks, Sam. I don't know what I'd do without you," she said honestly.

"Aw, ain't no trouble, Missy. You bein' the only gal on board, seemed to me you might need some lookin' after."

Maggie grinned. Even though she'd let everyone know from the onset of their trip she could take care of herself, he still watched over her like a sheep dog watching one of his flock.

On a whim she pushed back his hat and, using the wet cloth she'd used to clean up, she wiped a spot on his forehead. Before he could protest, Maggie rose up on her tip toes and gave him a big kiss in the only clean spot on his body. "Thanks again, Sam."

He turned every shade of red and purple before he hurried to his bedroll a few feet away from hers, hands shoved deep in his pockets. He plopped down and just sat there, a lopsided grin the size of Texas on his face.

It was then Maggie realized she had more than just one story to tell. Although on her way to Deadwood to write about the fire, to write about everything she could on how it started, how it affected the people, and how they were surviving, she had more great stories right here. Why did these men go to the Hills? What was the reason they risked their lives to find gold? Was it for lifelong riches or to rescue a widowed daughter alone with four children? She broke out one of her notebooks and started to write. A.E. wanted human interest stories. Well, he was going to get them.

Fort Laramie was wonderful! There was a real hotel, plenty of food, *good food*, lots of clean water and fresh air! Maggie ate her fill that night of chicken-fried-steak smothered in adobada sauce with fried potatoes in the Rustic Hotel's dining room and, by the time she finished eating, must have resembled a chipmunk hoarding food she was so full. She was given a small room and, after a long, leisurely bath, crawled into bed and fell into a deep sleep as soon as her head hit the pillow.

Maggie almost fell out of bed when the nerve-shattering peal of a bell tore into her dreams before the sun had even topped the rise. With her hair wild about her head and struggling to remember where she was, she finally broke through her sleep-induced fog to get her bearings.

A continuous knocking on the door drew her muddled attention. "It's mornin' Miss Douglas. Time to be up an' about an' on our way," Sam called from the other side between annoying knocks.

Still groggy, she fumbled around the small bedside table and found the oil lamp and matches. She lit the lamp, gathered her clothes and dressed. Uncaring of what she looked like, *why should it matter in that dusty, reeking stage?* she pulled her hair into a tail at the back of her head, tied it with a leather strip then shoved it all inside her cowboy hat.

"Mornin' Miss Douglas," Sam greeted when she stepped out of her room. "Didn't want ye to oversleep. George don't wait fer nobody, an' I'd hate to see ye git left behind." His hat was rolling between his fingers again and she couldn't help but smile.

She could think of worse places to get left, but was thankful for the old man's concern. "Morning, Sam. It's no bother. I appreciate your looking after me, but right now I have to…I'll be…I'll be right back."

Sam nodded, a gleam of knowing in his eyes.

Maggie excused herself and hurried away to take care of her morning needs. After cleaning up she met Sam and Tom back at the restaurant where they had ordered a breakfast of eggs floating in bacon grease, buttered bread and thick slabs of bacon. She sat down beside Sam and Tom and dug in.

"I hear it gits pretty rough from here," Sam mumbled around a mouthful of food.

"What?" She thought it'd been rough already!

"North o' here is where Injuns start showin' up," he said, his voice flat with foreboding.

Maggie swallowed hard. She'd heard the horror stories about what the Indians did to travelers they caught heading to the gold fields. Although she truly believed the Indians were treated badly, which, she also believed was one of the reasons they always seemed to be on the warpath, she didn't want to find out firsthand what they did in retaliation to the invasion of the Black Hills, lands sacred to the Lakota. All she wanted was to get to Deadwood, get her story, and get back. She had no interest in gold or getting a closer look at Indians along the way, regardless she felt they were mistreated.

Before breakfast was over two freighters, each with about ten men per wagon, pulled in behind the stage. The freighters were laden with shovels, pick axes, pans, buckets, lumber and every kind of implement instrumental in finding gold. There were extra rifles and ammunition, too, and she overheard some of the newcomers, stage passengers, drivers and guards discussing the benefits of having extra weapons and added men "just in case" of an Indian attack.

"The more men and weapons the better," one of the freighters said, the statement agreed upon by everyone in the conversation.

Maggie lingered as long as possible before re-boarding the stage in her usual cramped seat. It pulled away with the familiar pounding of hooves, jingling of harnesses, George's shouts and cracking whip as they headed out with the freighters following close behind.

After stopping at the Government Farm station to blow the horses, they headed on to Rawhide Buttes for the noon meal and Maggie already felt like a wrung out rag again. Whether from the constant bouncing and rocking, Sam's incessant chatter, or her nerves taught with worry over what they might encounter the farther north they went, she didn't know. All she knew was she was exhausted and the day wasn't even half gone.

At Rawhide Buttes Maggie stepped off the stage, stretched her back and legs, and scanned the station, surprised at the number of buildings that made up the depot.

"Thata way, Missy." Sam pointed to the depot where they'd take their noon meal before heading out again. George was shouting orders about changing the team and the rest of the passengers were already headed toward the depot.

Maggie stepped inside the building and was startled to find several women talking and giggling with the passengers and freighters who had pulled in right behind them. *Not very appropriately dressed women*, she noted, *although, what was appropriate, considering she was running around dressed like a man!* The four women stopped conversing and stared at Maggie, flanked by Sam and Tom. They eyed her as closely as she eyed them and Maggie wondered what they were doing there. *Was there another stage here she hadn't seen when they pulled in?*

A red-haired woman wearing a colorful, low-cut dress and fuzzy pantalets to match stepped from the others and walked toward Maggie. "You lookin' for work, honey?"

"Excuse me? What kind of work? I'm on my way to Deadwood."

"That's what they all say before they stop here an' decide they want to stay so's they don't have to face no Injuns."

Maggie looked askance at Sam who was beet red. Then it hit her. They were Soiled Doves! She knew in that instant her face must have turned six shades of pink to match Sam's. "I beg your pardon!" she shouted in a huff. "I'm Maggie Douglas, newspaper reporter for the *Cheyenne Sun* and I'm headed to Deadwood to report on the fire, not some, some..." She couldn't even get the words out she was so flabbergasted to be mistaken for a lady of the night. Especially dressed as she was!

"Fire? What fire?" the woman asked, all interest in Maggie gone.

"There was a huge fire there a few days ago that wiped out half the town and I'm going to write about it."

The woman chuckled. "Didn't know nothin' 'bout no fire in Deadwood. Must be why we ain't had too much traffic through here the last couple a days. 'Course, the boys that come through here don't do much talkin', if'n you git my meanin'?" The woman slapped Maggie's shoulder and snorted. She turned to her girls, who giggled in response.

"I do get your meaning." Maggie shook her head. She certainly never expected to be mistaken for a prostitute, but times were hard out here and finding women who would stay even harder. "I guess they wouldn't do much talking. No, ma'am, I'm not looking for, ahem, work, as I said." A thought struck her. "However, if you're interested, I'd like to interview you and your girls."

"What for?" The woman sounded insulted and Maggie tried to unruffle her feathers.

"Like I said, I'm doing a story on the fire in Deadwood, but I'm also talking to my traveling companions to find out why they're going to the gold fields and I thought, well, I thought it would be interesting to find out your stories. How did you come to be here, why do you stay, that sort of thing? *If* you're willing to share them, of course."

The woman pursed her lips and looked at the other three women watching her. Each one thought a moment about Maggie's request then one by one lowered their heads in agreement.

"How much will you pay us? You know our time ain't free."

Maggie had brought extra money with her to help with unexpected expenses and she considered this one of them. "How does a dollar each sound?"

"Five."

"Three."

The woman thought a moment. "You got yoreself a story, honey. 'Course, looks to me like you got your own story." She waved her hand at Maggie's clothing. "You tryin' to be another Calamity or somethin'?" She chuckled and slapped her leg causing loose feathers to float about.

"Not at all," Maggie defended. "I was born and raised on a ranch and these clothes are more comfortable *and* more functional for where I'm going. You can't get around this wild territory with a bustle or long train trailing behind you."

"No ma'am, you cain't." She stuck her right thumb at her chest. "They call me Mother Shepherd and these here are my girls, Sally, Betty, and Martha." The three women stepped forward and greeted Maggie. "Folks round these parts call me Mother 'Featherlegs'," she said with a cackle, "'cause of these here pantalets I like so much. Folks say they make my legs look like chicken legs, but I don't mind overmuch. It sets me apart from other—Mother's," she added with a grin and a sparkle in her eyes.

Maggie grinned back. This trip was getting more and more interesting by the minute. She was going to put together the best piece A.E. has ever read. Of course, that was if she lived long enough to write it.

They ate more beans and more cornbread for lunch. Maggie didn't think she'd survive another afternoon in that stinking stage, but was happy Sam and Tom had both taken baths at Laramie, their stench not quite as overpowering as it had been yesterday. *If only she could get their clothes washed, too, she might actually be able to breathe in their presence without gagging.*

"It could git rough this afternoon," George yelled at everyone as they were settling back on the stage. "Hang on tight an' have your rifles an' pistols ready in case you need 'em."

"Have the Indians bothered the stage lately?" Maggie asked, heart pounding.

The driver shrugged. "We usually git hit oncet, sometimes twice, a trip. Trick is to be ready for 'em."

Maggie felt like she'd swallowed a whole tomato and it was stuck square in the middle of her throat. *Well, I wanted to see*

Indians first hand. I guess there's a good possibility I'll get my wish.

"You men on top, be alert. Watch everythin' an' I mean everythin' round the stage. This here leg of the trip is the longest. It's thirty-five miles afore we reach Hat Creek Station. We'll stop 'bout half way at Running Water, change out the team, an' git on. We're gonna take it slow, which is gonna make for a long afternoon, cause if we run the horses they won't be worth a damn if'n we need 'em later. I know it and them Injuns know it, too, an' you kin bet they'll be a watchin' to make sure. The freighters are behind us with extra men and weapons, so they'll most likely take the brunt of any attack if'n there is one. They know what them boys is a carryin' in them big ole wagons an' they want it more'n what y'all are a carryin'. The closer we git to them Hills the more likely we'll see redskins, so be ready. Keep your heads an' you'll keep your hair," George shouted as easily as if he were ordering a meal, swinging up onto the driver's seat.

Maggie pulled off the bandana from around her nose and wiped the sweat beading on her forehead. Although the end of September, the heat inside the coach was oppressive, the air so thick and dusty she thought she'd have to cough up a lung to clear passage to breathe. Between the rank odors and the heat, if she hadn't been sitting down, she'd have passed out. The window flaps were lowered to keep out the sun and dust, but both seeped in, swirling around like sunlit dust balls.

"George, we got trouble!" yelled a man Maggie had heard called Hank, from up top.

Sam lifted the window flap beside him and whistled. Tom and the others pulled up their window coverings and tied them off. Maggie leaned into Sam, straining to see outside.

"Got us a bunch o' Injuns lined up on that ridge." Sam pointed.

Maggie spotted them and her heart went still. Up on the ridge were dozens of Indians. *Dozens!* She opened her bag and pulled Wally out. Having the cold metal in her hand made her feel better, but the number of Indians made her sick.

"Don't worry 'bout them, Missy. If'n they was gonna attack us, we'd a been hit already without knowin' they was ever there.

They's jest a watchin', checkin' our strength. Seein' if the horses is played out. Sure am glad we picked up them two freighters at Laramie," Sam said. "Give them Injuns a second think about attackin' us." He clicked his tongue and scanned the hillside again. "They's quite a few of 'em though," he added on a sigh. "Could give us a powerful piece o' trouble if'n they want to."

Maggie stared out the window at the Indians lining the ridge. They sat tall on their paint ponies, their black, braided hair falling in long chords down their backs or flying loose about their shoulders and bone breastplates. The horses were trim, but not skinny, the warriors sun-darkened, muscular and proud. These were the people being displaced by gold fever, by men who didn't care that they were destroying an entire people to find the yellow metal and, for a moment, Maggie felt sympathy toward the men perched like statues, watching and waiting.

There was a shot from one of the freighters and Maggie thought her heart would fly out of her chest and she'd swallow her tongue. A few of the Indian horses shifted, but the braves held the line steady. There was another shot and Maggie waited in anguish for what happened next.

Slowly their horses started to move, the riders advancing in one fluid line.

The coach picked up speed, rocking and bouncing wildly on the rough road.

"Best be gittin' to the other side of the stage, Missy. Keep your head down and give us as much room as ye kin," Sam said.

"Be ready boys!" Tom shouted, leaning over Sam, his rifle cocked and ready to fire out the middle window, the other three men crowded around the remaining window, guns ready.

"Hang on, Missy!" Sam steadied himself, rifle poised as the stage surged forward.

Maggie thought her teeth would rattle right out of her head. Ignoring Sam's directive to stay down she perched on her knees on the seat and was able to see the Indians racing alongside the stage, just out of rifle range.

"I think them son's o' bitches is playin' with us," one of the men across from Maggie growled, aiming and firing. They ain't fired a damned shot."

Maggie held Wally tight, praying she wouldn't have to use the pistol, but would if she had to to save her life. Right now the Indians weren't close enough to hit and *she* wasn't foolish enough to waste bullets she might need later, so she held on tight and stayed ready.

The coach rocked and rumbled forward for ten minutes before the Indians suddenly veered right, away from the stage. Turning around and lining up again, they shouted and whooped, waved coup sticks, lances and rifles at the passing stage like they'd just won a big battle. *Perhaps they had*, Maggie thought, *a psychological one.*

"Damn heathens *were* just playing with us," Tom shouted."

"Guess we was more'n they wanted to tangle with, since they didn't attack," Sam said, shoving his pistol in its holster. The other three men held their positions until the Indians were left well behind.

"Everybody all right down there?" George called from up top as the stage slowed down.

"We're fine," Tom yelled back.

"We're only a few miles from Running Water Station," George shouted. "We'll change out the team there an' git back on the trail right away. That means no pokin' around oncet we git there. You got as long as it takes to git this team changed to do your business an' git back on the stage. I ain't waitin' for nobody so y'all better be ready when I am. I plan to be at Hat Creek before nightfall."

Maggie took a huge, gulping breath. She'd seen her first Indians and lived to tell about it, so far. Her heart was pounding and she was breathing like she'd just run a race. Realization hit her. She *had* run a race—for her life—along with every man on this stage and accompanying freight wagons. She'd be happy if this was the last she saw of the Indians before they reached Deadwood, but knew there could easily be more and, with her heart hammering, she again wondered at her prudence in making this trip.

The teams were changed and the stage and freighters left the soddie station at Running Water fifteen minutes after their arrival, but in that fifteen minutes, Maggie found out just how vulnerable she was.

"Hello there, Miss."

Maggie whirled on the three rough-looking men standing in front of her. She didn't recognize them from the stage, so presumed they were from one of the freighters. She'd gone behind a small outbuilding to wash her face and neck before the stage pulled out again, thinking she'd disappeared unnoticed.

"What can I do for you boys?" She tried to sound confident, but wasn't sure she'd accomplished that feat.

The three chuckled low, making Maggie's skin crawl. "What do you want?" she asked angrily when none of them answered, only ogled her. As if nothing was amiss, she started toward her bag, lying on top of a fat, round splitting log, just out of reach.

One of the men stepped in front of her. Trying to keep up her façade, although her heart was pounding, she asked again. "What is it you want?"

"We don't mean no harm, ma'am. We's jest wantin' to visit. We didn't git no time to talk to them nice ladies…" the other two men chuckled behind him and he turned and shushed them. "We didn't git to talk to none of them ladies back at Rawhide Buttes an' it made us kinda lonely. We jest wanna talk, that's all."

"We don't have time to talk. The stage is leaving in a few minutes and we have to get back." She tried to walk around him to snatch up her bag, but he grabbed her arm.

"Let go of me." Her voice was hard, but her courage was waning.

"I'm tellin' ye, we don't mean ye no harm, Miss. We jest wanna talk."

Prompted more by anger than fear, she jerked her arm away and shouted. "You stupid sons-of-bitches! We're running from Indians and you think to accost me? Are you idiots?" She watched with satisfaction as their heads jerked back in surprise, their eyes wide. "We don't have better things to do than get the hell out of here?" Acting as though she had nothing to fear, she kept railing at them, while working her way toward Wally. "I've met tougher men than the likes of you three morons!" Their surprise was displaced by anger and they stepped closer, but by that time she'd grabbed the bag, opened it and had her hand on hard steel.

"I wouldn't if I were you." She raised the bag without removing the revolver.

The three men stopped in their tracks. "What you got there?" the leader asked.

"A five shot Colt that'll do a lot of damage to your sorry asses if you come any closer."

"You ain't gonna shoot us, lady." The first man took a step forward.

"But I will," came Sam's familiar voice from the other side of the building behind Maggie. He stepped to her right and cocked his pistol.

Tom stepped to Maggie's left. "Care to try me?" Tom waved his rifle at their chests.

"We didn't mean no harm," one of the other men whined. "Jest wanted to talk to her. We was only funnin' with ye."

"I don't consider being accosted 'funnin'!" Maggie shot back. "You don't *accost* a woman to *talk* to her. You scared the life out of me you fools!"

"Didn't mean to scare you, Miss. Truly we didn't," the last of the men said. "Like Dave over there said, we didn't git no chance to visit with them ladies back at Rawhide. We jest wanted to talk."

"We're done talking! And so are any future conversations we *might* have had," Maggie shouted. "Don't ever bother me again. And remember, I won't hesitate to use this if I have to." She slid Wally out of the bag and waved it at them.

"I believe you would, ma'am," said the man who'd grabbed her arm, his eyes wide. "I believe you would."

"An' if she don't, you kin bet one o' us will," Sam added, glancing at Tom. "Now git on out o' here."

The three men hurried away and Maggie felt like her legs turned to jelly the moment they disappeared. She plopped down on the splitting log and gulped air to keep from busting into sobs. "How can I thank you two?"

"Aw, we didn't do nothin'," Sam said. "We follered ya and was listenin' behind the buildin'. You had it under control—mostly." He grinned. "We didn't want no blood spilled, so we figgered it was time to show ourselves. Wasn't sure you *wouldn't* shoot them boys," Sam added with a twinkle in his eyes.

Maggie giggled and, as she did, broke into tears. "Guess I'm not as tough as I think I am, huh?" she said on a racking sob, tears streaming down her cheeks, her nose running.

Sam put his arm around her and handed her a dirty hankie. "Girl, you got more sand than most men I've met in my entire life—and that's considerable. Anybody can git the drop put on 'em. From now on you make sure you got that piece in your hand wherever you go. An' let me or Tom know where you're a goin' so's we can keep an eye on ye." He smiled and winked.

Maggie swallowed hard, swiped at the tears and blew her nose before nodding. "I can do that, boys. I sure can. From now on we're pards and you'll know where I am all the time."

"Come on you two, let's get back to the stage," Tom said. "George's about done changing out them horses and he'll be hell-bent to get under way."

Rounding the building, Maggie searched for her three attackers. She found them sitting on the first freighter watching her walk to the stage, flanked by her two grizzled protectors. Straightening her back she looked directly at each of them. She wanted no hard feelings, but she wanted it known she would not be man-handled by anyone. There'd been no time for them to do any real harm—other than scare the wits out of her. Perhaps they did just want to talk, but it was in her best interest to presume not. She raised her chin and nodded her head once. One by one, they nodded back before looking away in embarrassment.

Just before sundown George made quite a show of racing the stage into Hat Creek Station, a small town unto itself, the freighters rolling in right behind them. The station boasted a post office and a blacksmith shop, a brewery and a hotel where Maggie intended to bathe and stretch out for the night, a telegraph office, where she stopped before supper to let A.E. know she was still alive and halfway to Deadwood, and even a bakery where she planned to purchase a few sweet treats before their morning departure.

Thick beef stew and biscuits filled Maggie's belly while Charlie Hecht, the most recent owner of Hat Creek, regaled the passengers and teamsters with stories of how Indians had sneaked in and burned the original depot to the ground.

With Charlie's stories making her even more anxious about the rest of the trip, and wanting some privacy more than anything, Maggie excused herself by dropping a kiss on Sam's forehead and saying goodnight to Tom, George, Charlie and the others, still enthralled in the owner's stories. She hurried to the hotel and requested a bath in which she luxuriated for almost an hour. Her bath complete, her feet curled up under her in the bed, she wrote for nearly two hours about the day's experiences and how she felt before finally sliding between the sheets to find sleep. She wrote about her protectors and how they'd taken her under their wings. There were the beginnings of four stories of four women, forgotten by society, alone and, what Maggie considered, barely living in the wilderness, to be finished later. She penned her own feelings of helplessness at being caught unawares by the three teamsters, and fell asleep with a smile on her face and tales of excitement and hopes for new lives swirling in her head. She was anxious to be on her way and even more anxious to finish this journey so she could share her stories with the world—every one of them.

Chapter Fifteen

Whipping winds and cold drizzle greeted the passengers the next morning when the stage pulled out of Hat Creek Station, the freight wagons rumbling close behind as usual. Huge banks of dark gray clouds scudded across the sky threatening continuing, even heavier rain. For the first time since Maggie left Cheyenne, dust wasn't choking her and sweat wasn't dotting her forehead or soaking her clothes. Today's weather wasn't better, it was just different.

Maggie slid into her usual seat and waited while Sam and Tom settled on either side of her and the other three men crowded in across from her. *Maybe I can engage one or all of those three in an interview,* she thought, glad she hadn't stowed her pad and pencil with the rest of her bags. They were close at hand under the seat, just in case. *Maybe I can accomplish something other than being bored or shaken to death inside this smelly coach,* she mused with a sigh.

"Better git comfy, Missy," Sam said once settled. "This is gonna be a long, miserable day."

"Why?" She asked, not *really* wanting to hear the answer, the hair bristling on the back of her neck.

"We're headed into Dakota Territory—Indian country. Accordin' to George, we'll stop at Sourdough Dick's Old Woman Creek Station first. From there we'll keep north an' stop at Jim Mays' Station and be to his brother's place, Robbers Roost, by nightfall *if* we're lucky."

"Do you think the Indians will bother us again?"

Sam cocked his head in uncertainty and looked out the window. "Fact it's rainin' *might* keep them redskins away, but the rain makes for a whole 'nother set o' problems, Missy. We been a fightin' the heat an' dust the last couple o' days. Now we'll be a fightin' mud. Hear tell the ground turns to mush when it gits wet round these parts, makin' it real hard for man an' beast to git through. We may be diggin' ourselves out afore this day is done."

"Is it really that bad?" Maggie was frowning and foreboding raced up her spine. That meant getting out of the stage and being outside meant a better target for any Indians that might be around.

Sam closed his eyes and nodded. "Hate to tell ye it's so, but tis. Better yore ready for it, jest in case. So rest up, Missy, like I said, it could git a mite messy afore the day is gone."

Maggie laid her head back, closed her eyes and blew out a huge breath. "Seems every day gets harder and harder, huh, Sam?"

"It's a hard trip, Missy. But yore up to it. I know ye are."

She lifted her head and smiled at the old coot. "Thanks for your vote of confidence, Sam. I'll just have to make it through in one piece to prove you were right about me."

"You jest do that, Missy. You jest do it."

Maggie grew thoughtful. "How long before we reach Deadwood?"

"From what George tole me, after we leave Robbers Roost we cross the Cheyenne River an' head north to the Jenney Stockade for the night. From there, it's only a little over fifty miles an' two more stops afore we reach Deadwood." Sam's face was awash with pride like he'd just recited the Constitution of the United States. "If we make it through today, we *should* be done with the worst of it." He laid a gnarled hand over hers and patted it before he turned his head to the window and closed his eyes. "Git some rest, Missy. You're a gonna need it."

Maggie turned to Tom whose eyes were already closed. *How did they do that? Just lay their heads back and go to sleep?*

Their rest didn't last long. The road was rough, rocking and jolting the stage as it made its way through the sparse and dismal landscape. It was so rough there was no way Maggie could put pen to paper to interview anyone, so her writing materials stayed stowed. One minute the stage was rocking left and right, the next Maggie was being thrown to the floor. The longer and harder it rained, the slower the stage went, the horses and wheels mired in white/gray mud.

Later in the day they stopped at the Old Woman Station. The team was changed and the passengers stretched their legs before continuing north toward Mays Station. At Mays Station they ate while the horses were changed out then headed off again.

Maggie stayed close to the coach at each stop, unwilling to repeat what happened at Running Water.

They were halfway between Mays Station and Robbers Roost when the stage jerked to a stop, throwing Maggie and her fellow travelers to the floor again.

Tom crawled to the door, flung it open and stuck out his head. "What's going on, George?"

"Take a look," the driver shouted from above. "Stage won't move if the wheels cain't turn."

Tom whistled, sat down and hung his legs out the door. "I'll be. I've never seen anything like it before."

"What is it, Tom?" Maggie tried to see what they were talking about, but couldn't see over Tom's back.

"It looks like we're sitting in the middle of an ocean of mud, Miss Douglas. It's everywhere!"

"Which means," George said, scrabbling down from the driver's seat, "y'all are gonna have to git rid of it."

"How are we supposed to do that?" Tom asked. "Looks like stone."

"It will be if'n we don't git it off perty quick. You boys on top climb on down an' grab yoreselves a crowbar from back there in the box." There were moans and groans as the men up top made their way down, sinking deep in the mud as each one hit what used to be solid ground then grabbing crowbars from the box.

"Them boys behind us'll be doin' the same thing soon enough, but might be they'll have a few extra tools we kin use to help dig us outta here." George pointed inside the stage. "Y'all git on out, too. Ever'body needs to put their back into it. 'Ceptin' you, o'course, Miss Douglas. You stay where ye are. We'll take care o' this."

Maggie shook her head. If she wanted to prove she was equal to a man, she would damn-well pry mud or do whatever she could to help. "No, George. I'll get out with the others and do what I can."

George shook his head and snorted. "You're the damndest female I ever did meet, Miss Douglas. Have it your way. Grab a bar, shovel, pick, anything you kin to git that mud out o' the spokes an' from in between the wagon box an' bottom o' the stage. An' be prepared to do it agin ever' few minutes till we reach Robbers Roost. *If* we make Robbers Roost," he mumbled under his breath as he sloshed away, water sluicing off his hat.

Maggie pulled her bag out from under the seat and yanked out her slicker. Jumping out of the stage behind Sam and the others she sank to her ankles. When she lifted her foot, it felt like hands grabbing at her, trying to pull the boots right off her feet.

While George handed out crowbars and others searched for shovels and picks, Maggie worked her way to the front of the stage toward the team. The rain came in sheets and, despite her slicker, it didn't take long before it seeped inside any seam or opening that wasn't sealed tight in the coat. Her hat was soaked clear through in minutes, her head as wet as if she'd dunked it in a tub. Water dripped through the brim, into her eyes, down her neck, and into the slicker, saturating her collar. When she moved, her socks squished inside her boots, the water already having seeped in. Her boots were covered with thick, gray mud and she knew it wouldn't take long before it was caked to her calves. *Maybe I should have played the helpless female and stayed inside the coach? At least I'd be dry! Oooh, give me the heat and dust over pouring rain and mud any day. At least it's not cold—yet,* she thought on a sigh.

The horses were covered to their bellies with the gray muck. Globs of the oozing slop flung from their hooves dotted their backs and heads. They were no longer solid black, looking more like dapple-grays or appaloosas. *How could they even move in this quagmire? Easier without hauling a bunch of people inside the stage,* she realized, knowing the passengers would eventually be trudging right along with them.

Maggie made it to the rear horse. "Steady," she cooed. The horse's ears twitched as she sloshed her way closer, the sucking noise from her feet making the animals uneasy. "Shhhh, I'm gonna help you out of this mess." She laid her hand on the rear horse's flank, still talking to the animal. Slowly, she slid her palm over its rump and down its leg, pushing off as much mud as she could, tossing big, ugly globs as far away as she could. She was covered in sludge to her armpits one minute and washed clean from the heavy rain the next. Carefully, she worked her way around the outside of the team then stepped between them, sliding mud off each horse's legs as she went, the rain washing the last of their hides clean.

Lathrop found Maggie perched on the inner wooden hitching bar that ran from front to back between the animals. "Miss Douglas, you ought not to be in there!" he scolded, blinking to keep the rain from dripping into his eyes. "Them horses take off, you'll be in a heap a trouble!"

She frowned and lifted a muddy hand that was washed clean as she spoke. "Where will they go, George? They can barely move in this slop. Stage won't move if they can't, right?"

Lathrop pointed his finger at Maggie. "You got to be the damnedest female I *ever* did see!" Mud sucking at his feet, rain dripping from his hat, he turned toward the stage, but stopped before he took a second step. He whirled back around, a grin on his face, and pointed at Maggie. "'Ceptin for Miss Calamity, o' course!"

"I'll take that as a compliment!" Maggie threw her head back and laughed.

He shook his head, turned around, and continued his laborious trip toward the rear of the stage.

With everyone working together it took thirty minutes to get the horses, spokes and between the wheels and wagon-box cleared so the stage could move again. With some of the men turning the wheels, others pushing from the back of the stage, and George doing a lot of silk popping above the horses' rumps, the team finally jerked free and the stage found purchase on more solid ground. As it pulled away everyone jumped back on or inside, soaked and muddy from head to toe. Maggie couldn't decide which was worse, being water-logged or caked in mud. She'd thought the stage reeked before, but now it had the added odors of wet *and* muddy clothes. Sam pulled a blanket from under the seat and wrapped it around a shivering Maggie. No sooner had her teeth stopped chattering before they were out of the stage, doing it all over again with no sign the rain would let up anytime soon.

After the third evacuation, everybody just stayed outside, trying to keep the stage lighter and the spokes and horses' legs as clean as they could to keep the stage moving on what used to be the road, stopping every few steps to clean the mud off their own boots. Maggie kept a strong stick tucked in her belt for just such a purpose, wondering with every step if they'd make Robbers Roost before nightfall—or be forced to camp in this slop and at the mercy of the Indians.

It was late in the day before the skies cleared and the sun poked through. Maggie decided the rain *had* helped their cause as far as the Indians went, she hadn't seen one all day; but the day wasn't over yet. They'd spent so much time digging, pushing and pulling the stage out of the mud they didn't make the miles necessary to reach Robbers Roost before nightfall. Maggie had lost count how many times they'd dug themselves out before George called for everyone to gather round.

"I got bad news, folks. We'll be spendin' the night here."

There was groaning all around until George raised his hand. "I don't like it any more'n y'all do, but daylight's almost gone and in this muck, them horses cain't go no farther. They're played out. So break out yore gear an' find ye a spot over yonder," he pointed toward the stage and the freight wagons pulling up behind it, "to set out yore bedrolls. We'll dig out in the mornin', hopefully for the last time. If luck is with us we'll reach the Roost by mid-day—*if* the weather holds an' the sun stays high."

Maggie groaned. The last thing she wanted was to spend the night outside in this mess *and* vulnerable to Indians.

"Charlie, back there at Hat Creek," Lathrop continued, "sent along extra food, jest in case we wound up right where we are, so at least we'll eat." He pointed toward a small copse of trees. "We need wood for the fires. There's dry wood in the box to git 'em started, but we'll need more to keep 'em goin'. It'll be wet, but once we git 'em hot, that wood'll burn easy enough. Them freighters'll have dry wood, too, so we'll git more'n one fire a goin'. The more we got the better. It'll keep animals *and* Injuns away." He paused and pointed again. "There's a crick not far from here, so there's water for us an' the horses; but watch yoreselves along the banks. Injuns like to hide behind the rises." He paused again, looking at each and every man gathered, but his eyes stopped and held on Maggie. "Nobody goes nowhere alone. Nobody! Ever'body goes in twos or threes an' ever'body carries a gun. Y'all got that?"

There was unified agreement as everyone set off in pairs to find a spot to bed down. Tom and Sam had sneaked away just as George began his speech and stepped up beside Maggie as he finished.

"Come on, Missy, we'll show you where yore a sleepin' tonight." Maggie noticed a funny gleam in Sam's eyes.

Maggie grinned, thankful for Sam Whitmore and Tom Hanson. She looked around when they reached the stage, wondering where they'd set her bedroll. She'd told them where to find the oiled canvas to lay it out on the cold, muddy ground, but she didn't see it. She'd slept under the stars too many times to count, driving cattle with her father and brothers in the rain, heat and cold, but it wasn't one of her favorite things to do when it was as miserable as it was now. She did it when she had to and, unfortunately, she knew tonight was one of those times. Although the rain had stopped, she still wished they'd made it to the station so they could sleep inside without worrying about animals, more rain and, worst of all, Indians.

"We took care of ye, Missy," Sam said.

"I'm sure you did, Sam, but where?" Her eyebrows rose when she spotted her canvas poking out from under the *two* bedrolls below the coach. The three silent comrades were laying their oiled canvases down at the rear of the stage and others were setting up on the opposite side, attaching more canvases to the side of the stage, staking them like tents to ward off any more rain that might come in the night.

"Yore inside, Missy."

Her head jerked back and her face scrunched up. "In the stage? Inside that stinking stage?" *She had to bear it all day, could she bear it all night, too? If she had a choice, she might actually choose to sleep outside where she could breathe!*

"Yep, George agreed that's where ye should sleep. We aired it out fer ye, Missy," Sam said before she could protest again. "We uncovered them winders as soon as the rain stopped so it should be smellin' a might better by now," he added with another grin.

Maggie grinned back, her head shaking. "You're too good to me, Sam."

"Aw, tain't nothin' 'bout it. Jest want to make sure yore all right, that's all."

"Well, I couldn't have had better guardians than you and Tom if I'd asked." She kissed his furry cheek before he could stop her then turned to Tom, who was waving his hands to keep her at bay.

She laughed out loud and looked back at Sam who was blushing every shade of red there was. "Now Missy, don't go gittin' me all embarrassed an' such."

"All right, I'll stop with the gratitude. Where are you and Tom sleeping?"

"Down yonder, to make sure nobody bothers ye." Sam pointed to where the two bedrolls poked out from under the stage. His eyes sparkled and Maggie was sure she would sleep soundly, knowing both men were close and would keep her from harm.

Chapter Sixteen

"What will you do when you reach Deadwood, Sam?" Supper was over and Maggie was sitting in her usual place between Sam and Tom in front of one of three blazing fires. The two men had dragged a thick, downed tree limb from the woods on the other side of the road so they could sit on something other than the cold, soggy, ground.

"First thing I'll do is git me a drink." He grinned then scratched his head. "'Course, might have to go a ways to find one, since you're a tellin' us a good part o' Deadwod is gone."

Maggie nodded. "And after you find that drink, *if* you find a drink, what then?"

"Well, if'n Tom an' me kin git the equipment we're a needin', we'll light out into them Hills an' git what we come for." Hope sparkled in the older man's eyes.

Maggie scribbled her question and his answer before asking, "Aren't you afraid you'll run into Indians?"

He cocked his head and pursed his mouth. His lips disappeared into his beard and he looked like a wrinkled, mouthless, hairy face. "I try not to think 'bout it. Jest know I got to find me some gold," he said, looking like a man again. "It's the only way I kin figger to take care o' my little girl an' her young 'uns."

The interview went on for an hour and by the time Maggie was through she knew everything there was to know about Sam Whitmore. He'd owned two slaves and a small thirty acre farm in Tennessee prior to the war and, although already over forty, he fought for the southern cause, barely surviving Gettysburg. After the war ended, with no work, nothing left, and no place else for him to go, he went to live with his daughter and son-in-law, a former Confederate officer. It galled him sorely to ask for help, but he had no choice. When his son-in-law got sick and died it left his daughter, Molly, with four children, no husband and, in Sam's words, "a lame old man to boot," and few choices to help his girl.

"I liked that boy." Tears threatened with the simple statement, but with quivering lips and blinking eyes Sam held them back. "He took good care o' my Molly an' my grandbabies.

Took care o' me, too, a shriveled up ole Reb." He sniffed. "Weren't right the way he died. He were a good man, strong, smart an' dedicated to his family an' he jest withered away afore our very eyes. It 'bout tore me up. All they had was Joe an' me, an' I ain't worth a lick no more. Nobody'll take on a broken down, lame ole man to work for 'em. 'Specially not one that fought for the south an' has the limp in his leg to prove it. I got six months to find what I'm a lookin' for an' git back to my girl. After that, they'll lose their home an' won't have nowhere to go. I'm all they got an' I damn-sure ain't gonna let 'em down. Not unless I'm dead."

Maggie laid her hand on Sam's shoulder and the look of sadness in his eyes almost broke her heart.

"I gotta find me a stake, Missy. I jest gotta. I got nothin' else." He sniffed and looked up at the sky, clear of clouds and black as a velvet rug splattered with stars, sparkling like the gold he hoped to find.

With another sniff, Sam excused himself and wandered away. Maggie turned to Tom.

"I understand you fought in the war, too, Tom."

He nodded and chewed the top of his beard with his teeth. "I did. Fought for the preservation of the Union, but fought for a lot more'n that."

"Like what?"

"My life. My men's lives." He sighed heavily and repositioned to a more comfortable position on the thick branch. "You're too young to know, Miss Douglas, but when that war started, everybody thought it'd be over in a couple of weeks, a few months at most, but *nobody*, on either side, dreamed it'd last four bloody years." His eyes drifted upward and a tear formed in the corner of his eye before he swiped it away. "Lost a lotta good men in that damned," sorry Miss Douglas, "dang war. On both sides." He ran a hand under his nose. "We all thought we'd whip the other side and just get on with our business, but it didn't happen that way. It was a terrible time, and the time after it wasn't so good, neither. 'Course, I had it better'n Sam. I lived back east, while Sam was down south living with defeat and what went with it. Poverty, trying to rebuild their lives with nothing and the men that came after, carpetbaggers they called them, who took every little bit they had left. You name it, old Sam dealt with it." He shook his head and grimaced. "But no matter what side you were on, after fighting that long, struggling every day to stay alive, it's damned hard to get back to living a normal life."

Maggie smiled sadly, noticing he'd cursed again but was so deep in his thoughts he hadn't stopped to apologize.

"Couldn't eat, couldn't sleep, the clap of thunder would throw me into a tizzy, making me think I was back on the battlefield. I'd run around screaming at people to take cover, shouting that we were under attack and they needed to hide." He snickered, shook his head and ran a hand down his long beard. "People were afraid to come near me after a while." He lifted his hat and wiped some sweat that had beaded on his brow from the heat of the fire. "It was a terrible time, Miss Douglas, a terrible time."

He stopped talking and Maggie scribbled his words down as fast as she could so as not to forget anything. When she stopped writing, he continued.

"Now I'm ready to find a new life. It's been fifteen years since we put down our guns, but it's still with me every day. I figure I can forget it with a little gold. So here I am, me and Sam, going to find gold in those hills." He swung his arm north to encompass where the Hills should be in the darkness. "All I want is to die comfortable and not to have to worry about where my next meal comes from or if I'm gonna have a roof over my head. What I *don't* want to do is die a slobbering old fool with nothing and no one to take care of me." He sighed and Maggie sensed embarrassment. "I wouldn't mind finding a good woman to spend my last years with, neither. She don't have to be beautiful, just a gal who'll put up with me and keep me company in my old—er age," he added with another grin. "That's about the size of it, Miss Douglas." His lips tightened and he, too, looked like an old man with no lips, as he tried to tamp down the emotions threatening to bubble up from inside.

"What about your friendship with Sam? How did you two get together, having fought against each other in the war?"

Tom cocked his head. "It was tough at first, but we figured out pretty quick we needed each other. He's studied up on the

Hills. And me, well…" He looked over Maggie's shoulder and scanned the others around the fire. No one was paying them any attention and he leaned in closer. "Sold everything I had for a stake out here. Just hope there's equipment *to* buy once we git to Deadwood." He lifted his finger to his lips. "Don't tell anyone I got a stake, else we might get set upon by robbers. Or even one of those quiet fellas riding with us. It's hidden and nobody knows about it but me and Sam and now you."

"I won't tell a soul, Tom."

He grinned. "You were asking about me and Sam." He chuckled and clucked his tongue. "It was a might touchy at first. We both got a lotta bad memories coming outta that war, but every time it got tough we reminded each other the war was over, and the best thing we could do was help each other. So that's what we're doing. Hopefully, we'll get rich in the doing." He was grinning again and Maggie grinned back, as excited about the stories she would write about Sam and Tom and Mother Shepherd and her girls, as she was on the stories about Deadwood.

It was nine o'clock before she put her writing materials away, satisfied with her work and hoping A.E. would be as happy as she was. The fire was stoked and everyone wandered to their bedrolls. *Thank goodness it wasn't raining again,* Maggie thought, unable to imagine being any more soaked than she'd been earlier. Her clothes had mostly dried in front of the fire and now just a thin layer of mud covered her hair and clothes that wouldn't come off no matter how hard she rubbed, pounded or brushed.

Maggie stepped up into the stage, thankful she didn't have to sleep outside on the cold, wet ground. She dropped the window covers, slid her bag from under the seat and changed into her third set of dry, clean clothes, grabbed her blanket and settled on the thin seat as best she could. She laid down thinking how hard it was going to be sleeping on the uncomfortable seat and was dreaming in minutes.

"Miss Douglas, time to git up an at 'em," woke her the next morning.

"I'll be right out, Sam." Wiping the sleep from her eyes, she sat up and stretched. She tugged and pulled at the leather strip tangled in her hair until it finally came free and put her hair back up in another tail. Grabbing her hat from the other seat, she slapped it on her head, shivering at how cold and wet it still was from yesterday's rain.

Stepping outside, immediately sinking into the mud, she turned her face into the sun busting through the darkness with its warmth and promise for a beautiful day. Birds chirped, darted and soared between the trees and everyone was about rustling up the last of the grub and putting up bedrolls. Maggie sucked in a deep breath of fresh air, thankful to be dry and for Sam and Tom's continued kindness.

"We got a biscuit fer ye, Missy." Sam tried to hand her a leftover biscuit from Hat Creek.

"Now Sam, you know I can't do anything till I... Well, you know. I'll be back in a few minutes."

"Yes'm, Missy. You watch where yore a goin'. You got yore gun with ye?"

"I do, Sam."

"You go on an' take care o' yore business, but don't go too far. I'll be right here a waitin' fer ye."

Maggie waded through the slop toward the tree line and found a small cropping of bushes to shield her. She was buttoning up her pants when a noise not far away caught her attention. She grabbed Wally from the tree notch she'd set it in and listened, but heard nothing more. Anger tore through her and she sloshed her way toward where the sound had come from.

"You sons of bitches come out right now! Can't a woman have some privacy without worrying about the likes of you all spying on her?"

There was scrambling behind the bushes and, using the gun, she shoved them apart to reveal the interloper. Her knees almost buckled as she stared at the Indian with long, black, braided hair, dressed in light brown buckskins. He was slipping and sliding in the mud trying to gain his feet while wide, surprised eyes looked down the barrel of her gun.

The scream tore from her throat before she realized it. She screamed and screamed and the Indian scurried away as fast as he could, mud-covered from his feet to his chest. He jumped on a nearby horse and raced away through the muck before Sam and the rest of the party arrived at her side.

"What happened?" Sam grabbed her by the shoulders and kept her from falling down.

"It was an, an Indian."

There was a unified gasp around her.

"An Indian?"

"Where'd he go?"

The questions came in quick succession until she raised her hand to stop. "There was one Indian who was as surprised to see me as I was to find him. He lit out that way." She pointed in the direction he'd ridden away.

"Are you all right, Missy? He didn't hurt you or nothin'?" Sam gave her a quick look-over to make sure she was all right. "Let's git you back to the stage."

"An' git the hell out o' here." Lathrop pushed his way through the crowd. "Time to git on the road folks. Stage is leavin' so let's git a move on!"

It took no prompting to get Maggie back in the stage. In the time it took to scrape the slime off her boots she was ready to go. They were on the road in less than twenty minutes, the team hitched, food eaten, and utensils and bedrolls stowed. Maggie wasn't so naïve not to realize the Indian was probably a scout, sent to determine their strength. *What would he report? Would they meet him and his band up the road? Had she caught him before he made an assessment of their numbers?* Her head was hurting and she was still shaking as the stage jerked away through the mud. *This was* not *a good beginning to an otherwise beautiful morning.*

The sun stayed high throughout the day. Along with a strong wind that rocked the stage when it found enough solid ground to keep moving, it helped to dry the soggy earth faster. The travelers were forced to stop many times before they reached Robbers Roost, but at least there had been no Indian encounters or other mishaps along the way other than the soft ground that hindered their passage. Although adding more time to the trip, it was decided they would spend at least one additional day at the Roost before attempting to cross the swollen Cheyenne. Maggie was more than happy to stick around as long as they deemed necessary. She felt safe at the station, considerably more so than out in the open like they'd been last night. Although anxious to reach Deadwood, safety was paramount and she wasn't a fool not to realize that she got to do this trip all over again in reverse once her story was done. The return trip would be fraught with more perils than this one, adding highway robbers looking for easy fortunes by relieving passengers of the gold they carried to the usual worries of Indians and bad weather.

Throughout the day Sam and Tom regaled Maggie with stories of well-known gunfighters in the territory to help alleviate some of the boredom. "Daniel Boone May, jest Boone they calls him, is the owner of this here establishment we're headed fer," Sam said with a glint of reverence in his eyes. "Now he's 'bout the fastest gun in the Dakotas accordin' to folks round these parts. He's a U.S. Marshall, too, an' I hear tell, he's put more outlaws, robbers an' undesirables in the ground than the dreaded cholera." He paused and cocked his head when Maggie raised her eyebrow in question. "Well, mebbe not *that* many, but he's kilt a few." Sam smoothed his mustache and ran his hand down his beard. "Jest last year right 'bout this same time, he an' two other messengers was a waitin' north o' here at Jenney Station for the stage to pull in from Deadwood so's they could take over the trip down to Cheyenne. But the stage never come in like it was s'posed to. Them three headed toward Deadwood a lookin' fer it an' run smack into one o' them boys they was s'posed to replace ridin' fer help. Them four rode back to the station, found one o' the passengers kilt, one o' the other messengers wounded, the other one locked away, an' the gold from the stage gone."

Maggie smiled and tried to act like she cared. All she wanted to do was put her head back and close her eyes, but Sam prattled on and on until they finally pulled into the station hours later. Maggie was more than surprised when Mr. Daniel Boone May himself met the stage at the depot and greeted the passengers warmly, agreeing to join them for supper.

Gathered around the table that night, stage passengers and freighters alike fired question after question at Mr. May who stood at the far end of the long table in front of the fireplace, his right leg propped on a chair, a smoke in his mouth, answering their questions with a smile. His eyes, what Sam told Maggie folks sometimes called cat-eyes, were a color somewhere between yellow, green, and gray that gave him a restless look and sparkled during the telling of each story. With short-cropped hair, a mustache above an otherwise clean-shaven face, and fancy clothes, to Maggie he looked more like a politician stomping for votes or a gambler she'd find playing poker with Luke or Poker Alice, than a gunman.

"Tell us about Frank Towle," one of the silent coach companions asked, whom Maggie had heard called Brady early in the trip. She hadn't heard him or his companions speak ten words since their encounter with the Indians, so his question more than concerned her as to his interest.

"Well," Boone began, "not much more than a year ago me and another messenger by the name of Zimmerman were trailing the stage headed back to Cheyenne. Down near Old Woman Creek it was stopped by highwaymen. We were far enough behind that we got the drop on 'em and shot one, Frank Towle. We left him behind when we lit out after the rest of the gang, but they got away. When we got back, Towle was gone, too."

"What about Archie McLaughlin? Tell us about him," another of the silent companions Maggie'd heard called Jake asked.

There was a sudden, unexplained charge in the air. Maggie didn't know what it was, but she wasn't the only one who felt it, judging by the faces of everyone else in the room. These men knew a little too much about Daniel Boone May and his conquests.

Boone cleared his throat. "He was a road agent I was assigned to take to Deadwood with his men."

"But he never made it, did he May?" There was a hard glint in Jake's eyes and a sharp edge in his voice.

Boone cocked his head and his hand slid to his hip. His foot dropped to the floor and the cigarette was flicked away. "No, he didn't. The stage was stopped by masked riders, vigilantes who'd been set upon in one way or another by McLaughlin and his gang. They wanted justice—and they got it."

Jake jumped to his feet, rocking the bench seat under Maggie and the others sitting on it. "There was no justice. Archie was hung like a dog!" he shouted. "Him and Billy Mansfield along with him!" Jake's hand went to his gun, but in a blink, Boone's pistol was aimed and cocked.

"I wouldn't do that if I were you." Boone's voice was cool and steady. "Don't know who you are or what your concern is with those boys, but they deserved what they got. They were thieves and I just happened to be there when justice was served."

"We're Archie's brothers and that's not how we see it! You might as well have put the noose around Archie's and Billy's necks yourself." Brady's voice was deep and edgy now. He slid beside Jake, his hand hovering above his gun. The still unnamed brother stepped to Jake's other side. "You were supposed to *protect* them until you reached Deadwood and let the law decide their fate. You didn't do your job and now our brother is dead!" Jake shouted.

Boone tilted his head and lifted an eyebrow. "Would the law have had the chance to decide? Or did you and your brothers have plans to bust him and his boys out of jail before their fates *could* be decided?" Boone's voice dripped with sarcasm.

The brothers' eyes widened, a telling sign Boone had hit on what they really had in mind *if* Archie and his gang had arrived safely in Deadwood.

Boone stood his ground and Maggie watched in rapt silence, praying he could avoid gunfire. She'd thought she'd be safe here. Instead *she was caught right in the middle of a would-be shootout!*

"Boys, I did all I could, short of getting killed myself, to protect your brother and Billy. Those folks had killing on their minds and there was no way to talk 'em out of it."

"Well, we say you didn't try hard enough," the nameless brother said with a low growl. "You were supposed to make sure they reached Deadwood alive."

"So you could bust 'em out of jail when they got there?" Boone's voice was hard, but with a trace of humor. "Sorry your plans were ruined, but there was nothing I could do."

Boone took a step back, his gun still pointed at the brothers as the diners stood and scurried over benches and out of the line of fire. Sam grabbed Maggie and pushed her behind him. Tom slid shoulder to shoulder with Sam, shielding Maggie from harm. She peeked out through the scraggly hair between their heads, watching the scene continue to unfold.

"I'm sorry it came down to their getting hung, boys. I would have preferred a trial, but I was outnumbered. There was nothing I could do."

"And mebbe there's nothin' we can do to keep from killin' you right here, right now," Jake spat. "You're outnumbered again, but this time *we're* set on killin' *you!*"

"I may be outnumbered, but don't think I won't kill each one of you before I go down. *If* I go down." He waved his gun as if to remind them it was already aimed at their chests. He sounded so smooth, so sure, Maggie didn't doubt for one second he'd kill all three of these men before they could slap leather.

The brothers snorted, but uncertainty had leapt into their eyes.

"Nobody's been hurt so far, boys, so let's keep it that way. You've heard my side of the story. You can believe me or not, but if you still have revenge on your minds, be assured I'll send every one of you to a grave right beside your brother before you draw steel."

The brothers' fingers twitched above their pistols as they decided whether to draw down on one of the fastest-known guns in the area, whose pistol was already cocked and ready to fire. Suddenly, George Lathrop and John Noonan were beside Boone, guns drawn. Two freighters slid up on Boone's other side until five men faced the three brothers, guns ready.

"Looks like the odds have changed. I think it would be in your best interests to get the hell out of here and not be seen again. Next time I may not be so forgiving."

The moments stretched as the men stared at each other across the room. Nobody moved and nobody blinked.

"I'm giving you boys one last chance. Turn around and walk away. Now."

"So you can shoot us in the back?" Jake shouted, sounding less confident than he did a few minutes ago.

Boone shook his head and frowned. "I don't shoot a man in the back. If I'm gonna shoot him, I do it when he's looking me square in the eyes." He lowered his head, but his cat-eyes never wavered from their target. "Go on, turn around and git."

Without looking away, the brothers backed their way to the door and one by one slipped out into the darkness.

Maggie sagged against Sam's back when the door closed shut and the closest man threw the latch. "I don't know whether I was more scared being chased by Indians or in the middle of an almost gunfight!"

"Be glad it didn't come to that, Missy. Lead would a been a flyin' like sparks in that big ole fire we had last night. No tellin' who might a got hurt."

"But not me, Sam," Maggie said, giving him a big hug. "Not me. I had two of the best men in the world protecting me from danger."

Sam's head bobbed up and down and Maggie knew he was blushing again, even though she couldn't see his face. Tom stood still as a stone beside him, but she imagined he was blushing, too. *Thank you God,* she whispered under her breath, *for sending these two old soldiers to keep me safe.*

After the night's excitement calmed, everyone settled back into their seats and continued to question their host. Maggie listened, rapt, as one after another story unfolded from Daniel Boone May. At eleven o'clock he excused himself to his room at the back of the station and by eleven ten, bedrolls were spread and the travelers settled in.

Unable to sleep amidst the groaning, belching, farting, and snoring in the open room, Maggie sat up and wrote in the flickering candlelight, her bedroll tucked in the corner with Sam and Tom stretched out protectively on either side of her. She rolled story after story Boone had told them in her head, jotting down notes for later use.

So exhausted she couldn't keep her eyes open any longer, and despite the cacophony of noise in the open room, she finally slid between the blankets and fell asleep, feeling safer than she had since the trip began with protectors like Sam, Tom and Daniel Boone May. A prayer was on her lips that she would make it back safely to Cheyenne to write about everything she'd already been through—and had yet to experience.

Chapter Seventeen

Forced to wait at Robbers Roost for the river to recede following the heavy rains, the stage and freighters pulled out just after daybreak two days later. They crossed the still-high but passable Cheyenne River and continued north along more desolate terrain toward their final destination. Maggie sighed with relief when they reached Jenney Station, a one-room, log structure that offered little room and less comfort, but meant they were almost there. *One last night and they'd reach Deadwood. What was waiting for her there? Half the town was gone. Where would she sleep? Could it be worse than what she'd endured these past days? Well,* she reminded herself, *she'd asked for this assignment and she was going to give it her absolute best. Finding a place to sleep was not her highest priority. That worry is designated to writing the best story A.E.'s ever read.*

Following a cramped, uneventful night, the stage left Jenney Station on what was, hopefully, the last day of the trip toward Deadwood. After a stop at Beaver Station, tended by a man who introduced himself only as "Frenchy," and another stop at Canyon Springs, the station where Boone May had told the story about the southbound stage being robbed last year, the coach rolled without fanfare into a desolate, blackened Deadwood.

Entering on the south side of Sherman Street, Maggie, on a seat all her own now that the three brothers had vacated, stared wide-eyed out the window at the fire's destruction. Sam and Tom each stared in silence out the windows across from her on opposite sides of the stage.

What little, if anything, that remained of the buildings were blackened shells. Most had burned to the ground, but beside them something else was springing from the ashes. There were tents everywhere, making Deadwood look much like it must have when the mining town was first born, Maggie mused. Where a business or home had been destroyed, a tent stood in its place. As the stage rolled up the street, Maggie saw a fortitude and tenacity in the people they passed who greeted them with a wave or a nod, their dirty faces drawn with exhaustion, but with hope and determination in their eyes.

They crossed Lee Creek where a bridge no longer connected its banks, the charred remains rising from the water like an evil demon, its crooked fingers beckoning the unsuspecting to come closer so they, too, might become a part of the destruction it had caused.

Rumbling through the creek the stage turned onto Main Street, another blackened, desolate reminder of the carnage that had swept the town little more than a week ago. The stage pulled up in front of what Maggie presumed had been the stage office.

Although the town was mostly leveled, Maggie noticed something else. Amidst the wreckage and tents as far as she could see, rebuilding had already begun. Lots were cleared of debris and piles of wood, bricks and stone lined the streets waiting to build new strength and permanence into a town previously erected of highly flammable wood. Maggie wondered how it all got there, and decided it must have been hauled in by wagons from surrounding towns.

The stage door swung open and George Lathrop waited, his hand raised, to help her out.

"Been a long trip, Miss Douglas, but I got to say, aside from Miss Calamity, you're the best dang female passenger I ever did have." He grinned and Maggie noticed color creep up his neck.

She smiled, "Thanks, Mr. Lathrop. I'm hoping to conclude my business quickly and be on my way back to Cheyenne in three or four days. I know you'll already be on your way back, but I must tell you, it's been an honor riding with you."

"Me, too." He lowered his head, but not before Maggie saw him blush again. With a smile Maggie concluded compliments were not a usual part of George Lathrop's character—neither giving them *nor* getting them.

He helped her from the stage and she stood, transfixed, in the middle of the desolation, thankful to be on solid ground again. Passengers slid down from atop the stage, while John Noonan tossed bags from the roof and George pulled them from inside the rear box. Maggie hurried to retrieve her bag with the canvas and canned food in it. She turned, trying to figure out exactly where to put it so she could grab her other two bags, and ran smack into Sam.

The bag fell from her hand. "You scared the devil out of me," she said with a chuckle.

"Sorry, Missy." Sam picked up the dropped satchel. "Let me git that one fer ye. Tom, grab them others. You know which ones they are." Maggie grinned. They'd hauled her bags on and off the stage every day along the way so she had access to her clothes and writing materials and knew as well as she did which ones were hers.

"Thanks, boys. Whatever will I do without you while I'm here?"

Tom, always the more silent of the two, frowned and rubbed his beard. Sam, however, spoke right up. "Tom an' me been a thinkin' on that very thing, Missy. Don't look like we'll be a buyin' supplies anytime soon, leastwise not till they get more shipped in to the mercantiles. An' we won't be a gittin' into them hills without no supplies. O' course, we'll need a few days to catch up on our drinkin'…"

Maggie raised her eyebrows. "What are you trying to say, Sam?"

"Well." He scuffed his boot and the dust swirled like a small black cloud into the air. His face was beet red and Maggie couldn't help but smile. *How her feelings toward these scruffy men had changed. At first they'd only been two smelly old coots, but in the passing of time they'd become her protectors and friends.*

"Tom an' me figger we'll stick around a while till you git your story writ an' head back to Cheyenne. If'n that's all right with you, o'course."

Maggie grinned and threw her arms around him. "You bet it's all right, Sam," she said into his ear. "You boys can stay with me as long as you like." She released him and stepped toward Tom, whose hands were already splayed in front of him, holding her away. Maggie laughed out loud, ignored his plea and threw her arms around him anyway. He stood rigid only a moment before his body sagged and his arms went around her with a sigh.

"Thank you, boys. Thank you," was all she could manage between smiles and tears.

The next few days were both trying and exciting. Maggie had never seen such stamina in a people after experiencing so much loss. They worked from first light until total dark, many of them working by lanterns deep into the black night, laying foundations for the city emerging from the ashes. Their struggle reminded her of the Phoenix of ancient mythology; a bird of bright, multi-colored feathers that, when its life of 500 to 1000 years was about to end, burst into flames to rise bigger and stronger than before. To her that ancient bird was the symbol of Deadwood, rising from the flames of destruction to start anew, bigger, better and stronger than before.

Maggie didn't even try to find a room. She decided that living as the residents of Deadwood were living, in tents, suffering as they suffered day after day and night after night, with only a thin canvas between them and the elements, would add more realism to her story. After locating a spot to put up her canvas, with Sam and Tom setting up nearby, Maggie began her interviews with the townspeople. She ate the canned fruit she'd hauled along with her, but managed a few hearty meals of small game provided by Sam and Tom. It was shared with whoever was close enough to see or smell it cooking over the campfire they built with wood hauled in from the hills outside Deadwood on a sled Tom made from burned out timbers he'd found. There was little water and what there was had to be used for drinking. Bathing became secondary and, as the second day dawned, Maggie could barely stand herself, let alone Sam and Tom or anyone else she talked to. Her clothes were covered with a gray/black layer of soot that couldn't be rubbed, pounded or shaken off. Her boots were no longer brown, but an ugly black with gray streaks running through them, and her face was devoid of anything but grime and determination. Her hair stayed tucked under her hat so no one could see how badly it was in need of a washing. She felt dirty and exhilarated at the same time.

Tales of racing not only the fire, but the clock, became the underlying theme of what had transpired that early morning of September 26, 1879. Maggie spoke with men and women who told of being awakened in the middle of the night to a roaring wall of flames racing down the street.

Maggie sat on the starting level of a new home foundation interviewing a man named Arnold. Pounding and yelling echoed up and down Main Street, as well as on Sherman Street behind her. Wagons rumbled back and forth carrying lumber, bricks, stone, and all kinds of hardware, the rhythms of a city springing from the charred remains everywhere. The townspeople may have been surprised and devastated, but they were "survivors, ready to get back to living" Maggie wrote in her notes.

"Tell me exactly what you remember of that night, Arnold," she began.

Tears filled his eyes before he wiped them away. He cleared his throat. "Most I remember is not having any time. By the time anyone knew what was happening, it was already too late."

"How do you mean?" Maggie asked, scribbling at the same time.

"Fire started over there on Sherman Street in Mrs. Ellsner's Empire Bakery." He pointed and Maggie turned, but all she could see were white, flapping tent tops.

She turned back. "Go on."

He ran a dirty hand under his nose. "After the bakery it headed north to the Welch House. The hotel had about 75 guests who barely made it out before it went up in flames. That fire had a mind of its own, Miss, and it was of a mind to destroy this town."

"What about the firemen? Where were they? Why didn't they stop it?"

He frowned and shook his head. "The station house was one of the first things the fire chewed up. Ate the hook and ladder and hose carriage right off. Only thing left was a bunch of worthless hose with nothing to hook up to. Even if they could have hooked up to something, the water was blocked." He snorted. "Funny that the day before a new water-works station was tested; but even if there *had* been enough water to stop that monster, we had no way to git it to the buildings with the hose carriage already burnt up." He sighed and gazed off. "Have you ever felt so helpless you were weak with it?"

Maggie remembered her trip down another Main Street on a rail post in what seemed like another lifetime. She nodded and grinned. "I certainly do."

"Well, that's how every single person in this town felt—helpless. A light breeze fanned the fire that night, but we thank the Good Lord it weren't stronger or the entire town would a been wiped out. People grabbed what they could and ran." He pointed to the hills on the east side of Sherman Street. "Looked like ants at a picnic scrambling up that hill to git out of the way of that fire." He gazed at the hill a few moments before he continued. "Like I said, we grabbed whatever we could, but by then that was our children and the clothes on our backs. Everything else was left behind. We was lucky to escape with our lives that blaze moved so fast."

"Where did it go from the hotel?" Maggie asked.

"It hit Jensen Bliss's hardware store and when the powder exploded, it looked like the Fourth of July. By then most ever'body knew there was no stopping that monster and gave up trying. Lord, what a sight to behold. Sherman Street was ablaze, raining fire down over the town, while the bridge over Lee Creek burned bright over the water. Once it crossed the creek, it turned up Main Street and wiped out the town's most important businesses."

He hung his head and Maggie knew he was trying to hold back tears. She waited in silence, making notes, until he drew in a deep breath and continued. "We're figuring near to 300 houses and businesses was destroyed and about 2,000 folks is homeless. You seen what the town looks like now? It's a tent city with a few wooden shanties here and there, but it's the beginning of something new. We're gonna rebuild Deadwood even better than it was before." His eyes sparkled with the hope and determination Maggie'd seen in Deadwood's residents more than once since rolling into town.

"How are the people faring?" she asked. "What are they eating? How are they surviving day to day?"

He hunched his shoulders. "Best way they can. Them businesses farther up the road are helping out as much as they can by offering whatever they have to them folks what lost everything. Guess they figure it's the only way they can share in what the rest of us is suffering."

"It didn't take long for the community to start rebuilding," Maggie said. "How is it all being paid for?" She waved her hand to encompass the newly emerging structures up and down the street.

For the first time since their interview, a grin split his lips. "You won't believe me if I tell ya."

"Try me."

"Somehow the bank vaults, and what was inside them, survived the fire, so there's money to be had. Best part, though, is that," he chuckled again, "they're finding gold in the ashes and sifting it out to pay for a lot of this here rebuilding."

Maggie's brows furrowed. "What? The banks are *giving* money away and they're finding gold in the ashes to pay for all this!"

"Well, I don't know that them banks is *giving* the money away, but they're advancing it to them that needs it at low rates, and it's a fact. Don't have to go to the Hills anymore to find gold—it's in the ashes!" He laughed, slapped his leg, and strolled away, Maggie laughing as he went.

A woman helping her husband lay a new foundation around the tent standing in the middle of an otherwise empty lot was the next person Maggie spoke with. "I didn't have no time," the woman said, her voice solemn, "to do nothing more than grab my young 'uns and run into the hills. My husband ran out the door to find help, but everybody else was running, too, screaming, trying to get out of the path of the flames. The fire was coming right at us, eating everything in its way. The buildings glowed red and orange and looked—alive. And it— roared." She ran a hand under her nose and Maggie noticed dirt under her broken fingernails and a clean spot over her lip where she'd swiped her face with her hand. "When the powder exploded in the hardware store, we knew we was in big trouble." Tears ran down her cheeks, leaving more clean streaks on a face dirty with the work of rebuilding. She pointed to the hill behind Sherman Street. "We just grabbed the young 'uns and ran. The only thing with us when we reached the top of the hill was the clothes we was wearing and them.

"We come back to nothing; just a smoking, black pit. Everything we had was in our house and it's all gone. The town's pulling together, though. Them folks that still have are helping out those of us that lost everything. Business owners from the other end of town are helping, too." A sob broke free and she put up her hand. "I can't talk no more about it." She stood up and, without a backward glance, hurried to the other side of the lot where her husband worked.

More than anyone it was the children that broke Maggie's heart. Dirty faces with wide eyes peeked out from behind tent flaps or between tent rows as she walked along, looking for anyone who would talk to her. When some of the women agreed, most of the little ones hid behind their mama's skirts or held on tight to their mother's hand, as though afraid to let go and lose them forever, a telling story without words.

A few of the older children spoke up about that terrifying night. "Mama came screaming into the bedroom and jerked me and my brother outta bed so hard we fell on the floor," a boy who looked to be ten or eleven told Maggie. "Papa grabbed my little brother and Mama grabbed me and we just ran. I didn't know what was going on until we ran out the door and all I saw was that fire." He sniffed and tears streamed down his face. "I was so scared. I thought we was gonna die," he sobbed before he ran away in embarrassment.

Another woman spoke so low, Maggie could barely hear her. "We only had time to grab the children and run." Clinging to the woman's leg was a little girl of four or five, the woman stroking the child's dirty hair as she spoke. "They was all we had when we got up the hill." She fingered her soot-covered skirt. "This is the same dress I had on that night. It's all I got, 'ceptin' my child." She grabbed her little girl and started away. "I'm sorry, Miss, I can't talk about it no more."

So it went with survivor after survivor. Stories of racing a fire that ate everything in its path, of explosions and little time to escape. When it was over, Deadwood's people returned to homes and businesses destroyed and their lives in shambles, like the town around them. But they would rebuild Deadwood with their own sweat and blood and, from what Maggie could see, were well on their way to that end. The night of terror had passed and all that was ahead was the rebirth of a town, bigger and better than it had been before. It was only the future the people of Deadwood looked toward, not the past.

Chapter Eighteen

Standing beside the stage to Cheyenne, Maggie didn't even try to stop the tears slipping down her cheeks that sunny October day as she said goodbye to Sam and Tom. "You boys promise to be careful out in those hills? To take care of yourselves and watch out for each other?" She sniffed, lifted her hat and ran her fingers through her dirty hair, more than anxious to get to Robbers Roost and beg a bath. She'd managed to find a little water here and there during her stay in Deadwood, enough to keep her face and arms clean, but she was almost ready to sell her soul for a tub of water to immerse herself in for a thorough cleansing.

Both men shuffled their feet, their tattered hats rolling back and forth between their fingers. "We'll do that, Missy, you kin count on it," Sam said with a sniff.

"And you'll find me in Cheyenne on your way back?"

"Yes'm, we'll do that fer sure." Sam's eyes were rimmed red in his effort to keep his dignity.

Tom stood stoic, as usual, chewing on the top of his beard.

"Ever'body git aboard," the stage driver called. "Stage leaves in five minutes!"

Maggie's insides turned. Never would she have dreamed she'd become so close to these two raggedy men. She put her arms around Sam, who hugged her hard and long in return.

"You take care of yoreself, Missy, ye hear?" he said on a whisper.

She pulled back, more tears streaking her face. Maggie nodded and turned to Tom, expecting to see his arms raised against her. Instead they were open, beckoning her. She fell into his chest and hugged him tight.

"Thank you, Tom. Thank you both for everything you've done for me."

Tom stepped back, eyes brimming. "Miss Douglas, it was mine and Sam's pleasure to look after you." He leaned back toward her with a grin. "It gave us two old soldiers something to do."

A sob broke with Maggie's laughter. She hugged him one last time then kissed his cheek. "Goodbye, Tom. I'll never forget you."

"And I'll never forget you, Miss Douglas." He blinked his eyes several times to keep his threatening tears from spilling.

Maggie turned back to Sam and he reached for her one last time. She fell into his arms and they hugged until the driver stepped up behind them. "Sorry to break this up, folks, but I got me a schedule to keep. Time to git on in Miss."

"Go on now. We'll find ye in Cheyenne in a few months." Sam gave her a gentle shove toward the stage.

She stopped, her boot on the first step into the coach. "Promise?"

"Promise." Sam held up his right hand, kissed his crooked fingers then raised them in farewell.

Ten minutes later Maggie was on her way back to Cheyenne, one of four passengers inside the rocking coach and only a sack of mail up top. She didn't care who her fellow riders were. Her heart was too heavy to care. She had plenty of time to find out their stories in the coming days. For now, all she wanted was to put her head back and remember all she'd experienced thus far. And wonder what waited up ahead.

Sitting cross-legged on her bedroll that night at Jenney Station, working by candlelight on her stories, Maggie felt someone slide up beside her. She looked up to find the other woman passenger on her knees looking at her expectantly.

"I'm sorry, Miss Douglas, I didn't mean to disturb you." The woman worried at a dirty handkerchief.

Maggie sighed. She wanted to be left alone to write, but she didn't want to be rude either. "It's all right. What can I do for you?"

"My name is Ida James, Miss Douglas, and I just, well, I thought we could talk, get to know each other better, us being the only women on the stage."

Try being the only *woman on a stage and two freighters full of men*, she wanted to say, but smiled instead. "I suppose we can do that. What would you like to talk about?" Maggie put her papers aside to give the obviously lonely woman her full attention.

"Well, my name is Ida James, as I said, and you're Maggie Douglas."

"How do you know that?" Maggie asked. She hadn't spoken to anyone since she stepped foot inside the stage.

"I was nosey." Ida blushed. "I asked the driver. I thought maybe you were Calamity Jane."

Maggie sat a moment, unsure whether to take Ida's mistaken identity as an insult or compliment, then threw her head back in laughter. She'd been compared to Calamity Jane on more than one occasion since her departure from Cheyenne, but rather than be insulted, she chose to take it as a compliment. "No, I'm not Calamity, although a few folks have mistaken me for her because of my…" Her hand swept her dirty, disheveled clothes, "attire. Actually, I'm a newspaper reporter for the *Cheyenne Sun*. I just spent the last few days in Deadwood writing about the fire."

"Oh." Tears sprang to Ida's eyes. She worried harder at her handkerchief and Maggie wondered what hardship the woman had suffered there.

Maggie quietly waited for the woman to relate her story. It was several moments before Ida cleared her throat, ran a hand under her nose and said, "I lost my husband in that fire." She closed her eyes and laid the handkerchief reverently against her cheek. She took a deep breath of the once-white cloth. "This is all I have left of him."

Maggie touched Ida's hand and felt tears of her own rise. "I'm so sorry."

Ida sniffed and pushed down a sob. "It happened so fast. People were running, screaming, trying to get out of its way. Matthew and I were heading for the hills when we heard someone calling for help. He told me to wait." She sobbed quietly beside Maggie who put her arm around the weeping woman. "He let go of my hand, the hand holding this very handkerchief, to go find whoever was calling." She sniffed and took a moment to compose herself. "I screamed and begged him not to go, but he said he had to. 'What if it was you calling for help and nobody came?' he asked me, disappearing between two buildings to find whoever it was." She heaved a long, heavy sigh. "I never saw him again. The next thing I saw was a wall of fire rolling in around him. It came on so fast and was so hot the hair on my arms and in my nose curled up as I stood there." She stopped. Tears streamed down her face, the handkerchief crushed between her fingers. "I ran. I left him there to save myself." Ida turned into Maggie's chest and wept.

Maggie stroked Ida's back and rocked the distraught woman. "There was nothing you could have done," she said, trying to assuage Ida's guilt. "Your husband chose to go down that alley, to help someone in trouble. You couldn't have done anything but wait, like he told you. If he'd let you go with him, you'd be gone, too." Maggie continued to rub Ida's back as the woman cried into her chest. "He knew it was too dangerous for you, but he was willing to risk himself to help someone in trouble. From what I see he was a hero."

Ida sobbed harder and Maggie wondered what she could possibly say to make the woman feel better. She opted to just hold onto her and let her cry herself out. A few minutes later Ida sat back, brushed the tears from her eyes and cheeks and wiped her nose with the crushed handkerchief.

"I'm so sorry, Miss Douglas. I didn't mean to come over here and cry all over you like a baby. It's just that it, it still hurts so much." She sniffed. "I thought I could talk about it. Guess I was wrong." Her head dropped and she worried at the handkerchief again.

"Please, Ida, I'm Maggie. You talk and cry as much as you want. We women need to stick together." And Maggie meant what she said, realizing for the first time she'd never really had a "girl" friend to talk to or confide in. Her companions had always been her brothers, most women put off by her outspokenness and tough demeanor. Any other women she dealt with were business associates and not friends. She couldn't remember a single girlfriend in her life, and it felt good to open up to another woman. It was soul cleansing and tears slid down her cheeks right along with Ida's.

Ida chuckled and blew her nose with a different handkerchief. "I sure do appreciate your listening to me.

Matthew and I had been in Deadwood only a short while. We were going to be a part of something bigger by selling goods to the miners at our mercantile store," she said on a sigh. "The store and our little house were both destroyed in that horrible fire. Now what do I have? Nothing, not even Matthew."

"Where are you headed?"

"Denver. I've got a sister there who'll take me in until I figure out what to do. She's got four boys I can help out with. Maybe I'll find a job. I'll figure it out as I go."

"I'm sure your sister will appreciate any help she can get." Maggie grinned. "I can't imagine raising four boys. I grew up with two brothers and they were insufferable!" Maggie giggled and a few moments later Ida was giggling right along with her.

Maggie and Ida talked deep into the night. The next morning they, along with their two male companions, boarded the stage headed toward Robbers Roost. Maggie felt exhilarated after what she considered her "purging" conversations with Ida. By the time they finally closed their eyes, Maggie felt like she'd known Ida all her life, and Ida knew more about Maggie, including her trip down Main Street on a rail post, than anyone else in her life, even her family. For the first time, Maggie opened up about who she was and what she wanted—even told Ida about George, how she'd sent him away and was now looking for him. She felt free, happy to be able to share her thoughts and fears with another woman.

Feeling so open, she engaged the two male passengers in conversation when they got settled inside the stage. "I know I've been rather quiet since we left Deadwood, but my name is Maggie Douglas and you gentlemen are?" Maggie looked at each man opposite her.

The first man she addressed had on a fancy gray suit, black string tie and gray bowler hat. He sported a drooping mustache and had dark, penetrating eyes that matched his black, shoulder-length hair. He tipped his hat at Maggie and Ida. "I'm Frank Howard, ladies."

"And what is your occupation, Mr. Howard?" Maggie prompted.

"I'm a gambler. I was on my way to Deadwood when the fire struck. When I got there I walked into chaos. Not much for a gambler when the gambling houses and saloons have been destroyed and the ones still standing have been closed." He coughed politely. "Some committee was set up by the good citizens of Deadwood that shut them down and made a bunch of rules to keep 'unsavory' folks from taking advantage of the situation."

Maggie recalled the citizen's committee to which Howard referred and wondered if he was one of the unsavory folks they were trying to discourage from staying in Deadwood.

Howard frowned. "No saloons means no gambling and no gambling means no money for someone like me. So here I am, headed back to Cheyenne where a man such as myself can make a living." He paused and rubbed his chin. "Maybe I'll head down to Denver. Doesn't really matter I guess, a saloon is a saloon."

The other man leaned forward and offered his hand to Maggie and then Ida. "I'm Price Jennings, a salesman."

"And what do you sell, Mr. Jennings?" Ida asked.

"Fine spirits, ma'am. Fine spirits."

"Whiskey," Maggie countered looking Jennings in the eyes.

Jennings raised his chin and nodded. "Yes, ma'am, I sell whiskey. As Mr. Howard pointed out, once the saloons that were still standing in Deadwood were closed, there was no cause for me to stay. I tallied a few orders for when they have rebuilt," he patted his bag beside him, "but until such time as they're back in business, well, as I've already stated, there was no reason to stay. So I'm heading back to Cheyenne and other cities where I can still sell my wares." He grinned and cocked his head.

Maggie opened her mouth to ask Mr. Howard if he'd ever met Luke or Alice when there was a shot outside.

"Was that a gunshot?" Ida asked, wide-eyed, clutching her handkerchief to her chest.

"Sounded like it." Maggie peeked out the window and ducked when another shot rang out, but not before she saw three riders headed toward the stage. "We've got company."

"Stop that stage and throw down your rifles," one of the riders yelled, racing his horse up alongside the stage. "Do it quick!" He fired into the air again.

Maggie's skin bubbled. She recognized that voice! The men reined in beside the stage as it rolled to a stop and the driver and guard threw their weapons down at the horses' feet.

"Get down!" another of the masked riders shouted, dismounting and kicking the rifles away as the guard and driver scrambled down. "And you folks inside come on out."

Ida had a vice-like grip on Maggie's arm, and both men looked like hens cornered by a fox in a chicken coop.

When the passengers didn't emerge quick enough, the last of the riders pounded on the door. "Git on out here, now, or we'll shoot the driver!"

Maggie was the first to gather her wits. She threw open the door, hoping it would slam into the man on the other side, but it swung fully open. She crouched in the door way, still grungy and disheveled from the days she'd spent in Deadwood, hoping the McLaughlin brothers wouldn't recognize her in her unkempt shape.

"Come on, git on down here," said the voice Maggie recognized as Jake's. He reached up and jerked her arm so hard she almost fell out of the stage, but the driver caught her before she hit the ground. "Come on, come on, we ain't got all day," Jake shouted at Ida and the two men emerging behind Maggie, who was trying to get her balance.

Ida's eyes were wide, but no more so than their two companions. "Please sir, we're carrying nothing of worth," she moaned, crushing her handkerchief to her chest.

"Don't lie, woman. You folks just come from Deadwood. At least one of y'all has to be carryin' some gold."

Maggie recognized Brady's voice through the flour sack with holes cut in it for his eyes, nose and mouth that covered his head. He sounded much braver with the gun already in his hand, pointed at helpless men and women, than he had facing Daniel Boone May.

"Mister, I'm more broke than the day I stepped *into* Deadwood," Mr. Howard said in a shaky voice. He cocked his head. "My name is Frank Howard. I'm a gambler and, as you can see," he turned his pockets inside out, "there's no money to be had in Deadwood. I had barely enough to buy my passage back to Cheyenne."

The brother whose name Maggie had yet to learn stepped up to Mr. Howard, went through his pockets and checked around his waist. He stopped when he found a money belt strapped to Frank's back. "And what's this?" He jerked the pouch free.

Howard's eyes closed and he shook his head. "You'll find very little there."

The brother ripped open the pouch, pulled out a small wad of cash and counted it. He raised the bills in the air and shook his hand. "Thirty dollars? You've got thirty dollars! What the hell kind of a gambler are you?"

Howard harrumphed. "A broke one. The fire wiped out a good part of Deadwood. Whatever gambling parlors or saloons that survived are out of business. It doesn't make for a very lucrative business for a gambler, sir. What little currency I had was used for necessities until I was able to depart."

With a grunt McLaughlin shoved Mr. Howard away and whirled on Mr. Jennings. He waved his gun at the cowering man. "What about you?"

"I'm afraid I have the same sad story," he said between quivering lips. "I sell spirits, gentlemen. You can't *sell* much whiskey in a town that has been destroyed, its citizens destitute, and what few saloons that did survive are closed. Oh, there were plenty of men willing to relieve me of my burdens without compensation. Hoping I would give them a taste out of the goodness of my heart." He cleared his throat. "I am not that good, so what incentive is that for a man like me to remain in such a place? All I have is my reputation and my samples." He paused a moment and added, "Of course, you gentlemen are free to imbibe if *you* so desire." With shaking hands he held out the suitcase he'd been gripping close to his chest.

"What?" the unnamed brother asked Brady, his face scrunched in confusion. "What the hell did he just say?"

"He's a liquor salesman with nowhere to sell in Deadwood since the fire. All he's got is what's in that satchel and if we want a taste, we're welcome to it," Brady translated.

"Break it out then!" the nameless brother shouted.

Jennings handed the suitcase to Brady who put it on the ground and opened it, the bottles gleaming in the sunlight, his brother close beside him.

Jake stalked over, slammed the top shut, picked up the suitcase, and threw it at the salesman's feet. Mr. Jennings went to his knees beside the broken case, his eyes bulging as the contents from the broken bottles poured out onto the ground. His shoulders slumped and Maggie thought he would cry right there.

"We got better things to do than git drunk!" Jake's voice was thick with anger.

"We coulda drank it later," Brady whined. "After we was done here."

Jake stuck his nose in Brady's face. "We got to keep our wits, so shut up an' keep your eye on the driver and guard while I check them others."

Maggie's heart pounded and Ida's fingers dug into her arm. *Would they recognize her? And if they did, what would they do?*

She held her breath as Jake stepped toward her. "What have we here?"

He lifted Maggie's chin and eyed her. Her heart was racing and she tried to breathe normally, but wasn't succeeding. He cocked his head and lifted her hat. Her pony tail popped out and fell down her back. Jake stared. "I know you."

She shook her head.

He stepped back to view every inch of her. His head bobbed up and down and Maggie saw his lip curl inside his mask. "I do know you, which means you know us."

Jake turned to Brady. "Come here, look at what I found." He shoved the other brother toward the guard and driver, watching with their hands raised. "You keep an eye on them."

Jake pulled Brady in front of Maggie. "She look familiar?"

Brady stuck his face in Maggie's and she quelled the urge to spit in it. His eyes pinched and his head moved back and forth as he studied her. "Mebbe, mebbe not."

"Look harder. Look at her clothes! Look at her hair!"

Brady stepped back and eyed every inch of her. "I'll be damned, it's that reporter gal!" he shouted.

"And she knows who we are."

Maggie opened her mouth to deny it, but snapped it shut. These boys may be dumb, but they weren't totally stupid. They'd ridden together in the same stage for days, how could she convince them she wasn't who they thought she was? *She couldn't.*

"Jake," she began, "you're right. I do know who you all are even with the masks, but that doesn't mean things have to end badly. Nobody on this stage has any gold. Most of Deadwood has been wiped out by the fire. These men aren't prospectors, this woman is going to Denver to live with her sister after losing her husband and her home, and me, well, you know all I want is a story." She took a breath to still her hammering heart. Wally was in her bag in her right hand. Jake hadn't searched her yet and she hoped he wouldn't remember her constant companion. If she could keep him distracted long enough, she might be able figure some way to get the drop on him and maybe they'd all get out of this without injury. Maybe, she could swing the pistol at his head and knock him out like she had Thornton, but then she still had the brothers to deal with. Trying to work it out in her mind and keep Jake from finding Wally, she added, "Nobody's been hurt. If you just go away and leave us alone, nobody will say a word."

"So you say," Jake answered. "We haven't checked the rest of the stage yet. There could be a strong box under the driver's seat or up top. Stages don't leave Deadwood without gold."

Jake slapped Brady's chest. "Go check it out." He pointed at the front of the stage and thrust a thumb at the passengers. "I'll make sure they're not hiding anything." Brady headed toward the stage and Maggie tried to think of something to distract Jake so he wouldn't find Wally, but before she could think of anything he turned back to her. "Now, Miss Douglas..."

Maggie saw the gleam in his eyes through the holes in the mask and her skin crawled. She had to let him search her, unless she wanted to try and pull Wally out and draw on him—before he shot her. Knowing it was impossible her shoulders slumped in defeat.

"If'n I recall, you were right proud of a Colt pistola you kept with you all the time." He lifted his hand and wiggled his fingers. "Hand it over."

She raised the bag, but hesitated. He stepped closer. "Be a good girl, Miss Douglas, and give it to me." He wiggled his fingers again in impatience.

"Here!" She slammed the bag into his outstretched palm, satisfied by his grunt when steel met flesh.

His eyes gleamed with hatred when he heaved the bag away. "*Don't* do that again," he snarled.

"Do what?" Maggie feigned innocence.

Jake stuck his face in hers, his breath rank. She held her own breath, but stood tall. "You might be a woman, but don't think I won't make you pay if you do somethin' like that again." He touched her cheek with his fingers. "Just don't."

"How can I?" She cocked her head. "You took the only gun I've got," she said with a growl.

Jake edged closer. Maggie closed her eyes, waiting for the blow, but he jerked away and a moment later touched her shoulder before he began the violation of her body. She squeezed her eyes shut and held down her gorge while, as Jake pointed out to his brother, he searched for "hidden" weapons on her. She had to draw every ounce of inner strength she possessed to keep from falling down before he finished—or scratching his eyes out.

When the inspection of her body stopped and she forced her eyes open, Jake was stepping in front of Ida, who screamed like an injured cat the moment he touched her. She slapped at his hand and screamed through gritted teeth, "Don't you touch me! Don't you dare touch me you, you fiend!"

Maggie was afraid if the woman didn't stop carrying on she was going to swoon, or Jake was going to knock her into submission. "Stop it, Ida! There's nothing you can do," Maggie chastised. "Just close your eyes and pretend it's Matthew."

Ida raised tear-filled eyes to Maggie. "I, I can't."

"You can and you will, Ida." Maggie said more softly. "You have no choice. Now stop bellowing, close your eyes, and be brave."

Ida stared at Maggie a moment before she sniffed, raised her chin and stiffened her back. Her eyes closed, causing huge tears to slide down her cheeks. Her body shook as she cried in silence until Jake finished his inspection of her. He stepped back, pointed his gun at the helpless travelers, and waited for Brady to join him.

Done with his search of the stage, Brady stepped up beside Jake holding only Mr. Howard's thirty dollars and a bag of mail in his hands. Brady opened it, shoved his arm inside and felt around. When he pulled his hand out, all he had in it was a fist full of letters. He stood like a statue, glaring at his hand until, with a savage scream, he threw the letters into the air and they blew away. "Jesus, Jake. How could we pick the only stage outta Deadwood that don't have nothin' on it but mail and broke passengers?"

"Shut up!" Jake shouted as the letters tumbled away.

Maggie's body sang with warning. *Certainly they wouldn't hurt anyone over thirty dollars and some tossed mail!*

"What're we gonna do, Jake?" the unnamed brother asked, stepping beside the other two, waving his pistol at the guard and driver to let them know he was still watching them.

"I'm thinkin'," Jake shouted, his face red.

"Let's just take what we got and skedaddle," Brady said. "It's like the reporter gal said," he waved his gun toward Maggie, "nobody's been hurt so even if she does tell the law who we are, what difference does it make? We ain't done nothin' but stop the stage, take thirty damn dollars, and throw some mail away." He held up the money and the mail bag. "Come on, Jake. It ain't worth gittin' hung over. Let's just leave 'em be, get back in our saddles and head on outta here with our hides still attached." Brady snorted. 'Sides, as long as nobody's hurt, who's gonna come after us for thirty damn dollars?"

"I will," came the familiar voice of Daniel Boone May who stepped out from behind a tree thirty yards away with two pistols cocked and ready at his hips.

Maggie thought she'd collapse with relief. She had no doubt they would get out of this alive now—but the brothers might not fare too well. Ida sagged into her.

"You boys drop your guns and put your hands where I can see them. And pull those stupid masks off. We all know who you are." He stepped closer. "Don't do anything stupid, either. I've got two pistols with hair triggers pointed at your backs."

Brady and the other brother dropped their guns, pulled off their masks, and turned around, hands high. "We ain't hurt nobody, Mr. May," Brady whined. "You remember that. We ain't hurt nobody."

"That's the first and only smart thing you've done since I've had the displeasure of getting to know you three." May drawled. He waved the pistol in his right hand at Jake, who hadn't moved to comply to any of his requests.

"Come on Jake, don't make this hard," Boone drawled. "I don't really want to shoot anybody today."

"Jake, don't be no fool, now," Brady said. "Turn around and throw down yore gun. We're caught and there ain't nothing we kin do about it."

Jake's back was to May, his gun still on the travelers. "What if I was to shoot one of these here passengers?"

"It'd be a sad thing for them—and you," May growled. "You'd be dead before they hit the ground,"

Jake flexed his neck and gnashed his teeth. "Just how the hell did you git here anyway?" he yelled over his shoulder, his eyes, and gun, still on the passengers.

"Was on my way to meet the stage and guide them to the Roost. Heard the shots and here I am." Boone grinned. "What *am* I gonna do with you boys?"

Jake stared at the passengers and Maggie knew he was trying to decide whether to draw on one of the fastest guns in the territory or throw down his gun and live to see another day, although that day and many to follow might be from a jail cell. His eyes grew hard and his fingers tightened on the grip of his gun. He whirled left, but before he could target May, he was jerked back in the opposite direction like a scarecrow in a gale wind from the force of the bullet that hit him, and was face down in the dirt a split second later. Brady and the other brother went to their knees beside their fallen sibling.

"You shot him in the back! Said you wouldn't shoot a man in the back," Brady yelled.

"I didn't shoot him in the back." May walked up, kicked Jake's gun aside and rolled him over with his foot. Blood gushed from a wound in Jake's chest. "I looked him straight in the eye before I shot him, just like I told him I would." May pulled the mask off Jake's head, his eyes wide. "Looks like he saw it coming," May said matter-of-factly.

"You gonna shoot us, too?" Brady asked, a quiver in his voice.

"Not today, boys, not today. You're goin' to Custer City and the Marshall there can deal with the two of you."

The driver and guard tied the living McLaughlin's to their horses, while Boone, Howard and Jennings heaved Jake across his horse's back and bound him to the saddle. Ida kept a tight hold on Maggie and Maggie tried to console the frightened woman while trying to stop her own quaking hands and racing heart. She'd survived yet another confrontation on this journey. How many more would she face before reaching Cheyenne—and live to tell about?

Chapter Nineteen

Disappointment, relief and anxiety rode Maggie's emotions like the team of horses racing into Cheyenne, tossing the stage and its passengers around as it rumbled into town. Part of Maggie was disappointed the trip was over; a journey fraught with danger, excitement and new friendships she would remember all her life. Another part of her was relieved she'd made it back alive, and another was more than anxious to finish her stories and present them to A.E. She couldn't wait to see Luke, too, but realized that, although it had been over two weeks since she'd left, the only time she'd really missed him or even thought of him was now.

The stage slowed with much braking and *whoaing* before it rolled to a stop in front of the depot where the horses blew, shook their heads and stamped their feet. Maggie heaved a sigh of relief that the trip was finally over and she could worry about something other than Indians, thieves, being sandwiched inside the stinking stage, and back-breaking bad weather. She didn't get up when the stage came to a full stop. Instead she sat still, eyes closed, thinking back over the last leg of the trip. She smiled when she realized that *without* the excitement of the Indians and bad weather such as they'd encountered going *to* Deadwood, the trip home was so boring following their encounter with the McLaughlin brothers, she and Ida had resorted to singing. They'd even recruited the men in harmonious rounds to keep their minds from turning to total mush in the dark, rocking carriage.

Mr. Howard and Mr. Jennings took no time to exit the stage. There were no heartfelt goodbyes like she'd exchanged with Sam and Tom in Deadwood, only the rush to be gone.

Maggie and Ida were the last to get out and faced each other on the sidewalk.

Ida grabbed Maggie's hand and squeezed. "I'll remember you always, Maggie Douglas. I'm a stronger woman for knowing you."

Maggie laughed. "Me? How?"

"You've shown me what it's like to stand on your own. You're strong and brave and speak your mind and handle any situation with dignity. I want to make a difference in this world, like you do. If I can't do so with children of my own, I'll start with my sister's. Perhaps I'll learn to teach school," she paused and a grin crossed her lips, "or maybe I'll become a newspaper woman, like you, and go off on adventures in search of the big story. Maybe I'll even look into the women's movement."

Maggie didn't know what to say. She'd never inspired anyone the way she, obviously, had Ida. She was just a woman trying to make her way, but realized that without even trying, she'd made a positive impact on this one woman's life.

Ida squeezed her hand again. "I wish you luck in finding George," she whispered.

Maggie hugged her new friend. "And I hope you find what you want in your new life, Ida." She held the woman by the shoulders to look at her. "You have a lot of living to do. You may not want to think about it now, but somewhere along the way you may find someone else to share that life with and you'll love him like you did Matthew. But then again you may not, and if that happens there's more for you out there than just having a husband and taking care of children. Find it, Ida, and be happy whatever it is."

Ida blushed and tears sprang to her eyes. "I know you're right, but I just can't think about loving someone other than Matthew. I'll never love anyone the way I loved him, but that's not to say someday I won't find a man to love—differently." She paused. "What I *can* think about is making a difference for myself. I realize *I* matter, too. If I meet a man along the way, so be it. If not, well, I'll do just fine on my own. You taught me that."

"When do you leave for Denver?" Maggie asked to change the subject, uncomfortable with Ida's praises.

"Monday morning. I'll miss you terribly, but I'll manage," Ida said on another grin.

"Shall we have dinner tonight or tomorrow?" Maggie asked, feeling the anxiety of separating from this kind woman to whom she'd opened up more than anyone else in her life.

Ida shook her head. "You have to get that story ready for your boss and don't have time to mollycoddle me. Besides, you need to track down Luke to let him know you're back. It wouldn't do for me to interfere in your homecoming."

She'd told Ida all about Luke, how he'd rescued her from being trampled to death, showed her around town, become her friend and, how she feared he'd fallen in love with her. "He'd understand," Maggie began but was stopped with a finger across her lips.

"Don't be silly. Besides, I need my rest. I'll be looking forward to some quiet solitude before I have to climb back inside that coach again. Believe me I'm looking forward to as much time as I can get on solid ground with a few good meals, as many hot baths as they'll let me have, and a comfortable bed." She touched Maggie's hand again. "You go find Luke. I'll be fine."

"You're sure?"

Ida nodded. "Go."

They hugged fiercely one last time. "You'll keep in touch?" Ida asked.

"I will. And you'll do the same?"

"I will," Ida promised before they went their own ways, hands raised in a final wave, Ida's handkerchief clutched between her fingers.

Maggie watched her new friend walk away, tears threatening to explode, before she stepped inside the stage depot.

The clerk looked up from behind his desk. "Yes, ma'am?"

Maggie pointed to where her bags had been stacked by the driver on the planked sidewalk just inside the depot door. "If I may be so bold to ask, would you please watch my bags until I return? I have an errand and will be back shortly to retrieve them."

He nodded and smiled. "Yes, ma'am."

Maggie hurried across the street to the Inter-Ocean, anxious to find Luke. She couldn't wait to see the look on his face when he saw her. She was still in her denims, boots and cowboy hat and was drawing stares from many passers-by, but she ignored them. She felt free. She had, at least, been able to wash at Robbers Roost, luxuriating for over an hour before the water grew cold and she had to get out, but not until her hair squeaked and her body glistened. And she got to do it all over again at Fort

Laramie, so at least she arrived in town looking clean and like a woman, albeit still *dressed* like a man.

Her boots snapped on the hardwood floor when she stepped inside the gaming room of the Inter-Ocean. It took a moment for her eyes to adjust as she looked around for Luke. She couldn't find him in the sparsely crowded room and wondered where he was. It was Saturday night and, even though it was early, he should already be dealing. Maggie felt an odd stirring of uncertainty and hurried to the Inter-Ocean office. She'd gotten to know "Big" Ed Chase in the time she'd known Luke. Mr. Chase would know where Luke was at.

Maggie knocked on the office door. Ed opened it with a smile. "Miss Douglas." He eyed her clothing with a raised eyebrow.

"Good evening, Mr. Chase. I'm sorry to bother you. I've just gotten back into town from Deadwood so I must apologize for my appearance." She was suddenly self-conscious of her appearance in front of the well-dressed man.

Chase smiled and nodded his head. "I understand, Miss Douglas. And how was Deadwood?"

"Sad, Mr. Chase. More than half the town is gone, but the people are survivors and they're already rebuilding."

He nodded and smiled. "What can I do for you?"

"I'm looking for Luke. He should be working tonight, but I can't find him."

Chase cocked his head. "You don't know." It was a statement, not a question.

"Know what, sir?" Maggie's skin pricked.

"Luke's gone."

"Gone! Gone where?" she cried.

"He left two weeks ago."

"Two weeks ago!" Maggie could hardly contain herself. *Luke was gone? How? He must have left just after she did. Did he know he was leaving? Why hadn't he told her?* The questions rolled around in her mind until she realized Mr. Chase was speaking again.

"He's managing the Long Branch in Dodge City...Kansas," he added as though she didn't know where it was. "Hated to see him go, but it was a good opportunity for him to run his own place."

Maggie nodded, the wind taken out of her, her excitement at being back in Cheyenne gone. She felt betrayed, bereft and lost. *How could he have left without telling her? What would she do without him? Why hadn't he told her?*

"I'm sorry, Miss Douglas. I have to get back to work. Let me know if I can be of further help." Chase shoved a cigar in his mouth and stepped back into his office leaving Maggie confused and alone in the hallway.

All Maggie wanted to do was run. After all she'd been through these past few weeks to come back to this! *She felt so betrayed. Luke was gone. What now?*

Her back went up. She was alone. That was how she'd come to Cheyenne and that was how things were again. Maggie had her wits and that was what she was going to use. Luke had given her direction and friendship when she'd arrived. Now it was time to stand on her own and go forward with everything she'd learned.

Hurrying back to the depot she hired a hack to take her and her bags to the boarding house. Mrs. Harris met her at the door, eyeing her attire with her usual glare of disapproval.

"Welcome home, Miss Douglas. I presume you'll be changing into something more appropriate now that you're done traipsing across the country," she said, arms crossed over her large chest.

Was everyone against her today? Even Mrs. Harris who had applauded her for doing a man's job? Why was it all right to do a man's job, but not dress like one? Maggie sighed and shook her head.

"Hello to you, too, Mrs. Harris. I'll get into proper clothing as soon as my cases are put in my room and I've had a bath." She turned to the driver and handed him a coin. "Put my bags in the yellow room at the top of the stairs, please."

The driver nodded and pulled her bags from the hack.

Maggie stepped past Mrs. Harris, who seemed put out that Maggie didn't stop to talk with her, but she was too worn out. It had been a long, difficult trip. All she wanted was that bath she'd mentioned and to curl up in her bed. She didn't even want to work on her stories until after she sulked a little. Tomorrow being Sunday, she'd work all day on her Deadwood article and hand it to A.E. on Monday. She was anxious to tell him all about the other people she'd written about in her travels, too, hoping he'd be as excited to run their stories as she was to write them.

She took the stairs slowly, barely able to lift her feet, as though a hundred pound weight was lodged on her back. At the top of the stairs she went into her room, the hack driver lugging all three bags up behind her. He dropped them inside her door, tipped his hat and hurried away. Maggie didn't even say 'thank you' when she closed the door behind him.

Maggie looked around the room, both glad and sad to be back, and noticed an envelope on her pillow. Running her fingers over the paper, she knew it was from Luke. Tears formed in her eyes. *Had she thrown Luke away the same way she had George? Was she too selfish to love any man? Ever?*

Plopping down on the bed she opened the envelope, careful not to tear it.

My Dearest Maggie,

By now you've learned I'm gone. Please believe I didn't leave to hurt you, but to save myself the pain of knowing you will always love another. I tried my best to win you, but you've already given your heart and, it appears that once given, it is forever out of reach to anyone else. I hope someday you find George and he discovers just how lucky he is—for your sake.

It was time for me to move on and I've taken a position managing the Long Branch Saloon in Dodge City, Kansas. It's what I wanted to do, what I needed to do, to stop the ache in my heart.

I was so worried for you when you left for Deadwood and by now you understand that great fear; that is if you survived the trip to receive this letter. I even let A.E. know just how foolish I thought he was for allowing you to go, no matter you begged him. He sputtered and spat and in the end, defended his decision to send you. You are a strong woman, Maggie Douglas, as headstrong as any woman I've ever met. You do as you feel you must, so I am compelled to do as I must to save myself further pain.

You will always be my friend and I will think more than kindly of you the rest of my life. Perhaps we will meet again someday in my travels. I pray you find the happiness you seek and I pray, some day, I find mine. However, if your feelings toward me have changed during your journey, you know where to find me—but not for long, so tarry not.

With love, admiration, and friendship,
Yours,
Luke

Fat tears slipped down Maggie's face and onto the letter, the wetness spreading like the sadness filling her heart. She crushed the letter to her chest and cried out loud, wishing things could be different. Wishing Luke weren't right in all he'd said. She'd given her heart to one man then thrown him away. *Did she regret it? Of course she did, but did it change what had happened? If given the same circumstances, wouldn't she do the same thing again? Hadn't she done exactly that with Luke? She'd been given a second chance and thrown it away, just like she had George. Would she survive this blow? Yes. She was a survivor and, although she hurt today, she would feel better tomorrow and the next day and the next. She would make it through this disappointment and any more that came along because* that's *what Maggie Douglas did.* She raised her chin and wiped her eyes. It was time to get on with it. She had things to do.

The temperature was cooling down and Maggie wrapped a heavy shawl around her shoulders as she left the boarding house following a huge breakfast with the other lady boarders. She hadn't spoken more than five words with any of them since coming to the house, but this morning they fired question after question at her about her trip. Maggie surmised the three widow women, Mrs. Clark, Mrs. Hampton, and Mrs. Wentworth, were all waiting for their next husband to come along, biding their time at Mrs. Harris'. Maggie managed a cheerful smile and answered all their questions before she was able to pry herself away with the excuse she had to get to the *Sun*.

Once again in her sensible skirt, blouse and boots, Maggie pushed out of the boarding house door. There was excitement back in her step. She'd cried herself out about Luke. *There was nothing she could do. Nothing she wanted to do. Luke was a friend—a friend who had chosen to leave. She'd cried and berated herself as a fool for throwing two good men away. How many women got the chance to have one good man in their life, let alone two? Luke was a gambler,* she'd reminded herself. *Was that the kind of life she wanted? Following him from town to town in smoky gambling halls with dangerous men and loose women? No,* and the more she reminded herself of that fact, the more she came to terms with and accepted his departure and her feelings of betrayal.

The skirt swirled around her ankles and it took her a while for her to feel comfortable in it again. She'd grown to love the non-restrictive denims she'd worn throughout her trip to and from Deadwood, but knew they weren't acceptable for a woman in Cheyenne.

Maggie had numerous errands before she went to the *Sun*, the first stop the telegraph office.

A bell jingled as she pushed through the door. "Hello, Miss Douglas. How can I help you today?"

"I'd like to send a telegram, please."

"Yes, Miss Douglas." The clerk nodded, having sent several previous telegrams for Maggie. He grabbed a pencil and paper and readied himself to take down her message.

"This will go to Mr. Stuart Douglas at the Lazy D Ranch near Kansas City."

"The man scribbled then looked up, ready for the rest of her message.

Maggie pursed her lips, unsure exactly what she wanted to say.

"Miss Douglas?"

She shook her head. All she wanted was to let her father know she was all right. She'd been wiring him twice a month since her arrival and didn't want him to wonder why she hadn't contacted him for so long and have him show up in Cheyenne looking for her.

Pa,

I've just returned from Deadwood to report on the horrific fire that struck there. I waited until my return to inform you so you wouldn't try to stop me from going. It was exciting and my story will run in the Cheyenne Sun *this week. I will forward copies. All is well. I'll be in touch soon.*

Love, Maggie

Maggie also placed her monthly advertisements.

A.E. was waiting for her when she arrived at the *Sun.* "You're back!" He hurried to meet her when she came in the door. "I'm anxious for that story, Miss Douglas. Hand it over," he said with a grin and an outstretched hand.

She pulled her papers from a folder and handed it to him, but before she let go added, "I came away with more than just one story about the fire, A.E. I got a bunch of human interest stories like you asked me to get. I haven't finished them all yet, but I'll have one every day for more than a week if you want them."

"You give them to me and I'll read them. If they're half as good as your other articles, you can bet they'll run." He slapped the paper Maggie was still holding and she let go, speechless at the confidence he'd shown in her work.

Staring down at the copy and without looking up, he shoved open the gate. The door slapped shut behind him, and he sat down at his desk. Maggie held her breath and went to her own desk to wait. Mr. Burns' was nowhere to be seen so she assumed he was off on a story somewhere.

She watched A.E. read her copy, recalling every word she'd written over and over again until she got it right:

FROM THE ASHES OF DESTRUCTION
Like a Phoenix, Deadwood Rises!

Where the largest, richest town in the Dakota Territory once stood, where common people reached for their dreams, prospectors went in search of the elusive yellow metal called gold, and hope blossomed for both, now stands the charred remains of what was Deadwood. In one of the most horrific fires ever in the Territory, the rolling wall of destruction left in its wake only blackened symbols of what used to be the town's major business district and nearly 300 homes.

The fire, which started at Mrs. Ellsner's Empire bakery on Sherman Street, became a rolling inferno once the powder in a nearby hardware store ignited. The fire was described by survivors as a "monster" that pulsed with life as it worked its way along Sherman Street. In a race against time residents ran for the hills to the east of Sherman Street with little more than the clothes on their backs, clutching their children, while embers from the roaring fire rained down upon them like a summer shower bringing destruction instead of refreshment.

Finished with Sherman Street the fire ate its way across the Lee Creek Bridge and took less than 30 minutes to spread its fingers onto Main Street, destroying many of the town's most important businesses. Although Deadwood boasted a fire department, it was one of the first victims of the flames. The hook and ladder apparatus and hose carriage were both destroyed, leaving behind only a few worthless feet of hose to assist in dousing the flames—if water could have been reached.

After the fire had spent its wrath, Deadwood's displaced telegraph operator set up a temporary station on a bluff a mile and a half from town with only a barrel head for a desk. Contacting General Sturgis at Fort Meade some twenty miles away, troops quickly arrived to assist the destitute with food and housing and to keep those with thieving on their minds from robbery and lot-jumping. The soldiers came with ten wagons and two ambulances to transport those who would go to Fort Meade for shelter in the Fort's graciously opened barracks. All saloons in Deadwood have been closed until such time as normalcy is re-established and a Citizens Normalcy Committee appointed to help toward that endeavor.

However, amidst Deadwood's devastation something miraculous grows. Like the mythological Phoenix that rises from the ashes of its destruction, wings spread and ready for flight, Deadwood, too, is rising. Lots were cleared of debris as soon as the cinders cooled. Wood, brick and stone are being hauled in from neighboring towns. The pounding and sweating has begun *with the building of brick foundations for a new and improved Deadwood that rises to replace the tent city currently housing the displaced.*

Smudged faces greet visitors bold enough to enter this burnt-out town, but in those dirty faces is the determination of a people with a mission, that mission to rebuild their town stronger and better than before. Described to be "half-crazed" as they scrambled into the hills to save themselves, these courageous people quickly pulled up their boot straps and did what was necessary to begin rebuilding.

Help has been extended by various merchants from back East and St. Paul, Minnesota, with mining and commercial ties to Deadwood; however, most residents merely said "thank you," and choose to rebuild on their own, alongside their neighbors with only their mettle and determination. Local businesses not destroyed help where possible and bank vaults, the contents of which somehow survived the sweeping flames, have been thrown open to advance money with little or no interest to residents in need of assistance.

The citizens of Deadwood are a determined people. I am proud to have met them and had the privilege of living amongst them for but a few days. It is this reporter's opinion that Deadwood, like the mythological Phoenix, shall rise from the ashes bigger and better than before.

The story concluded with the dry information of what businesses had been lost, who had insurance coverage and who didn't before she closed the piece. Maggie watched A.E. read it once, then again. *Did he like it? Enough to run it? Had it been a wasted trip? Would he ever send her on another story as important as this one?* Her mind was tumbling when he stood up, strode back through the gate, and stopped in front of her desk.

Maggie stood up, heart pounding. She sucked in a huge breath. "Well?"

He shook his head and Maggie's heart fell. *He hated it!*

"I never would have believed it."

"What, sir?"

"That a woman could write such a fantastic story!" His voice rose with each word and he was smiling and hopping with excitement by the time his sentence was finished. "This is wonderful, Miss Douglas. Wonderful! It'll run on tomorrow's front page." He sucked in a deep breath. "Congratulations!"

"Thank you, A.E. I'm so happy you like it." She tried not to gush, but it was hard. It'd been the only thing on her mind for two weeks.

"What about these other stories you mentioned."

Maggie smiled from ear to ear. She was as partial to those tales as she was the fire story. "I wrote about the people I traveled with, A.E. About the two old soldiers who became my protectors, the three brothers who turned out to have a vendetta against Daniel Boone May, the owner of Robbers Roost Station and a U.S. Marshall. About the Soiled Doves who ply their wares along the trail."

She took a breath, ready to continue, but A.E. stopped her with a raised hand. "That's more than enough. Write them. After reading this, I don't even want to see them until they're ready to run. There'll be a new story every day until you run out. Deal?" He offered his hand.

Maggie grabbed his hand. "Deal!" She couldn't contain herself. Although she'd agreed not to anymore, she threw herself into A.E.'s arms. He laughed right along with her, both knowing they had something special in the tales that would follow about the people who survived the trip to Deadwood and all that went with it.

Chapter Twenty

Maggie,
Thank God you're safe! And you're damn right if you'd even hinted what you had in mind I'd have hopped the first train out there to stop you—or had the sheriff put you in jail to keep you from such foolishness!

Maggie crumpled the telegram in her fist. *What did it take to make him proud of her? If it had been James or Edward that had done what she did, her father would have been riding around the county shouting what a great accomplishment his sons had made, but when it was his daughter, all she got were stern words.* She un-crumpled the paper and smoothed it on her lap, her heart like a stone in her chest.

Although what you did was foolhardy, it was brave, Maggs, and I'm damn proud of you, as are James and Edward. They went to town so they could tell anybody and everybody that would listen how their little sister rode the stage to and from Deadwood and faced Indians and robbers to report on the big fire there. From their excitement, you'd think you had become the first woman president. But it was close in our estimation, Maggs. I'll admit, I mentioned it to a few folks myself. We're damn proud of you, damn proud, but don't go off and do something like that again, leastwise not until my heart settles from your last adventure!
Pa

Maggie crunched the telegram in her hand again. If she hadn't already been sitting on her bed, she would have fallen down. *Her father and brothers* were *proud of her!* He hadn't even alluded to it, he actually *told* her.

She laid down, the missive clutched close to her heart. They were proud; her father and brothers were proud! She fell asleep with a smile on her face, her last thought that if she did nothing else in her life, she'd made her family proud and *that* was an accomplishment in itself.

A month had passed since Maggie's return from Deadwood and the article on the fire ran on the front page of the *Cheyenne*

Sun. Since then she'd been inundated with congratulations on what a great story she'd written, and told more than once how surprised everyone was, knowing of course, the underlying statement was that they were surprised a *woman* had done such a good job.

She'd dazzled them a second time and a third and fourth, with her tales of the journey itself and the people she'd met. Each day for more than a week Cheyenne's citizen's eyes were glued to the *Sun* as they read about Sam Whitmore and Tom Hanson, Mother "Featherlegs" Shepherd and her girls, Ida James, George Lathrop and John Noonan, and three brothers with revenge on their minds. She'd regaled her readers with stories of Indians and bad weather, of fear and courage, of friendship and determination.

Even Mr. Burns admitted they were some of the best pieces he'd ever read and confided he was envious, wishing he'd been the one to write them.

Maggie was adjusting to life without Luke. She spent every day at the paper then went back to the boarding house where she had a cup of tea and visited in the parlor with the other ladies for a few minutes before heading to her room, exhausted and happy to find her bed, asleep before nine o'clock. She hated to admit she was lonely, but she was. She missed Luke's friendship and guidance and the more she missed Luke, the more she missed George. She was close to accepting she'd never find him. It had been almost six months of continued advertisements in almost half a dozen papers. *If he hadn't responded by now...* It was as Luke had said, George was in the wind. Maggie knew she should give up, but her heart just wouldn't let her, if for no other reason than to tell him how sorry she was for throwing him away, for throwing *them* away.

She wrote and rewrote wires to Luke apologizing, but every time she finished it was rolled up in a ball and tossed away.

The pages of the calendar flipped toward a new year and Maggie tried to immerse herself in her work, but the stories didn't excite her like the fire or her journey had. She was always on the lookout for something bigger. Cheyenne was quiet these days and Deadwood was rebuilding. Nothing inspired or challenged Maggie and she realized she was bored as much as she was lonely.

It was New Year's Day 1880 and A.E. had asked Maggie if she wouldn't mind coming in to write a piece about Cheyenne's past. She'd spent a quiet New Year's Eve in the privacy of her room, reading and, since she had nothing else to do today, here she was. She presumed Mr. Burns had nothing to do, either, since he was already at the *Sun* when she arrived.

Maggie had been scouring the *Sun's* archives all morning looking for old stories to include in her article about Cheyenne's past. There were pieces on the discovery of gold in the Black Hills, tales about Wild Bill Hickok and Calamity Jane, Indian attacks on the very stations she'd visited on her way to and from Deadwood, the building of the Elephant Corral, and the emergence of Cheyenne from its Hell-on-Wheels days to its growing sophistication. She even found a story on Phatty Thompson and his trip to Deadwood with his wagonload of cats and Charley Utter's arrival from Denver with *his* wagonload of prostitutes.

There was one article that caught Maggie's eye. Something she'd never seen or heard before. It was about two men, gunfighters involved in a classic gunfight back in 1877. Although it happened only three years ago, it seemed to Maggie as though it must have taken place in another town. Cheyenne had changed much in those few years since then, with little of those wild and wooly days remaining.

She settled in and read:

Cheyenne Sun, March 10, 1877

"Yesterday, March 9, 1877, Jim Levy, a noted gunfighter in the Territory, was involved in a shootout with C.H. "Charlie" Harrison, another well-known pistolier and gambler in the Territory. Following a disagreement that began at Shingle and Locke's Saloon*, possibly stemming from remarks Mr. Harrison made about Mr. Levy's Irish/Jewish heritage, the men took their argument outside. The two men wound up facing off in a duel in front of* Frenchy's *on Eddy Street. Although Mr. Harrison was an accomplished marksman, he fired first, yet wildly in his*

excitement, and missed Mr. Levy. It being Mr. Levy's turn to shoot, and with plenty of time to site his quarry, Mr. Levy did just that, taking his time before he raised his gun and shot Mr. Harrison, striking and injuring him. Although injured, Mr. Harrison managed to walk to Dyer's Hotel where he was checked out by a doctor, given a positive prognosis, and where he remains today."

Maggie lifted the March 10th copy and noticed another article behind it:

Cheyenne Sun, March 23, 1877

"Following the shoot out on March 9th between Jim Levy and Charlie Harrison that began at Shingle & Locke's *and ended outside* Frenchy's *on Eddy Street, it has been learned that Mr. Harrison, who fled to* Dyers Hotel *after the confrontation, has succumbed to wounds sustained in that shoot out and has died..."*

Maggie glanced up, the article forgotten when she spotted Mr. Burns. He'd been working at his desk for over an hour, but now sat cradling his face in his hands, staring down at the paper as though he had no idea what to do with it. Maggie got up and walked to the front of his desk, laid her palms on top, and looked down at what he'd been working on. There was nothing on the page—not a single word.

"Harvey, what's the matter?"

Burns' head snapped up, a glazed look in his protruding eyes. "What? What did you say?"

Maggie cocked her head. "What's wrong with you? You've been sitting there for over an hour and haven't written a word."

"Oh, yes, I..." He put his head back in his hands and stared down at the blank paper, as though Maggie hadn't spoken.

"Harvey, what *is* it?" Maggie stepped to her co-worker's side and laid her hand on his shoulder. He jumped up like he'd been hit with the rock from David's slingshot. His chair skittered away from the desk, his eyes were wild, and his chest rose and fell like he'd just run a race.

Maggie raised her hands in the air where he could see them. "Harvey, it's all right. It's me, Maggie. What is wrong with you? You're as jumpy as a jackrabbit in a nest of vipers."

The man swallowed and wiped his mouth and forehead with a handkerchief he pulled from his pants pocket. He slid his chair back behind the desk and plopped down into it. When he looked up, the pain in his eyes made Maggie want to weep.

"What is it? What's has you so upset?"

"It's not what's happening now, Maggie. It's what happened eighteen years ago today."

Maggie did a quick calculation in her head. "January 1st, 1862? During the war?"

Harvey nodded, drew a ragged breath, and sniffed. "That's the day they burned Dayton."

"Who burned Dayton?"

"That damned Jayhawker Lt. Colonel Anthony and his damned Seventh Kansas Cavalry, that's who." His eyes were pinched and his voice was hard, as though the mere voicing of the man's name caused real, physical pain.

Maggie recalled hearing her father and brothers discussing just such an issue years after the war was over. They'd talked about how the Jayhawkers crossed the border, before *and* during the war, causing all kinds of damage to Missouri's people and property. Her brothers, having been too young to fully understand, had argued that it was wartime and that the Jayhawkers fought for the preservation of the Union. Her father, although having fought for the Union, argued they'd been of no better ilk than Missouri's Bushwhackers and had, in fact, perpetuated the formation of Quantrill and his men in retaliation for the Jayhawker raids that left behind decimated fields, burnt homes, dead men and displaced and destitute families all along the Missouri border.

"Would you like to talk about it?" Maggie asked, hoping to help her colleague in any way she could, even if it meant just listening.

His lips flattened into a straight line and he breathed deeply through his nose before he said, "Don't know. I haven't spoken of it to anyone for years."

"Maybe it'll help."

"Maybe." He sat quietly, his lips working, his fists rolling. Finally he looked up. "Maybe I will. Told you I would someday, guess today is as good a day as any."

Maggie stepped to her desk, grabbed her chair and pulled it up beside Mr. Burns. She sat down and waited, her hands curled together on her lap.

"It was the first day of the New Year of eighteen hundred and sixty two," he began, his voice tight. "I wasn't in town that day, else wise I'd be dead." He spoke the words matter-of-factly.

Maggie leaned forward and laid her hand over Harvey's fisted one. "Go on."

"I didn't read about what happened until days later in the *Kansas City Times*." He paused, his eyes searching the ceiling before he continued. "I hurried home, but there was nothing to hurry home to. Nothing left but one house, and we all knew why that house still stood. He was a Union man.

"The story is that Colonel Anthony, hold up at Camp Johnson near Morristown outside Harrisonville and about 25 miles north of Dayton, was alerted that a contingent of Rebels were in Dayton recruiting and burning out Union supporters. He and his troops headed straight away to engage the Rebels, but by the time Anthony and his men got there his quarry was long gone."

Maggie sucked in a breath and waited.

"Anthony's men weren't to be denied. They took revenge on the folks in town, taking what they wanted, burning their homes to the ground, leaving the women and children to face the bitter cold with no shelter. There were only three men in the whole town that day, and every one died that morning. One man, mistaken for a Confederate captain who had the misfortune of having the same last name, was killed fleeing his home. The other two were taken from their homes and shot and every house, except the one, was set to the torch. My family home was among those destroyed. My mother and sister were put out into the cold with nothing but what they were wearing and what little the soldiers so kindly allowed them to carry out."

He looked up, his eyes red-rimmed and haunted. "Both caught pneumonia and died. I thank God I was with them when they passed." His head lowered and his voice grew hard again. "As refugees in a corner of my aunt's home in Austin."

Maggie felt as though her heart stopped beating. Her body ached with sorrow at what he had suffered. It had been eighteen years since that day, but to Harvey Burns, it was might as well have been yesterday, as it was to many who had fought. Whether they'd sided with the North or South, Maggie realized it could very well take generations before memories of the struggle were forgotten, transgressions forgiven, and the war was really over.

Maggie decided it was time to cheer Mr. Burns up and put work aside for a little while. She jumped up and grabbed his hand. "Come on, Mr. Burns, it's a new year and we're going to put our sour moods aside and celebrate with some lunch. We've both been cooped up in this office for too long and need a break."

"I don't know, Miss Douglas. I'm supposed to finish this piece."

"Well it doesn't look to me like you've made much progress." She smiled and tapped the blank paper. "I won't take no for an answer." She tugged at his hand when he continued to protest. "Mr. Burns, I insist. My treat," she added as extra incentive, knowing Mr. Burns was a bit of a tightwad.

His chin came up and a slight smile crossed his lips. "Well, if you insist, I imagine I could use some distraction to dispel this black mood I find myself in."

"Good! Shall we then?"

Burns offered his elbow and the two left the *Sun*, hoping to rid themselves of the black moods that had descended upon them.

A few months later the bell jingled above the door of the *Sun*. Maggie sighed, absorbed in her article, not wanting to be disturbed. She looked up and her breath caught.

"Sam! Tom!" She jumped up and ran to the two men, barely recognizing them in their fancy clothes and almost clean-shaven faces. "You're back! You're safe! Oh, I'm so happy to see you!" She was rambling and she knew it, but she was so excited to see them she couldn't contain herself.

After the hugging was over, she whirled around and led them to the gate. "A.E.! This is Sam Whitmore and Tom Hanson, the two men I wrote about on my trip to Deadwood."

A.E. came through the gate, hand extended. The three men shook warmly. "Welcome, gentlemen. Maggie has spoken very highly of you two."

"She did, did she?" Sam's eyes sparkled with humor.

A.E. leaned forward. "Indeed she has." He pumped their hands again and added, "I would personally like to thank you for taking such good care of our Maggie on your trip." He stepped toward the gate. "I'll leave you three to get reacquainted. Good to meet you two." As quickly as he'd arrived, A.E. was back at his table, setting type for the next day's edition of the paper.

Maggie turned to Mr. Burns, sitting at his desk awaiting introduction. "Mr. Harvey Burns, these are the two men I wrote the articles about, Mr. Sam Whitmore and Mr. Tom Hanson."

Burns stood and shook their hands. "And a good job she did, too. I'm very pleased to meet you and would like to thank you again for taking care of our Maggie while she was on the trail."

Maggie grinned, she'd never heard herself referred to as "our Maggie" before and it warmed her. Sam was beaming and Tom was grinning, too.

"So you did write them articles you interviewed us about," Sam said.

"I did, and they were very well received. I'll get you each a copy before you go. People have been asking me questions about you and Tom since they ran. You've become quite the celebrities in Cheyenne," she added with a sparkle in her eyes.

Sam snorted and Tom looked away, silent as usual.

Mr. Burns excused himself and went back to his desk so the three could continue their visit.

"So, you *look* like you found gold. Did you?" Maggie asked under her breath.

Both men nodded, grinning from ear to ear. "We did, Missy. We did. Found enough to make us rich men." Sam leaned over and whispered, "But don't tell anyone, I'd hate to be relieved of my wealth before I get home to help my little girl or Tom can track down that woman he's so anxious to marry."

Tom shoved his friend's shoulder. "Hush up, Sam."

Maggie clapped her hands like a little girl she was so delighted they'd found what they were looking for. "And your daughter? She knows you're safe and coming home?"

Sam nodded. "That she does. An' jest in time, too. We've only got one more week afore they put her an' her children out on the streets. Which means we're only here for the night. We'll be a headin' out tomorrow mornin'.""

Maggie was sad they couldn't spend more time, but happy they'd stopped to let her know they were alive, found what they'd gone looking for, and were on their way home.

"Where are you staying?"

"Well, we decided on the Inter-Ocean, since you spoke so nice about it an' all," Sam said.

"Wonderful. Why don't I meet you there in, say, two hours? I'll be through here by then and that'll give you boys time to check out the faro tables and paint your tonsils with a few drinks before I get there."

Both men blushed. "Sounds like a fine plan, Missy. A fine plan," Sam said.

"Very well, you boys head on over to the Inter-Ocean and I'll meet you there in two hours. We can have dinner and you can tell me all about your adventures."

Sam stroked his closely cropped beard, as though yearning for the rest of it that was no longer there. "We'll be a seein' you then."

After more hugs, the two men left the *Sun* and Maggie hurried to finish her work, anxious to meet her friends and catch up on the four months since their departure in Deadwood.

Dinner was joyous! The three friends talked and reminisced deep into the night before Sam and Tom excused themselves to get some sleep before the train left in the morning. Reluctantly they departed, Maggie feeling as lost and alone as she had on her return from Deadwood and finding Luke gone. Sam and Tom's arrival and quick departure made her realize just how lonely she was, how fruitless her search for George had been, and that there was really nothing that kept her in Cheyenne any longer. Not even her job. She'd succeeded in busting into a man's domain by becoming a reporter—and had done it well. Although well-respected around town, she had no real friends; no one to confide in like she had Ida on her return from Deadwood. She wanted something more in her life, something that mattered. She wanted George and the pain of realizing she would never find him drove a wedge into her heart that made it hard to breathe.

Saying goodbye to Sam and Tom for the last time made her realize that, regardless of all she'd accomplished so far in her life, she was still alone. That night she made a decision that would change her life—again—forever.

Chapter Twenty-One

Maggie let the tall, gangly man twirl her around the dance floor. She was bored with her life *again*. Leaving Cheyenne in 1880, Maggie had stopped in Dodge City, Kansas, to find Luke and make amends, but by the time she arrived, he was already gone, headed down the road toward his next adventure. After a six month stopover at the ranch to decide what to do next, feeling lost and unappreciated, Maggie rejoined the women's movement, causing another rift between her and her family who wanted her to stay at the ranch. The movement was gaining momentum. People were beginning to listen, and the place to be for such happenings was Washington, D.C. She put her fears aside, pulled out the fancy dresses she'd shoved in a trunk after her horse mishap in Cheyenne, re-packed them, said goodbye to her family this time, and off she went to begin the next chapter in her life.

Washington society was exciting. For a time Maggie was happy to be in the middle of it, but amidst all the commotion she was still alone. Regardless she was constantly busy, she still went to bed at night alone and lonely. Women surrounded her after each rally asking question after question about her life, where she'd been and what she'd seen. Men fawned over her, but the only things that came to her mind whenever she thought of any kind of relationship were Thornton's betrayal, Luke's desertion, and her inability to find George.

Maggie was feeling more-than sorry for herself, wishing the evening would hurry to a conclusion, when the music stopped. Tonight was just another in a string of fundraisers for the cause. She danced with men she didn't care about, smiled when she wanted to cry, and socialized when she wanted to be alone in her misery. *How could she have so much and be so miserable?* Her dance partner, who was so unimportant she couldn't even remember his name, offered his elbow and guided her from the dance floor. She felt unappreciated, unloved and useless. *What the hell is wrong with you?* she chastised, walking from the dance floor, her back rigid, wanting only to escape her escort's fawning hands and inane questions.

Standing at the refreshment table, something crawled up her spine and lodged at the base of her neck. She stiffened. Someone was watching her. Slowly Maggie turned and searched the room table by table. She thought her knees would buckle when she spotted him across the room staring a hole right through her!

She put her drink on the table, excused herself from her dance partner and hurried toward him. Her heart was hammering and every step felt like she was wading through the mud she'd fought so long ago on her trip to Deadwood. George! She'd found him! Somehow, after all these years of searching, he was here, right in front of her! Tears shimmered in her eyes, but she held them back. It wouldn't do to cry in front of him.

"George!" she cried, grabbing his hands in hers. "I can't believe it's you. What are you doing here?"

He was smiling, but in a moment his face become a mask of the hurt and anger she knew he must feel toward her. "Business," was his curt response. "I might ask you the same thing."

Maggie heard the recrimination in his voice, the challenge. Her smile faded and she rose to the challenge. "What are you doing here?" she asked again.

"Not looking for you, if that's what you think."

She took a quick breath, but regained herself just as fast. *If only he knew...* A slow smile crept across her face. "Did I indicate that you were?" Her eyebrows rose with the challenging question.

"No," George snapped. "And I'm not. I'm here on business with my brother."

She turned to the handsome man beside him, recalling George's stories of how they'd grown up together and how Blue had saved him at the Battle of the Little Bighorn. "Blue, right?"

Blue raised his glass and nodded then turned questioning eyes to George.

"And this must be Amy, correct?" Maggie smiled and nodded at George's sister-in-law.

Amy nodded back, a wry smile on her face.

"There now, all the introductions are done. We can enjoy ourselves," Maggie'd waited too long for this reconciliation and she wasn't about to let George slip away. She grabbed him by the hands and pulled him out of his seat.

The music had started again. "A waltz. I love the waltz. Dance with me." Maggie didn't care what dance it was, she just wanted to be close to George. In his arms, to smell him, feel him, and revel in the fact she'd found him! That he was flesh-and-blood and not a figment of her imagination.

He followed her to the floor, but once there he pushed her away and just stared at her. What she saw in his eyes made guilt wash over her like a sluicing wave. There was anger, joy, fear, and pain, so much pain. She felt it as easily as if he'd put it to words.

"Was it worth it, Maggs? Was leaving me and your family worth this?" His hand encompassed the lavish hall and she realized he believed she'd been in Washington all this time, wearing fancy dresses and elbowing with the rich who could help the cause. He had no idea where she'd been and what she'd endured since their separation, didn't know the pain, suffering, and searching she'd done in those years just trying to find him.

She laid a finger across his lips. Maggie didn't want to talk about it right now. Any of it. All she wanted was to be with him and enjoy whatever time he allowed her. A tear formed in the corner of her eye before she could swipe it away at the thought of losing him again. At the thought he would send *her* away this time.

"Please, no questions. I just want to enjoy being with you again. Hold me, George. Please hold me, just like you used to." She laid her face against his. Electricity tore through her, and from the way George reacted, she knew he felt it, too.

In that moment, Maggie Douglas, reporter, women's suffragist, cowgirl, and woman of the world knew without a doubt she couldn't let George Hawkins go again and that she'd do whatever it took to keep him.

George reached across the settee and touched Maggie's entwined hands. Other patrons of the hotel gawked at their closeness, but Maggie ignored them because they didn't matter. George did. She was nervous as a cat. All she wanted was to tell him how sorry she was and how much she still loved him—had always loved him. Tell him she was a fool, but that she'd had to do what she did in order to be satisfied with her life with the hope that someday they'd find each other again and make a life together.

Last night he'd tried to walk away. He'd turned his back on her, told her she'd hurt him too badly for him to let her do it again. She'd begged him to give her a chance to explain, and after commenting on how he'd never seen Maggie beg, he'd agreed to meet her this morning in the lobby of her hotel. She spent a restless night, hoping and praying he'd be there when she went downstairs and had nearly tripped and fallen when he was right where he said he'd be.

"All right, Maggs. I didn't press you last night. But I'm *damn* tired of waiting for an explanation—if you really intend to give me one." George's voice was hard and Maggie didn't blame him. She'd thrown their love away like yesterday's garbage and he wanted to know if it had been worth it.

"Oh, George, I never meant to hurt you."

"You damn well did." His eyes snapped with anger.

She lowered her head and looked down at her lap. "I know. And I'm truly sorry."

"Was it worth it?" He'd asked her that question last night, but she'd skirted answering it, not wanting to explain anything she'd done in a room full of people. She wanted him alone with his full attention on her. He wanted that answer now. He raised her chin with his fingertips so she could look into his eyes. "Was it?"

She took a deep breath and squeezed her hands in her lap. She licked her lips then took another breath. She had to make him understand that at the time it was the right choice. Had she not done what she did, they might well be together, but unhappy, her longing to do things she'd never done and resenting George for keeping her from doing them.

"In many ways, yes, it was worth it. I've grown up since I left the ranch. Times haven't always been easy. I've learned to survive on my own. A woman trying to make it alone is not an easy task." She turned tear-filled eyes to George. "But I've accomplished much that I'm damn proud of." She sighed, unlaced and re-laced her fingers. "There were so many things I wanted to do, George—with Mrs. Anthony, for the Indians, for the women of our country. All Edward, James and Father did from the time I was old enough to marry, was badger me *to* marry, but wouldn't accept anyone I chose—least of all you, George."

His face hardened with the lie. Alone last night in her hotel room, Maggie had decided not to tell George the joke was on both of them. That her family had, in fact, accepted George and was rooting for him to sweep her off her feet and marry her. She felt the blow to his pride might push him away again, so she decided to tell him what she'd told him before. That they did not, and would not, ever accept him as a viable suitor in her life.

"Me! You said you never spoke about us to them," he said a bit too loudly, drawing more hard stares from other hotel patrons.

She couldn't look him in the eyes when she lied, "Father isn't a stupid man and neither are my brothers. They had an idea something was going on. They confronted me one evening when you were still riding fence. I lied and told them there was nothing between us, but I could see in their faces they didn't believe me. And again, as they have in the past, they reminded me of everything wrong with you and why they would never accept you."

George heaved a sigh. "I had no idea."

Maggie felt terrible at the deception, but now that she'd started, she couldn't stop. "It wasn't that they didn't like you, George. They liked you too well. They were determined I'd marry someone proper who could take care of me and give me the kind of life I'd grown up with. You weren't that man."

His face showed the betrayal he felt and she touched his shoulder. "I'm sorry. So sorry. I couldn't tell you, even though you were so insistent that we tell them about us. I didn't want to hurt you. And I knew their rejection would hurt you badly." She paused to gather her thoughts, and decided to tell him exactly how she felt. "I loved you, George, I truly did, and I would have fought to be with you against my family *if* I hadn't had things to do on my own, just like you did." She looked deep into his eyes. "And did you do them?"

George smiled. "I've managed to accomplish a few things. Not been so successful in others." He cocked his head as though to remember those things, while absorbing all Maggie had just said.

"Tell me," she whispered. She wanted to know it all. Every little detail that had happened in his life in the years they'd been apart. "Tell me everything."

They left the hotel, walked and talked for hours, and as the day progressed, George's emotions melted against Maggie and the years fell away like water through a sieve.

"I became a teamster, Maggs, bringing annuities to the Indians."

Maggie squealed with delight, happy he'd done what he set out to do. "So you did help the Indians?"

"As much as I could. Came up against a corrupt system that made it hard to get worthwhile goods to the Indians without it being stolen and replaced with inferior goods I wouldn't give to a dog."

His voice had grown hard and Maggie knew the passion he felt; the same kind of passion she'd felt when writing about the fire and the people on her journey to Deadwood.

"I saw Red Cloud at Fort Robinson." He stopped and a shadow crept over his face.

Maggie squeezed his hand. "Go on." They were sitting across from each other at a table in the hotel restaurant, their empty dinner plates still in front of them.

"I was at Fort Robinson when Dull Knife's people were brought in after they fled their reservation down south. And why did they flee that reservation?" he asked, not waiting for an answer. "Because the conditions there were terrible." He paused a moment before he continued. "They wanted something better for their people, but in their trek north they were intercepted by soldiers and taken to Fort Robinson. What happened there was unconscionable."

Maggie had read an accounting in the *Sun* of what happened after Dull Knife's people had surrendered at Fort Robinson then had tried to escape when they refused to return to their reservation in the south as they'd been ordered.

In an effort to force them into submission, they were locked inside the cramped barracks they'd been housed in, built to hold 75 men and much too small for the 150 people forced to live there. The doors were chained and they were guarded twenty-four hours a day. Rations were cut, and they were given no wood for the stove to keep out the bitter January temperatures.

Somehow they'd managed to conceal a few guns before their imprisonment and on the night of January 9, 1879, they used those guns to escape. They were chased down, the braves killed trying to protect their families as they fled, and many of the women and children succumbed to the bitter cold before they were far enough from the fort to be free. Few survived and those that did were brought back to Robinson and imprisoned again. It was a horrible story and Maggie felt a stabbing in her heart, knowing George had been there and somehow felt responsible for not being able to stop it.

Maggie realized then she hadn't been able to find George because he hadn't been near Deadwood or anywhere she'd placed her advertisements. She almost heaved a sigh of relief knowing he hadn't chosen to ignore her. He'd never *seen* any of her ads.

Trying to shake the sadness that had washed over him in his telling of what happened at Fort Robinson, she told him how she'd gone to Boston and worked with Miss Susan B. Anthony and Miss Lucy Stone. As though talking about someone else's life, she recalled the adventures she'd had between Boston and Washington, including her trip to Cheyenne and Deadwood, how she'd learned and matured. For the first time in a long time Maggie didn't feel alone. She felt alive and looked forward to tomorrow. She'd found her love. Now she would do whatever it took to keep him.

They spent the next few weeks forgetting the world around them. Every day was spent catching up on each other's lives.

"I've been extremely busy since I arrived in Washington," she declared during lunch in Ferguson's Restaurant, situated within eyesight of the famous Ford's Theater where President Lincoln was killed.

George crunched on a piece of fried chicken. "Tell me about Mrs. Anthony and what she and you have been doing to stir up all the ladies of our great nation." George's eyes were gleaming and Maggie wasn't sure if he was baiting her or truly interested in what she'd been doing for the cause. She chose to believe he was interested.

"Well, Mrs. Anthony has been tireless in trying to get women the vote."

"I remember she was already doing *that* from my lessons before you left," George reminded her with a grin.

"Yes, all right." She waved her hand. "She's been very busy since then. She travels the country speaking to the women of our nation, telling them to fight for our right to vote, just like men do."

"Is she making any headway?"

Maggie suspected he was only asking to make her happy, but again, chose to answer as though he were really interested.

"I believe she is. Oh she, and I for that matter, has been run out of many a city on a rail." As soon as the words were out of her mouth she wanted to pull them back, praying he didn't ask more, not ready to divulge her most humiliating moment to him. Someday perhaps she might open herself up and tell him, but not today. Hoping to keep him from asking more, she hurried on. "She does manage to get her point across before she leaves. I've helped her organize many of her rallies. The National Woman's Suffrage Association is growing every day. You should *see* how the refined ladies of this country get all worked up!" By the time Maggie finished she realized that, although she was lonely, she *had* done well in her years with the movement. It *was* making progress and someday women *would* vote the same as men.

"And what about your other causes?" George asked.

"Which ones?"

"The Indians? Your right to drink and smoke like a man?" he teased.

She snorted, thinking about how many times she'd been mistaken for Miss Calamity Jane because of her clothes and her language. "I've grown up a good deal since I left the Lazy D, George. Those causes aren't as important anymore."

"The Indians aren't?"

"Well, I haven't given much thought to them. I've been otherwise occupied since I left, although I did get to see them first hand on my trip to Deadwood. I still believe in their plight, I just haven't done anything about it. What could I do?" she asked.

"Well I've seen what's happening to them first hand and it's a sad sight to see."

"From what you've told me, it sounds terrible."

"It's not all terrible." He paused and looked into Maggie's face. "Actually, I have some very nice memories."

"Such as?"

"I'm no longer just George Hawkins to the Lakota," he said with pride.

Maggie laughed. "Well, who are you then?"

"I'm Wasicun Cantewaste. White Man of Good Heart."

"White Man of Good Heart," she repeated. "Hum? And why is that?"

"Because I've fought more than one battle to make sure the goods I bring the Sioux for their annuities are good and usable. I make sure their flour isn't filled with weevils and the blankets aren't full of holes. I guess they recognized my efforts and, as a way to show their respect, gave me that name."

"I'm impressed." She leaned back against the chair and studied him. "What else?"

"I'm here on their behalf, although I seem to have forgotten that now that I've found you again."

Afraid she'd taken him from a very important task, and not wanting to be the cause of more hardship for the Indians, she leaned forward, serious. "Don't give up your dreams, George. Not for me. Especially not after what I did to you." She cringed after the words were out, afraid he would do just that.

"I don't intend to."

"Well, tell me what you intend to do." Her heart was pounding now, afraid he would tell her he was leaving to finish what he came here to do. Leave her behind, as she'd done to him.

"Blue has made his way into some very important circles here. He's working on getting me an introduction to Hiram Price, the new Indian Commissioner. I want him to appoint me to the Indian Bureau and assign me to a reservation."

"As an Indian Agent? I hear they're all corrupt."

"Which is exactly why I want to be given a post. So I can watch over at least a small portion of the Indian population and make sure they get what they should. Not the garbage the current agents allow them to receive. I'd make damn sure what gets onto my reservation is edible and usable."

She touched his hand, electricity flowing up her arm, again fearful he was telling her he would leave soon. "I'm happy for you."

"I haven't been appointed yet. And if I am, it still doesn't mean I'll be able to make a hill of beans of difference for those people."

"But you'll try. Damn hard, too, I'm sure."

George nodded.

And in that moment Maggie knew her greatest fear could be realized. If George were awarded this appointment, she could lose him again.

"I talked to Commissioner Price." Blue was leaning against the door frame of the kitchen in the small rental home he and Amy were living in during their time in Washington.

George leaned forward in his seat at the table and Maggie waited beside him, anxious to hear what Blue had to say about his meeting with Commissioner Price.

"And?" George asked.

"If you're interested, he'll assign you to the Standing Rock Agency in Dakota Territory as a sub-agent. He's already got an agent in place who has no intention of giving up his position right now."

"That's the best he can do?"

Maggie held her breath. *He'd been offered a post. What would that mean for them?*

"You've got to start somewhere, George. And that's not normally at the top. I was lucky to even get in to see Price. He's very busy and doesn't know me from any other struggling lawyer here in town. He gave me five minutes to state my case and I was lucky enough to get the appointment for you. Take it or leave it."

George turned to Maggie. She nodded and smiled. *This is what he's wanted for so long. She couldn't stand in his way. He had to find his way the same way she had.* "This is what you've wanted, George. What you've been working for. Perhaps not on the grand scale you'd hoped for, but it's a beginning. I think you should take it." Her heart pounded and she prayed she wasn't throwing their relationship away again, only this time being noble!

He looked up at Blue, waiting for his answer. "Can I have 'till tomorrow to think it over?"

"Sure, but I'm not the one chomping at the bit to get an appointment like that. Remember, since the Little Bighorn, I was the one who knew what I was going to do to help my people and you were never sure *what* you could do to help them. Well, this is your chance. What the hell are you waiting for?"

Blue stammered to silence when he looked at George, then at Maggie, and realized not *what*, but *who* it was George was waiting for.

"Fine," Blue said. "Tomorrow. But I hope you know what you're doing."

Maggie read the censure in his voice. She'd already rejected George once and Blue wondered if she'd do it again.

Later that evening at dinner George broached the subject again.

"I want to take that position at Standing Rock," he told Maggie.

"I think you should. It's what you've worked for all these years." Every word she spoke betrayed what she really wanted to say. She wanted to beg him not to go, to stay with her and start the life they were meant to have. Instead she remained silent and waited.

"It doesn't pay much. Only about a thousand dollars a year, but I'd be doing what I want. Helping the Sioux and Northern Cheyenne."

"I know," she whispered, wondering why he was telling her about the pay. "I think you should take the appointment."

"I'd still be fighting all the crooked agents and transport companies, like I have the past few years. But now I'd have more power to make sure things are better." George sighed. "I know I should do it and I appreciate what Blue has done in getting the appointment from Price. There's only one thing holding me back."

"And that is?" Maggie's heart was pounding. She could only hope...

"You."

She caught her breath and her eyes filled with tears. She couldn't have said a word if she wanted.

"I have to know what you feel, Maggie, in your heart. You loved me once. At least you said you did. Could you love me enough to go with me? To work with me side-by-side, doing what we both know is right?"

They were the words she'd been waiting to hear. She threw herself into his arms and kissed his face, then his lips, regardless of who was staring at them. "I do love you, George. I've never stopped loving you. I should have trusted you. Should have trusted the love we felt for each other. I was selfish and foolish and a child." She paused and took a deep breath. "If you'll let me, I'd like to try and make up for the pain I've caused you. I want to go to Standing Rock with you."

"Are you sure?" he whispered, his mouth brushing over her ear when he hugged her. "It would be a hard life, Maggs. We'd work from sunup to sundown without the comforts you have here."

"And I'd love every minute of it," she said honestly. She was bored and needed something meaningful to fill the void inside her. She'd found George and they could do what they'd both wanted for a long time. Help the Indians. "I could work with the children and with the elderly. Teach the women to sew with the materials you bring them, instead of hides." She was suddenly so excited she couldn't stand it. "I could open a school. Help the children get a start in our society in case they're ever allowed to leave the reservation. I could teach them how to read and write. Oh, George! There's so much I could do to help you. And them." She could fulfill so many dreams. She took George's hands into hers.

"Let's do it, George Hawkins. Let's go to Dakota Territory and make a difference." The thought of going back to the Dakota Territory excited her, too. She'd learned much while she was there, but now she'd return with the man she loved and do what they'd both wanted to do for a long time. They'd help the Indians—and make a difference at the same time.

Chapter Twenty-Two

They were to leave for Standing Rock tomorrow morning. Most of what needed to be done before their departure was done and Maggie looked forward to hers and George's final dinner in Washington. She was anxious, had already waited too long to let him know how she really felt about him, and tonight she was going to show him.

Maggie took great care in dressing for the evening. She wore a demure white dress that buttoned up the front with a black silk ribbon that tied in the back and form-fitting long sleeves. Her long, unbound hair fell to her waist in a riot of black curls under a wide-brimmed hat that drew the attention of many a passerby on her way to George's hotel. She was flushed with anticipation when she arrived, anxious to consummate their love, hopeful he would let her. Too many times he'd pushed her away with his old-fashioned ideas. Tonight she was going to show him how much she cared, no matter what it took.

She rapped on the door. The moment he opened it Maggie knew George more than appreciated her appearance, his eyes raking over her like a traveler deprived of water. He drank in every curve of her body and took his time about it.

"Are you going to invite me in, or make me stand out here all night while you gawk?" Her voice was husky, sensuous, and it had the desired effect she'd hoped for. His mouth snapped shut and he came to attention.

"No, of course not." He cleared the doorway allowing her entrance to the room.

She glided inside, noticing the lace-covered table in the middle of the front room set for two with fine china and clean white cloth napkins propped up on the plates. Candles in the center of the table gave the room a warm glow. *Perhaps George is hoping for the evening to end the same way I do*, she thought with a grin.

"You're beautiful." George's voice cracked like a schoolboy.

"Thank you." Maggie smiled and scanned the table. "I see we have a similar ending in mind for the evening." Her voice was playful. "You needn't ply me with alcohol to make me compliant, though, George." Her chin jerked toward a chilling bottle of champagne. She traced a finger over George's cheek and she felt gooseflesh ripple over his skin.

"Ah, so much for the challenge," George said, his eyebrow rising.

"I never was much of a challenge when it came to you, George Hawkins. If you recall, *I* was the one who tried to give myself to you. On a platter, if I recall correctly. The one who tried to seduce you—and failed." She felt the old mischief creeping up and smiled. "I recall you were quite the old woman about it."

George groaned. "I respected you, Maggs. I wanted you and you know it. From the minute I laid eyes on you. But I wasn't going to rut like an animal in heat," he defended.

She laughed and he closed the distance between them. He grabbed her shoulders and covered her lips with his, as though to prove to her tonight would be different. She melted into him, wanting this almost more than the air she breathed. It was what she'd been seeking for so long. Their lips mingled and when George finally pulled away he stood in front of her with a silly grin on his face.

"Not bad, eh?"

She raised an eyebrow and a strange feeling tore through her. "Been practicing?" Her voice dripped with sarcasm—and jealousy?

"And what if I have?" He waited for her reaction.

She threw her head back and laughed. "You've learned well, my darling." She was not about to let him know she *was* jealous. She stepped forward and ran her fingers deep into his thick hair. "But there'll be no future practicing except with me." Here and now she was giving him notice that from now on, he was hers and no one else's.

George howled with laughter. "You're jealous! Maggie Douglas is jealous."

"I am not!" She tried to deny it, but couldn't. The thought of him in the arms of another woman sent rivulets of anger snaking up and down her spine, but she couldn't let *him* know that! To keep her pride intact, she hurried on with, "But if I'm going with you to Dakota Territory, I'll go as the only woman whose mouth your lips are going to touch."

"You're damn right you'll be the only one, Maggs." George suddenly became serious. He stepped to the dresser and withdrew a small box from the top drawer, then turned and took her right hand into his. He opened the black velvet box and exposed a small ruby ring with small diamonds set on each side of the larger stone.

"Come as my wife, Maggs, as Mrs. George Hawkins."

Maggie couldn't believe she was hearing the words. She'd searched for him for so long, had come to believe she'd never find him, and he was asking her to marry him! Her breath caught and her eyes filled with tears.

"Oh, George." Her voice was rough and low. "You asked me that so long ago. I laughed at you and made a fool out of you when I left. I can't believe you'd ask me again."

"I love you, Maggs. I've never stopped, even though I thought I'd lost you. And when I saw you again on that dance floor, no matter how hard I tried to tell myself I didn't love you, I was lying. I want you with me. Always. But I want you to come to Standing Rock as my wife, to work together toward our common goal. Can you do it, Maggs? Can you be my wife? Can you give up all this?" He waved his hand to encompass the hotel room and city that surrounded it.

She couldn't speak, only stared at the ring. He took it out of the box and slid it onto her finger. Her mind was rolling. This was all she'd wanted for so long and now, *did she have doubts?*

George lifted her chin and their eyes met. Her eyes brimmed with tears and through the blur she could see the uncertainty in George's face.

"Maggs?"

Her heart was thundering, her breath quick. In an instant she saw herself and George working with the Indians, helping where they could, carving out a life of hard work and the rewards of that hard work. She looked up, all the love she had for George swelling in her heart. "I can and I will, George." She nodded her head and gazed down again at the ring on her finger.

"You will?" He sounded incredulous and Maggie giggled.

"Yes. I'll marry you and I'll follow you wherever you go. We'll be partners and we'll make a difference. I swear," she said, and meant every word.

"What about your father and brothers?" George asked.

"My family has learned by now they can't control me or what I do. I've been on my own for too long for them to even think they can dictate to me anymore. They haven't *approved* of what I've been doing for all these years, so this won't be any different. I do what Maggie Douglas wants to do and she wants to marry you!"

Her eyes glinted with mischief as she leaned into his chest. Her hand closed around his neck and her lips traced his ear. "Trust me," she whispered. "I'm all yours."

He wrapped her in his arms, breathed in her scent then ran his fingers through her curls.

"Love me," she said. "Love me like you'll never leave me." As she said the words, fear washed over her. She'd offered herself to him more than once only to be rebuffed. *Would he do so again?*

She was swept up into his arms as though she were a feather. He carried her into the separate bedroom and placed her on the bed, her hair fanning out around her head and neck like a black velvet cloak.

They jerked upright at a knock on the door.

"Dinner!" they shouted in unison, eyes wide, faces red, laughter on their lips.

"Forget dinner, I need other food." George jumped up and ran into the front room, pulling the door closed behind him so Maggie remained unseen. She heard the outer door open and the waiter entered. Trays clattered onto the table, silverware clinked into place.

"Will that be all, sir?"

"Yes, yes, that's all. Thank you, thank you." The sound of George's voice washed over Maggie and she thought it was the sweetest thing she'd ever heard. From the impatience she heard in his voice, she imagined George hurrying the waiter out the door and she was giggling by the time he pushed back into the room and hurried to the bed.

He slid up beside her and, other than wiping her threatening tears of joy away, she hadn't moved since his departure.

"Now, where were we?" he asked.

"Right here." She ran her hand down the length of George's body, feeling his excitement grow with each movement of her hand.

His lips found hers as he fumbled at the buttons on her dress.

Without leaving her lips, George managed to unbutton her dress and undid her lacy undergarment. Slowly he peeled the material away from her skin to expose her breasts. She was in unfamiliar territory. She'd never done more than taunt and tease a man, although she acted like she'd done a lot more. George's eyes moved up and down her body and a rush of embarrassment tore through her.

She was shaking, but didn't know whether it was fear he might still reject her, or her body's expectation of what was to come.

"Is something wrong?" he asked, his head cocked in uncertainty.

She shook her head almost imperceptibly.

George didn't speak as he ran his hand across her left breast, then the right. Her nipples puckered at his touch and her whole body sang a song she'd never heard before. She sighed and shifted to give him better access. She wanted more, she wanted all of him. He rolled the pink tips between his fingers before his tongue swept down to lave at each. Her breath caught and she squirmed beneath him.

As he suckled, she jerked his shirt out of his trousers and off his shoulders. She hurriedly undid his belt while his lips continued to feast on her breasts and belly.

"I've missed you so much," she whispered, shoving his pants down over his slim hips. He wriggled free and she touched him. She was being bold, she knew it, but this was the Maggie Douglas George Hawkins loved. The bold, adventurous, outspoken woman. Not some shriveling flower.

George leaned back, a strange gleam in his eyes, and Maggie feared she'd gone too far.

"This is one time you won't dominate me, Maggs. Tonight I'm the boss." His voice was a deep growl.

He crushed his lips to her breasts again. Her fingers dug into his hair and she pulled him closer. She wanted him to be part of her, to be as close as two people could be without being one. He sucked and laved while his fingers roamed and explored her most intimate places. She was writhing, calling his name, not certain what she was calling for, anxious to find out. His mouth slid down to the point of her pleasure and she thought she'd come right up off the bed when he began to nip and suck. Her fingernails scratched at the bedclothes, then at his back. She'd never felt such pleasure!

Then his lips were on hers again. Their tongues wrestled and fought for domination. But George wouldn't concede. She went where he led her until she couldn't breathe and her body cried for release.

"Please, George, I can't take much more." Her body felt like it would shatter into a thousand pieces with his next touch.

He slid into her—and jerked to a stop. He stared down at her, taking in her shy smile and the tears running down her face. He believed she wasn't a virgin, and she was happy to prove him wrong.

"It's only been you I've ever wanted, George. Finish it."

She raised her hips, forcing him to break the lining that made her his. Her breath caught and he stilled. She tried not to cry at the pain the intrusion brought, but it was worth it to prove to George she'd never been with another man. That she was his and only his.

"The pain will stop soon, Maggs. I promise." He sounded wounded and so sorry he'd hurt her. He smoothed her hair from her face and gently kissed her lips, giving her a moment to accept him. Slowly, he began to move again. The more he moved, the more the pain abated and the pleasure returned. Her kisses grew impatient and he moved faster.

They rocked each other with passion. Sweat rolled off their bodies, soaking the sheets beneath them.

They exploded together, shattering like precious vases thrown to the floor. She held onto him like a lifeline, never wanting to let him go, never wanting to forget this feeling, wanting to experience it again and again throughout her life. She had found her love and she would never let him go.

She was breathing heavily when he rolled to her side. Her hair was plastered against her face and body, her lips swollen.

She gazed into his eyes and she gently touched his cheek.

"I didn't know," he said, confusion in his voice.

She laid a finger across his lips. It didn't matter. She was his and that was *all* that mattered. "I do love you, George Hawkins, with all my heart and soul and I want to spend the rest of my life doing what makes you happy."

She reached around his neck, drew him to her, and showed him again just how much.

She was in his arms, George staring at her when she woke.

"Good morning," he said with a smile.

"Good morning." She grinned sheepishly then stretched like a cat. "What time is it?" *It wouldn't do to stay abed all day, although she would like nothing more than to do just that. They had things to do before they left for the agency.*

He grabbed his timepiece from the side table. "Eight o'clock."

"Eight o'clock!" she shouted. "I've got to go!" She jumped to her feet and raced about the room, gathering her clothes and shoes, pulling them on as she collected them. "How am I going to explain myself to Mrs. Dowd when I run into the boarding house at this hour looking like this?" Her hair was a wild mess, she knew she had to be flushed, and...

"Since when did Maggie Douglas care what anybody thinks?" George goaded. "I recall a time when she would have told old Mrs. Dowd to go to hell. That it was none of the old biddy's business how she spent her time—or with whom."

Maggie stopped her scurrying and glared at George. "I've changed, George. I've...I've grown up." And she had grown up. Although appearances weren't everything, the correct one certainly helped. *She was leaving so what did it matter; but why leave with everyone thinking she was some harlot!*

"Um, you certainly have." He was staring at her half-clad form and she could almost see his mouth watering.

"Are you going to lie there and gawk all day, or are you going to get up and help me? We have a train to catch, don't we?"

"Yes, we do. But not until you have a decent breakfast and we make several stops."

He had a strange glint in his eyes. *What was he up to?* "Stops?"

"Um hum." There was that gleam again.

"What kind of stops?" She furrowed her eyebrows.

"One, to get Blue and Amy and tell them the good news. Two, for breakfast. And three, no, I think I'll let you wait for three." His smile was smug and his eyes still gleamed.

She glared at him, but her lips were curled in a wry smile. "What are you up to George Hawkins?"

"You'll find out soon enough."

"Fine!" She remembered old Mrs. Dowd and the other gossiping biddies at the boarding house. "But I have to go right now. If we're going to be on that train, I have to gather my things now."

She swung around, smoothed her hair and dress back into place and smiled innocently. "And what time shall Mr. Hawkins come to collect me?"

"It's eight now. Our train leaves at twelve-thirty. That gives us plenty of time."

"For what?" She was bubbling with excitement.

"Our stops. You'll see. I'll be around to Mrs. Dowd's at nine o'clock. I'll get Blue and Amy first then collect you and we can come back here for a late breakfast."

"Then what?"

"Be patient." He brushed her nose with his finger then placed a quick kiss on her lips.

"Fine," she huffed. "I'll be patient, although you know it's not one of my virtues." She raced out of the room, slamming the door behind her. She had much to do in preparation of her next adventure.

Chapter Twenty-Three

Blue and George hauled Maggie's cases down the boardinghouse stairs and loaded them into the buckboard Blue had rented. While the men fussed with the bags, Maggie and Amy chattered like magpies in the backseat, before everyone headed to breakfast. For the first time since opening up to Ida, Maggie felt a true kinship with Amy. She'd survived the Civil War and later captivity amongst the Lakota, where she'd fallen in love with her captor, Blue, so she understood much of what Maggie had survived throughout the years.

After breakfast George blindfolded Maggie, helped her out of the buckboard and led her into a building, their footsteps echoing off the walls and ceiling once inside.

George slid the kerchief away. "Surprise. Stop number three."

Maggie's eyes grew wide as realization dawned. She was in a church, a huge, beautiful church, adorned with flowers and stained glass windows depicting all manner of Christian stories, with her new friends on either side of her. She began to cry. Although not normally a crier, she just couldn't help it. Maggie threw her arms around George's neck and kissed him all over his face, leaving wet trails up and down his cheeks.

Blue stood to George's right, Maggie was on George's left, and Amy was beside Maggie. Maggie was handed a tiny bouquet of flowers she was told Amy hastily picked from the garden in the front of the church. The minister, his back to the altar and facing the two couples, was smiling, waiting for the signal to begin.

Everyone quieted and the minister spoke about commitment and faithfulness, saying the words that would bind Maggie to George for the rest of her life. She should be afraid, but she'd never been more sure of anything in her life.

Before she could change her mind, or talk herself out of it, she repeated, "I, Margaret Douglas, do take you, George Hawkins, to be my wedded husband. To have and to hold, from this day forward." Her eyes glistened with tears of joy.

She stopped speaking and waited as the minister spoke the words for George to repeat. George stood silent. Fear washed over her. *Was he having second thoughts? Had he changed his mind?* Her mind whirled as he just stood there, staring at the minister. Her heart caught and she held her breath.

Finally, drawing a deep breath, he repeated each sentence the preacher had spoken, the words that would make her and George Hawkins husband and wife.

"You may kiss the bride."

George leaned toward Maggie and kissed her full on the mouth, drawing guffaws from Blue and Amy and cleared throats from the minister and his wife, who was standing in the pew behind them.

"Hello, Mrs. Hawkins," George whispered when he pulled away.

"Hello, Mr. Hawkins." Maggie's eyes were damp. There was so much joy and love in her heart she thought she'd bust.

Suddenly, Blue and Amy were congratulating her and George, hugging them and giving them well-wishes. There were good wishes from the minister and his plump, sniffling wife, too.

Before she could think, Blue and Amy had whisked George and Maggie away to the train station.

They were on the platform waiting for the train, Maggie standing beside her new husband, when Blue began the final goodbyes. "It was good to see you my brother." Blue put his hands on George's shoulder. "It's been too long between visits. And you should visit Ben and Sarah more often, too," he chastised.

"I go to Kansas City whenever I can between runs," he defended. "Spent a couple of Christmases there."

Blue smiled. "It's good to see the laughter in your eyes again, my friend. It was gone for too long."

George nodded and Maggie prayed that light was in his eyes because of her. She knew she certainly felt renewed and more alive than she had since leaving the Lazy D so many years ago.

A whistle blared in the distance, signaling the arrival of the train. The two couples stepped toward the tracks and waited as the train chugged its way to a lumbering stop in front of the station house.

Amy touched Maggie's shoulder. "Now don't you forget about us. We'll be here in Washington until Blue finishes his apprenticeship—or they kick us out." She giggled then grew more serious. "George is a good man, Maggie. Take care of him."

"I will." She glanced lovingly at her husband then turned back to Amy. "I promise."

Amy grinned and pulled Maggie into an embrace. Sniffing, Amy stepped away and Maggie stepped back to George.

"I guess this is goodbye," George told Blue. Maggie knew it pained him greatly to say those words to his friend and she hoped that now that they'd found each other, they'd find a way to see each other more often.

Blues lips pinched and he nodded. "I know you will do well with your appointment, George. You're a good man, named so by The People themselves. Wasicun Cantewaste *is* a white man with a good heart. Don't ever forget that and don't let anyone try and tell you otherwise. Keep those sons-of-bitches in line, George. The People need you," Blue said with a grin at having learned the white man's slang, and using it.

George closed his eyes and nodded. "I will." He turned to Maggie and took her hand in his. "At least I'll have help this time around. And trust me," he said in a sarcastic tone, "she'll keep *me* in line."

The four laughed and hugged one last time as "all aboard" echoed up and down the platform.

Clutching Maggie's hand, George led the way onto the train and settled in a seat by the window. Maggie crowded beside him, peeking out the glass, waving one last time to her new friends still standing on the walkway outside.

"Take care of yourself, my brother," Blue shouted. "Take care of that new wife of yours, too!" Maggie heard the muffled command through the glass.

Amy was waving and crying, her hair fluttering around her face in the wind. "Be careful," she shouted. "Take care of each other!"

The whistle blew several times, announcing their departure. Amy waved furiously now. Tears streamed down her cheeks. Maggie cried in silence at all she'd gained and lost. She'd gained a new life and George, but she was losing another friend.

George raised his hand, put his palm against the glass, and held it there.

Blue stepped to the edge of the platform and raised his hand to the glass, too. As he did, Maggie noticed the scar that ran almost the length of his palm, stark white against his dark skin. The same scar George bore. She recalled the pledge George told her he and Blue had made to each other as young men. They were brothers, made so by the mingling of their blood.

"Brothers," Blue mouthed as the train jerked forward, picking up speed with each grinding turn of the wheels.

"Brothers," George said back. "I'll make you proud!" he shouted as the train chugged away from a stone-faced Blue, his hand still raised, Amy sobbing beside him.

Maggie sat beside her new husband in heart-breaking silence as Blue and Amy disappeared in a cloud of smoke. The train lumbered forward, faster and faster, hurtling her and George toward an unknown future, one she looked toward with great excitement—and much trepidation.

The train rolled to a stop in Kansas City and Maggie's heart beat faster. This was where her journey had begun, where she'd gotten on the train that took her east to fight for the cause, and left George and her family behind. She searched the platform for her father and brothers and waved frantically when she spotted them. George was waving, too, but at a couple she presumed were Ben and Sarah. Without waiting for her husband she bounded unladylike from the train and into her father's outstretched arms. The smile he held for her said everything. He was still proud of her. He held her tight and she reveled in the feel of his still strong chest and comforting warmth.

There was a tap on her shoulder. "Are you forgetting someone?"

Maggie pulled from her father's embrace and fell into James' open arms and then Edward's. She felt like a little girl again with the spark of pride back in her family's eyes.

"It's so good to see you!" Maggie cried.

"How would we know?" Stuart chided, as her father always did, but there was a grin on his face. "You never write."

"I've been busy," Maggie defended, realizing her father was teasing her. "I wrote and told you I'm coming to see you as a married woman. That should make you *all* very happy. Now you can stop badgering me!"

"Indeed it does make us happy. And Maggs," Stuart leaned forward and whispered, "he's a fine husband, too. We're happy you found him." His eyes gleamed and Maggie melted into his arms again.

Realizing they didn't know the whole story, Maggie whispered into her father's ear, "George doesn't know you and James and Edward actually knew all about our relationship and approved. I never told him. He still believes you would have rejected him."

Stuart stood back. "Why didn't you tell him?"

"Because I didn't want him to feel the betrayal I felt when *I* found out. I didn't want him to think we've wasted all these years not being together. That if you'd said something, I might have stayed, because I most likely would have gone anyway," she said with a frown.

Her father frowned back. "I don't like lyin' to the boy, but we'll play along and not give you away." He paused and his eyes sparkled with mischief. "May even let him think we still disapprove to make it more convincing..."

"Don't you dare!" Maggie slapped her father's shoulder and the two giggled at the shared secret.

"Disapprove about what?" James asked, stepping closer to his sister while Edward craned his neck to hear what was going on.

"Shhh. Pa will explain later."

Someone cleared their throat and Maggie turned to see George and a dark-haired man standing beside him and a blond woman on his arm. "Maggie, this is Sarah and Ben."

Maggie disentangled herself from her own family and stepped toward Sarah with her hand extended. Sarah looked at her proffered hand, moved it aside and pulled Maggie into a warm embrace.

"It's so nice to finally meet you. We've heard so much about you over the years," she said, tears glistening in her eyes as she pushed back from her new daughter-in-law.

"And this is Ben," George introduced before the conversation with Sarah could continue.

"I'm honored, sir," Maggie said before Ben hugged her, too.

"It's about time George finally tracked you down and married you," Ben said on a smile. "I thought that boy would never settle down—unless he found you. Welcome to the family, Maggie."

Maggie looked askance at her husband, whose face was turning red. Exposed! Ben had just confirmed that throughout their years apart, George had always cared for Maggie. A smile lit her lips and more love for her husband exploded in her heart.

Stuart Douglas cleared his throat. Maggie hurried to her father, hooked her arm in his and led him toward the others. "Ben and Sarah, this is my father, Stuart Douglas, and these are my brothers, James and Edward."

The formal introductions concluded, everyone stepped forward to shake hands.

She stood rooted to the spot, happier than she'd been in too long to remember.

"How long are you here?" Stuart asked once everyone had greeted one another.

"Two days," Maggie answered.

"Same old Maggie, here one day and gone the next. That's our girl!" Her father's words were said with a smile and everyone laughed, even Maggie. She'd come full circle, accepted by her father and brothers for who she was. A woman with a life of her own in which she'd accomplished much—and even *found* a husband to boot. Literally.

The two days flew by in a whirl of getting to know George's surrogate parents and reacquainting herself with her own father and brothers. Everyone stayed at White Oaks while George and Maggie were in town, and Maggie loved it *almost* as much as she did the Lazy D. She and Sarah slipped away more than once, the older woman telling her all about being captured by the Lakota, how she and Ben had come to own White Oaks, and how

Blue had come to them. Maggie listened intently, realizing how much Sarah had suffered to be where she was today, happy with a loving husband and family, albeit an unconventional one, consisting of a half-blood Lakota, a cavalryman, a Rebel, a Yankee, and even two former slaves they included amongst them. They were wonderful as far as Maggie was concerned and she was more than happy to be considered one of them.

Maggie's heart opened to Sarah like a book unfolding. Her kindness and warmth filled the emptiness Maggie had held inside for so long, growing up without a mother with whom to share her doubts, fears, and accomplishments. Now there was Sarah to confide her doubts and victories with. Maggie told her all about her adventures, from Boston to Deadwood and everything in between, including being ridden out of town on a rail, which she related without embarrassment.

Ben and Stuart exchanged cigars and stories of the war, who they'd ridden with and when, compared information about raising cattle, selling them, and even the new-fangled barbed fence they used, while George and the brothers saddled up and explored every inch of White Oaks. They were all instant friends and Maggie felt like she'd never been happier, like she'd found everything she'd been looking for.

Too soon it was time to leave, but this time there was pride in her father and sibling's eyes when they kissed her goodbye. There were no rebukes for going off to do something they didn't approve of or think she *couldn't* do. She'd proven she could do *anything* she set her mind to.

Although she cried when she left her new family, she was anxious to get to Standing Rock. She had more to do in her life and it was time to do it. She'd accomplished so much and for the first time since she left the Lazy D, she realized it. Another new life called to her, a life that would be difficult yet more fulfilling than anything she'd done so far. It was time to close another chapter in her life and begin a new one.

PART IV

STANDING ROCK

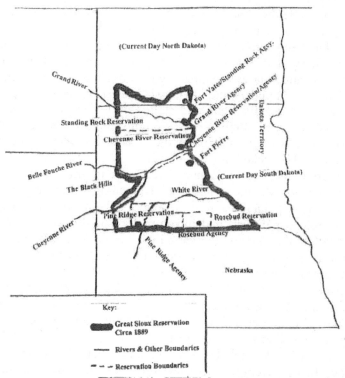

This map is a compilation of numerous different maps
and is for visual aid purposes ONLY – NOT TO SCALE

THE GREAT SIOUX RESERVATION – CIRCA 1889

Chapter Twenty-Four

George and Maggie stood outside the agency building watching the Sioux men go to the table. Some as young as ten years old made their marks and walked away, averting their eyes when they noticed George and Maggie watching them. The newly married couple had been at Standing Rock for several months now and knew most of what went on inside the reservation and what was happening now made them both sick.

"They don't understand, do they?" Maggie asked George.

George shook his head and sighed. "They have no idea. If the good Reverend Hinman gets enough signatures, he can put a bill in front of Congress to annex the 14,000 square miles they're asking for." He sucked in a deep breath.

George had come home every night this past week explaining to Maggie what was happening. How Reverend Hinman was at Standing Rock to make an offer to buy 14,000 square miles of Indian land in return for 25,000 head of cattle and 1,000 bulls. The good reverend was smug in the idea that his offer was a good one, but George had laughed in his face then went throughout the reservation, telling The People not to sign his paper, hoping they would listen. The People just didn't understand. All they understood were the threats they'd gotten that they'd lose their annuities and their people would starve or freeze if they didn't touch the pen.

"And who do they have to fight for them in Washington besides Blue?" George asked absently, watching the parade of men to the table.

Maggie squeezed his arm. *This could be the opportunity he'd been waiting for. He could fight for The People. He could make even more of a difference to these people who had so very little, and much of what they* did *have was thanks to George's efforts.*

"They'll have you." Maggie's heart was pounding. She knew what she was doing. In the time they'd been here they'd pounded out a life, one that included helping The People understand what was happening to them, as well as educating them in the ways of the white man so they could, someday, be absorbed into the white man's world and survive, while helping them keep their dignity, despite what was being done to them.

George whirled on his wife. "You mean it? You don't mind?"

"Of course not, as long as you take me with you." She was anxious to return to Washington. She wanted to see Blue and Amy and catch up with them, as well as the women's movement. She didn't miss working for the cause at all, but she did want to know if all she'd put into it had helped to move it forward.

George grabbed her by the waist and twirled her in a circle. "You bet I'll take you with me. And we'll fight 'em, Maggs. We'll fight 'em with everything we've got!"

The train ride to Washington was long and cold, but George and Maggie complained little. They just snuggled closer. They were too intent on reaching their destination to let a little boredom and frigid air put a damper on their plans.

"There they are!" Maggie heard Amy's voice as she descended the steps of the train. Amy was waddling toward them, holding her back, a huge smile on her face. Moments later Amy was cradled in George's arms when Blue strode up beside them.

"Hey, mister. You know my wife well enough to hold her like that?" Blue drawled, a smile on his face.

"I certainly hope so." George released Amy and grabbed Blue in a hug. The two grunted and growled like circling bears, slapping each other on the back, laughing when they parted. "How the hell are you, you old warrior?" George asked. "Looks like you keep fit." He slapped Blue's stomach. "No extra baggage here!"

Blue laughed and punched George in the shoulder. "Looks to me like you're staying fit, too, brother. You throwing buffalo at the 'Rock'?"

"You know there aren't a lot of buffalo near the agency. Buffalo hunters ran them off a long time ago." George's voice was low and solemn.

Blue puckered his lips and nodded. "I guess game is pretty scarce in those parts." It wasn't a question, but a statement as to how much the area had been decimated by white hunters.

Feeling forgotten and wanting to turn the somber conversation, Maggie stepped out from behind George. "Does anyone remember that I'm here, too?"

"Maggie!" Amy shouted. "I'm so sorry. I just..."

"Don't explain, Amy. Just come here and give me a hug. Look at you!" Maggie raised Amy's arms to view her friend's protruding belly. "You're a sight!"

"Only three months to go. Three months I'm afraid I might not survive. I detest being in the motherly way," Amy complained in a loud whisper. "I stay home and hide my belly like it's something to be ashamed of."

All Maggie had fought for over the years leapt into her brain. "Don't you *ever* be ashamed of that life you're carrying inside you. For any reason or any one." Maggie stepped forward, took Amy's arm and led her away from the men. "Unfortunately, it's just the way it is around here. You know these stuffy old hens." Maggie pinched her nose and eyes and stiffened her back. "It's just not done," she trilled.

The two women laughed and embraced. "It's so good to see you, Amy. And you," Maggie swung back toward Blue. "Give your sister-in-law a big hug!" Maggie ordered.

"A pleasure." He wrapped his arms around her tiny waist. "Ummm, I'd almost forgotten what it feels like to hold someone with such a tiny waist."

Maggie and Amy both slapped him on the shoulder for his comment. He threw up his hands.

"All right, all right. I was teasing." He grabbed his wife around the waist and kissed her into silence. "Just look at how much more I've got to love."

Maggie laughed heartily, happy to be here with her dear friends. During their visit, George and Blue would try and stop Hinman from stealing the 14,000 acres from the Indians. Maggie prayed they would succeed. The People needed someone to speak for them who understood what was happening. George was that man, Wasicun Cantewaste, a white man of good heart, and he would do whatever he could to keep more land from being stolen. She knew it as sure as her name was Maggie Hawkins.

Maggie accompanied George and Blue to the hearing. Amy had stayed at home, uncomfortable, both physically and from the stares and sneers she received at being in public in her "delicate condition" so close to her confinement. Maggie was sitting in the audience when George jumped up in response to something said by a member of the commission.

"I protest!" George shouted. Blue jumped up from the seat beside him.

"And who the hell are you?" a congressman yelled back.

"I'm George Hawkins, sub-agent at the Standing Rock Agency, Dakota Territory."

"And what, exactly, do you protest?" the congressman asked.

"Everything these men have told you!" George shouted.

Maggie watched Newton Edmunds, the chairman of the commission heading the effort to claim the lands from the Sioux, turn beet red. Beside him Reverend Hinman's lips twitched and his eyes turned to slits in his effort to contain his anger. Maggie smiled. George was making them crazy.

"Sir," George began, "I've seen how those people are treated. The majority of Indian agents are corrupt, lining their pockets with money stolen from Sioux mouths. I've seen entire shipments of a year's worth of annuities stolen and replaced with garbage. Food I wouldn't feed a starving dog. I swore when I took this position I'd do something to make a difference. And I don't plan to leave here until everyone has heard what I have to say."

Maggie wanted to stand up and cheer she was so proud of her husband.

"Continue," the congressman requested.

George spoke about how badly the Indians were treated, about the poor conditions on the reservations, of how the majority of Indian agents were corrupt and without scruples.

"I was there when the illustrious Reverend Samuel Hinman came to Standing Rock to get the headmen to sign away more of their land. He threatened them. Told them he would stop their annuities from coming in, promised they would starve and freeze to death without them. So they signed." He paused and took a deep breath. He scanned the faces of the congressmen and scowling Edmunds and Hinman.

"I was there when they signed. I watched boys, children perhaps ten or twelve years old, but not yet male adults as stipulated in the Laramie Treaty of 1868, make their marks on a piece of paper they knew nothing about. Please, gentlemen, if you have any conscience about what we've done to these people, don't allow this bill to pass. Please."

George sat down. Blue plopped down beside him, clapped him on the back, and whispered in his ear.

Maggie's heart was pounding. She watched the congressmen confer, Hinman's face tight with rage. She waited in silence hoping and praying they would come to the right decision. Not to pass a law that would grievously harm the Lakota—again.

"Here's to George Hawkins!" Blue hoisted his wine-filled glass, some of the liquid sloshing over the sides.

"Here, here!" Maggie and Amy raised their glasses, pride washing over Maggie like the liquid slogging over Blue's glass. George had won. The congressmen had listened and the bill did not pass.

"I just did what was right." George raised his glass, his face flushed from the compliments.

"Well, by God, you did a damn fine job of it!" Blue shouted.

The four took a drink and set down their glasses.

"And here's to Beveridges," Blue shouted, obviously feeling the effects of the wine he'd already had.

"Why Beveridges?" George asked.

"Because this hotel accepts Indians. I thought it appropriate for you and Maggie to stay here for just such reasons and it would be most appropriate for us to celebrate our victory here!"

Three more glasses were raised in a toast to Beveridges in a celebration that lasted until exhaustion claimed Amy and Maggie and Blue excused themselves to their hotel.

"You were wonderful," Maggie told George as they slid into bed.

"I didn't do much. Just told the truth."

"A truth many people are afraid of. If I haven't told you already, George Hawkins, I'm proud of you, proud of what you're doing and proud to be your wife." In the waning hours of the night, she showed him just how much.

Chapter Twenty-Five

The following years at the Standing Rock Agency proved to be more than challenging, but were highly rewarding for Maggie. Hers and George's rapport with the Lakota grew as George watched over the annuities that flowed through their section of the Great Sioux Reservation, and Maggie helped The People in any way she could.

It was well-known George often butted heads with William T. Hughes, the agent in charge of Standing Rock, while doing what he could to help The People. The headmen addressed him only as Wasicun Cantewaste to show their respect toward his efforts to make their lives a little easier.

Finally ready to pursue her own way of helping the Lakota, Maggie had George order the supplies needed to build the school she had dreamed of for so long. Using food as an enticement, she enlisted the aid of every Lakota man who would come to help build it. George taught them how to use a hammer and nails, and Maggie encouraged them, although she jumped right in beside them, swinging a hammer where she could.

Day after day she supervised the school's building from the simple plans George had drawn up, getting as many blisters as the braves while doing her share of the work. Soon the women came too, curious at first, but eventually pitching in by bringing more food and helping with small jobs like bringing supplies or water those who needed it. Within three months a one-room schoolhouse stood next to the agency building with enough rough-hewn tables and benches to seat twenty students.

Maggie turned in a circle in the middle of the new school, her arms spread wide. She sighed. It was done. For so long it had been just a dream. Now it was a reality. Tears filled her eyes, but she wasn't sure whether they were from happiness or the fear that no one would come.

She pulled out the chalk tablets George had ordered from the Montgomery Ward "wish book" that were stacked in the desk drawer at the front of the room and laid them on the first two tables. A room-sized chalk board stood beside the desk facing her would-be students. There were text books, tablets, a lesson planner, and lots of hope. Maggie'd put all her efforts into this school and prayed The People would embrace it with the spirit in which it had been built.

Everything was ready for her students. Students that didn't come.

Maggie paced. She'd arrived at eight this morning, anxious and ready. She went from her desk to the front door then back to her desk. As the day warmed, she stepped outside and peered around the building to see if anyone was coming. She rang the big bell that hung on a high pole outside the front door then rang it again an hour later. Still no one came, not even out of curiosity, not even the men or women who had been there day after day to build the school. She swallowed her disappointment and reminded herself that nothing worth having was easy. Tomorrow was another day and she'd be right back here doing the same thing, waiting and hoping.

For a week Maggie went to the school, ready for the one child whose parents would let them go to the white lady's school. And for a week she was alone in a building built for others.

The second week began much the way the previous had ended—until mid-morning. Maggie was at her desk, reading through her lesson plan, making changes she'd already changed a dozen times the week before, when she sensed someone else in the room. Slowly, she lifted her eyes to find a Lakota woman she recognized as one who'd come to help with building the school standing just inside the door. Maggie's heart thudded and hope flowed through her. *All it took was one.*

Maggie hurried to the woman, a big smile on her face. "Welcome! Come in." She extended her hand and led the reluctant woman to one of the benches at the back of the room. She assumed the woman was there to ask questions about the school for one of her children, and Maggie was more than willing to tell her what she had in mind. That was *if* she could communicate it to her. Although Maggie tried her hardest, she still wasn't mastering the Lakota language as quickly as she'd like.

Maggie waved her hand around the room. "School."

The woman looked at her blankly then scanned the room with a hard stare.

Maggie whirled her hand around again. She went to the front of the room and lifted the tablets so the woman could see them then went to the big board and wrote the word "school" on it. "School," she said again, hoping to convey some understanding of where she was, hoping the woman might supply the Lakota word.

The woman raised an eyebrow and looked around, uneasy.

Maggie again encompassed the room with her hand. "School."

The woman blinked and slowly said, "Wayawa."

Excitement burst through Maggie. "Wayawa," she repeated, bringing a reserved smile to the other woman's face. She nodded and repeated, "Wayawa."

Maggie pointed. "Table."

The woman cocked her head. "Wagnawotapi."

They went back and forth several times before Maggie finally pronounced the word well enough for the woman to nod.

Maggie realized she didn't know the woman's name, or the woman hers, so she put her thumb to her chest. "Teacher." She pointed at the woman and tilted her head in question.

The woman thrust her thumb into her own chest. "Cetan."

"Cetan," Maggie repeated, bringing a smile to the woman's face. She pointed back at herself. "Teacher."

"Tee—cher," Cetan managed on the second try.

Maggie's smile could have lit the room had it been dark. She bobbed her head up and down and repeated the woman's name and, pointing to herself, said the word teacher over and over. Maggie pointed to the table again, raised her shoulders and frowned at having forgotten the word.

The woman tried to hide a grin, but Maggie laughed out loud, bringing a full smile to Cetan's face. "Wait!" Maggie cried. She jumped up and retrieved one of the small chalk boards so she could write down exactly what Cetan said and *remember* it.

Cetan watched her closely as she gathered the chalk and board and sat back down on the bench beside her. Settled, Maggie started over so she could get everything written down this time. She waved her hand around the interior of the room.

"Wayawa," Cetan answered.

Maggie wrote it on the board then tapped the table.

"Wagnawotapi," the woman responded.

Maggie scribbled then pointed to the woman's chest. "Cetan."

Cetan's head went up and down and her eyes sparkled. She pointed at Maggie. "Tee-cher."

Maggie smiled and clapped her hands as a feeling of accomplishment spread through her like a cold drink on a hot day.

Throughout the morning Maggie pointed, the woman responded, and Maggie wrote down everything she learned. Near noon, the woman left, but not before she understood Maggie wanted her to come back tomorrow.

She did come back the next day, and the next day, and the next, each woman helping the other breach the wall of language that separated them. By Friday they greeted each other warmly and conversed on a raw level, but understanding more and more of what was said.

The following week the woman arrived with a child of about six years old she called Wanonah. The little girl hid her face in her mother's deerskin dress, but in a short time she was giggling and learning with her mother. The girl had huge almond eyes, sleek black hair and reminded Maggie of the little Indian girl whom she'd met with her grandfather at the pond at the Lazy D when she was a girl herself. Hope washed over her, as though the girl from her past was there in spirit to help make the school a reality.

As the days progressed, mother and daughter came to the school every morning by ten o'clock and the three pointed and spoke, with Maggie adding at least one more word to her tablet each day. The little girl giggled and Maggie and her mother exchanged much. Maggie packed lunches and they ate and learned well into the afternoon.

After the second week mother and daughter moved to one of the tables at the front of the room. The little girl scribbled on a chalk tablet when Maggie printed numbers and letters on the board at the front of the room. Cetan seemed to want to learn as much as Wanonah so Maggie gave her a tablet, too, and encouragement coursed through her.

The second month began with another mother and her son of about seven or eight years old stepping through the door. They joined the finger pointing with Cetan doing as much of the teaching as Maggie. The two children giggled and learned and soon, there were four students who came without their parents, then eight, until Maggie had twelve students anxious and excited to learn. As the school blossomed, so did Maggie, finally able to make the *real* difference she had longed to make for so long. The mothers learned as much as the children—and Maggie learned more than all of them.

George and Maggie saw many changes at "The Rock" during the years there. In 1881 as a way to help "make the Sioux as white men," a new Indian agent was sent to preside over the Standing Rock Agency. His name was James McLaughlin and he became known as White Hair to the Sioux.

In early 1883, Sitting Bull was released from Fort Buford, where he'd been held since his surrender, and was allowed to join his fellow Hunkpapa at Standing Rock. In September of that same year, Sitting Bull traveled to Bismark, South Dakota, and spoke during the celebration to drive in the last spike of the Northern Pacific Railroad. He gave a flowery speech and received a standing ovation. But George learned later through his friends at the agency that Sitting Bull had done nothing but hurl insults at the white crowd. The army interpreter had translated what the crowd *wanted* to hear, instead of what the great chief had really said.

Also in 1883, Maggie and George had a child they named Mary Elizabeth. She was the crowning glory of their little family and their greatest joy. Throughout her pregnancy Maggie kept a strong presence at the agency school and picked up right where she left off after Mary's birth.

Because of his new popularity between the Sioux and the whites, Sitting Bull was whisked away in the summer of 1884 to speak in fifteen cities throughout the country. In 1885, Sitting Bull joined Buffalo Bill Cody, another old warrior, in his Wild West show which drew tremendous crowds and made the great chief even more popular. When asked to accompany Buffalo Bill to Europe with the show, Sitting Bull declined. He was needed at home. The government was again attempting to grab more of the Black Hills.

"I just don't understand it," Maggie complained to her husband. She was sitting on the settee in the small front room of their cabin at the agency, mending. "Why can't the government just leave them alone? Why do they have to continue to take more and more from them? They're a defeated people. They've got so little left. Why can't they just leave them alone?"

George shook his head. "I don't know, Maggs, but I damn well hope to help stop it."

"Wasn't the Dawes Severalty Act passed to *help* the Indians?" Maggie asked. It seemed no matter what they did to try and help The People something always came along to tear it away.

"Yes and no. And I'm not so sure it's going to save them from losing their land."

"But it gives each Indian so much land of their own, doesn't it? According to their age and family status?" Maggie argued, not understanding how something set up to *give* the Lakota their own land, could hurt them.

"It does that, but what about all that's left over? *That's* what the government is trying to cede. And, in the process of giving all this land to the Indians, the government is *also* attempting to assimilate them into white society at the same time."

"Oh," Maggie sighed, understanding dawning. They'd offered enough to appease The People, knowing there'd be land left over that would need to be distributed—and the government would step right in to take their portion, while still working to "make them as the white man," in the process.

"A new commission's been formed to look into cutting the Lakota lands into six smaller reservations. It'll leave nine million acres to be thrown open to settlers."

"Nine million acres!" Maggie shouted. She shook her head in disbelief. "Of prime land, I suppose." Now she understood. The Great Sioux Reservation, which included the Standing Rock Agency, was about to get cut into six smaller reservations to house the different tribes. But in that division, the Sioux Nation would lose nine million acres of prime land, lost forever to the greed of the white man.

George frowned and nodded.

"We have to stop them." Maggie's eyes glistened with anger. She was tired of fighting a losing battle, trying to keep what belonged to the Indians *for* the Indians, when the government constantly worked to take it away.

"I'm going to get the chance in a few days. The new commissioners are coming here to convince Sitting Bull and Gall to sign the papers. I have to convince them otherwise—without McLaughlin finding out," George said on a sigh.

Mary clung to her father's neck as he headed out the cabin door the next morning for the council lodge to speak with Sitting Bull. Anxious to know everything that happened, Maggie followed her husband out the door, extracted her daughter from his neck, got a kiss and a promise.

"You'll come home as soon as you're finished to let me know what's happened?"

"I will, Maggs. I'll come straight home and tell you everything."

The morning dragged like a plow horse tilling corn rows in a clay field filled with stones. Maggie couldn't concentrate on anything except whether George could convince Sitting Bull to keep The People from signing away more land because they just didn't understand what they were signing and afraid they would lose what little they had if they did.

Maggie and Mary were side by side doing lessons at the table when Mary turned Maggie's face toward hers and laid the palms of her little hands on her mother's cheeks.

"Sing, Mommy." Mary's eyes were wide and sparkled with childhood innocence. Love burst through Maggie and she pulled the only child she would ever have close to her and hugged her tight, silently thanking the Lord she was still alive after a birth that had nearly killed them both. Mary was given everything they could in their little world between Fort Yates, the army post that kept watch over the Standing Rock Agency, and the actual reservation where The People lived. The child had grown and blossomed between cultures, taking the best of both and forsaking the worst. She was bright and beautiful with long, dark curls like her mother, had chubby little-girl cheeks, and spoke

Lakota as well as she spoke English. Her playground was the reservation, her playmates the Indian children Maggie taught. Everyone loved her. She was sunshine and happiness, bringing that happiness with her wherever she went. She brought laughter when the children were sad, and gave them whatever she had that they didn't. Maggie made doll after doll for her daughter that was given away to others almost as quickly as she gave them to her daughter.

Mary was an anomaly. She didn't see color, only friends she hadn't met yet, judging them for what was in their heart. Many times she turned a sour-faced brave into a doting, smiling "uncle," anxious for her next visit with flowers or cookies her momma had made, or just the little girl's presence and the smile that came with it.

"What do you want to sing?" Maggie asked.

Four year old Mary leaned forward, pooched out her lower lip and said in a deep voice and a twinkle in her eyes, "Hot Cross Buns, Momma."

"Hot Cross Buns it is."

"Hot cross buns! Hot cross buns!
One a penny, two a penny,
Hot cross buns!
If you have no daughters,
Give them to your sons
One a penny, two a penny,
Hot Cross Buns!"

Mary clapped and sang what words few she knew until Maggie finished the tune.

"Sing it again, Momma."

Maggie ran her fingers along her daughter's cheek, the child so precious to her it made her chest tighten with love—and fear of losing her. With a nod, Maggie sang it again.

"Sing another one, Momma," Mary chided when *Hot Cross Buns* had been sung three times and Maggie refused a fourth.

"How about Little Cock Sparrow?" Maggie relented with a tweek of Mary's nose that made her giggle.

"Yes, Momma. Do the sparrow song."

Maggie launched into *The Little Cock Sparrow* as Mary clapped and flitted around the room, flapping her arms and chirping like a bird.

> *"A little cock-sparrow sat on a high tree,*
> *A little cock-sparrow sat on a high tree,*
> *A little cock-sparrow sat on a high tree,*
> *And he chirrupped, he chirrupped so merrily.*
> *He chirrupped, he chirrupped, he chirrupped, he*
> *chirrupped,*
> *He chirrupped, he chirrupped, he chirrupped, he*
> *chirrupped,*
> *A little cock-sparrow sat on a high tree,*
> *And he chirrupped, he chirrupped so merrily.*

Maggie and Mary sang song after song while Maggie waited for George and news of the council. She was almost to the point of forcing her way into the council lodge to find out what was going on, knowing she absolutely *couldn't* do such a thing, when George finally returned.

"Well? What did they say?" Maggie met her husband at the door. She dragged him inside and led him to the table, as excited as Mary had been singing songs before Maggie shooed her daughter outside to play, unable to sing another song, exhausted, her throat sore.

"I told Sitting Bull and Gall the commissioners were coming and that they were going to try and get them to touch the pen to split up the lands into six parcels, one for each tribe."

"And?"

"And, I told them they can't sign; told them that no matter what, they can't touch the pen to the commissioners' paper. I don't know if they fully understand, but I'm hoping Sitting Bull understood enough that he'll keep them from signing. The most we can do now is hope."

A month later George charged into the cabin, picked Maggie up and twirled her around in a circle. "We did it! We did it!" he shouted, hugging her tight before he set her back on her feet.

"They didn't sign?" Maggie cried with laughter. She was breathless, giddy from her twirling.

"Not enough. Those commissioners were here for almost a month and didn't get Gall *or* Sitting Bull to sign. All they got were twenty-two signatures, not nearly enough to cede the land. We won, Maggs! We won!"

He twirled Maggie around again and she laughed with him, but at the same time she wondered just how long *this* victory would last.

Maggie checked the basket she was carrying filled with bread, chicken and fruit. She and six year old Mary had come to Fort Yates to surprise George. He'd become a very busy man over the past years, one who often forgot to eat his noonday meal. So on this mid-summer's day of 1889 Maggie gathered up their daughter, hitched up their rickety wagon, and trekked to the fort to oversee today's meal for her husband.

"Now you be nice and quiet when we go inside to see your Papa," Maggie told a squirming Mary while she finger-combed her child's mussed hair.

"All right, Momma. But I *really* want to play with Sakari," Mary pouted.

"You remember what I said, now, be still when we go inside. You can play with Sakari later."

"Yes, Momma," Mary agreed on a heavy sigh.

Maggie lifted her hand to push through the door, but stopped short of the frame.

"Damn it!" she heard George yell. "Why won't they just leave it be?"

"Calm down." Maggie recognized the other man's voice as that of James McLaughlin, the Indian agent over George.

"Don't tell me to calm down. You're in it with them. You'd be happy to see these Indians beaten down," George countered.

"That's a lie!"

"And you're full of shit and you know it," George shouted back. "From the time you got here you've tried to convince Sitting Bull and Gall that the best thing for them to do would be to sell off the land. That the only way their race will survive into the future is to become like the white man. But damn it, James, you don't *give* them anything to be a white man with! They've got no tools to plant with and not enough beef or land to start a ranch. What have they got other than what our illustrious government deems to give them?"

"Momma? Why is Papa cussing?" Mary asked, concern on her face.

"Shhh. Be still, Mary. We don't want to disturb your Papa."

"Is Papa fighting?"

Maggie shushed her daughter again. She didn't want to miss anything that was said.

"I have a job here and I'm doing it the best I know how." McLaughlin's voice was controlled.

"You're a puppet, James, and you do what the puppeteers in Washington tell you to!"

"That's a lie, too!"

"Then tell me why word has been circulating around the agency that White Hair has been telling the headmen they'll have to sell their land soon or it'll be taken away? Isn't that what the powers in Washington told you to say?"

"It's the goddamned truth!" McLaughlin yelled. "If they don't sell this time, the government is going to come in and take it away. They're tired of trying to bargain with the Indians. This time they'll just take it."

Maggie felt as though she'd been hit in the gut. When it came to the government they were ruthless in their pursuit of the Black Hills. She was pulled back to the conversation inside when George asked, "And what's the going price this year, James? The same poor fifty cents they offered last year?"

Maggie was getting more and more nervous, not liking the direction the conversation was going in.

"Word is they're going to offer a *dollar* and fifty cents." McLaughlin sounded smug.

"My, we're getting generous in our desperation aren't we?" Sarcasm was heavy in George's voice.

"Don't make it sound like it's my idea. I told you, I'm just doing my damn job!"

"And so am I," George shouted, "which is to help these people. To make sure they're not cheated by low-life mercenaries—or our government. Seems to me you're working for the other side these days, James."

"Damn you, Hawkins," James hissed. "I do what I'm told. I know you never have and I've let you operate that way because these people like you. Listen to you. But this time stay out of it. Do you hear me? Stay out of it."

A sense of foreboding washed over Maggie. McLaughlin's words were deliberate and spoken as though he knew something George didn't. Maggie sucked in a deep breath and gooseflesh ripped up her arms.

Mary tugged on Maggie's sleeve. "I'm hungry, Momma. When can we see Papa?"

"Soon, Mary. We have to wait until your Papa and Mr. McLaughlin finish talking."

Mary crossed her arms and harrumphed. "They're fighting, Momma. Just because I'm only six doesn't mean I can't tell when Papa is fighting."

Maggie leaned over her daughter. "Yes, Mary, but now is *not* the time to go in there. Please, be still so I can hear what they're saying."

Mary sucked in a breath and groaned, but there was a grin on her face and a sparkle in her eyes, as though happy to be a part of her Momma's secret spying on her Papa.

"Why, James?" Maggie heard George ask his superior, hoping she hadn't missed anything.

"Like I said, they're tired of waiting for the Indians to give in. They're threatening this time to go against the treaty. They want that land, George. And they plan to get it however they can."

"And what trickery are they using this time? Aside from threatening to steal the land if they don't sell?"

There was a pause before McLaughlin responded. "They're sending George Crook out here to convince them."

"Crook? Three Stars Crook? The man who chased them down like dogs, while we ate horsemeat and slept in the slop and rain without even a tent to keep us dry trying to catch them?" George's voice was incredulous.

"They trust Crook. He's one of the few generals who *has* kept his word to the Lakota. If anyone can convince them, it's him," McLaughlin said.

Maggie knew all about Three Stars Crook, the man who had led the Horsemeat March in 1876 chasing the Lakota after the Little Bighorn. George had told her all about him and what had happened during one of the worst times of his life. George, among Crook's men, had eaten, slept and ridden in the rain for months. They rode straight into winter following the Lakota and some of the men even froze to death at Fort Pierre in the general's zeal to catch the Indians that had delivered Custer's defeat at the Bighorn.

Oh yes, Maggie knew all about General George Crook, and everything she knew about him she disliked.

It was July 27, 1889 when General George Crook arrived at the Standing Rock Agency. Maggie and Mary stood with the rest of the crowd outside the headquarters building waiting to get a look at the famous general. Crook dismounted his horse and stepped onto the porch. He looked shabby and disheveled from what Maggie could see of the great man. His gray flannels looked like he'd been in them for a week and his hair and beard were both in need of a trim. Not exactly what she expected of the great man.

George made his way toward Crook who was headed toward the door and Maggie held her breath. Her husband turned to her, as though for luck, and she flashed a smile. *Here we go...*

"Do I know you?" Maggie barely heard Crook ask George when her husband stepped in front of the man. George doffed his hat and lowered his head in greeting.

"Yes, sir," George answered. "I served under Anson Miles during the horseme...during the Sioux campaign of '76, sir."

"Ah," Crook pursed his lips. "A campaign I would just as soon forget."

"Me too, sir. It's not one of my better memories of the cavalry."

"And what are you doing now? Why are you here?" Crook continued toward the door, George beside him, Maggie straining to hear what the two men said.

"I'm the Indian sub-agent here," George said.

"Indian agent?" Crook turned to George, surprised. "I should think you'd have had enough of Indians after our ill-fated campaign."

"I feel they've been mistreated, sir." They started through the door, but McLaughlin stepped in front of George and the general.

Maggie stared as McLaughlin extended his hand, as though George weren't even there. "Welcome, General Crook. I'm James McLaughlin, Indian Agent for Standing Rock Agency. As soon as you're settled, I'll introduce you to the headmen." In the space of a few moments McLaughlin whisked Crook away and left George standing red-faced on the porch.

Maggie thought she'd swallowed an apple her throat was so tight. She didn't know what to say to her husband when he stalked back to her. She sighed and shook her head. "I'm sorry. Maybe you can catch him at another time."

"Maybe," but his voice belied his uncertainty, and his anger.

Once James got his claws into Crook, Maggie knew George would have little chance to speak to the general alone, let alone tell him his thoughts. A bad feeling washed over her, one she knew wouldn't go away until Crook did.

"Crook has been talking to The People for the last week, but none seem inclined to do as he asked," George told Maggie, who was slicing bread at the table for supper.

"He was frustrated as hell that he hasn't been able to sway Sitting Bull and The People, Maggs. I thought we'd won, but then Crook told James to do whatever it took to convince them to sign the land away." He ran his fingers through his hair. "He told James to threaten them, even scare them. I tell you, Maggs, it made me sick to think about it."

Maggie laid her hand on her husband's back. The government's attempts to take the Black Hills from The People seemed never ending. *Well, this was just another day and another fight,* she told herself, steeling herself for what was to come.

"That wasn't the worst of it, Maggs. Crook included me personally in his order to speak to The People to try and sway them to sign. I can't do it, Maggs. I just can't." His fingers slid through his hair again. He shook his head and frowned.

"What will you do?"

"It's not what I will do, it's what I've already done."

"You went to Sitting Bull, didn't you?" Maggie's heart was pounding. *If McLaughlin or Crook knew...*

George nodded. "I'm afraid it won't help. I told him Crook and McLaughlin want the three-fourths signatures of all the men required by the Laramie Treaty, but because Crook is threatening them, The People are afraid. Neither Sitting Bull nor Gall want to sign and Sitting Bull actually *asked* me to go among his followers to convince them not to. Told me I have to convince Crook I'm working to get them *to* sign, while in fact, I'm telling them *not* to."

He shook his head and pursed his lips. "If they find out what I'm doing, I'll lose my position here, then what help will I be to The People?"

"They're what?" George yelled at the young brave who brought the news a few days later.

"They're holding a secret council with John Grass, one of the other headmen, instead of Sitting Bull."

Maggie couldn't believe her ears. They were trying to cede the land without including Sitting Bull or Gall!

George was on his feet. "I've got to warn Sitting Bull." He charged out the door.

Maggie busied herself as best she could, like she always did when George was gone and she was awaiting news of what was going on. She baked and mended. She even went to the school and worked on her lessons for next week.

It was hours before George slammed back through the door and Maggie had to calm him down between tirades and explanations of what had happened when they arrived at the council lodge.

"The sentries wouldn't even let us in, Maggs. It wasn't until Sitting Bull started hurling insults at the guards, reminding them they were Lakota and should be ashamed of themselves, then threatened them before we were finally let in."

He sighed and rolled his shoulders as though he had a huge weight there he couldn't dislodge. "He lied, Maggs, as easily as a man says a prayer, McLaughlin lied. He sat right there and told Crook that Sitting Bull had been informed of the meeting. That he and his followers knew all about it." He shoved his fingers through his hair. "We were too late, Maggs. I yelled and McLaughlin lied, and while we shouted at each other, the other headmen were shuffled to the table, touched the pen, and gave away nine million acres of Indian land."

Chapter Twenty-Six

It was a lazy Sunday afternoon in the Drying Grass Moon, October of 1890. Maggie was inside preparing dinner and George was on the steps of their cabin, whittling yet another doll for Mary.

Stepping in front of the porch a young warrior named Hokala, Badger in English, asked George, "Have you heard the talk?"

Maggie stopped her work, wiped her hands on a cloth, and walked to the door, her curiosity piqued, thankful she could now understand most of the Lakota language.

"What talk?" George asked without looking up from his chore.

"Kicking Bear, one of our Minneconjou brothers, has come to Standing Rock from the Cheyenne River agency to tell The People about a new Messiah. He traveled far to see this Messiah who spoke with him and told him many things."

"Like what?"

"He gives The People hope that someday the whites will be driven from our lands and things will be as they were."

"And who is this so-called Messiah?" George's tone had changed. There was interest now and it made Maggie even more curious about this Messiah Badger spoke about.

"His name is Wovoka, a Paiute who says one day our ancestors will rise from the dead and drive away all whites. He says the Indians of all nations who dance the Dance of Ghosts will rise above the land and watch as the earth is cleansed of all white men and becomes as it once was. Buffalo will again roam in herds of thousands and wild horses will run free through the tall grasses. When the earth has returned to how it was in the generations of our grandfathers, those who were raised will be lowered back to the earth and our people will live with their ancestors, as we have always lived. Hunting, moving with the seasons, living free."

George groaned and Maggie's breath caught.

"Tell me more."

Maggie pushed through the door and stood beside her husband, anxious to hear everything the young warrior had to say.

"Wovoka has decreed a sacred shirt must be worn when we dance."

"And what does this sacred shirt do?"

"It makes the wearer strong." The youth paused, as if uncertain how much to say, especially in front of a woman. "It will make him invincible."

"To what?" George asked, concern heavy in his voice.

Maggie felt claws of fear rake up her spine. This was not good.

Arrogance crept into Badger's eyes and he drew his back up straight as a lance. "To the soldier bullets if they try to stop us."

Maggie clutched the cloth she was holding at her stomach as though it would stop the fear building there. She sucked in a deep breath and tried to calm her racing heart. The ramifications of what Badger said were staggering. If the Indians believed all they had to do was wear a mystical shirt that made them impervious to bullets and dance the Ghost Dance, they'd be raised up during a rapture of some kind that would wipe out all whites. The possibilities of what could happen at these reservations made Maggie shudder. For both the Indians *and* the white men who ran them—including her, George and Mary!

"My words anger you?" Badger asked.

"No, my friend." George dropped his hand on the boy's shoulder. "They don't anger me. They frighten me."

Badger smiled. "You should be frightened."

Maggie stared at the young brave, his back straight, his eyes glistening with defiance and another chill ran up her spine.

"When is this great cleansing supposed to happen?" George asked.

"In the next springtime."

"Jesus," George whispered.

"Yes, Wovoka is what your people call Jesus or Christ. The Messiah. Understand, I have no bad feelings for you or your family, Wasicun Cantewaste. You try to help us and your hearts are good. You are a kind man, unlike most whites I've seen. But your people have had their time to rule the earth and done poorly. "Now it will be our turn."

Badger left and Maggie sat down beside George on the porch. She took his hand into hers. "Maybe it's not as bad as you think," she whispered, knowing it was, but unable to voice it.

"Maybe not as bad? How could it be good?" George almost shouted. "All of a sudden these people have something to hope for. Something to pray for. The destruction of all whites and the return of their lands to the way they were before white men ever touched these shores!"

"But maybe it's just like our religion. We pray to Christ, our Messiah, maybe it's the same thing," she hoped.

George shook his head, pulled his hand free and sighed. "No, it's not the same thing, Maggs. Christians aren't praying for the destruction of another race. These people are waiting for our decimation. They think by wearing some damned, mystical shirts, bullets won't hurt them. Can you imagine how many people will be hurt if it comes to a test of that belief?"

"Do you think it'll come to that?"

"I don't know. I damn-sure hope not, because if it does, there will be a lot of innocent blood spilled."

Maggie closed her eyes and sighed. This Ghost Dance, although intended to be peaceful, would not end well for The People.

The Ghost Dance spread through the reservations like a wild prairie fire. Within months The People throughout the reservation system danced day and night, praying to Wovoka and the ultimate destruction of the white man.

"Is the situation really that bad?" Although Maggie knew it was bad at Standing Rock, she hoped it was different at other reservations. At Standing Rock the majority of The People danced all the time, forsaking everything else. They danced until they dropped from sheer exhaustion and when they regained their strength, they danced again. One by one Maggie's students stopping coming to school and instead—they danced.

Maggie picked up George's empty dinner plate and Mary played in front of the hearth with a new doll Maggie had recently finished, hoping her child would keep it a *few* days before she gave it away.

"McLaughlin's done it again." George finally said, Maggie almost forgetting what the question was.

"What?" Maggie put the plate back on the table and sat down beside him.

"You know McLaughlin's been running scared of Sitting Bull and the Ghost Dance. He blames Sitting Bull for the dance's spread. Remember he threatened to have the chief arrested if it didn't stop?"

Maggie nodded.

"Remember the list I told you about that he sent to General Miles with the names of all the Indian 'dissenters' on it?"

Maggie nodded again, her stomach tightening. McLaughlin had wired the Indian commissioner on two occasions complaining about Sitting Bull and the Ghost Dance, but it wasn't until after the second, frantic wire, that General Nelson "Bear Coat" Miles finally asked for a list of those involved with the Ghost Dance. McLaughlin had happily complied and put Sitting Bull's name at the top of the list.

"What's McLaughlin done now?"

"Well, when Miles saw Sitting Bull's name on that list he decided to handle things himself."

"How?" Maggie ran her hand up and down George's arm hoping to calm him a little.

"He sent Buffalo Bill Cody out here to convince Sitting Bull to go to Chicago to talk to Miles and work things out."

"Why didn't you tell me? I had no idea Cody was here."

He shook his head and frowned. "I didn't want to add to your worries. With the students leaving school and The People dancing all the time, I didn't want to make things worse."

Maggie sighed and pursed her lips. She didn't like not knowing everything that was going on, but she certainly understood George's rationale. She lifted her head. "Cody? I presume that's the same Buffalo Bill whose Wild West show Sitting Bull starred in?"

"The same. When Cody got here, McLaughlin wouldn't let him near Sitting Bull."

"But if he was under orders from Miles, McLaughlin didn't have a choice. Did he?" Maggie was confused. *If Miles himself had ordered Cody to come here to get Sitting Bull and bring him back to Chicago, how could McLaughlin ignore that order and get away with it?*

"You'd think not. But James wasn't going to let Cody see Sitting Bull without a fight. He wired Washington, protesting Cody's visit. Back and forth the wires went. James said Cody no longer knew Sitting Bull the way he had five years ago. He said the chief had changed and that Cody wouldn't be able to alter his thinking." George drew a breath. "I watched him give every reason under the sun why Cody shouldn't speak to Sitting Bull."

"What happened?"

George shrugged his shoulders. "Miles rescinded his order and McLaughlin escorted a very unhappy Cody off the reservation."

"What now?" For the first time since coming to the reservation Maggie felt the first misgivings of fear. "Do we have anything to be afraid of?"

George took Maggie into his arms. "If McLaughlin would just let it go, I'd say no. But the more he stirs things up..." Maggie tensed and he pushed her back at arm's distance.

"Maybe I should send you and Mary to the Lazy D."

"Don't you even spend half a second thinking on it, George Hawkins! We're a team. I married you for better or worse. I'm made of good, strong stock, you know that."

"I know that, Maggs. But what about Mary?"

"These people love our Mary. No one here would hurt her. I'd bet my life on it." As soon as the words were out of her mouth she wanted to pull them back, wondering at their truth, wondering if she was trying to convince George or herself that no one would harm Mary. *Wondering if she was willing to take that chance and make that bet if things turned bad?*

George crashed into the cabin, the door slamming behind him, the frigid December air following behind him.

Maggie's heart tumbled in her chest at the harsh intrusion and Mary's eyes were wide with fear. Maggie jumped up from where she was sitting cross-legged in front of the blazing hearth and hurried to her husband, noticing an armed soldier through the window standing on the porch as she passed by.

"George! What's wrong with you?" she chastised. "What's going on?" It took one close look at her husband's wild eyes and she knew the worst had come. "Oh dear Lord, they're going to arrest Sitting Bull, aren't they?"

George paced in front of the fire, stopping every few steps to warm his hands. "I've been ordered, under guard," he swung his arm toward the porch, "to remain here while James gets ready to arrest Sitting Bull." He paced again and shoved his fingers through his still sandy-colored hair, although graying at the temples. "I have to talk James and Colonel Drum into letting me go, too. He paused again, his shoulders slumped, and he shook his head. "I couldn't stop them from killing Crazy Horse, Maggs. I couldn't stop them from slaughtering Dull Knife's people at Fort Robinson. I *have* to do whatever I can to save Sitting Bull."

He was rambling and Maggie knew it was from his deep-seeded guilt that he hadn't been able to keep Crazy Horse from being killed when he was arrested years ago. George somehow felt responsible for not making the guards understand the Oglala chief would rather die than be put into a cell; but by the time they realized he spoke the truth, it was too late and the great war chief was dead, killed with the help an agency policeman, a former follower. Maggie also knew he was haunted by the tragedy at Fort Robinson in '79, when Dull Knife's people were killed.

Maggie stepped in front of her pacing husband, took his hand, and led him to the bench at the table. "What, exactly, is going on?" she asked, afraid to hear the answer, but needing to know everything.

"Miles finally sent the order to arrest Sitting Bull; but the soldiers from Fort Yates aren't going to make the arrest, Maggs. McLaughlin talked Drum into sending the agency police instead, which will humiliate Sitting Bull and make the situation that much more explosive. I've got to get back there and convince McLaughlin and Drum to let me go with them. I may be the only thing between Sitting Bull and his death."

Maggie wanted to protest, but knew she couldn't. They were at Standing Rock to help The People and this was part of it, no matter how scared she was for her husband. She closed her eyes and nodded. "I'll do whatever I can to help."

George and his escort left a few minutes later. Maggie kissed him goodbye and tucked Wally into his belt under his coat.

The night dragged. Maggie felt helpless, again, as she waited for George's return. Mary felt the tension, too, and had curled up beside her mother in her parent's bed, sucking her thumb, something she hadn't done in years.

Maggie's mind tumbled, remembering the day she'd found George after searching for him for so long. The day they'd married, the day she'd accompanied Wasicun Cantewaste through the gates of the Standing Rock Agency and how they'd done everything they could to make it a better place for its people. She sighed, rolled over and beat her feather pillow. A tear slipped from her eye then another. Everything they'd accomplished over the years at Standing Rock was in jeopardy, as was George's life in his effort to stop what might happen. She felt as impotent as she had the day Paul Thornton ran her out of town, a feeling she had prayed she'd never experience again.

The clock ticked on and her mind ticked right along with it. Just as the cock crowed outside she drifted to sleep, but was abruptly awakened a short time later when George slammed into the cabin, a look of utter defeat surrounding him.

Maggie slid out of bed, covered Mary and joined her husband on the floor in front of the hearth where he sat cross-legged, staring into the coals of the smoldering fire.

"Sitting Bull is dead, Maggs. Crow Foot is dead and chaos is running Standing Rock right now."

Maggie's stomach clenched and tears filled her eyes. She didn't know what to say or do to help assuage her husband's pain. She scooted beside him, took his hand in hers and squeezed it. "Tell me what happened."

"I went with the agency police hoping to avert all this, Maggs. To save Sitting Bull." He hung his head. "I failed again."

His voice trailed to a whisper and Maggie knew without question he again held himself responsible for not being able to stop disaster.

"Stop talking like that, George. You've done more than most men have for the Lakota—and they know that. What happened

happened because of McLaughlin, the Ghost Dance, and The People themselves, certainly not because of you."

George breathed deeply through his nose, closed his eyes, and nodded slightly. "Sitting Bull came out peacefully. We were standing on his porch when Catch-the-Bear, one of Sitting Bull's followers, lifted his blanket, raised a rifle and shot Bull Head, who was standing right next to Sitting Bull." George's eyes were bloodshot, his hair a wild mess, and his back slumped.

Maggie knew Bull Head was the head of the agency police and that he would have been the one sent to arrest Sitting Bull.

"Bull Head raised his rifle to shoot Catch-the-Bear, but because of his own wound he was unsteady. When Bull Head fired he fell over and it was Sitting Bull he hit, not Catch-the-Bear."

Maggie gasped. Sitting Bull was shot by one of his own people! Her nerves sang with fear and warning and tears filled her eyes. "Go on." She tried to sound calm, but knew she was failing.

"People were screaming and running and then Sergeant Red Tomahawk just stepped up to Sitting Bull and shot him in the head."

If Maggie hadn't already been sitting on the floor, she would have fallen down.

"Crow Foot tried to reach his father, but was swallowed up by the crowd as the Ghost Dancers swarmed on Red Tomahawk."

George fell silent and Maggie thought about Sitting Bull's son. Crow Foot was not yet a man, but old enough to understand his father was dead, killed by one of his own people, an agency policeman, an Indian turned white man. Dread covered her like a putrid blanket as she waited for George to continue.

"I ran to him, Maggs. I ran to Sitting Bull, but there was nothing I could do. He was already gone." He lifted haunted eyes. "Then there was shooting everywhere. The smell of spent powder floated on the air, reminding me of the fight at the Little Bighorn." He swallowed. "Suddenly everything went quiet." He snorted. "You want to know why the shooting stopped? It stopped because everyone was watching Sitting Bull's white show horse. He was standing off to the side doing the tricks he'd done when he performed with Sitting Bull in Cody's Wild West Show—and we were the crowd there to watch him. The horse was dancing, Maggs, and everyone stopped to watch. It was eerie in the moonlight, eerie and foreboding. He only danced a little while before he stopped and wandered away as though nothing were amiss. The silence lasted long enough for the horse to amble away before everyone started shooting again."

"Oh George, it must have been horrible."

"That's not the worst of it, Maggs. I was holding Sitting Bull in my arms when Crow Foot emerged from the middle of the crowd and started waving at the policemen, shouting for Sitting Bull's followers to seek revenge on the police, the 'bad-hearts' he called them. Crow Foot yelled for them not to let Sitting Bull's killers live to see another day." George looked down at his hands, folded around Maggie's. "The crowd went after the policemen, attacked them with anything they had. Crow Foot charged one of the policemen who had a rifle already leveled at the boy's chest. I screamed for Crow Foot to stop, but he didn't hear me. Again, I couldn't do a damned thing and Crow Foot is dead, too.

"By the time Drum and his troops got there a half hour later, Sitting Bull and his son were dead, Bull Head and Shave Head, Bull Head's second in charge, were both wounded and so many others, policemen and Sitting Bull's followers alike, were dead or dying."

Maggie absorbed all George told her, feeling like a hole had just opened in her heart. "So what's happening now?"

"The People are running. They're preparing to join Red Cloud and his people at Pine Ridge."

"But they'll freeze!" Maggie shouted, a chill racing through her body to remind her how bitter it was outside and how cold it was sitting in front of a dead fire.

"What would you do, Maggs, if it were your people? Your family that had been killed? Would you wait around for the soldiers to come and kill you, too, which is exactly what they expect to happen."

Maggie sighed. "I'd run just like they are. What's James doing about all this?" She thought about the pompous ass who had started all this. *If he'd only left them alone…*

"James was running around like a cat with its tail on fire. I finally got him to sit down and listen to me. I told him to round up the headmen that aren't fleeing to Pine Ridge and calm them down. Promise them nothing was going to happen to them in retaliation. Told him the *only* thing saving *him* from the Lakota right now was the Ghost Dance and their belief that they don't have to worry about killing him for revenge—that he, along with the rest of the white race, will all be wiped out in the rapture next spring."

"And where does that leave you?" Maggie asked, knowing she wasn't going to like his answer.

"I'm going after those who are fleeing to try and stop any more bloodshed. I have to speak for them, Maggs, to any soldiers they might come upon. Explain why they're off the reservation. Stop this from getting worse than it already is."

Maggie saw the weariness in her husband's face, but she also saw the determination. He was going and no matter what she said, she wouldn't talk him out of it. *They'd come here to help the Indians,* she reminded herself for the second time in days. *They'd come to make a difference. Well, The People never needed more help than they did right now*

Unlike the last time she'd questioned why they were here, this time Maggie *was* afraid.

"What about me and Mary?" she asked, able to speak again.

"Don't worry, Maggs. The remaining headmen have assured me you and Mary will be safe. There's nothing to worry about. They know you had nothing to do with Sitting Bull's death."

"I'm not concerned about me. It's Mary..."

"Stop. You'll both be fine. These people are in shock. I heard them talking after Sitting Bull's death." He pulled Maggie's hand up and kissed it. "They believe so strongly in what Wovoka preaches they aren't concerned with revenge. They believe the white man will be wiped out next spring anyway. Why lose more of their people exacting revenge?" George told her, his voice strong and full of conviction.

"And what about you?" Maggie asked.

"I'll be fine. Badger is riding with me to make sure The People understand why I'm there."

Maggie forced a smile and wrapped her arms around her husband. Everything in her told her this was going to get even worse for The People. She wouldn't try and stop George from doing what they both knew he must and she prayed he could do *something*. If he couldn't, she feared he would carry it with him for the rest of his life, just like he did Crazy Horse, Dull Knife, and now would carry Sitting Bull.

"Please be careful. I don't know what I'd do if something happened to you."

George took her by the shoulders. "These people trust me, Maggs. I have to try and help them. If I can speak for them at Pine Ridge or to any soldiers they may meet, I want to make their passage as easy as possible."

"I understand that. I'm just afraid for you."

He pulled her back into the circle of his arms. "Shhh. Badger has become a good friend. He'll be sure they know why I'm there. If I'm not afraid, you shouldn't be."

"You're not afraid?" Every nerve in her body snapped with fear, even though she knew it was the right thing to do. Something he *had* to do.

He shook his head.

"Then I guess I'm afraid enough for both of us." She buried her head in his chest to keep him from seeing that fear.

A little more than a week later, George stumbled through the door of the cabin, dropped his belongings on the floor and staggered to one of the two chairs in front of the blazing fire. He plopped down and laid his head back.

Mary, anxious to see her Papa, flung herself onto her father's lap as soon as he landed in the chair. She wrapped her little arms around his neck and squeezed. Her eyes and mouth puckered and her face turned red with the strength she exerted with her hug.

"Papa, papa! You've come home! I missed you so," Mary cried, lavishing kiss after kiss upon her father's cheek.

Maggie laid down the quilt she'd been piecing together for Mary's bed and hurried to her husband. She didn't think she'd ever seen such relief or love on a man's face as she did when George wrapped his arms around his daughter. His eyes closed and a peace seemed to envelop a chin covered with a week's worth of beard, eyes with huge, black circles under them, and disheveled, greasy hair.

He'd never looked more wonderful as far as Maggie was concerned. As the days passed after he left with Badger, Maggie had grown more and more fearful her husband wouldn't return. When word finally came over the wire of the massacre she'd stumbled around their home for days, not knowing if George was one of the casualties, while the families of those who had fled to Pine Ridge mourned and wailed, their voices carrying throughout the reservation like banshees. Her heart ached, her daughter cried for her Papa, and every day Maggie's resolve lessened, until her dirty, wonderful husband stumbled through their door.

When Mary finally relinquished her hold over her Papa, Maggie slid beside him and hugged him, her heart swelling with relief and more love than she thought imaginable. Tears streamed down her cheeks at that relief and she buried her face in his neck and cried.

It was several minutes before she could ask him what happened.

"It was like the Little Bighorn all over again, Maggs, but in reverse," he eventually managed. "The dead were everywhere, mowed down by the Hotchkiss guns where they stood or sat." He stopped and Maggie could see he was fighting to keep his gorge down at what he'd seen. "A mother nursing her babe was killed," he swallowed, "while the child still nursed at her teat. It was a massacre, Maggs, one I'll never forget as long as I live," his voice low so Mary wouldn't hear.

The haunted look in George's eyes made more tears rise in Maggie's eyes. She held his hand as they sat side by side at the table and he recounted everything that had happened that deadly December day in 1890.

"Of all the bad luck, it was the Seventh Cavalry that was to bring Sitting Bull's people in. I told Major Whitside, in charge when Badger and I came on them, that all The People wanted was to go to Pine Ridge to join Red Cloud, but Whitside said he was under orders to take them to their camp at Wounded Knee Creek." George turned red-rimmed eyes to his wife. "Whitside was, at least, kind to The People. He fed them that first night, gave them tents and even put a stove into Big Foot's lodge because the old chief was sick and he knew it. When Colonel Forsythe relieved Major Whitside, I knew something bad was going to happen. Forsythe recognized me from when I rode with the Seventh and treated me like a pariah. He wouldn't even shake my hand when I offered it. Once he took over, it was all over before it began and I couldn't stop it. Again, I couldn't stop it."

His head sagged and he drew in a ragged sigh and Maggie knew he again held himself responsible for what happened that day when over three hundred men, women and children were killed then left to freeze where they lay when a winter storm rolled in.

"Forsythe insisted the Lakota still had weapons hidden on them, even after his men had searched their tents and even stripped them to make sure nothing was hidden on them." He stared off a moment before continuing. "They had nothing left, not even their dignity, Maggs, when Yellow Bird, a medicine man, started shouting about their Ghost Dance shirts and how the soldiers' bullets couldn't hurt them. I knew we were in real trouble then. Yellow Bird started to dance. Others joined and before I knew what was happening the guns were belching and The People were slaughtered."

Maggie ran her hand over his back, trying to soothe his pain, the pain she felt, too, knowing Sitting Bull, Crow Foot, Big Foot, Badger and so many innocents had been killed because, again, the white man wouldn't listen.

"All I could do was run. I found a ravine and slid down into it. There were families hiding there and mothers shielded their children against me until they realized who I was. They trusted me to help them, and I swore on my own life, I would. We waited until the guns turned away and I showed them where to run. With the grace of God, Maggs, we managed to survive, but we were the only ones."

A sob erupted from his throat and Maggie felt helpless to ease his pain. In that helplessness, she could only imagine the impotent rage he felt at not being able to stop more Lakota deaths at the hands of the U.S. Government.

Chapter Twenty-Seven

After a two week visit to the Lazy D, George and Maggie were snuggled on a settee just beyond the hearth in the front room of White Oaks. The fire snapped and popped, casting its light throughout the room, warming everyone within its reach. Maggie scanned the faces of those around her. She burrowed closer to George, the man she loved with all her heart whom she'd discarded in what seemed like another lifetime, and luckily found in this one. She gazed at her daughter, born between two worlds who thrived within both and took only the good from each, wrapped in her Aunt Amy's arms. The child was being taunted by her Uncle Blue and Cousin Luke, Amy and Blue's eight year old son, while Grandma Sarah playfully tried to wrest Mary from their clutches.

Maggie studied Ben and Sarah, strangers who took George and his father in when they had no place to go when George was just a boy. When an angry, thirteen year old half white, half Lakota boy came to them in need of a home, Ben and Sarah gave it to him, along with the love and support he needed to grow into manhood. Ben helped mold George and Blue into the men they would become with strong ideals and sound judgment and Sarah gave them the love they needed to thrive and blossom into loving men.

Maggie's eyes fell on Blue, George's brother by blood, the man who had saved George's life at the Little Bighorn so many years ago. He'd become "as the white man" and learned the law so he could help his people in their continuing fight against the United States Government. Her eyes lit on Amy, her dear friend who had suffered throughout her early life, but was kind and strong in spite of it. They were all different—yet somehow through their struggles, this mismatched group of strangers had become a family.

Ben had fought for the Union in the War Between the States, while Amy had suffered deeply in the south in that same war. Blue was considered a mongrel, a half breed, yet he had grown to become an honorable man who fought for the good of his people. Sarah, captured by the Lakota before the Civil War, had raised an angry half Lakota child as her own, and loved him as she would have those she'd been unable to bear herself. George, a man who fought at the Little Bighorn against the Indians, now fought *for* the Indians with every breath he took.

Sadly, she was reminded of the nightmare of the massacre at Wounded Knee Creek and how the court had ruled for Colonel Forsythe with a mere slap on the wrist. Following the debacle, Forsythe was relieved of his command by General Miles. However, at his court martial the Colonel testified on his own behalf as to what occurred that December day and, after days of testimony, Forsythe was given back his command by the Secretary of War as though nothing had happened.

Not allowed to testify during the proceedings, but in the audience every day, an outraged George had jumped from his seat and shouted in protest when the court gave Forsythe back his command. Although proven time after time at the court martial he'd acted that day with incompetence, Forsythe returned to duty receiving little more than a reprimand for the atrocities he'd committed.

"Are you all right?" Maggie asked, gently rubbing the length of George's arm. She knew where he was when he stared in silence into the distance. It was something he did often since that day at Wounded Knee Creek.

George leaned toward his wife. "I was just thinking."

"I know where you were. It *still* weighs on you, doesn't it?"

"What?"

"That you couldn't stop it."

George sighed and Maggie couldn't help but smile. She knew her husband very well—and he knew it. She turned her husband's face to look her straight in the eyes. "I'm going to tell you something George Hawkins. And you're going to listen." The room was suddenly quiet, everyone watching except Mary, still rolling and giggling from the tickling she'd just received from her Uncle Blue.

George smiled. "Yes?" he drawled.

Maggie's voice was hard. She wanted him to hear every single word she said to him—and understand it. "You did what you could to save those people. If I recall, you managed to save fifty, isn't that correct?"

Heads nodded around the room in agreement.

George nodded, too.

Maggie touched his face with her fingertips. "George, you couldn't have stopped what happened that day. It was a disaster waiting to happen. You can't surround three hundred and fifty Indians with five hundred soldiers and not expect trouble." She took a deep breath. "You did what you could. You managed to save fifty innocent women and their children in the process. Stop beating yourself up. Pat yourself on the back. Even if you'd saved only one that day, you succeeded."

He looked deep into her eyes and Maggie knew he was working it through in his head.

George glanced around the room and each of his family nodded, telling him without words they agreed and were proud of him.

"You gave The People hope, George," Blue whispered from across the room. "You are Wasicun Cantewaste, White Man of Good Heart, a name given to a man of honor and someone they trusted. Someone they believed in. Someone who has made a difference in their lives."

Amy whispered "Amen," a wide smile on her face as she gently rocked George and Maggie's child in her arms.

"We're all very proud of you, George. You treated the Indians with dignity and honor and tried to help them whenever and wherever you could. No other man could have done more," Ben added.

Sarah was nodding beside her husband. "Yes, George, we're all very proud of what you've done for The People. Don't ever let anyone take that away from you." Tears slid down her cheeks.

George took a deep breath. "Thank you," he whispered and it seemed to Maggie all the tension he'd held inside for so long melted away. His head snapped up and he took Maggie's hand. "I couldn't have done any of this without Maggie. I never would have accomplished anything if she hadn't been there for me." He kissed her and she knew everything she'd lived through in her life had brought her to this place. To George and Mary, to Ben and Sarah, and to Blue and Amy. If the choices she'd made had been different, her whole life would be different. She'd be at the Lazy D or a ranch somewhere close, married into a life she'd settled for, not one she'd worked toward or earned. She would be angry and resentful toward her own family and whomever she'd married. For the first time she was content. She didn't look forward to the next adventure. She was happy right where she was.

Like a book, its pages flipping quickly by, the past ten years flashed before her—the day she said goodbye to George at the Lazy D, Boston, the Cause and Paul Thornton, the day she was ridden out-of-town on a rail, Luke, Poker Alice, two wonderful old geezers who took her under their wing on her trip to Deadwood, and the humility she learned there, A.E., and finding George again. So many things flashed before her she couldn't help the smile that spread across her face.

George's head cocked. "What is it?"

Tears filled her eyes. "Do you remember when we first met at the Lazy D?"

"Of course, how could I forget? I thought you were the wildest most beautiful thing I'd ever seen and I told myself to stay well away from you." He smiled, but love sparkled in his eyes.

Maggie grinned back. "Ah the truth comes out. I'm glad you didn't succeed."

George snorted. "You wouldn't let me."

"No, I recall I chased you mercilessly, until you let me catch you and then *I* ran away."

"You did, but that's ancient history. We're here and we're together, that's all that matters. Now, what were you asking?" he said with a sparkle in his eyes having turned her question in another direction.

"Do you remember that we told each other we 'had things to do' and wanted to 'make a difference' for the Indians?"

His lips pursed and he nodded.

"Well, George Hawkins, I think between the two of us, we've made one hell of a difference, and I'm damn proud to say so."

Mary sat up from her aunt's lap, a huge grin on her angelic face. "Momma's cussin' again."

The room erupted in laughter.

299

"Some things never change, Mary girl," George shouted over the laughter.

Maggie knew her face was aflame. She was laughing with everyone else when George nibbled on her ear and whispered, "Thankfully, my darling Maggs, *some* things *never* do."

The End

AFTERWORD

This book is a work of fiction; however, I have tried to stay as accurate as possible to the history contained herein, while introducing factual characters.

Luke Short was a gambler who spent much of his time after 1879 working the gambling circuit that ran from Denver to Cheyenne to Deadwood with fellow gambler and lawman, Bat Masterson. According to my research he lived in Cheyenne and worked for "Big" Ed Chase at the Inter-Ocean Hotel dealing Faro from 1876 through mid- to late 1879. By the fall of that year he left Cheyenne and took a job managing the Long Branch Saloon in Dodge City, Kansas. Later that same year he was known to be running games in Leadville, Colorado.

Poker Alice was a real gambler who was followed and revered by many because she was a winner in a man's game, yet still very much a woman.

Taunton is a real town outside Boston and the facts on the sign outside the city when Maggie arrives are correct.

The city map included is a compilation of several Wyoming city maps dated from 1883 to 1886. As Maggie's story in Cheyenne begins in 1879, these locations may or may not be completely accurate, so have been edited as necessary to fit my story.

According to my research Margaret "Mother" Shephard's establishment was "on Silver Springs Road, near Muskrat Canyon, about 1 ½ miles south of the Niobrara County line…at a point where the stage driver would "blow the horses" after the fifteen mile run from Silver Cliff."

Daniel Boone May was, indeed, owner of Robbers Roost and a U.S. Marshal, a few of whose factual exploits are recounted in this story, including the shooting of Frank Towles and hangings of Archie McLaughlin and Billy Mansfield; however, the three McLaughlin brothers are fictional and were added for dramatic purposes.

The Standing Rock Agency was established within the Great Sioux Reservation after 1876, but became the Standing Rock Reservation after it was split into six parcels, one for each tribe and left nine million acres that were opened to white settlers.

GLOSSARY

Adobada sauce – A sauce for meats. *Happy Trails A Dictionary of Western Expressions, Robert Hendrickson*

Buck the Tiger – An historical term meaning to play against the bank in a game of faro. Faro was called *the tiger* because professional gamblers carried their faro outfits in boxes with a Royal Bengal tiger painted on them and tigers were also painted on the chips. *Happy Trails A Dictionary of Western Expressions, Robert Hendrickson*

Dawes Severalty Act - 1887, passed by the U.S. Congress to provide for the granting of landholdings (*allotments,* usually 160 acres/65 hectares) to individual Native Americans, replacing communal tribal holdings. Sponsored by U.S. Senator H. L. Dawes, the aim of the act was to absorb tribe members into the larger national society. Allotments could be sold after a statutory period (25 years), and "surplus" land not allotted was opened to settlers. Within decades following the passage of the act the vast majority of what had been tribal land in the West was in white hands.
http://encyclopedia2.thefreedictionary.com/Dawes+Severalty+Act

Free Love - In 1855, free love advocate Mary Gove Nichols (1810–1884) described marriage as the "annihilation of woman," explaining that women were considered to be men's property in law and public sentiment, making it possible for tyrannical men to deprive their wives of all freedom. *From Wikipedia, the free encyclopedia.*

Freezeout – A poker game requiring each player to drop out when s/he loses a predetermined amount of money, until one player is left with all the winnings. The game appears to have been played in the West in about 1855. *Happy Trails A Dictionary of Western Expressions, Robert Hendrickson*

Hell-(bent)-for-leather - The truly odd thing about "hell bent for leather" is that it appears to be a combination of two other phrases: "hell bent" and "hell for leather," which also dates to the late 19th century. "Hell for leather" specifically referred to riding a horse very fast, the "leather" in question being either the saddle or, more likely, the leather crop used to "incentivize" the poor horse. "Hell bent for leather" doesn't make any more literal sense than "hell for leather" did, but the fact that "hell bent" is more widely understood undoubtedly led to the fusion of the two phrases. *The Word Detective*

Phoenix - A phoenix is a mythical bird with a colorful plumage and a tail of gold and scarlet (or purple, blue, and green according to some legends). It has a 500 to 1000 year life-cycle, near the end of which it builds itself a nest of twigs that then ignites; both nest and bird burn fiercely and are reduced to ashes, from which a new, young phoenix or phoenix egg arises, reborn anew to live again. The new phoenix is destined to live as long as its old self.
From Wikipedia, the free encyclopedia.

Road Agents – robbers, bandits. A highway man, the term first recorded in 1863. *Happy Trails A Dictionary of Western Expressions, Robert Hendrickson*

Silk Popping (Silk Popper) – A historical term for a stagecoach driver, who popped his whip. *Happy Trails A Dictionary of Western Expressions, Robert Hendrickson*

Slap(ping) leather – Drawing a pistol in a gunfight. *Happy Trails A Dictionary of Western Expressions, Robert Hendrickson*

Suicide Gun – Cowboys early in this century called the Colt .32 (and similar guns) a *suicide gun* because it lacked the power to stop an assailant dead in his tracks and thus often led to the death of the man who fired it. It was no match for the .44-caliber gun most gunfighters carried. *Happy Trails A Dictionary of Western Expressions, Robert Hendrickson*

It is coincidence that Archie McLaughlin, the man hung by vigilantes, (and his fictional brothers) has the same name last name as James McLaughlin, the (factual) Indian Agent at the Standing Rock Agency. As I am aware, there is no relation between them.

304

References Consulted

Cheyenne Photos, 1870's—Wyoming Tales and Trails (internet website)
www.wyomingtalesandtrails.com/cheyenne70S

Cheyenne Photos II—Wyoming Tales and Trails (internet website)   www.wyomingtalesandtrails.com/cheyenne2

Cheyenne Photos IV—Wyoming Tales and Trails (internet website)   www.wyomingtalesandtrails.com/cheyenne5

Ladies' Victorian Clothing and Living History Accessories (internet website)   www.ladiesemporium.com

Frontier Gamblers (internet website)
www.frontiergamblers.com/page44 (Luke Short)

Legends of America (internet website)
www.legendsofamerica.com/we-pokeralice.com (Poker Alice)

Soiled Doves, Prostitution in the Early West by Anne Seagraves, 1994 Wesanne Publications, USA

Happy Trails, A Dictionary of Western Expressions by Robert Henderson; 1994 Facts on File Books

Black Hills Visitor Magazine (internet website)
www.blackhillsvisitor.com

Wikipedia (internet encyclopedia)   www.wikipedia.org

City of Sin and Ashes (internet website)
www.deadwoodmagazine.com/archivedsite/Archives/Ashes
Deadwood, SD Fire, Sept 1879/ GenDisasters Genealogy in Tragedy, Disasters, Fires,... (internet website)
www.gendisasters.com/south-dakota/7270/deadwood-sd-fire-sept-1879

The New York Times, New York, NY 27 Sept 1879; 28 Sept 1879

Digital Deadwood-Fire of 1879 HistoryLink Data (internet website)
www.digitaldeadwood.com/historylink/events/fire1879

Caught Between Three Fires, Cass County, Mo., Chaos & Order No. 11 1860-1865, Tom A. Rafiner, Xlibris, 2011

The Burning of Dayton, Jackie Polsgrove Roberts, Two Trails Publishing, 2006

Everyday Lakota, An English-Sioux Dictionary for Beginners, Joseph A. Karol, M.A., Assistant Editor, Stephen L. Rozman, Ph.D., Copyright 1971 by The Rosebud Educational Society, St. Francis, SD

Peter's Quotations, Ideas for Our Time, by Dr. Laurence J. Peter, Copyright 1977 by Bantam Books

About the Author...

Diane was born on "The Jersey Shore" and spent much of her youth on the beach, but for the past 20+ years she's lived in the Kansas City area. She currently resides south of Kansas City with her husband, horses, and a multitude of cats. She has two grown children and five grandchildren. She's always loved the old West and history of the Civil War period. Her favorite movie is Dances With Wolves, an inspiration for the first book in the White Oaks Series. Having parents from both the "North and the South" and a cousin whose parents were reversed, they called each other "Yebels" as children and, imagined themselves, as children will do, 150 years ago fighting different sides of the war in their games.

As a kid, Diane played "Cowboys and Indians" more than she did Barbie, and it comes through in her writing, as she relates stories of the struggle of common people and what made this country great.

When Diane isn't working on her next book in progress, one can find her curled up on the sofa engrossed in a good book or watching and old western movie. She currently is employed as a legal administrative assistant at a major law firm in Kansas City.

Diane would love to hear your comments on the books... e-mail her at dlrogers2@peoplepc.com.

Made in the USA
Middletown, DE
02 April 2021